On the Bro'd

Mike Lacher

A PARODY OF JACK KEROUAC'S *ON THE ROAD*

AVON, MASSACHUSETTS

DEDICATION
TO BUFFALO WILD WINGS, FOR EVERYTHING

Published by
Adams Media, a division of F+W Media, Inc.
57 Littlefield Street, Avon, MA 02322. U.S.A.
www.adamsmedia.com

ISBN 10: 1-4405-2906-X
ISBN 13: 978-1-4405-2906-1
eISBN 10: 1-4405-3130-7
eISBN 13: 978-1-4405-3130-9

Printed in the United States of America.

10 9 8 7 6 5 4 3 2 1

Library of Congress Cataloging-in-Publication Data
available from publisher.

This book is an unauthorized parody of *On the Road* by Jack Kerouac. It has
not been approved, licensed, or endorsed by the author's estate, its publisher,
or any licensee.

This book is available at quantity discounts for bulk purchases.
For information, please call 1-800-289-0963.

Contents

Part One

What Up

CHAPTER ONE

A NATTY LIGHT-SLUGGING HERO
OF THE SOUTHWEST

I first met Derek not long after Tryscha and I hooked up. I'd been real hungover but I won't tell you much about it, except that it was a result of a six-foot-five douchebag and a beer bong. It totally blew. When Derek Morrisey cruised into town, he got my life on the bro'd bumpin'. I'd always wanted to roll West to try In-N-Out burgers and scope hot actress chicks, but I always got too hammered at frat parties in Ohio and had to sleep it off the next day. Derek is an awesome road trip buddy because he knows how to fucking party. I heard about that dude from Chaz Kerry, who'd reshared some Facebook status updates written by Derek from the Arizona State Beta Phi Omega house. I was stoked about Derek's status updates because they were funny as shit, asking Chaz to rate some pictures of girls he hooked up with the night before. Sometimes Carl Marcus and I texted about the status updates and wondered if we could ever hang with the epic Derek Morrisey. This was like forever ago, when Derek was just a young Communications major instead of the crazy fucking jagoff he is today. We heard that Derek was sick of ASU and was transferring to Ohio State; and we heard that he was cruising in with some slam piece named Maryann.

One night I was playing flipcup at the Ohio State Delta house and Chaz and Tom Grover told me Derek just got in and was crashing at the Holiday Inn Express near East Campus. Derek had rolled up the night before, his first time ever in Columbus, with his hot-ass stacked trixie Maryann; they busted out of his Land Rover, checked his phone for some grub, and plowed into a Buffalo Wild Wings, and since then B-Dubs has always been a favorite place in Columbus for Derek. They threw down cash for mad-good wings and brewdogs.

Derek was always spitting shit like this to Maryann: "Yo, babe, we're at OSU, and even though I haven't laid down the plan for you, we gotta forget about whatever stupid shit happened between us in Phoenix and just start thinking about where we're gonna pregame tonight . . ." and whatever like he always did back then.

I rolled up to the Holiday Inn Express with my buddies, and Derek opened the door wearing his lacrosse shorts. Maryann was totally topless; Derek was totally getting his bone on, 'cause he thought boning was the most tits thing in the world—although he had to do some jobs and whatever to keep beer in the fridge. You could tell that he loved his junk from how he stood around, checking out porn on his iPhone, but pulling a mad fake-out, so you thought he was listening to you and not looking at phone porn, saying a bunch of "Hell yeas" and "Right ons." I thought Derek was sorta like a less assholey The Situation—ripped, funny as shit, with spiked hair—a Natty Light-slugging hero of the Southwest. And for real, he had been in the hospital for alcohol poisoning before hooking up with Maryann and coming to Ohio State. Maryann was a nine-out-of-ten with a Mystic Tan and a crazy rack; she chilled on the edge of the couch with her iPhone and her oversized Dolce & Gabbana sunglasses, looking sorta like a less-hot Megan Fox in that first *Transformers* movie. And like most hotties, she could be a total bitch. That night we all slammed Bud Light Limes 'till sunrise, and in the morning, while we sat around hungover as shit, Derek got up like a total pimp and asked Maryann to make us some food. "We gotta have some breakfast burritos, babe." She had some kind of bitchfest about it and I peaced out.

Next week, Derek told Chaz Kerry that he totally had to learn how to play the acoustic guitar; Chaz said that I played some awesome Oasis songs at a party a while ago and that he should come to me for advice. Meanwhile Derek had gotten a personal trainer job at Bally Total Fitness, had a fight with Maryann in a Hooters—can't believe that fucking dude took her there—and she was so pissed that she told the cops Derek was holding, and Derek had to get the fuck out of the Holiday Inn Express. He had nowhere to crash. So one night when I was blasting through my first P90X workout DVD in my apartment there was a knock on the door and Derek was there, hammered, smelling of Axe Body Spray in the dark of the hall, all like, "What up, I'm Derek. You gotta teach me how to play 'Wonderwall.'"

"Where's Maryann at?" I asked, and Derek told me that she'd flipped her shit and hauled ass back to Phoenix. We rolled out to slam a few brews 'cause we couldn't hang around my roommate Ty, who was totally putting the moves on this hottie. As soon as he met Derek he knew he'd try to pull the robbery on his lady.

We went to Buffalo Wild Wings and I told Derek, "Dude, I know you didn't just come to me to learn how to play acoustic, and honestly the only things I know are how to play chords in first position and how to make sensitive faces to the hotties watching me play." And he was like, "Right on, bro, I feel you and I thought of that, but you know it's all like, you know and shit . . ." We talked about things I didn't get and neither did he. Back then, Derek didn't know what he was talking about; he was just a young player who wanted to become a legendary pimp, but on the DL he was already pretty close to pimp status, and after he chilled with Carl Marcus for a while he got all in it with all the pimp terms and frontin'. But we were like natural bros, and I let him crash on my couch as long as he promised to road trip it West with me.

This one time when Derek was drinking Natty Light at my place—he had already hit the gym earlier—Derek said, "Come on bro, we gotta meet these hotties, hurry up." I was like, "Chill the fuck out, we'll roll out as soon as I finish these lunges," and they were some of the hardest lunges in the whole P90X system. Then I geared up and we headed out to hang with some chicks.

We rolled into the party scene of South Campus, passing around Derek's flask; I was starting to get pretty buzzed like Derek. He was a totally solid dude and, even though he could be kind of a douche, it was only because he was like crazy-focused on partying and laying any hottie within arm's reach. He was being sort of a douche to me and I knew it (crashing at my pad and learning the acoustic guitar, etc.), but I didn't give a shit and we still partied like hell—no bitching and moaning. I started to learn how to party from him as he learned how to play acoustic guitar from me. Whenever I played stuff, he was like, "Hell yeah, I love all those songs." He watched me play classic Lifehouse songs, all like "Yeah! That's the best fucking song!" and "No fucking joke!" and then he slammed a Natty Light. "Bro, there's so many good fucking Lifehouse songs. How to even *begin* to learn all of them . . . "

We were at Dave & Busters and nuclear explosions practically blasted from Derek's Oakleys as he talked about boning chicks. He talked about it so graphically that buzzkills left the arcade to get away from his gross-ass talk. But he was pimping; at ASU the dude spent a third of his time at the bar, a third in the sack, and a third at the Beta Phi Omega house. Townies saw him running around, no shirt, with a forty duct-taped to each hand, or sneaking around to get into some Alpha Phi hotties' rooms, where he spent hours just going at it.

We went to a party at Alpha Tau Omega—we were supposed to meet up with a pair of hotties by the flipcup table but they didn't show up. We went over to his buddy P-Rock's room where Derek shotgunned a beer and whatever, and then rolled out. That was when Derek partied with Carl Marcus. A legit thing happened when Derek met Carl Marcus. Two total players that they are, they wanted to get wild together ASAP. One jacked arm fistbumped with another jacked arm—one belonging to the beer-slugging player with the lacrosse shorts, the other to the MGD-chugging player with the popped collar who is Carl Marcus. After that I didn't get to hang with Derek that

much, which was sorta lame. Their vibes totally tangled and I
was a prude next to them; I couldn't shotgun PBRs as fast as
them and could only do like eighteen to twenty shots at a time.
The whole insane clusterfuck of everything that was to come
began then; it would mix up all the bros I knew in one massive house party stretching across the American Night. Carl told
Derek about his crew, P-Rock; D-Rock; Jenni; C-Rock in Texas;
J-Rock in Toronto; and M-Rock wandering in Times Square,
fucking drunk out of his skull. And Derek told Carl of players at ASU like T-Rock, the ripped-as-hell bouncer and online
poker genius. He told him of J-Rock, B-Rock, his old school
bros, his frat buddies, his hookups and *Hustler* mags, and his best,
worst, and most strategic fantasy football draft picks. Carl and
Derek rolled into parties together, bonging brews, which later
became totally stupid and lame and annoying. But then they
strutted down the streets like total pimps, and I strutted after as
I've been doing all my life, because the only bros for me are the
awesome ones, the ones who are mad to chug, mad to party, mad
to bone, mad to get hammered, the ones who never turn down
a Natty Light but chug, chug, chug like fucking awesome players exploding like spiders across an Ed Hardy shirt and in the
middle you see the silver skull pop and everybody goes "Fuck
yeah!" Wanting like hell to learn how to be a total pimp like Carl,
Derek was all up in his face with a need to get wild: "Bro, Carl,
listen to this—I'm being fucking real here." I didn't hang with
them for a couple weeks while they ramped their partying up to
epic proportions.

Then it was March, the time for spring break, and all my
bros were getting ready to hit Cabo or Cancun. I was busting ass
through the fifth disc of P90X and after I finished tricking out
my triceps, and after a trip to Miami Beach with Ty, I got ready
to beast it West for the first time.

Derek rolled out earlier. We had a party at the Bar Louie
in the Arena District. We got real hammered and took some
pictures with our phones. Carl turned his Ed Hardy hat to the

side and looked badass. Derek showed his sick bicep tat of an ASU Sun Devil pissing on an Arizona Wildcat. My picture made me look like a fucking RoboCop who'd kill anybody for anything. Carl and Derek saved their pictures as their iPhone backgrounds. Derek was rolling back to ASU; he'd finished his first semester in Columbus. I say semester, but the dude never went to class and mostly just worked as a trainer at Bally. The most badass personal trainer in the world, Derek can get a fat chick through like ten squats, spot a hottie at the elliptical, motor over to her, spit game so hard you'd think you were watching Cassa-fucking-nova on crack, get her into the back office, beast it, get out, tell the fattie good job, max out on the bench, then spot another hottie and do the same thing all over again; he worked like that without pause for four to five hours every Tuesday and alternating Wednesday wearing his uniform, Sun Devils lacrosse shorts, a sideways visor, and Adidas flip-flops. Now Derek had a hilarious new tee to hit the road in—red with "Female Body Inspector" written across it—and an acoustic/electric Fender guitar that he was going to start playing at ASU as soon as he re-enrolled. We noshed on some sliders and Bud Light in Bar Louie, and then Derek hauled ass into the night. I had to bust out West once summer break happened.

And this was how my road trip started, and the shit that happened later is too off-the-chain not to spit at you.

The fact that I was a party god and was always looking to get wild wasn't why I wanted to hang with Derek more, and it wasn't 'cause I'd pretty much banged every hot chick on the Ohio State campus; it was because, even though he was total West-coast style, the dude was like some long-lost bro. The look of his spiked hair with the frosted tips made me remember back when I was chilling in the frat houses and dorm rooms freshman year. His Hollister shirts clung to his abs like spray paint. And in his voice I heard the voices of old bros from high school. All my other bros were cool as hell—Chaz the natural lady-slayer, Carl Marcus and his off-the-chain double-fisted party vibe, Old

Brad Lewis and his awesome WTF sense of humor—or else they were sort of assholes like E-Rock, who always had to get in fucking fights or J-Rock who was always ready to fuck up anybody over flipcup. But Derek's awesomeness was just as sick and killer and off-the-chain, without any of the asshole shit. And the way he could be a douche wasn't really all that shitty; it was kind of a kick-in-the-dick of American awesomeness, a totally West Coast dose of awesome from the quads of Arizona State, something sick as hell. He was only a douche when he needed to be. Besides, all my OSU bros were fighting to maintain their awesome reps on campus, but Derek just crashed the party, hungry for kegstands and boning; he didn't give a shit if people didn't want him there, "as long as I can nail that little hottie, bro," and "as long as we can *eat* some fucking *wings*! I'm fucking *starving*, let's *pound some wings right now!*"—and off we'd rush to eat, 'cause, you know, "dudes gotta fucking wing it."

A western player of epic proportions, Derek. Although Ty told me he might be *too* big a douche, I could see some awesome times in the future. And I even knew there'd be some fucked-up times dealing with Derek's totally asshole moves in shitty sports bars and Sunglass Huts, why the fuck should I give a shit? I was a young player and I had to get my party on.

Somewhere along the line I knew there'd be hotties, foam parties, everything. Somewhere along the line the bottle service and a VIP table would just be handed to me.

CHAPTER TWO

TOLEDO IS A BITCH

In July, after having pulled down a couple thousand from online poker, I finally got my shit together to roll to the West Coast. My buddy Ricky Bronco had sent me some texts from San Francisco, telling me to roll out there and party on his dad's yacht. He swore he could totally get me laid in international waters. I texted back and told him I'd be cool with getting laid on land as long as the chick was at least an eight-out-of-ten and drinks were free. Ricky had a place in Mill City and said I could spend some time boning and drinking while we waited for his dad's yacht to get out of dry dock (it was having surround sound installed). Ricky was crashing with his slam piece Liana; he said she had a posse of hot friends and everything would be raw as hell. Ricky and I played lacrosse back in the day; he was from Miami Beach and a pretty hard-core dude. He was expecting me to roll up in about ten days. My parents were fine with my trip West; they didn't really care because my grades at OSU were fine and only a couple of my DUI charges were going to stick. The only drag was they wouldn't let me take the Land Rover, but I decided I'd hitch my ass there. I'd save cash for beer, meet some awesome dudes on the way, and smash with mad hotties with cars. Leaving my P90X DVDs in my DVD rack, and locking up my tequila so Ty wouldn't bogart it, I packed my North Face bag full of party essentials and rolled out for the West Coast.

I'd been MapQuesting shit on my iPhone for a couple days, checking out awesome bars along the way, and there was a long-ass yellow line called I-80 that led from Teaneck, New Jersey, clear to San Fran. I figured I'd just hang on 80 and I started moving. I had to haul ass to Toledo to catch I-80. Thinking like mad about all the tail I'd slay in Chicago, Denver, and then San Fran, I took a city bus up to Worthington and got out near the bank of the Olentangy River.

I started hitching up Route 23. Five non-hottie-filled rides got my ass to Toledo, where I found an onramp for I-80. Toledo was boring as hell and it started raining like a bitch when I got there. I had to get under some trees to stop getting drenched and I started to get angry. I was like 120 miles north of Columbus; the whole time heading here I'd been pissed that I was moving north instead of west and now my ass was stranded. I busted ass to a closed Subway and stood under the overhang. Overhead the clouds sent down thunderclaps that were loud as shit. All I could see were closed gas stations and restaurants without liquor licenses. "WTF?" I punched the wall of the Subway; it was hard as fuck. "All these dudes are having an awesome time! I can't believe I'm not there! When the hell will I get there!"— and whatever. Like forever later, a car stopped at the closed Subway; the dude and two chicks in it were looking at a map or something. I strutted over and gave a "what up" nod to them; I looked like a raw mess. I was soaked and my North Face bag was as dirty as shit. I had been wearing flip-flops, which are comfy as hell for hanging, but total bullshit for standing under an overhang in a rainstorm in Toledo. Luckily the dude and chicks let me in and hauled my ass back to fucking Columbus, which was at least better than being stuck in Toledo for the rest of forever. "Anyway," the dude was like, "there's barely any girls along I-80. Everybody knows that hotties flock to I-70," and he was probably right. My MapQuesting had been dumb as hell, like it would be easy to roll down one yellow line across MapQuest and not even print out some fucking directions.

It was less wet in Columbus. I had to roll back to my apartment in a city bus with a bunch of not-hot bitches who were talking about some bullshit conference—bitch-bitch, whatever-whatever—and I was crazy pissed about how much poker cash I'd wasted. I wanted to get moving and instead I'd dicked around all day going up to Toledo and back like an idiot; it was like a keg party where some asshole loses the fucking tap. I had to get to Chicago tomorrow, and that was no joke, so I grabbed a Southwest flight, drained most of my Rapid Rewards points, and figured, whatever, I'd just have to beast it in Chicago fast.

CHAPTER THREE

WHERE THE FUCK IS MY PHONE?

I t was a dumb plane ride with whiny-ass babies and stew-
ardesses that could be hotter. I downed one mini bottle of
Dewar's after another, until we got up to cruising altitude and
flew straight across Indiana. I landed in Midway in the afternoon, got a room at the Holiday Inn Express, and grabbed some
sleep. With half my poker dollars left, I brought the party to Chi-
town after exploding my nap bomb.

I checked out the hotties on Lake Michigan and Jägerbombs,
yard-long beers, and one shitshow after another in Wrigleyville,
where some grenades followed me like a fucking disease. At this
time, Kanye West was blasting like hell everywhere and the clubs
on Weed Street dropped the beat. As I pumped my fist, I thought
of all my bros from one end of the country to the other and
how they were really all in the same vast game of flipcup, getting ultra-hammered. And then for the first time since I was like
six and my family went to Disneyland, I headed out West. I had
to get out of Chicago traffic, so I rocked a bus to Joliet, Illinois,
posted up by the road after some margaritas and appeteasers at
the Chili's, and got my hitch on. I'd made like a baller from
C-Bus to Joliet and had totally wrecked my online poker cash
and Rapid Rewards points.

I got a ride on a Bud Light truck and the truckdriver
showed me all the truckstops where he had gotten his smash
on with trucker chicks. Around three o'clock, after a Bloomin'
Onion and a Miller Light at an Outback Steakhouse, some chick
stopped for me in a Sebring. I sprung an undercover chub as I
ran after the car. But that chick was a not-hot cougar, and wanted
help driving to Iowa. I figured whatevs. Iowa was sorta close to

Denver where Derek was, and once I rolled up to Denver I could beast it. The chick drove for a couple hours and made us go look at a stupid old monument or something, like we were fucking idiots, and then I got my drive on. And even though I'm not into driving anything that can't off-road, we blasted through Illinois to Davenport, Iowa. There I saw the Olive Garden, offering a Never Ending Pasta Bowl in the summer haze and low-priced happy hour drinks and a T.G.I. Friday's—with wings, onion rings, and a large drink menu—just across the street. The cougar had to keep rolling on some other road, so I got out.

It was getting dark and I drank like ten to twelve Natty Ices then strutted to the outskirts of town and nearly tossed my shit. A bunch of dudes were heading home from work in Tauruses, Civics, and whatever other stupid rides, just like idiots drive all over wherever. A dude hauled my drunk ass up to a boring-ass intersection near a field. It sucked there. A bunch of farmers drove by and looked at me like I was some kind of asshole; I flexed my neck; don't fuck with me. No trucks anywhere. Some cars rolled past and a douche in a tricked-out Civic cruised past me with his bullshit music blaring. It got totally dark and I was stuck there, totally fucked. It was so dark and there weren't any lights anywhere; in a second I'd be totally invisible. Then finally some jagoff from Davenport gave me a ride back. My ass was right where it had been before.

I sat in an Outback to think things over. I pounded a Bloomin' Onion and a Miller Lite; that's the stuff I noshed on for my whole trip, 'cause it's filling and pretty fucking delicious. Then I decided to stop fucking around. After a nice scope session on the Outback's lady bartender, I rocked a bus out to the edge of town, sorta near some truck stops. The trucks were seriously big, and in a hot second a dude pulled over to give me a ride. I bolted for it and was stoked as hell. The driver was a crazy motherfucker—a huge fat crazy motherfucker with a lazy eye and deep-ass voice who like went batshit crazy on the road and couldn't give two shits about me. Which meant that I could

chill for a hot second, because the dumbest thing about hitching is that you have to talk to all the douchebags so they don't
regret picking you up; you have to make them think you think
they're cool, which is all lame as hell when the only thing you're
shooting for is to lay a damn nap bomb. The trucker yelled over
the music and I just yelled back, and we got our chill on. And
dude cranked straight to Iowa City and told me some funny-
ass shit about how he dodges cops or whatever. When we rolled
into Iowa City he saw another truck coming up on us and did
me a solid by blinking his lights. The other dude slowed down
to pick up my ass, and in a hot second I was in another truck,
ready to haul ass across the night, and I was stoked as hell. And
this new trucker dude was as off the chain as the other trucker
dude and just yelled crazy shit too, so all I had to do was chill.
Now I could see Denver looming ahead of me, way the fuck out
wherever, across the Texas Roadhouses of Iowa and the On The
Borders of Nebraska, and I could see the vision of San Francisco
beyond. The trucker hauled ass and spat stories for a little, and
then, when we rolled up into this city in Iowa where a couple
years later Derek and I were pulled over after we shoplifted some
PowerBar Gel, he passed out for a few hours in his seat. I set off a
nap bomb too, and took one XL piss on the side of a Citgo, with
the prairie chilling out past the car wash and the garbage smelling like a Bacardi Girl who's had one too many.

The trucker woke up like crazy at dawn. Off we rolled,
and a hot second later the Pizza Hut/Wing Street of Des Moines
appeared ahead over the green cornfields. Dude had to get his
Wing Street on and I refuse to eat wings that don't come from
Buffalo Wild Wings, so I kept going to Des Moines, nabbing a
ride with a couple of d-bags from University of Iowa (fuck the
Hawkeyes—for real); and it was so lame to sit in their Ford Focus
and listen to them talk about nerd shit and their lame football team
as we rolled into town. Now I wanted to rock some legit sleep. I
rolled up to the Holiday Inn Express to grab a room; motherfuckers didn't have shit, so like by reflex I wandered toward the Texas

Roadhouse—and there are a ton of them in the Des Moines metro area—and I ended up in a Red Roof Inn by the Texas Roadhouse's killer patio, and spent a long day passed out on a twin-sized bed. I woke up when the red neon Texas Roadhouse sign was turning on and that was a totally stupid time because I couldn't find my phone—my ass was in Iowa, beat as shit, in a lame Red Roof Inn that didn't even have continental breakfast, hearing the maids doing whatever, and the couple banging next door, and some kid whining above me, and it was all crazy annoying, and I looked at the HBO-less TV and for real couldn't figure out where the hell my phone was. It was real stupid; I needed my phone to play *Angry Birds*, and I hadn't checked Facebook in a day, maybe two. I had left it inside the pocket of my jeans that were inside my bag and so I never even heard it ring, so maybe that's why I couldn't find my phone on that stupid day.

Since I found it I had to get a fucking move on and stop bitching, so I picked up my bag, said peace out to the dickwad at the front desk watching *Two and a Half Men*, and went to eat. I noshed on a Bloomin' Onion and a Miller Light—which was getting more delicious the more I ate it, the Bloomin' Onion bigger, the happy hour specials a little less heinous. There were the most off-the-chain thickets of hotties all over Des Moines that afternoon—a bunch were total high school chicks—so I couldn't risk some jailbait situation, but I was totally looking forward to beasting of-age chicks like crazy in Denver. Carl Marcus was all up in Denver; Derek was doing his thing; Chaz Kerry and Tom Grover were chilling there, it was their hood; Maryann was hooking up with Derek there; and I'd gotten some texts about a crazy fucking crew there like Rob Riggins, his hot-as-shit sister Beth; the hot waitresses Derek chilled with; and even my dude Ryan Minor, who I played mad beer pong with at OSU. I was stoked as hell to see all of them. So I had to skip those jailbait hotties, but I'm being real when I say that Des Moines has the hottest jailbait in the world.

Some tool with a tricked-out Escalade, a total poser ride, took me a couple miles, then some farmer and his son grabbed me and hauled me to Adel, Iowa. Then near the parking lot of a Joe's Crab Shack, I bro'd up with another hitchhiker, a total New York dude, a player who'd been pulling mad cash in venture capital but now was going to Denver to chill. Seems like the dude was trying to leave some shit in NYC behind, probably like a heinous grenade or something. He was thirty and kind of a guido asshole and I wouldn't have partied with him normally, but I was hurting for some party bros. This dude was wearing some Under Armour Tactical gear and didn't have like a bag or anything—only an iPhone and a tax-free bottle of Grey Goose that he picked up in New Hampshire and he wanted to hitch together. I should have been like "Naw," since he seemed like he'd be pretty dickholey after a while, but we ended up grabbing rides together; some dude took us to Stuart, Iowa, which turned out to be a major shitshow. The two of us waited for what seemed like forever by the CVS there, looking for some cars 'till it got dark. We talked about stuff like fantasy sports and hookups and whatever, then we just played games on our phones. Shit was boring. I figured I'd house some dollars for some brews so we rolled up to a sports bar and domed some Natty. This dude got legit hammered, and kept yelling shit at me that I couldn't even understand. I didn't totally hate the dude, mainly because he had a crazy fucking alcohol tolerance. We tried to get more rides in the dark and fucking nobody came by. Shit dragged on forever. We tried to sleep on the bench outside the CVS, but the automatic door opened and closed all night and we couldn't sleep at all, and big trains were being noisy outside. We could have tried to jump on a train, but we didn't know anything about that; we weren't some kind of poor assholes who did that kind of stuff. When this dude saw a Greyhound to Omaha cruise by at the asshole of dawn he jumped on and sat down— I had to pay for his fucking fare, cheap dickwad. Teddy was the dude's name. He was sorta like my cousin's husband from Jersey. Most of the reason I rolled with him was 'cause it was sorta like having an old bro along, a shotgunning, only-sorta-douche kind of dude to party with.

The bus rolled into Council Bluffs at like 5 A.M.; I checked
that shit out. I'd heard that back in the day there were mad wet
T-shirt ragers around there before everybody started heading to
Cabo for spring break; now there were just boring houses, looking
dumb as hell with their green lawns. Then we rolled into Omaha,
and for real, I saw my first legit cowboy, a rough dude in a hat getting hammered on Bud inside a beige booth of a Pizza Hut Italian
Bistro, looking like he could totally be a bro at a Delta party except
for his outfit. We got off the bus and strutted up the big-ass hill,
an annoying hill that was a total dick move on geology's part, then
got our hitch on at the top. This player in a Yankees hat picked us
up and told us that the hotties of the Platte were just as smoking
as the hotties of Cabo. At first I thought this was totally dumb but
then we passed a Hooters that overflowed with total smokeshows
and a couple of eight-out-of-tens, and I thought that maybe dude
knew what he was talking about. A little later we were chilling at
an intersection and this other cowboy dude, who was like literally five hundred years old, hollered at us and asked if we could
drive. Both of us had licenses, but I was sort of toasted from sucking on Teddy's Grey Goose. This old dude was trying to get two
cars back to Montana. His wife was waiting around Grand Island
in Nebraska and then she could take over the driving. By then,
he'd be rolling north, so we'd need to get the fuck off. Still, we
could roll a solid hundred miles through Nebraska, so we signed
on. Teddy drove one car by himself while the old dude and I took
the other car, and as soon as we got into some open road, Teddy
started to beast it like hell at ninety miles an hour. "Goddamn it,
what the hell is he up to?" the old-ass dude asked and hit the gas to
catch him. It felt sorta like *The Fast and the Furious: Tokyo Drift*. For
a hot second it seemed like Teddy was gonna jack the car—and he
totally could have. But the old dude kept on his ass and got him to
pull over. "Damn, boy. You're gonna get a flat at that speed. Can't
you relax?"

"Oh shit, bro, was I really rocking it at ninety?" said Teddy. "I
totally didn't notice it with the asphalt being all smooth and shit."

"Just take it easy and we'll all get to Grand Island in one piece."

"Right on." So we kept cruising. Teddy had chilled out and probably even needed to lay a nap bomb. We kept hauling ass through Nebraska, checking out the abundant hotties of the Platte.

"During the depression," the cowboy was like, "I used to bed ladies on freights at least once a month. In those days, you'd see hundreds of fellas getting lucky in a flatcar or a boxcar, and they weren't just bums, they were all kinds of fellas out of work and going from one girl to another and some of them just making eyes at 'em. It was like that all over the West. Brakemen let you have all sorts of sex in boxcars in those days. I don't know about today. Nebraska's nothing like that today. Soon as that dust cloud rolled out, there wasn't no action left for a fella in the whole goddamned state. They can give Nebraska back to the Indians for all I care. I hate this shit state more than any place in the world. Montana's my place now—Missoula. You roll up there sometime and see God's ladies." A little later I passed out in his front seat when he stopped spitting stories—which was too bad because he spat some pretty awesome stories.

We got off at an exit to pound some grub. The old-ass cowboy had to get a tire fixed, and Teddy and I rocked it in an Outback. I heard a Kanye ringtone, the awesomest Kanye ringtone you've ever heard, and into the Outback walked a ripped-as-hell Nebraska player with a deep crew of dudes; his Kanye ringtone blasted over the plains, across the whole raw world and beyond. All the chicks wanted on that. Dude didn't have a shred of fat on him and was like a magnet for women. I thought, Dude, check out that bro spit game. The West is legit, and I'm all up in it. Dude just rolled into the Outback and called for the waitress who served the choicest Bloomin' Onions in Nebraska, and I chowed one with a frosty Miller Light on the side. "Babe, sling me some grub before I gotta start sucking snatch for nutrients." And he threw himself in a booth and went "for real, for real, for real. And throw some Aussie Fries with it." I felt like the most amazing player of the West was chilling next to me. I wished I was Facebook friends with him so I could check out what other shit he'd been up to besides pounding appetizers like a champ. Off the fucking chain, I thought, and the old cowboy got his tire fixed and we hauled ass to Grand Island.

We hit Grand Island in a hot second. The cowboy left to find his wife and do whatever while Teddy and I got back to hitching. A couple of lamewads picked us up—nerds, freshmen, rural dicks in a four-cylinder-at-best Pontiac—and let us out in some crappy rain. After that, some silent old dude—who the hell knows what his deal was—dropped us in Shelton. Teddy looked bummed as hell. He looked at the water tower that said SHELTON. "Fuck me," Teddy was like, "I've been in this town before. It was years ago, during a lacrosse road trip, at night, late at night when everybody was at a clutch house party. I went out on the front porch to spit some game, and there I was on the porch alone with a total grenade, and I looked up and see that name Shelton written on the water tank. Bound for a night with a horse-face, hammered as hell, and I only stayed for a few minutes, weighing the options or something, and off we went to her room. I've hated this shithole ever since!" Our asses were trapped in Shelton. Sorta like in Davenport, Iowa, most of the cars were just full of farmers, but one time we saw a Tahoe, and Tahoes are super lame, with d-bags at the wheel and their girlfriends bitching about whatever, and sitting back not realizing that they can't really off-road.

The drizzle increased and Teddy started shivering like a bitch; he was kind of a bitch. I pulled a black North Face fleece from my bag and Teddy wore it. He bitched less. I felt totally gross. I bought a mini-bottle of Captain Morgan in a gas station. I downed the bottle and sent Derek a text. We tried to grab a ride. That stupid water tower was totally rubbing it in our faces. A train passed. It was full of Amtrak assholes. Those assholes busted out West like we wanted to. It started to rain like a bitch.

This weird dude in a hat pulled over and came over to us; he looked like a rough dude. We got ready for a fucking rumble.

He walked all slow and shit. "You guys headed anywhere, or just looking for a good time?" That didn't make sense to us, but somehow it was totally awesome.

"What up?" we were like.

"Well, I own a little strip club that's a few miles down the road and I'm looking for some old boys willing to work and make a buck for themselves. I've got a couple of bouncer jobs, you know, the kind where you keep guys from touching the girls. You boys want to work for me, you can get thirty percent of the door."

"Free drinks?"

"You can get two trips to the buffet per night but no drinks. You'll have to pay at the bar. We open early on holidays." We put that in our brains. "It's a good club," he was like, and stood there waiting for us to decide. It was pretty awkward-times-ten and we didn't know how to handle this, and I knew I didn't want to get tangled up with a strip club with a buffet. I had to get shit started with my dudes in Denver.

I was like, "Naw man, I'm hauling ass as fast as I can and I don't think I have time for this." Teddy thought that would be pretty dumb too, and the dude peaced out to his ride and busted out. That was it. We cracked up about it and imagined what would have gone down if we'd said yes. I had visions of a dank and dirty place on the plains, and the mad racks of Nebraska strippers getting their jiggle on, with the pervy audience looking at everything with boners, and I know I would have felt like a total skeez-bag watching to see if any of the creeps started touching. And the neon lights flashing in the flatlands darkness, and, to top it all off, the expensive-as-hell prices of the drinks and me wanting to get the hell to Denver—and having to avoid the strippers' advances because they'd totally want to get with me but stripper chicks are nasty.

Teddy pulled a total douche move next. Some kind of shitty trailer came by, hauling a bunch of trash and driven by some weird dude. He pulled over for us. We ran to it and the driver

was saying like he could only fit one of us; like a King Douche
Teddy got in and they took off, and motherfucker was still wearing my fleece. The fleece was gone; I had like six others anyway and North Face is sort of over so I didn't mind so much. I
hung around in lame-as-hell Shelton for forever. Denver, fucking Denver, when the hell was I gonna get to Denver? I was like
inches away from just going to grab another Bloomin' Onion
when some dude in an Elantra stopped for me. I chased that shit
down.

"Where you going?"

"Denver."

"Well, I can haul you a hundred miles up the road."

"Dude, you saved my life."

"I used to get my hitch on, that's why I always pick up a
bro."

"I would too, if I had my fucking Land Rover." So dude
drove me and he talked about his lame self and I set off some nap
bombs 'till Gothenburg, where the dude dropped me off.

CHAPTER FOUR

SHIT IS RAW

The most epic ride in my life went down next, a huge-ass RV, with a bar in back, and like seven bros all chilling out in it, and the drivers, two legendary players from Minnesota, were giving rides to pretty much everybody on that road. They were the most ripped, chill-as-fuck couple of bros in America, both wearing Pony polos, Diesel jeans, and aviators; both jacked-up and tan as hell, with broad gofuckyourself grins for any douche that tried to step to them. I ran up, was like "Can I nab a ride?" They were like, "Fuck yeah, get in, shit is raw."

The RV sped off before I could sit down, but a bro grabbed me and I nabbed a seat. Somebody threw me a can of Natty. I shotgunned it in the air-conditioned, party-filled air of the RV. "Fuck yeah, let's do this!" yelled a bro in a New Era hat, and the driver jacked the RV up to eighty and tore it up. "We've been getting hammered in this shit since Des Moines. These players never stop. Every now and then you have to yell to get them to stop for a piss, otherwise you have to piss in the RV bathroom, and another dude already puked all over it."

I checked out my fellow bros. There were a couple of young bros from rural North Dakota named Chad wearing Cornhuskers hats, which is what like everybody wears out there, and these dudes were looking for some wild scenes; their dads let them have an awesome summer road trip. These two other bros from Ohio were also named Chad, football-playing bros, eating Big Macs, cracking up, and they were just partying all over the country.

"We're gonna get wild in LA!" they yelled.

"What are you gonna do there?"

"More like *who* are we going to do there!"

There was this other dude named Chad who looked like a total redneck. "Where're you from?" I was like. We were sitting next to each other, shotgunning; there was no way you could shotgun standing up cause the RV had shitty suspension. The dude turned to me, finished his brew, and was like, "Montana, bro."

And then there was Mississippi Chad and his buddy. Mississippi Chad was a this lanky tan dude who surfed couches across the country, never making real dough but just chilling, slamming brews, and keeping up a real solid natural tan. He hung out in the RV double-fisting, staring into his beer for hours without saying anything, then all of a sudden he looked at me and was like, "Where the fuck *you* headed?"

I told him I was rolling to Denver.

"I got a slam piece there but I haven't smashed with her for like ever." He talked like a real raw dude. He was legit. His buddy was young as fuck, like sixteen, wearing the same sort of busted gear; I mean that they wore out-of-date polo shirts stained by the splash of beer pong and the ash of cigars and the shit on their buddies' couches. The kid was quiet as fuck and he probably was running from like a psycho grenade or something. Montana Chad tried to give them shit with his d-baggy smile. They didn't give a fuck. Montana Chad could be a real dick. His asshole grin sorta pissed me off the way he got all in your face.

"You got any cash?" he was like.

"Fuck no, maybe enough for a case of Natty 'till I get to Denver. What about you?"

"I know where you can score some."

"Where?"

"Just bust into a bedroom at a frat party and steal that shit. Cash and DVDs, you feel me?"

"Yeah, but that's sort of a dick move."

"I'll do that when I really need some dough. Headed up to Montana to see my bros. I'll have to get off this whip at Cheyenne and roll up some other way. These motherfuckers are going straight to Los Angeles."

"For real?"

"For real—if you want to hang in LA you got a ride."

I thought it over; being able to haul ass through Nebraska, Wyoming, and Utah in a hot few seconds, and then blasting through Nevada the next day and cruising into Los Angles after that almost made me change my mind. But I needed to get my ass to Denver. I'd have to peace out at Cheyenne and figure out how to get there.

I got stoked when the two Minnesota bros driving the RV pulled over in North Platte to slam grub; I totally wanted to hang out with those dudes. As we came out of the RV they fistbumped with everybody. "Piss it up, bros!" one was like. "Nosh o'clock!" the other was like. They strutted into Johnny Rockets and we all strutted after them, and ate some Rocket Double burgers and flavored coke while they pounded onion rings and brewdogs like it was their job. They were tight; they were going to LA for their fantasy football draft and having a good fucking time doing it. On the way to LA they picked up everybody who looked like they wanted to party. This was like the fifth time they did this; it was totally tits. They partied everywhere. They chugged like whales. I tried to chill with them—I was awkward as fuck and just looked like an idiot—and all they did was give me a couple of badass nods and two flashes of bright white-stripped teeth.

All the dudes from the RV were in the Johnny Rockets except Mississippi Chad and his buddy. They were chilling in RV, getting pretty drunk and sleeping. Shit was getting dark. The bros who were driving were doing a quick workout to stay loose. I knew I had to use the time to go buy a case of Natty to keep the party bumpin' 'till sunrise. They were like, "Yeah bro, make it fast."

"I'll totally let you nab a couple cans!" I was like.

"Nah bro, we only drink Miller products."

Montana Chad and the Nebraska Chads came with me on the beer run. They threw a few dollars my way, and Montana Chad a few, and I bought a 30 rack. Some loser dudes watched us go by from their stupid offices; everything there seemed boring as shit. It was just a whole bunch of flat nothing past every stupid street. I felt like I had to take a wicked dump in North Platte, I didn't know why. Turns out I went one Bloomin' Onion too far. I blasted that out of me, got back on the RV, and rolled out. It got dark fast. We all shotgunned a Natty, and all of a sudden everything around was just like desert or something, a ton of sand and whatever the fuck grows in sand. I was like "Fuck."

"What the hell is this?" I asked Montana Chad.

"We're in the legit West, bro. Feed me another Natty."

"Fuck yeah!" the high-school Chads were like. "Ohio, eat these nuts! What would our buddies say if they saw us now? Bam!"

The bros up front had switched to let the less-drunk brother drive; dude gunned it like crazy. The road got really bad: all humped out with ditches and shit, and the RV drifted from one side to the other—luckily not when other cars were coming the other way or we'd have totally murdered them. Dudes could for real drive. The RV flew like a G6 through the Nebraska chode—the little part that sticks out over Colorado. It hit my brain that I was close as hell to Colorado, not there yet, but so close it felt like I could piss on it. I got stoked as fuck. We shotgunned some Natties. Our shirts came off, we arm-wrestled. I felt like Christian Bale in *Terminator Salvation* when he blows up Skynet.

From nowhere, Mississippi Chad took a break from his shotgunning, looked at me, and was like, "This shit reminds me of UT-Austin."

"Are you a Longhorn?"

"Fuck no, I'm an Ole-fucking-Miss Rebel." And that was for real how he said it.

"Where's your lil' bro from?"

"He got into some kind of shit during a college visit at Ole Miss, so I offered to do him a solid. Lil' bro's never been out on his own. I do him solids as best as I can, he's only a kid." Although this might sound totally racist, even though Mississippi Chad was white there was something straight-up gangster in him, sorta like my dude Eddie Hammer, who pounded Four Loko on OSU campus, but a rawdog Hammer, an off-the-chain Hammer, beasting it all over the place all the time, Vail in the winter and Key West in the summer, all 'cause the dude couldn't crash anywhere for more than a week without banging somebody's sister and because he had a ridiculous credit limit on his Visa.

"I've chilled in Ogden a couple times. If you want to ride on to Ogden I know some hotties there who have bangable sisters we could smash with."

"I'm going to Denver from Cheyenne."

"Fuck, plow straight through, dudes don't get a ride like this every day."

Shit sounded good. But how bangable were the sisters? "How bangable are the sisters?" I was like.

"They're the hotties that most bros would slice off a nut for; you're liable to blow your dick when you see them."

During sophomore year I went on semester at sea with this crazy dude from Louisiana we called Big Jim Halverson, Ronnie Jameson Halverson, who knew he wanted to be a bro since he was little. He was eight and saw this bro come up to compliment his mom's rack, and she was totally frigid, and when the bro went off in his Cherokee the little bro had said, "Mom, what's up with that guy?" "That's a disgusting bro." "Mom, I want to be a bro when I grow up." "Shut your mouth, no Halversons will ever become bros." But dude never forgot that shit, and when he grew up, after a little time playing football at LSU, he did become a bro. Big Jim and I spent a ton of nights slugging brews and spitting game at sea-faring hotties. Mississippi Chad's alcohol tolerance was so similar to Big Jim's that I had to be like, "Did you ever party with a bro called Big Jim Halverson somewhere?"

And he was like, "You mean the tall-ass motherfucker with the jacked-up triceps?"

"For real. Dude was from like Ruston, Louisiana."

"Fuck yeah! Louisiana Jim he's sometimes called. Right on, I have totally hung with Big Jim."

"And he used to get his workout on in the East Texas Crunch gym?"

"Crunch is right. And now he's all about 24 Hour Fitness."

And that was right on the money; and it blew my skull that Mississippi Chad had for real partied with Jim, who I'd been texting for pretty much ever. "And he used to get his workout on in the New York Athletic Club?"

"Aw dude, I don't know."

"I guess you only partied with him in the West."

"Totes. I've never rolled to New York."

"Well fuck me, I'm stoked you partied with him. This is a big-ass country. Yet I fucking knew you must have partied with him."

"Yeah dude, I partied with Big Jim pretty hard. Always generous with his fifth of Jägermeister when he's got one. Mean-ass brawler too; I saw him flatten a fifth-year senior on the porch of the Beta house over a game of beer bong with one punch." That was Big Jim all over; dude always took beer pong so seriously; he looked like Brekin Meyer, but a ripped-ass Brekin Meyer who loved Jäger.

"Hell yeah!" I shouted, and I shotgunned another Natty, and was getting pretty awesome-crunk. The fucking awesome fun of playing *Madden* on the RV's Xbox wiped away the bitter Natty aftertaste, and the crunkness hugged me like a blanket. "Cheyenne, I'ma blow you up!" I was all like. "Denver, look out for my dick!"

Montana Chad pointed at my Urban Outfitters flip-flops, and was like, "You fucking think you could even play a half-court game in that shit?"—looking serious as hell, of course, and the other bros heard him and cracked the shit up. I can't deny they were sort of lame shoes; I wore them 'cause I didn't want my feet to sweat like balls, and except for the rain in fucking Toledo they were totally clutch shoes for the trip. So I had to crack up like hell with them. The flip-flops were totally jacked by now too, with the straps falling off and they stunk like ass. We shot-gunned another beer and cracked the shit up even harder. Like in *2 Fast 2 Furious* we hauled ass through some jank-ass towns in the dark, and passed Ford Escorts full of fugly bitches under the stars. They scoped us driving by, and we saw them lick their lips from inside their stupid cars—those ugly bitches wished they could get with us.

There were also a good amount of hotties around; they were home for break. The Dakota Chads were fidgeting. "I think we'll bust ass out of here at the next piss call; seems like there's mad tail around here."

"All you gotta do is beast it north when you run out of slam pieces," Montana Chad was like, "and just follow the hotties 'till you get to Canada." The Dakota Chads weren't impressed; they thought he was full of shit.

All this time the little blond bro just chilled; occasionally Mississippi Chad leaned out of his Buddhistic chug-trance over the rushing blast of *Madden* and said something funny as shit in to him. The little bro cracked up. Mississippi Chad was doing him a solid, clutch and raw. I couldn't figure out what was up with those dudes. They had no iPhones. I let them check Facebook on mine; I thought they were all right. Dudes were gracious as fuck. We balled it through another jank-ass town, passed another line of tall stacked hotties in PINK sweatpants clustered in the dim light like moths with boobs looking to bone, and returned to the dark shit, and the Hardee's sign ahead was pure and bright as we dropped Jägerbombs over the endless stretch of American night, about a shot a minute, and no pussies refusing any chal-lenge to chug anywhere. And once I saw this cow standing in the tall grass of a rundown house as we flew by. It looked fuck-ing stupid.

When we got to the next town, Montana Chad was all like "I gotta piss, bros," but the dudes didn't stop and the RV kept cruising. "Bros, I gotta get my piss on!" Montana Chad was like.

"Piss out the window," said somebody.

"What-fucking-ever," dude was like, and as we all watched (no homo), he balanced up on the back of the couch, opened the window, and stuck his junk out the window. Somebody texted the bros driving up front so they'd know the awesome prank that was getting set up. And just as Montana Chad was about to get his stream on, the driving dudes started zigzagging the RV at like seventy miles an hour. Montana Chad stumbled for a hot second; we saw him totally soak the side of the window; he struggled to get his junk pointed right. Dudes swung the RV. Slam, Montana Chad fell off the couch, pissing all over himself. While we were laughing like hell, he was swearing like a little whiny bitch. "Not cool; not cool." He had no clue we were pranking his ass; he just kept trying, hella-pissed. When dude was finished, his jeans were soaked, and now he had to wipe the piss off his Oakleys, and with a most pissed-off look, and everybody cracking the fuck up, except for the weird-ass blond kid, and the Minnesotan bros totally losing their shit in the front. I handed him a Natty to make up for it.

"What the shit," he said, "were those motherfuckers doing that on purpose?"

"Yeah, bro."

"Fuck me, that's fucked up. I pissed out the window in Nebraska and everything was fine."

Next we cruised into some shithole called Ogallala, and the bros driving were all like "Piss break!" and it was beyond hilarious. Montana Chad stood by the RV, still raging as hell for pissing on himself. The two Dakota Chads said peace out to us 'cause they wanted to start cruising for tang here. They disappeared into a dark bar down the street where iPhones were glowing and where some dude in Adidas windpants said they could snag some bangable ass. I had to eat a Bloomin' Onion. Mississippi Chad and his buddy came with me. I strutted into some seriously awesome shit, an Outback Steakhouse with a fucking two-dollar draft special. People were getting crunk, while Linkin Park rocked out over the stereo. Shit got wild when we rolled in three deep. Mississippi Chad and the blond dude just stood there, with no game; all they wanted was a Bloomin' Onion. There were total hotties, too. And one grade-A smokeshow made eyes at the kid and he never picked up on it, and that was pretty lame.

I bought a Bloomin' Onion for us; they were grateful as fuck. It was time to get the crew back in the RV. Now it was like midnight, and we were grade-A hammered. Mississippi Chad, who'd done more crazy shit on the road than any of the other motherfuckers, said we should all go up on the roof and car surf. In this manner, standing on top of the RV going balls-out down the highway, we had the most raw time as the mad-frigid air turned our Nattys into slushies. Shit got crazier the more we shotgunned brews. We were all up in Wyoming now. Surfing the RV, I stared straight into my iPhone, loving the Facebook posts I was making, loving how hard I rocked it since Toledo after all, and getting super pumped for the times I'd have in Denver— however shit would go down. Then Mississippi Chad started to sing a sick Linkin Park classic. He dropped it in an awesome, raw-as-hell voice, with a Durst-esque rasp, and it was killer, all about how there's something inside that pulls you beneath the surface and shit.

I said, "Holy shit, I forgot how awesome that band is."

"Best fucking band in America," dude was like.

"Bro, I hope you get to where you're going and slay mad tail when you do."

"I always end up slayin' a little somethin' somethin'."

Montana Chad was dropping some nap bombs. Dude woke up and was like, "Yo, player, how about you and me trawl for tang in Cheyenne together tonight before you peace out to Denver?"

"Fuck yeah." My drunk ass was ready for action.

The RV rolled into the edge of Cheyenne and we saw the towering lights of a Sonic, and then from like nowhere came a big-ass crowd all over everywhere. "WTF, it's like a bunch of lame cowboys," said Montana Chad. A whole bunch of lame dudes, fat men in fucking stupid boots and big-ass cowboy hats, with their fat wives in cowgirl shit, hung out and did whatever lame shit at this stupid festival in old Cheyenne. There was probably some cooler stuff in the new part of town, but all these assholes were in Oldtown. Blank guns went off. The saloons had shitty draft specials. It was crazy, and at the same time I was like What the fuck: on my first trip to the West there was all this lame, poser bullshit that wasn't legit at all. It was time to peace out from the RV; the Minnesotan bros weren't into this scene. I felt sorta sad when I realized that I'd never see these dudes again. "You'll have no chance of pulling tail without me," I cracked up. "You're all cool as shit, but you have no game!"

"Shut the fuck up," said Mississippi Chad. And the RV rolled out, balling through all the posers who had no idea about the awesomeness of the bros inside, shotgunning brews like badasses on a mission. I forced myself to throw up so I could rally.

CHAPTER FIVE

HUNGOVER LIKE A PRO

M ontana Chad and I started getting our bar crawl action on. I had like a hundred bones in my wallet, and dropped a fat eighty of them that night. First we hung around the fat cowboy tourists at the Applebee's bar, the Friday's bar, the Chili's bar; then I tried to pour some grub into Chad, who was crunk-staggering all over the place from sucking down so much Natty: the dude sucked at drinking; he got real sloppy, and in no time he'd be grinding up on some busted action. I swung by an Outback to refill my gut after puking, and I saw this waitress who looked totally like Shakira. I demolished my Bloomin' Onion, and then I wrote some shit on the check. The Outback Steakhouse was hella-quiet; all the losers in town must be eating somewhere less delicious. She checked out the back of the check and cracked up. I had written a limerick about how I wanted to bone with her.

"I'd love to, baby, but I have a date with my boyfriend."

"Can't you drop his ass?"

"No, no, I can't," she said in a way that showed how much she totally wanted to bone with me, with her Outback nametag looking all hot on her rack.

"I'll come by later and maybe you'll change your mind," I was like, and she was like, "Yeah, bring it." I scoped her for a little longer and polished off another Miller Lite. Then her boyfriend showed up to try to get her to head out. I could tell he probably couldn't bench much more than the bar. I swiped her ass real fast on my way out. Shit was like mad outside with all these lame fat dudes getting A-plus hammered and shouting and whatever. It was a fucking mess. Some Indian dudes were walking around

the crowd looking all pissed in some kind of feathers or something. Montana Chad had gotten totally hammered.

He was all like, "I just wrote a Facebook message to my dad
in Montana. AT&T sucks and it won't send. You think you can
find some goddamn WiFi to hook up to?" Dude was too hammered to function; he tossed his phone to me and staggered into
a sports bar. I went to a Starbucks, got online, and looked at the
message. "What up dad, I'll be back Wednesday. Everything is
chill with me and I hope stuff is chill with you. Chad." I thought
the dude was pretty cool but now I could see what kind of lame
stuff he wrote to his dad. I met up with him at the sports bar.
We snagged a couple ladies, a hot-ass blond chick and a chubby
grenade. They sorta sucked, but we needed to get our smash on.
We went over to a shitty club that had a brutal dudes-to-chicks
ratio and I dropped a fat wad on Bacardi Ices for the chicks and
MGDs for the dudes. I got re-crunked and felt chill as hell. I
was focused like a sex laser on the blond hottie. I grinded up on
her and she was totally feeling it. The club started to really suck
so we went out to the street. I checked my phone; the hot, ever-
flowing text messages of booty calls from back home were there,
burning. The two chicks wanted to head to the bus station, and
'cause we're gentlemen we went with them, but then it turned
out that they were meeting some dickhole sailor dude, and this
dickhole was rolling with a bunch of his dickhole buddies. I was
all like, "What the shit?" The hottie wanted to go back home
to Colorado. "I'll ride the bus with you," I was like, hoping for
some back-of-the-Greyhound action.

"No, the bus stops on the highway and I'll have to walk
super far. My Uggs are totally new and I don't want to get them
dirty tonight."

"Come on, babe, it'll be like a nice walk."

"Shut up," she was like. "I've gotta get out of here and move
to New York or something. I'm so over this shit. Cheyenne is
like the only thing around and there's like no cool people here.

"New York is lame as hell."

"Bullshit," she said like a champion bitch.

There were like literally a million people in the bus station. Tons of assholes were wandering around, getting on buses and whatever. The blonde hottie left me hanging and started getting all up on the sailor and the others. Montana Chad was dropping a nap bomb on a bench. I checked my phone. The AT&T service is the same all over the country, always showing like three bars but never actually making fucking calls and it gets me pissed in a way that only AT&T can. It was exactly like being in Columbus, except my data service was a little faster. I was pissed at the way my trip suddenly got less awesome, not getting laid, and fucking around in this shithole, trying to smash with this frigid hottie and blowing too much of my online poker cash. It made me crazy pissed. I hadn't slept in like forever so I decided not to let that frigid hottie know what a bitch she was and instead rock some sleep; I conked out on a bench with my North Face bag, and straight up passed out 'till like 8 A.M. when all the stupid assholes passing by woke me up.

I came down with a weapons-grade hangover. Montana Chad had peaced out to Montana or wherever. I rolled over to the 7-Eleven next to the bus station. And in that 7-Eleven, for the first time, I saw on a bunch of shelves, a huge shitton of Broncos merchandise. I took some aspirin. I needed to roll to Denver stat. I domed some breakfast, a decent Denny's Grand Slam, and then I walked out to the road. The stupid cowboy festival was still happening; everybody was at some dumb rodeo, and it would be all the same stupid shit again. I was like "fuck that noise." I had to party with my Denver crew. I drank a 5-Hour Energy and went to a travel plaza where a couple of freeways went off toward Denver. I took the one that looked like it had the best food. I nabbed a fast-as-hell ride from a lame Connecticut dude road-tripping in his Taurus, probably getting no tail; he was like some kind of East Coast d-bag. He talked forever; I was ultra-hungover from all the drinking. When we went over some bumps I nearly chunked it on the dashboard. A few miles later when he dropped me in Longmont, Colorado, I got my shit back together and was ready to get back on the party train. I peaced out.

Longmont was awesome. There was a killer porch party at this big house that some dudes lived at. I asked the fat dude on the couch if I could hang there, and he was like "Def;" so I sprayed on some Axe, tilted my cap, grabbed a brew, and scoped the super hottie in the Tebow jersey. I got hammered there for a couple hours, the only shitty thing was this asshole who kept pushing for the keg. I was partying in Colorado! I kept getting psyched. Fucking clutch! Fucking clutch! Fucking clutch! I'm making it! And after a couple hours filled with kegstands and beer pong, I put my shirt back on, made out with the Tebow jersey hottie, and peaced out, raw and awesome as Tebow himself, and got a Bloomin' Onion at an Outback to rescue my beer-blasted stomach with some deliciousness.

BTW, this crazy hot chick served me the Bloomin' Onion; she was totally vibing me too; I was pumped, it totally compensated for all of last night's bullshit. I was like, "Hell yeah! How sweet is *Denver* gonna be!" I strutted over to the road and snagged a hot ride with this Denver business dude in his new Cherokee. Dude cruised it at ninety. My brain got into pumped mode; I checked the map on my iPhone to see how close we were. Past the sprawling outlet stores all glowing beneath the shimmering Nike and Hilfiger signs, I'd finally be all up in Denver. I imagined hanging in a Denver bar later, with the whole crew, and they would see how awesome I was, wandering West across America to bring the party, and the party I had brought would be totally off the fucking chain. The business dude and I talked about whatever, and in a hot second we were going past Sports Authority Field in Denver; there were sports bars, tailgates, tons of parking, and the distant downtown squeals of hotties, and now I was all up in Denver. Dude dropped me by the stadium. I strutted with the most stoked-up feeling of awesome ever, among the drunk dudes and football chicks of Sports Authority Field.

CHAPTER SIX

GO BRONCOS, BITCHES

B ack then, Derek and I weren't super tight, so as soon as I rolled into Denv-town I wanted to chill with Chaz Kerry, natch. I hollered at his cell and heard his ringback music—it was early Bizkit, which is hilarious and fucking raw. Chaz is a lanky-ass blond dude with a Josh Hartnett look that helps him slay tail by looking all sensitive; if I was a chick, I'd hit that. Dude is a total Western baller who's smashed in Texas Roadhouse bathrooms and went all-state in high school football. He's like a crazy film buff. "The shit that I think is awesome Sam, about Will Ferrell movies is how he's always like funny as shit in like every situation. In *Semi-Pro* there's like this part where he's playing basketball but he's wearing these shorts that are like way too fucking small. Shit dude, that got my shit!"

I saw from Chaz's Facebook check-ins that he was noshing down on some wings at the local Buffalo Wild Wings. I texted him and the dude rolled by and grabbed me in his old Hummer that he used to go off-roading on sick weekend trips. Dude rolled up in lacrosse shorts and an Aéropostale shirt. I was kicking back on my North Face bag shooting the shit with the same dickhole sailor who knew that hottie bitch, asking him why the fuck she was such a bitch. Dude was too plowed to say anything. Me and Chaz rolled out and Chaz had to swing by an ATM to grab some cash. After that Chaz needed to pick up his MacBook from the Apple Store, and then other shit, meanwhile I just wanted to go slam some beers. But like the whole time I kept thinking: What shit is Derek up to right now? Chaz wasn't hanging with Derek anymore, 'cause some kinda drama happened, so dude had no clue where he was at.

"Is Carl Marcus up in this bitch?"

"Yeah." But dude didn't hang with Carl either. This was when Chaz Kerry started pussing out on our crew. I was gonna go drop a nap bomb up in his crib that day. Then later I could move over to Tom Grover's place where my buddy Ryan Minor was staying. There was definitely some drama up in all this shit, and the drama totally split the crew: Chaz Kerry, Tom Grover, and Ryan Minor, and the Rigginses, all being sorta dicks to Derek Morrisey and Carl Marcus. And I was stuck in the middle of all of this.

The rest of the crew was just totally jealous of Derek. Derek's dad was a total badass, like the biggest badass in all of Denver, so Derek was genetically predisposed to being a badass. He was his dad's wingman at bars when he was in kindergarten. Little Derek would steal brews from under the bar and sneak them back to the Golden Tee machines where his dad was chilling. At the Englewood Hooters, he broke the state record for eating cheeseburgers and went to third base with a waitress. Ever since he could read he was getting hammered. His prime move was jacking some Mike's Hard Lemonades, offering them to chicks, taking them up in the mountains, and getting his Rocky Mountain bone on before getting plowed at the first sports bar he came to. His dad started as a lame-ass middle manager, but then became the marketing director for the Denver Nuggets, which is more awesome than anything, and was always handing out free skybox tickets to games. Derek had a couple of half-brothers from his mom—she divorced when his dad got awesome—but they were totes jealous of him. Derek's only real bros were regulars at Hooters. Derek and Carl were like the new party-slaying monsters of Denver that summer, them and their crew, and they partied in Carl's condo right next to Hooters, a sick condo where Carl, Derek, me, Timmy Snipes, Todd Dinkel, and Ray Jeffries all got wild. I'll spit more about these dudes in hot second.

Around like 2 P.M. I laid a nap bomb in Chaz Kerry's room while his mom cooked and Chaz played *Madden* in the basement.

Chaz's dad was hella-old and always told slow-ass stories about whatever shit he did on a farm when he was little, like dude rode ponies bareback, which sounds pretty gay to me. He taught some kind of English shit in Oklahoma, then he did like insurance or whatever around Denver. He still had a bunch of business cards, which were extra boring. What was clutch was he had hooked up their TV with Netflix Instant. He got a forty-inch LG and hooked it up to the Internet. It had Netflix already installed—or something—so you could just watch Netflix without any other boxes. I turned it on and started watching *Step Brothers* underneath a big poster of *Scarface* and it was just as hilarious as always. I tried to grab some sleep but it was just too hilarious to stop watching. Finally the movie ended, so I headed downstairs. Chaz's dad asked me what I thought of the TV setup. I said the TV was a little small but built-in Netflix is super clutch, for real. That old dude was pretty solid. He did say some total bullshit about he like invented Netflix before Netflix happened and he could like be a millionaire if he sued. But that was pretty clear bullshit; if he thought up Netflix then my dick is like twelve-feet long. That night we noshed down on the food his mom made, some chicken parm with a mad good breading. But where the fuck was Derek?

CHAPTER SEVEN

PULLING THE DOUBLE SMASH

The next couple days were legit as hell—and totally raw. I started crashing at Tom Grover's parents' crib with Ryan Minor. The place was crazy big and the fridge was jammed with brews, and there was a hot living room where Minor chilled in his boxers watching ESPN Classic—a pretty funny, chubby fucker, who could turn on the sickest party vibe in the world when given a few generous shots of Jäger. He sat like that on the sofa, and I did chin-ups in the doorway, wearing only my Buckeyes sweats. Minor had just finished watching the classic OSU-Miami 2002 national championship game. It was awesome. The Hurricanes had a killer offense but the Buckeyes had a brick-wall defense. The game is like neck and neck. The Canes are up by a TD. Then the Bucks are up by a TD. And then at the end there's the crazy pass interference call. It's as fucking amazing now as it was then. Minor and I were pretty solid bros; he totally respected the Bucks. Minor was into skiing, just like most Denver dudes. He showed me pictures on his phone from a ski trip to the Alps. "For real, Sam, if you came with me on a sick trip to the Alps with some vicious Swiss hotties, then you'd stop just getting hammered at Outback all the time."

"I get you. But you know I fucking love Outback Steakhouse. Straight up, Minor, if you just knew how much awesome shit I pounded on my trip."

The Rigginses' place was pretty nearby. The mom was a MILF who owned part of a pool-less Best Western and had five sons and two daughters. Rob Riggins was buddies with Tom Grover and was for sure the pimpest son. As soon as Rob and I shotgunned a beer together we were hella-tight. We got hammered in some sports bars and Irish pubs. Rob's sister was named Beth, and this chick was like a category five smoke-show—straight-up Western spank bank material. She was Tom Grover's slam piece. Meanwhile Minor, who was just chilling in the apartment with me, was smashing like crazy with Becky, Tom's sister. I was like the only dude getting no play. I kept asking around, all like, "Where's Derek at?" Everybody just gave me bullshit.

Then shit finally went down. I got a Facebook message from my boy Carl Marcus. He told me where his condo was at. I was like "What's shaking in Denver? I mean what the fuck are you *busting up?* What's the fucking deal?"

"You're gonna shit a knife when I tell you."

I flew like hell to meet him. He was interning at an investment bank; fucking Rob Riggins called him from a payphone, and pranked him saying that I boned his aunt. Dude totally thought I had boned his aunt. And Riggins was like, "Gotcha. Sam's in town," and told him where I was crashing.

"And what's Derek's deal?"

"Derek's dick is like a foot deep in Denver. You gotta hear this shit." Turns out Derek was totally pulling the double smash on these two chicks in different hotels: Maryann, his gf, and Carly, this new chick. "When he's not blasting those chicks he hangs with me."

"What kind of shit is that?"

"Derek and I are making absolutely epic business happen. We're trying to get hammered with absolutely no ralphing and no blueballs every night of the week. We've had to chug 5-Hour Energy. We stand on opposite ends of the beer pong table, ready to rumble. I've been telling Derek what a badass he could be, become Brewmaster for Coors, lay an NFL cheerleader, or become the sickest dude since Jeter. But dude keeps rushing into fights with big douches. I always get his back. He punches and yells, amped up. Dude, Sam, Derek is always getting caught up in that stupid shit." Carl was all like, "For real."

"What's the plan?" I was like. Derek always had a plan up in his dome.

"It goes down like this: I finished my internship a half-hour ago. Meanwhile Derek lays pipe to Maryann over at her hotel so I get on my party shirt and do some grooming. Then at like one he busts ass over to the La Quinta to see Carly—and natch Carly and Maryann have no idea that he's pulling a double smash—and he bones with Carly, and then I roll up like a half-hour later. After that the two of us go out—Carly is usually a total bitch about it 'cause she hates me—and we'll like go party or just chill here and get hammered and play beer pong and *Madden* 'till sunrise. We used to party for even longer, but Derek is getting all pussywhipped by these chicks and can't bro it as hard as we want. He rolls back to Maryann after that—and dude is probably just gonna be dumping her ass soon anyway. Both those chicks say that they love Derek."

Carl told me about how Derek started hooking up with Carly. Ray Jeffries, who was on Derek's rec league football team, met her at a club and took her back to his place; thinking he was hot shit, Ray called up the whole crew to come hang and check out how hot she was. The whole crew chilled for a while, doing a few shots and trying to get up on Carly. Derek just leaned back and checked his phone. When everybody was peacing out, Derek found Carly on Facebook, friended her, sent her a message saying he'd be back at four, and rolled out. Carly totally locked out Ray and then smashed with player-of-the-year Derek. I needed to go hang with that motherfucker. Derek could totally score me some tang too; he knew like every hottie around Denver.

I rolled through the sick streets of Denver with Carl. The bars were so plentiful, the hotties so fine, the promise of cheap-ass drink-and-shot combos so awesome, that I was afraid I'd wake up. We headed over to the hotel where Derek was railing Carly. It was a nice-ish La Quinta with full breakfast but the pool in the back wasn't big enough to do laps in. We took the elevator. Carl knocked and then ran like hell behind the ice machine to hide; Carly would go Terminator-bitch if she saw him. I waited in front of the door. Derek opened it with just a New Era cap on his junk. There was a brown-haired hottie on the bed, with her choice ass covered in Aéropostale short shorts, who looked at me like "What the fuck."

"Motherfucking Sa-a-am!" said Derek. "Well fuck me—no shit—yes, you're here—you sonofabitch you finally beasted it on the road. Well, shit, for real—we gotta—yes, yes, for real—we gotta, we gotta do this shit! Hey, Carly." And dude turned to her. "This is Sam, we got wild in Columbus together. This guy has never been to Denver before and it's like totally clutch for me to take him out and just drown him in snatch."

"How long are you going to be out for?"

He checked his phone and was like, "It's like one-fourteen. We'll be chilling for like a couple hours, so then I'll be back for another hour of rawdogging together, mad-ass rawdogging, babe, and then, you know, like I said before, I gotta go and get into work like crazy fucking early in the morning—which I know is weird but I totally told you about it." (Derek was totally lying so he could party with Carl, who was still hiding like a pussy.) "I gotta get my pants back on and get back to partying, to life, to beers and shit, you know, 'cause now it's like *one-fifteen* and I gotta get things started."

"Whatever, baby, can you come back by three?"

"Babe, I told you, I gotta have two solid hours. You get me?" And dude went over and made out with her for a little. There was a big blown-up photo of Derek on the wall, taken in Cabo, with his huge package bulging from his swim trunks, taken by Carly. It was awesome but it felt a little gay to look at it. Everything was weird.

We busted out; Carl met up with us by the La Quinta front desk. And we proceeded down the narrowest, strangest, most confusing La Quinta floor plan that ever happened, 'cause who puts the gym on the other side of the hotel from the lobby? We shot the shit in the parking lot. Derek was like, "Sam, I've got this choice piece of tail you could smash with right now if she's done working." He checked his phone. "Her name's Tina, she's totally smoking, a little bit of a prude about some shit which I've tried to get her to chill out about and I think you can make it happen, you stud. So we'll roll over there now—we gotta bring beers, 'cause they've got some themselves, but shit!" he said almost dropping his phone. "I'm totally gonna blast her sister Mandy later."

"What the fuck?" Carl was like, "We were supposed to just chill and play *Madden* tonight."

"Yeah dude, after."

"Fuck this Denver bullshit!" yelled Carl to the sky.

"Isn't this dude fucking hilarious?" said Derek, checking his phone real quick. "Do you believe this dude? Do you believe him?" And Carl started doing his funny-ass crunk dance in the middle of the road just like he used to do in Columbus and it was still hilarious.

'Cause my poker cash was a little low, I was all like, "How the shit are we gonna buy brews out here?"

"I can totally hook you up with a job," Derek was like, all serious and shit. "I'll blow up your phone once I'm finished boning Maryann and roll up to your place, say what up to Minor, and take you over to my buddy's temp agency, where you can grab a job in a hot second and pull some dough come Friday. I did it a couple weeks ago 'cause I've been dropping too much cash on these chicks. Friday night for real us three—the three amigos of awesome—gotta get hammered at a Broncos game, and it'll be an awesome time . . . ." And whatever like that.

We rolled up to the waitress chicks' crib. The waitress chick I was supposed to bone was still at work; the waitress chick Derek wanted to smash was home. We chilled and had some drinks. I was supposed to holler at Rob Riggins. I did. Dude came over in a hot second. For real, this dude busted in, ripped off his Under Armour and started grinding up on this Mandy Bellingfort chick who he never met before. Beer can pyramids crashed to the floor. It was like 3 A.M. Derek bolted to go bone Carly for an hour. Dude boned on schedule. The waitress chick I was supposed to smash with came over. We needed to get rolling, and we were getting pretty sloppy. Rob Riggins called up his dude with a Yukon. He drove over. Everybody got in the whip; Carl was trying to shotgun beers with Derek in the back seat, but the ride was too bumpy. "We can chill at my crib!" I was like. So we went over there; as soon as the car pulled up to my place I jumped out and did a hilarious drunk break dance on the lawn. My keys totally fell out; I could get some copies. We busted ass into the place. Ryan Minor tried to keep us out in his boxers.

"Dudes! Tom Grover is gonna be pissed if you trash his place!"

"WTF?" we all shouted. Shit was wild. Riggins was getting to second base in the grass with one of the waitress chicks. Minor was being a real dick. We were gonna call up Tom Grover and tell him Minor was jerking off on his bed. But we just decided to hit up some bars. I blacked out and came to in the street with my fucking AmEx missing. Such a total drag.

I hauled ass to Tom Grover's place to get some rest action on. I texted Minor and he let me in. I wondered if Derek and Carl were playing some *Madden*. I'd find that shit out later. I was crazy drunk, and I slept like a fucking champ.

CHAPTER EIGHT

DENVER DELTS

The whole crew started planning a wild trip up in the mountains. We started planning shit in the morning, then I got a text out of the fucking blue—that Teddy dude I road tripped with for a hot bit; he remembered that I said I'd be in Denver. I had to get back my fleece. Teddy was crashing with his slam piece near Colfax. Dude was looking for jobs, so I told him to come by so Derek could hook him up. Derek busted in, amped up as hell, while Minor and I were slugging protein shakes. Derek was too amped to even sit for a second. "I've got a ton happening so let's move it."

"Just chill a second for this dude Teddy to swing by."

Minor thought how amped up Derek was was pretty hilarious. Minor had come to Denver just to chill. He treated Derek like he was a douche. Derek didn't give a shit. Minor would be all like, "Morrisey, what's this shit I hear about your dick being like one-inch long?" And Derek sucked down an energy gel and was like, "Whatever, whatever, fuck that noise," and looked at his phone, and Minor cracked up. Sometimes I felt like a dick hanging with Derek—Minor thought he was a total douche and a dumbass. Natch he was just jealous, but I still wanted to show all these dickholes how raw Derek was.

We picked up Teddy. Derek didn't really give a shit about him either, and off we rolled across Denver to nab some jobs. Working was gonna be totally dumb. Teddy kept fucking yammering like all the time. We talked to this dude at a temp agency who would take both of us; we had to get in at like 8 A.M. and shit didn't stop 'till like six. This dude was like, "I need some committed team players."

"I'm all over this," Teddy was like, but I thought the whole thing sounded a little lame. I had like a ton of other awesome shit I had to make happen.

Teddy went in to work like an idiot; I was like, "Fuck that." I had a place to crash and Minor had a bunch of food and booze, and I could always dip into my parents' credit card. So I lit shit up. The Rigginses had this huge rager. The Riggins MILF was like traveling somewhere. Rob Riggins sent a Facebook invite to like everybody on the planet and was like, "Just bring some Natty and Jäger;" then he started following up with some chicks. I texted a bunch of them for him. A king-sized truckload of hotties rolled up. I texted Carl and asked him what he and Derek were getting up to. They were gonna hang at like 3 A.M. I rolled up there when the party got un-hot.

Carl's condo was in a new granite building near a Hooters. You went in the lobby, past the doorman, took the elevator, and went through a hallway and came to his place. He'd made like a man cave fit for Zeus: a king bed, a fifty-inch plasma TV, 5.1 surround sound speakers that oozed Monday Night Football, and a jacked-up Bowflex that he rigged up when he maxed out the normal kind. He showed me his daily workout. He called it "Denver Delts." Carl woke up in the morning and did two hundred pushups while alternating hands; he did one hundred pull-ups in the doorway and they looked hard as fuck. A couple reps on the makeshift Bowflex decimated his upper arms. His shoulders, his jacked-up shoulders that you could see from the other side of the club from any place at the bar, were ripped like a god. His whole upper body was jacked and stacked and ripped as fuck. He called Derek, who couldn't hang with his workouts, a "pussy at squats." He referred to him as "Delt-less Derek" who "couldn't do fifty pull-ups to save his own dick from a fire." He spent a ton of time in his man cave writing in this journal where he kept track of all his workouts—every rep and set.

Derek rolled up right on time. "Shit is set" he was like. "I'm gonna dump Maryann's ass and start crashing with Carly in San

Fran. But Carl, first we gotta beast it over to Texas so we can chill with Old Brad Lewis, who I haven't partied with yet but you dudes won't shut the fuck up about him. Then I'll roll up to San Fran."

Then those dudes got in their groove. They set up the beer pong table and stood across from each other. I chilled on the couch and saw all of it. They began with some rapid-fire shots; tried to psyche each other out, blocked it out; tried to crack each other up so they'd miss the shot in the rush of everything; Derek pooched a shot but swore he could still win, getting focused as hell.

Carl was like, "Remember we were hitting some at the driving range and I wanted you to go hit on the hottie lady golfer at like that second, you took a wicked slice and totally hit that kid in the face."

"Fuck yeah! Of course I remember; and oh shit, you gotta hear, this real wild party at Stacy's that you gotta hear about, for real, 'cause it's so amazing . . ." and two new funny-ass stories got started. They cracked up and played some pong. Then Carl asked Derek how much he could bench and on the real if he wasn't lying to him about how much he could bench.

"Why you always gotta be like that?"

"Just be real with me."

"Yo Sam, you've seen me bench, you're chilling there, what do you say?"

And I was like, "It's not always about the amount of weight, Carl. It's about reps too. We always think about weight but it's about reps."

"Shut the fuck up! You're talking total bullshit like some kind of Curves trainer!" Carl was like.

And Derek was like, "That was pretty stupid, but Sam can say whatever shit he wants, and for real, don't you think Sam's an all-right dude, coming this long-ass way to chill and watch us play beer pong—Sam's aight, Sam's aight."

"Don't call me fucking 'aight,'" I was like. "I just don't know why you guys are talking about benching when shit like P90X yields way better results. It's fucking stupid."

"You're being a downer."

"What's your fucking deal?" I was like.

"Be real with him," Derek was like.

"No, you be real with him," Carl was like.

"Fuck this noise," I said and laughed. I needed to lay a nap bomb. "I want to lay a nap bomb," I said.

"Little Sam always wants to lay a nap bomb." I shut the hell up. They got back to playing and bullshitting. Carl was like, "Remember when you borrowed that condom to lay that waitress who gave us free sliders?"

"No, dude, it was onion rings! Remember, at Houlihans?"

"I was confusing it with Ruby Tuesday. When you borrowed that condom you were all like, like, 'Carl, for real, I just need to borrow this,' as if, like, you meant that you were gonna give back that gross-ass condom!"

"No no no, I didn't mean to be gay like that—oh man, remember that one night we were at Buffalo Wild Wings and Maryann was in the bathroom and when, you dropped your fork into my lap and you grabbed it and totally swiped my dick, which I think we both knew was totally gay as hell. You think it isn't?"

"Fuck no! Because you forgot that—aight let's be cool. No homo…" And forever, like forever they bullshitted this bullshit. I opened my eyes at dawn. They were finishing their hundredth game of beer pong. "'Cause when I just said that I needed to grab some sleep *because* of Maryann, 'cause I gotta get over there by ten, I didn't mean to say that like I was bored playing beer pong, but only, *only*, 'cause I gotta, for real, totally and without a fucking doubt need to grab some sleep, I mean, I'm tired as fuck, I'm totally fucking beat."

"Pussy," said Carl.

"I'm fucking tired. Let's stop the pong."

"You can't stop the pong!" yelled Carl super loud. There were birds outside.

"After I make this shot," Derek was like, "We'll stop playing, we'll just call it a draw, and we'll grab some sleep."

"You can't stop the pong like that."

"Stop the fucking pong," I was like. They were like, "Whaaaa?"

"Dude's been faking nap bombs and has just been chilling. What's in your skull, Sam?" I told them my skull thought they were crazy motherfuckers and that I listened to their stupid and hilarious bullshit like a dude watching a UFC fighter who's got like no control but just punches like crazy at whatever 'till the bell rings. The dudes laughed. I flipped them off and was like, "Bullshitting like this, you'll both end up like total douches, but I still wanna party with you dudes."

I busted out and looked back through the window of the condo, and Carl Marcus's crazy-jacked deltoids grew red as he challenged Derek to a pull-ups contest.

CHAPTER NINE

WHAT WOULD DANE COOK THINK?

That night I took off on the sick road trip to the mountains we'd been planning so I didn't hang with Derek or Carl for like almost a week. Beth Riggins borrowed her boss' sick ride for the weekend. We brought some raw party clothes and rolled out to Central City, looking sharp as hell. Rob Riggins was driving; Tom Grover chilling in the back; Beth up front. I'd never partied up in the Rockies before. Central City used to be a mining town with a grade A ton of silver that some old dudes found. They got rich as fuck fast as hell and built some stupid opera house in middle of their crap mining town. Some puss-ass opera singers came through to sing there. Then the grade-A ton of silver turned into a grade-A ton of nothing and Central City cleared the hell out, 'till some new dudes rolled in and decided to get shit started again. They built a casino with an amazing comedy club, and every summer bombass hilarious comics came out and tore it up. It was like solid good times. People came from all over to check the comedy shows out, even some famous people. The town was fucking packed with idiot tourists when we rolled in. Minor was scoping the tail scene. He was getting pretty stoked, turning on his big lady-slaying smile to all the chicks and high-fiving and pounding knucks over everything. "Sam," he shouted, pounding the rock, "check out the tourist tail up in this. Can you believe this place just had puss-ass opera like fifty years ago? Now it's the shit."

"Yeah," I was like, then to be funny I was like, "Except your weak ass is here."

"Motherfucker," he cursed. But he went off to get his party on, Becky Grover all up on him.

Beth Riggins was a solid hottie. She hooked us up with this timeshare a little ways away where we could all crash for the weekend; it was free as fuck if we just cleaned it up. The place was built for mad parties. It was a pretty nice timeshare but it was dirty as hell; it had an above-ground pool that was like covered in shit. Tom Grover and Rob Riggins got to it and started cleaning like hell, and it was a ton of work. But they worked on a thirty-rack of Keystone while they cleaned so it was aight.

I was gonna go check out the matinee at the comedy club at the casino with Beth. I borrowed Tom's nice-ass blazer. I'd just rolled into Denver a couple days ago looking like shit; now I was pimped out to the max, with a smashtastic chick with me, downing martinis, and chilling like a baller. If only Mississippi Chad could check out this shit.

Dane Cook was performing that day. I was like, "Holy shit!" about the stuff that was coming out of his mouth about relationships. I was almost crying. That's totally what I think about relationships too. I was so amped about seeing the show that for a while I forgot about like everything else in the world and got lost in the great hilarious sounds of Dane Cook and the off-the-chain-funny details of his stories.

"Hey, Sam, did you have a good time?" this dude Daniel D. Douglas asked me outside the club. Dude booked the comedy club.

"Fuckin' A, Fuckin' A," I was like. "Dane Cook is my hero."

"I should see if I can get you backstage to meet him," he went on, but the asshole totally forgot about it when he got a bunch of text messages and peaced out.

I rolled back to the timeshare with Beth. I took off my baller gear and pitched in with the cleaning and Keystone drinking. It was taking forever. Ryan Minor was just chilling in the breeze-way not doing a fucking thing, just having a Keystone and a hoagie. While we were busting our asses with Swiffers and sponges he talked on his phone. "Bro, you gotta roll with me over to Berlin and slam lager and scope German chicks, you'd have the best time. The South of France is extra-tits in the summer, the nude beaches, the parties. Come on, dude," he said to his buddy on the phone. "Take the stick out of your ass and let's see how wild we can get in Europe." It sounded sorta like *EuroTrip*.

We hollered at some chicks walking by the timeshare. "Come help us clean this shit! We're throwing a badass party tonight!" The ladies helped us. Now a massive crew was slinging Swiffers. Then a bunch of the dealers from the casino, who were pretty weird dudes, swung by and helped clean. Our cleaning shit done, Tom, Riggins, and I decided to get our groom on in hilarious style. We went across town and snuck into the casino's hotel penthouse where a dude told us Dane Cook was staying. From the lobby we had heard the beginning of his second show. "Let's do this," Riggins was like. "Nab some of his shit and we'll get our groom on." We also stole some product, cologne, shaving cream, and totally took showers in Dane Cook's bathroom. "Isn't this the fucking realest?" Tom Grover kept being like. "Grooming up with Dane Cook's product and towels and body spray and gel?"

That night was sick. Central City is hella-high up in the mountains; you can get hammered way faster, but then you get tired as shit, but then you can get even more hammered. We came down the frontage road toward the lights of the casino parking garage; then we headed over to hit some of the bars. Everything was empty since the tourists were all at the casino. We chugged down some XL beers. The TouchTunes was bumpin'. Through the backdoor you could see a hottie in the moonlight. I was like, "Pop the hood!" It was game time.

We rolled back to the timeshare. Everything was ready to go for our rager. The chicks, Beth and Becky, cooked up some nachos and wings, and then we did some shots and started pregaming for real. When the evening Dane Cook show ended, a whole herd of hotties cruised into our crib. All us dudes sprang some form of chubbies. We grinded up on those hotties. We didn't have any jams, nobody had the cord that connects an iPhone to laptop speakers. Shit got packed. The beer supply got low. We made a ton of beer runs. Everybody was getting rowdy. I wanted Derek and Carl to be partying with me—but they'd totally steal all the hotties for themselves. They were like the dude with the CamelBak full of Jäger, never stopping the party, the jacked-up players of America, a new bro generation that I was slowly joining.

The dudes from the casino's house band showed up. They began covering "Freebird." They also played awesome shit like "Hotel California" and "Where the Streets Have No Name" and great long sick guitar riffs from "Carry on My Wayward Son." The snatch selection was terrific. We took chicks to the backyard and made out. I got this one chick onto a bed and was like two inches from smashing her when from nowhere all these teenage dickbombs from town busted in and totally ruined the vibe by coming on too strong to the ladies—they totally fucked our rager. In like five minutes all the tang cleared out and it turned into a huge sausage party that was like lame-times-ten.

Rob, Tom, and I had to get the hell out and hit some bars. Minor had peaced out; Beth and Becky had peaced out. We stumbled our drunk asses into the street. All the casino tourists invaded all the good bars. We couldn't hear shit. The weird Daniel D. Douglas dude who booked the club was hanging around with everybody and shooting the shit. I saw him chilling with some dudes from Spain. Then he was talking up this MILF; then he was chilling with some younger dudes outside. Then he shook my hand and didn't even get that we'd met before. I couldn't believe this asshole got to meet dudes like Dane Cook as part of his job.

There was one of the opening comics in the bar who I guess was pretty funny; Daniel Douglas told me I should go chill with him but I thought that might be kinda lame; his name was some guido shit like D'Annunzio. He was chilling with his lady. They were looking pretty lame at some table. An asshole Argentinian dude was at the bar. Riggins pushed him to get some space; the Argentinian got mad pissed. I had to hold Riggins' Bud Light while he punched the shit out of this dude's face. It was a TKO. Shit got crazy; we all got the fuck out. Luckily it was too crazy for the cops to find us. We were totally in the clear. We got some more drink on. We found Minor dragging his drunk ass up the street. "What the hell is happening? Any fights? I'll fuck them up!" Everybody cracked up. I wondered what Dane Cook would have thought, and looked up and saw keggers in the moon, and saw ghosts of old players, and thought things over. All across the dark Eastern expanse of America parties were winding down with whispered drunk dials, except in this ravine where we raged; and toward the West a few parties kept going as new kegs rolled in and were tapped and drank, and led to fights and hookups and Taco Bell runs in the dark drunken land. We were on the rocky tits of America and all we could do was text—across the night, eastward over the Plains, where somewhere a bullshit cop was probably walking toward us with open container violations, and would arrive any minute and kill the party.

Riggins had to go back to the bar where he laid that dude out. Tom and I thought that was bullshit but we had his back. Riggins stepped to this opening comic D'Annuzio dude and totally threw a Jägerbomb in his face. We had to drag the crazy motherfucker out. We met up with the dude who sells Dane Cook's merch and grabbed some brews at another bar. Of course Rob called our waitress a fat bitch. This crew of townies looked pissed; they wanted to rumble. They were all like, "Get out of here in ten seconds." They probably had weapons so we didn't want any. We hauled our drunk asses back to the timeshare and completely passed out.

I woke up the next morning and rolled over; I'd totally stolen five pint glasses from the bar. I tried to check Facebook; I didn't get service. Tom Grover had crashed out in the bed too. We were hungover to the extreme. We had Doritios and what was left of the keg for breakfast. We packed our shit.

My head was fucking pounding. When we walked out to the car Beth totally tripped and faceplanted. I had to pretend it wasn't kinda hilarious. We got her ass off the ground. We loaded back into the car. Our hungover-as-fuck journey back to Denver began.

All of a sudden we busted downhill and saw the sick scene of Denver with heat rising from it like a tanning bed. We shotgunned a couple beers. It was time to beast it to San Fran.

CHAPTER TEN

KANYE SEX-MIX

I hollered at Carl later and he told me that he'd totally been chilling in Central City with Derek.

"What were you up to?"

"You know, we hit up some parties and bars and then Derek jacked a paintball gun from Sports Authority and we blasted shit with paintballs the whole way home."

"I didn't see you."

"We were probably too hammered to know anything that was going on."

"Dude, I'm gonna roll out to Fran."

"Derek talked to Tina and you could totally smash with her tonight."

"Well fuck, my ass is staying." I had to get some play. I sent text messages all over the place asking hotties for some booty calls and all of them airballed; after tonight I would be back on the tail wagon, as soon as I smashed with Tina.

So I took Tina Bellingfort back to my place. I got her to chill with me on my bed after some bullshitting out in the living room. She was an aight chick, like a seven-point-five-out-of-ten, but prude as hell. I told her I was crazy good at sex. I wanted to show her how crazy good I was. We went at it, but I didn't have my Kanye sex-mix and it sucked. She sighed like a total bitch. "So what kind of music are you into?" I was like. That's my standard question for chicks.

"Whatever," she was like. "Stuff like Black Eyed Peas and whatever." She yawned. I was like, "What the fuck, babe?" and couldn't believe she was yawning after boning. I tried to convince her to smash some more; I needed a real quality smash before I rolled out to San Fran. She just rolled over like a total bitch. I lay on my back, staring at the ceiling fan and wondering why some chicks have to be so annoying to smash with. We said maybe we'd hook up in San Fran.

As I took that chick home I realized that I had to rock out of Denver. After dropping her off I chilled out on the patio of an Irish pub with a bunch of bros, and hearing them talk about funny stories made me need to get back to having an awesome road trip. Sometimes a chick would pass by and one of the bros would holler at her. They talked of parties up north. It sounded pretty solid. I wanted to go back to Tina's place and bone her proper and see if she'd loosen the hell up. Society has always gotta make boning so uptight; you can't just bone and get out. Not even breakfast—just straight up boning, 'cause life is holy and you just gotta do it. I heard the crowd roar at Sports Authority Field. I wanted to get the party started.

Minor and I shot the shit and had some bedtime beers. "Have you ever seen the 1984 Boston College-Miami game? It's the fucking realest." We pounded knucks. We'd chill together in San Fran. I texted Riggins. "peace out bro hollr if ur in sf." I tried to text and call Carl and Derek—dudes just didn't answer. Tom Grover swung by my crib and was like, "Peace out, queer." We called each other "queer" as a joke. "Hell yeah," I was like. I kicked it around Denver for my last couple days. I thought every awesome dude around Larimer Street might be Derek's dad; Old Badass Morrisey, the Regulator. I grabbed a drink at a sports bar where Derek and his dad chilled and where this one time Derek got hit on by this old grenade with a mole who had totally hooked up with Derek's dad before. There was this midget chick selling newspapers outside, she was totally like Mini-Me. I strutted up Curtis Street, which is pretty lame; total chaches in graphic tees; trash, vacant Blockbusters, Zipcar parking spots. Beyond the vacant Blockbusters was America, and in America was an awesome time. It was time to do this shit.

I swung by Carl's crib at dawn. I did some reps on his jacked Bowflex, laid some nap bombs, then tall-ass Todd Dinkel rolled

up with his dude Ray Jeffries, and Timmy Snipes, who I'd heard
was pretty good at Texas hold 'em. Carl showed off to everyone
his mad benching skills. I checked my phone, totally over the
whole thing. "My pecs are on fucking fire!" Carl was like. The
whole crew rolled out and strutted up a street between a couple
of Starbucks. "I used to scope tail over here," Chaz Kerry told
me once. I wanted to see that; to hang in Denver five years ago
when all these dudes were in high school, and in the sunny hungover morning of springtime in the Rockies chasing mad ladies
up the joyous alleys still full of Blockbusters—the whole crew.
Except for Derek, who was off getting wild lone-wolf style like
a badass.

I rolled over to Teddy's slam piece's place with Ray Jeffries
to get my North Face fleece, the one he totally jacked in Shelton.
I got it but it was totally fucked up, all stained and rumpled like
hell. Ray peaced out and told me he'd shoot me a text in San
Fran. Fucking everyone was rolling out to San Fran. I played
some online poker and made some cash. It got light outside and
Tom Grover took me to the bus station. I dropped some of my
new poker cash on a bus ticket to SF and I cruised out around
two. Tom Grover gave me a "peace out" nod. I rolled out of the
epic, raw scene of Denver. "For real, I'm gonna party here again
and definitely get laid more," I swore to myself. I got a Facebook
message right when I was leaving. It was Derek saying that he
and Carl might roll out to San Fran with me; all of a sudden it hit
me that I hadn't hung with Derek for more than like five minutes the whole time.

CHAPTER ELEVEN

DUDE'S GOTTA HAVE NUGS

I was like crazy late getting to Ricky Bronco's place. I was bored as hell for most of the bus ride, but I did get more amped when we started getting closer to San Fran. I watched some episodes of *The Sopranos* on my phone, finished season one as we crested the mountains; then got deep into season two when we were rolling into Salt Lake City—the middle of season two is aight, it definitely picks up later. Then I switched over to watching *Reservoir Dogs*, its badass guns and funny-ass lines make it seem better every time I watch it—I wished like hell I could see it again for the first time, 'cause it's one of the best movies ever, and it was beyond amazing the first time I saw it. Then we were in fucking Cali. It was crazy warm—I wanted to go shirtless stat. But I couldn't do that on the bus; I'd have to get some tanning in later; all the dudes around looked way tanner. I dropped a heavy nap bomb as we crossed the Oakland Bay Bridge; I didn't wake up 'till we were at the bus station in SF and all of a sudden it was go-time again. I strutted out of the bus station feeling like a tired motherfucker, and then I was all up in San Fran—a ton of hills and weirdos and shit. I scoped the scene a little. Homeless dudes begged me for change. I heard Kanye blasting from somewhere. "Shit, I am gonna do this up later! But I gotta go meet up with Ricky Bronco."

Ricky lived in Mill City, which is this town of sorta shitty houses that were built for something during some war; it had like no nightlife, none at all, nothing to do but sit on your dick. There were some stores and restaurants but almost nowhere had draft specials. It was, I'm guessing, one of the lamest communities in America; and one of the lamest places I've ever been. I checked the Facebook message the dude had sent me like three weeks ago:

Ricky Bronco
Yo, Parker. If I'm not around when you roll in, just bust in through the window.
-R

So I climbed in the window and Ricky was totally there in bed with his lady Liana—the bed he told me a few days later that he stole from a mattress store; that drunk asshole seriously made off with a bed and got it all the way home. That's just the tip of the crazy-motherfucker iceberg that is Ricky Bronco.

I gotta tell you everything that went down in San Fran 'cause it's like crucial to everything that goes down later. Ricky Bronco and I met in our high school lacrosse team; but what really made us tight was my ex-girlfriend. Ricky hooked up with her first. He came up to me at practice one day and was like, "Parker, put down that Gatorade, I need some fucking help." I got off the bench and capped my Gatorade. It was before I knew that Gatorade barely actually hydrates in high-performance environments; I used to drink that shit all the time in high school. "All right, don't spill your 'Rade. I've found the most bombass chick and I am going straight to third base with her in like five hours." And he made me go meet her. And for real just a couple of days later, she was totally on third base with me. Ricky was a tall, dark, ripped Floridian (he looked sort of like a young Paul Walker); because he was Floridian he had to tan all the time; his bronze was perfect, head to toe. He liked to dress like a baller and go out with stacked blondes and throw mad cash around. Dude wasn't pissed I pulled the robbery on his girl; it just made us tighter; that dude was crazy solid and thought I was awesome, which is fucking right.

When I met up with Ricky he was going through some total bullshit that happens to a lot of solid bros after gradua-tion. His dad froze his trust fund so he had to make some dough working as a stupid security guard at this barracks across the canyon. Liana was a hottie but could be a real bitch and she was on his case like constantly. They spent all week busting ass for money and went out on Saturdays to drop a few hundred in a couple hours. Ricky chilled around the house in lacrosse shorts and a Gamecocks hat. Liana wore some expensive shit. They just sat around and bitched at each other nonstop. I'd never seen so much bullshit. But then on the weekends, they'd act all cool and hit the town like ballers.

Ricky woke up and saw me hauling my ass through the window. He laughed like fucking crazy, like louder than fucking anybody. "Fuck me, you just busted right in through the window like some kind of fucking ninja! What's your fucking deal? You're like crazy late!" He high-fived me, swiped Liana's ass, he cracked open a brew and kept cracking up and yelling "fuck me!" so loud you could probably hear it from goddamn space or whatever. "A fucking ninja!" he screamed. "Like a fucking ninja!"

I rolled through Sausalito on my way, and so I was like, "I noticed a bunch of hotties walking around Sausalito."

"You noticed a bunch of hotties around Sausalito!" he kept cracking up. "Fuck me!" He thought this was like crazy funny or something. "Babe, can you believe the shit coming out of this dude's mouth? A bunch of hotties in fucking Sausalito! Fuck me! No shit! Fuck me! No shit!" Dude got red as hell from laughing. "You're a funny motherfucker, Parker, you're like the fucking man, rolled up, busted in like a ninja! Fuck me! No shit!"

I wondered if Ricky was fucking high, 'cause he thought everything was so hilarious. I always thought he was high when we played lacrosse; dude would go insane with pranks and just lose it at anything. I don't think he really smoked that much though. He was just crazy. Maybe he was just like naturally high all the time, which would be sort of awesome. The dude had like no cash and was strapped to this bitch, but at least he was like high all the time and I knew we were gonna straight-up tear it down in San Fran.

Ricky and Liana crashed in the bed and I crashed on the couch. Ricky didn't want me to fuck Liana. He was like crazy serious about this shit. "Don't try to like stealth-rail her. You can't pull that shit on me. I'm being totally real here." I scoped Liana. She was a hot piece, an eight-point-seven, but she was a raging bitch to me and Ricky. She wanted to marry a rich dude. She had been like poor or something in Oregon. She totally regretted ever hooking up with Ricky. One weekend he'd acted like a huge baller and dropped a few hundred bones at dinner and he looked like he was totally loaded. But then his trust fund got locked down and they moved into this shit hole and she just stayed. She got some job in SF but she had to haul-ass in a stupid bus to get there. She was pissed as fuck at Ricky for it.

Ricky wanted to get rich by producing a series of workout videos. Dude was going to make all these connections and like some kind of Hollister-clad angel, make us all rich; Liana was gonna work on it too. Ricky was going to talk to this friend of this dude who knew his other buddy's dad, who I guess produced the Insanity workout videos and was also tight with Billy Blanks. So the first week I was there I just chilled in the house, working like hell on a raw new workout plan that I thought would be cool to these producers, but what sucked was that it was just way too extreme. Ricky couldn't even get through the Day One regimen, and so he didn't even try Day Two and just sent it to this producer dude. Of course Liana was way too much of a weak bitch to even give it a shot. I spent like all the time pounding energy gel and working out. Finally I was like, "This is bullshit;" I'd rather just have a job; my lactic acid burns were killing me. A shadow of "what the fuck" came over Ricky's face—he was always getting all "what the fuck" about the lamest stuff. But he was all right.

He hooked me up with the same stupid security guard job he had. I did some stupid interviews, and the assholes gave me the job. The police chief swore me in and gave me like legit cop stuff like a badge and a tazer, so I was like some kind of bullshit cop. Derek and Carl and Old Brad Lewis would have laughed their dicks off if they knew I was a cop. There was a stupid uniform so I had to get some stupid pants; for a while I borrowed Ricky's pants; since he was way less fit and was sort of pudging up they didn't fit at all and I looked like an idiot. Ricky had me borrow a real fucking gun that he had.

"Why the hell are you packing?" I was like.

"When I cruised out West last year I was chilling with my uncle in North Platte, Nebraska, and dude offered me this sweet gun, which I took, natch, and got back on the road."

And I tried to tell him how hard I partied in North Platte, slamming Natties with the boys, and he just gave me a high-five and told me I totally cracked his shit up.

Using my iPhone as a flashlight, I hauled ass up one side of the canyon, walked on the busy-ass road like some kind of poor person, hauled ass down the other side, almost fell and lost my shit, and went past a gas station where there were always these weird dudes eating donuts out front. Then I had to haul my ass down this little dusty road—it was sorta like when there are like backwoods races in *The Fast and the Furious* franchise or any other sweet driving movie that has scenes like in the woods or wherever. I took my gun out and pretended like I was an FBI agent trying to stop Vin Diesel. After hauling ass up one more hill I got to the barracks. It was all overseas construction workers crashing in the barracks. They needed to crash there while they waited to roll out to wherever. Most of those dudes were like on the run or something, probably from cops or bitches. There were hard dudes from Georgia, real sketchy dudes from Massachusetts, and other crazy motherfuckers from wherever. Since the parties overseas would suck, the dudes got hammered here. We were just supposed to make sure they didn't tear shit down. The main office was this shitty boring room with a bunch of desks. We just sat around, checking our phones and being super bored while the old cops shot the shit.

All the other cops except me and Ricky were total assholes and douchebags. Ricky and I were just chilling and pulling down some cash, but all these assholes wanted to get all David Caruso and shit. They told me I'd get fired if I didn't break up a party a week. That shit went against like everything I believe in. But for real, I ended up partying the most and getting the most hammered in the barracks when things got off the chain.

This one night I was totally alone for like six hours—just me chilling; and the dudes in the barracks got like beyond wild and hammered. It was 'cause the Giants won big that day. They drank like freshmen trying to impress their older frat brothers. I sat in the office chillaxing, reading Facebook updates on my phone, then all of sudden I heard shit blowing up out there. I rolled out. The barracks were lit up and bumping like everywhere. Music was cranking; bottles were getting thrown. I had to be a dick and shut it down. I went over to one door and knocked. Some dude opened it like a crack.

"What's going on?"

I was like, "I need you dudes to keep it down"—or some kind of fucking RA bullshit like that. The dude slammed the door on me. I couldn't believe how stupid this shit was. It was one of the top-five dumbest things I've ever done. I knocked on the door again. They opened up. "Yo," I was like, "I don't want to be a dick, but it's my stupid job to tell you to keep shit down."

"Who are you?"

"I'm a guard here."

"Never seen you before."

"Dude, I'm legit."

"Why the hell do you have that stupid gun?"

"It isn't mine," I felt like an idiot. "I borrowed it."

"Have a drink, for fuck's sake." Sounded pretty good to me. I slammed two.

I was like, "All right, dudes? You'll keep it down, dudes? I'll get mad shit for it if you don't."

"We read you," they were like. "Go do your shit. There's more beers here if you want some."

So I went around and it happened again and again, and in no

time I was totally astro-hammered. I was supposed to put up the flag at dawn on this big-ass flagpole, but I was so crunked that I put it on upside down and then passed out at home. I got in the next night and all these douche cops were looking pissed as hell at me.

"You know anything about a lot of noise here last night? We got a bunch of calls from people who live around here."

"Beats me," I was like. "It's crazy quiet now."

"All the guys are gone. You were supposed to keep things quiet last night—the chief is real mad at you. Do you have any idea how much trouble you can get in for putting the American flag upside down on government property?"

"Upside down?" Oh fuck; I hadn't realized how hammered I was. I did that flag shit every morning like a robot.

"You bet," said this fat-ass cop who used to be some stupid prison guard. "Only a total asshole would do a thing like that." The other cops were all pissed too. They were always getting all pissed; they took everything way too seriously. They all had guns and messed around with them. They were totally looking to bust a cap. Ricky and I were like prime targets.

The prison guard cop was pretty old and crazy fat, and he couldn't get enough of this fake cop bullshit that he'd been all up in for like forever. He showed up every night in his pathetic '87 Toyota and just sat there being a dick. Dude took everything seriously like he was Dick Tracy or some shit. Sometimes he'd tell stories about being a huge dick. "Me and Slug" (this younger douchebag cop who thought he was saving the world) "beat the hell out of this guy in Barrack G. The guy bled all over the place. You can see the stains everywhere. We pounded him all over the place. Slug and I took turns punching him in the face 'till he was almost dead. The guy said he was gonna kill us when he got out of jail, but we haven't heard a damn thing." He thought his dick was like six-feet long 'cause this dude had never come back and tried to fight him.

The douche fat cop wouldn't shut up about how cool he thought his stupid time working at a prison was. "We had

those men totally broken. They did whatever we said. Just like
machines. I owned those boys. Worked there for twenty-plus
years. Nothing ever went down on my watch. They were scared
of me. Some guys don't control the prisoners, and they end up in
real trouble. Like you—you let those assholes get away with too
much." He took a bite of a Pop-Tart and looked at me all mean
and shit. "They'll take advantage of you that way."

I knew it. I was like, "I don't want to be some kind of asshole cop."

"Well you signed up for the job. Either do the job or get the
hell out. They swore you in. Justice needs to be served."

I felt all like "Fuck." I'd just wanted to party on Ricky's
dad's yacht and instead I ended up stuck in this hellhole.

The other asshole, Slug, was tall, kinda-jacked, in a stupid
crew cut and real twitchy—like a UFC fighter going nuts. He
decked himself out like an old-school Texas Ranger. He had a
revolver down low, with an ammo belt, and carried an Indiana
Jones whip or some shit, pieces of leather hanging everywhere,
like a way-not-hot dude dominatrix. He was always showing me
wrestling holds—reaching around me and trying to lift me. Since
I'm lean but jacked, I could have broke his ass with the same
hold; but I never let him know it because wrestling is pretty gay.
I'm sure all wrestlers aren't gay; I just don't want to get into that
shit. The dude was always hoping to arrest people. This one time
when just the two of us were working he got like crazy pissed.

"Those guys out there won't shut up. I told them they had
to shut up two times. Three strikes, man. Three strikes. Come
with me so we can arrest their asses."

"Dude, just chill. I'll talk to them," I was like. "Just chill."

"No way. We've gotta regulate." I was like, "Ugh." This
sucks. Me and him went over to this room where dudes were
being loud and Slug went in like a dick and broke up the party.
I've never felt like such a total dick. This is the fucking problem
with America. Everybody goes around being a dick 'cause they
think they have to. Why they fuck does it matter if some dudes

get hammered and have a good time? Slug needed to prove how big a dick he could be or something. I had to come help him in case things got violent. It could have. All the guys were pretty rough dudes from the South. We marched all these poor fuckers to the office in a line.

One of the dudes was like, "Tell that stupid jerkass to chill out. We're gonna lose our jobs over this bullshit."

"I'll work it out."

When we got back to the station I told Slug to take a lap. But he was all trying to be raw and a dick. He was like, "Three strikes. Three strikes."

"Come on, man," the Southern dude was like, "This is bullshit. What if I lose my job?" That jerkoff stayed cold as ice and for real wrote them up. He ended up arresting a dude and let the others off. The police truck came and grabbed him. All the other dudes walked back hella-pissed. "Why's that guy gotta be such a dick?" they were like. Then one dude got all up in my face. "Tell that jagoff that if my brother isn't out tomorrow I'm going to bust his ass so hard. So I passed that on to Slug but dude didn't give a shit. I guess that dude got out of jail and things were cool. That crew of dudes peaced out; a new gnarly crew rolled in. Without Ricky I would have gotten out of this shitshow in like a hot second.

But Ricky and me hung out on duty alone all the time, and that's when advanced-level shit blew up. As we were making rounds, Ricky kept checking all the doors and trying to bust into one. He kept being like, "Someday I'm totally gonna train a dog so it's like a super thief that can break into rooms and pickpocket. I bet you could make it so if you made the dog smell money all the time it would only nab cash. And I bet you could make it only take twenties, like if you pulled some real advanced *Dog Whisperer* shit." Ricky seriously sounded high sometimes; he wouldn't shut up about that dog for like weeks. There was one time he did find a door unlocked. This was a real crappy idea so I kept walking. Ricky tried to open it all quiet like a ninja. As soon as he opened it, the fucking supervisor was standing right there. The dude and Ricky did not get along. Ricky once was like, "Who was that UFC fighter we saw the other night—the one who's a big-ass ugly tank of a dude and absolutely pulverizes dudes in the cage with like one hand?" Dude was talking about Brock Lesnar. "Yeah dude, yeah dude, Brock Lesnar. That dude has a jacked-up face just like Brock fucking Lesnar." It was fucking ridiculous that the only time he found an open door it was Brock Lesnar's room. Brock was sleeping but woke up when Ricky started fucking with the door. He was wearing lame-ass pajamas. When he opened the door he looked extra pissed and extra busted.

"What do you think you're doing?"

"Aw, you know, I just thought this was like where the cleaning supplies are. I was just looking for a mop."

"A mop?"

"Uh—you know . . ."

I got his back and was like, "We gotta clean up where some dude ralphed in the hallway."

"There are no cleaning supplies here. It's my room. Pull a stunt like this again and you're fired. You read me?"

"Some dude just ralphed upstairs," I was like.

"Get your damn mop from the janitor's closet down the hall." And the dude stood there and waited to see us grab a mop and carry it upstairs like a couple of assholes.

I was like, "Jesus fucking Christ, Ricky, you're always getting us into shit. Can't you just cool down? Why do you gotta be stealing like such an asshole all the time?"

"This is how I do, you read me? You can't teach this old player new tricks. You keep saying asshole stuff like that and I'm gonna start calling you Brock Lesnar."

Ricky could be a real whiny bitch. Since leaving high school where he was god, things went sour for him; he dropped out of college to finance a killer startup; the business tanked and his dad took away his trust fund; he spent every night thinking about how he could get some wealth on. He had to get back on top; there was no end to how pissed he was; this crap was gonna go long-term.

The most choice action was the barracks cafeteria. After we made sure none of our asshole cop buddies were gonna see us and narc on us, I'd give Ricky a boost up through the window that dude always made sure was unlocked. I had more lean muscle mass and solid vertical, so I got in on my own. I realized a fucking dream and made bacon and onion ring nachos. Then we got Ziploc bags and loaded them down with Doritos and bratwursts, and then checked for other deliciousness in the kitchens. A lotta times I grabbed bags of frozen chicken nuggets to take home. "You know what they say," Ricky would be like. "Dude's gotta have nugs."

One time Ricky took forever filling a big box full of chicken nugs. Shit wouldn't even fit through the window so Ricky had to like condense all the nugs. That night when I was working alone after Ricky peaced out, I went down into the canyon to see a naked hottie in a farmhouse window. (Ricky had seen a naked hottie in the window, and she was supposedly totally stacked.) I heard this crazy noise out in the dark. It sounded like some kind of big-ass vicious wolf, all huffing and puffing and whatever. I was ready to shoot it in the face. Then it turned out it was just Ricky lugging his big-ass box of nugs. Dude was bitching like whoa 'cause it was super heavy. He managed to bust out of the cafeteria with like the motherlode of nugs. I was all like, "Bro, WTF is up? I thought you left."

But he was all like, "Parker, you know this shit, *dude's gotta have nugs*." And he lugged those nugs off into the darkness. I already told you about how raw that trail back to the house is, shitty as hell for hoofing it. He dropped his nugs in a ditch and came back to me. "Sam, I can't get this home. Do me a solid and help me haul it."

"I'm fucking working."

"I'll cover for you while you're gone. Carrying that shit sucks. We've just gotta get those nugs home, and that's fucking that." He wiped his face. "Dude, I mean it, Sam, that we're bros, that we're in it together. That's the straight up truth. The Brock Lesnars, the cops, the Lianas, all the bitches and buzzkills of this world, are trying to bring us down. We gotta watch each other's backs. They're jealous as fuck of us and wanna ruin our reps. I'm serious. I know what's up."

I was finally like, "What the fuck happened with partying on your dad's yacht?" We'd been doing this shit for ten weeks. I was having a shitty time and hadn't gotten to have any sick yacht parties like Ricky promised. I'd only chilled in San Fran one night. My life was stuck in that stupid house, with Ricky and Liana bitching all the time, and this crazy lame job.

Ricky went off to score another box of nugs. I hauled that shit with him on that backwoods *Fast and Furious* road. We dumped out the nugs in a big-ass pile on the table at their place. Liana checked it out.

"Dudes and chicks gotta have nugs." She was into it. I realized that pretty much all Americans like to nosh on chicken nuggets when they're hammered. I was def into it. I even began to have nug-slamming contests with Ricky. The other cops thought we were idiots; they saw us almost puke; they thought we were total jerks; they were just pussies who couldn't hang. Years of experience had made them into super pussies compared to Ricky and me.

Sometimes Ricky and I would go and try to shoot some shit like birds. Ricky sneaked up crazy close to one of the birds and blasted the .32. Motherfucker missed. His big-ass laugh made me feel fucking deaf. "Dude, I gotta take you to the Banana King."

It was Saturday; we got on some going-out shirts and busted over to San Fran. I thought maybe shit would be cool. Ricky's big-ass laugh blasted everywhere we went. "You gotta post about the Banana King on Facebook," he was like. "Don't fucking forget. The Banana King is the rawest time. Check this out." The Banana King was a shitty Caribbean-themed bar on the corner. I was crazy bored. Ricky slapped my back and tried to get me to try the pineapple burger. "When you post about this shit make sure to tag me." I kept telling him the Banana King was fucking dumb. "Until you try the fucking pineapple burger you're never gonna know what you're talking about," Ricky said like a dick.

There was a big-ass rusty boat out in the bay that was just chilling there. Ricky wanted to go out there, so one time we packed some nugs and took a boat out there. Ricky brought like wire cutters and some other shit. Liana got seriously naked and lay down to get her tan on. I scoped her rack from the higher deck. Ricky went down to the boiler room, and 'cause dude was so fucking broke, tried to find fucking copper. I slammed brews in some old room in the boat. It was a pretty raw old ship and I bet it was like totally pimped out back in the day, with fancy-ass furniture and a sick bar. I could feel the ghosts of the ballers of the seas. It would have been tight to hang with these ballers. Babes hung off the sides. There'd probably been a pimp sea captain sitting right here eating like lobster and banging chicks on the waves.

I met up with Ricky in the boiler room. Dude had tore shit up. "Nada. I thought I could score some copper, at least fucking something. A bunch of assholes must have gotten all the good shit first." It had been chilling in the bay forever. Whatever douchebag stole the copper was probably long dead by now.

I was like, "I'd love to throw a vicious party here with the hotties hanging off the sides and the music blasting and a beer bong fixed up to the mast."

Ricky was mindfucked; he thought I was even more awesome. "Sam, that would be beyond off the chain. Do you realize how legendary that party would be? I'll score a boat and ferry the hotties back and forth all night."

"Hell yeah!" I was like. Ricky went over to Liana. I wanted to jump down from a mast and get myself all up in her, but couldn't do that shit to my boy. Bros don't get themselves all up in other bros' slam pieces.

Meanwhile I started getting my party on in San Fran more; I spat all the game in the world to lay some pipe. I even wined and dined this one chick 'till sunrise without a whiff of play. She was some bitch from Minnesota. There were a crazy ton of gay dudes. Sometimes I'd be rolling in San Fran and I swear these dudes would check me out and I'd be all like, "Step off! I'm all about snatch!" That showed them. I never understood why they always had to probably be all up on me. It was just the gay shit of San Francisco and the fact that I'm pretty ripped. I can't hide my pecs in any shirt. I walked by a CVS and wanted to run in, grab a pile of condoms, and run and get it on with Liana. Then we could go wherever to get our beast on. It was clear as fuck I needed to get out of San Fran before I lost my motherfucking skull.

I wrote a ton of texts to Derek and Carl, who were partying with Old Brad out in Texas. Dudes were looking to come hang in San Fran. In the meantime, it got real lame between Ricky and Liana and me. It started raining like crazy and the bullshit started piling up. Ricky had taken my workout video idea to LA with Liana, and shit-all happened. The fitness video producer was totally hammered and didn't care about them; they chilled around his Malibu beach house; they started bitching at each other at a party; and they peaced out.

Then there was the fucking racetrack. Ricky saved all his money, like barely anything compared to what I pull in a solid couple days of online poker, dunked his ass in cologne, got Liana to come, and we rolled over to the Golden Gate racetrack to get hammered and win dollars. To show you what a douche that dude was becoming, he made us preparty at this shitty Buffalo Wild Wings-wannabe bar, and invited some asshole he knew from football camp who ordered expensive-ass microbrews and then peaced out without paying. I was like, "What the fuck?" Of course I had to pick up the tab. That guy was a fucking asshole. Ricky barely even knew him. "Chillax," Ricky was all pretending it wasn't bullshit. "I'll totally hit you back sometime."

We kept rolling to the track. He made crazy dumbass bets on idiot horses and in like no time he was broke as hell. With the last of all our cash he made another dumbass bet and blew it. We

had to beg for a ride back to San Fran. At least I was getting my
road on again. A dude gave us a ride in his sick Audi. I chilled
up front with him. Ricky was making up all this crap about how
he'd lost his wallet or whatever. "I gotta be straight with you," I
was like, "we lost our all our money at the track, and to keep this
from going down again, from now on we'll just go to a fucking
off-track betting place, huh Ricky?" Ricky got all embarrassed
and whatever. The fancy dude finally told us that he ran the racetrack. He dropped us off at this mad-fancy hotel and then disappeared into a thicket of hotties and booze, his pockets stuffed
with cash, his strut like that of a total baller.

"Oh fuck me!" Ricky was like all douchey. "Parker gets a
ride from the fucking owner of the racetrack and is all like, 'Let's
go to an off-track place!'" He grabbed Liana's ass. "What a fucking weirdo. There must be a lot of hotties in Sausalito. Fuck
me!" He cracked up.

That night it rained like fuck and Liana was being a total
bitch to both of us. All of Ricky's dough was gone. The rain was
getting crazier. "It's gonna be like this forever," said Ricky. He
changed out of his baller suit and into his lacrosse shorts and
nasty Gamecocks hat. He stared at the old beer cans on the floor.
Some nugs thawed on the table. This was ultra-lame.

"This is so stupid," Liana was like. She was looking to bitch
out on somebody. She started getting all up in Ricky's face. He
was busy scrolling through his Facebook friends to see who owed
him cash. He posted shit on their walls. I dreaded the day he'd
write stupid shit on my wall. Lately I'd barely had time to play
online poker, so I didn't buy much food per week. 'Cause I'm
a solid dude, I tried to throw in some more. But Ricky thought
I was being a cheap asshole, so he'd started making dick moves
like taping the grocery receipts to the wall like an asshole. Liana
thought Ricky and I were like holding out cash from her, which
is totally psycho. She was a nuclear bitch.

Ricky bitched back at her. "Where the fuck else are you
gonna go?"

"Johnny,"

"*Johnny?* That little asshole who works at the track? Sam, can you believe this? Liana is gonna get her smash on with a cashier at the track. Get ready to pick up horse shit with him."

Shit got shittier; it rained like a bitch. Liana had lived there first, so she was gonna kick Ricky and me out. Dude packed his REI bag. I was terrified of being alone in this rainy dump with that bitch. I had to mediate. Ricky called Liana a slut. She posted some nasty stuff about him on Facebook. Ricky e-mailed me some fucked up pictures of her and told me to post them on Facebook. Liana flipped out and was gonna go get a cop, like for real that dickhole prison guard we worked with. Thank Christ that dude wasn't around. She came back drenched and pissed. I stayed out of it in the corner with my eyes plastered on my phone. Why had I come here? Where was my fucking party yacht?

"And one more thing, you stupid dick," Liana was like. "I'm never gonna make you those fucking nuggets or those nasty-ass wings and watch you stuff your face and turn into a fat-ass in front of my fucking face."

"It's cool, babe," Ricky was like all quiet. "It's totally cool babe. When I started hooking up with you I didn't expect things to be all happy and great and it's all cool. I tried to be a solid dude for you—I tried my best to be a solid dude for both of you; you've both let my ass down. You've both been total assholes," he was like all serious. "I thought shit would work out with us, that shit would by totally awesome; I tried, I tried to sell that workout video. I hooked Sam up with a job; I spent mad cash on your fancy clothes; I tried to show you guys awesome times in San Fran. You were dicks; you were both total dicks to me in return. So I'm gonna ask you for the last solid that I'll ever ask you for. My dad's visiting San Fran next Saturday night. I just want you to come hang at dinner and act like I'm cool and that everything is cool so he'll unlock my trust fund. Liana, act like my lady, and Sam, act like my bro. I'm gonna borrow like a few hundred for Saturday night. I gotta make sure my dad has an awesome time and is totally cool to unlock my trust fund."

I thought this was weird. Ricky's dad was a crazy rich doctor who balled around Vienna, Paris, and London. I was like, "You're saying that you're gonna blow a few hundo on your dad? He's like rich as fuck! You'll be broke, dude!"

"It's cool," said Ricky all quiet and sorta like a pussy. "I just want one thing from you—just make me look cool and improve my rep. I think my dad's all right and I gotta get my cash unlocked. He's coming with my hot stepmom. We gotta show him a good time." There were times when Ricky seemed like a really desperate pussy. Liana got onboard, and thought meeting his dad might be tight; she thought he might have some awesome rich friends, if Ricky was still gonna be poor as hell.

Then it was Saturday night. I'd gotten the fuck out of my shitty job, since they were gonna fire my ass anyway and I needed to party on my last Saturday night in SF. First Ricky and Liana met up with his dad at his hotel; I had played some online poker earlier and got hammered at the hotel bar. I rolled up to the room late as hell. His dad opened the door, a rich tall dude in a custom Armani suit. "What up!" I was like when I met him. "Mr. Bronco, what's shaking? Let's tear shit up!" I hollered, which I intended to mean like, "Let's do this, let's have a good time," but I don't think the dude got it. The doctor looked at me all weird. I had already sorta fucked over Ricky. He looked pissed as hell at me.

We rolled over to this pimp North Beach restaurant called Alfred's, where Ricky dropped mad cash to pay for a shitton of drinks and food. Then the rawest thing happened. I ran into my dude Ryan Minor at the bar! Dude had just rolled into town and was looking to party in SF. He was grade-A hammered. He was a total wreck. Dude came over and pounded knucks and we did a Jägerbomb. He parked his ass next to Ricky's dad and leaned over the dude to talk to me. Ricky was fucking ballistic.

"Who the hell is this?" Ricky said trying not to rage it.

"Ryan Minor, college football historian," I tried to say without losing it. Liana was in total Bitch Force One mode.

Minor began talking at Ricky's dad. "So do you like dudes?" he yelled.

"Excuse me, but I have a wife."

"Oh, I heard you like dudes." He was deliberately pissing him off. I thought about that one time he tried to stop us from partying in Denver, but that was old news.

I got over all that kind of shit. I leaned back and I got hammered. I started spitting game at the doctor's hottie wife. I pounded so much booze that I kept having to jump over Ricky's dad to go chunk it in the bathroom. I was getting mad sloppy. It was time to get my dick out of San Fran. Ricky was gonna be pissed at me for a long time. It was sort of crappy of me since we used to be tight but he'd been a real dick lately so whatever. He could go fuck himself. Things had gotten so totally fucked since I'd first started texting him in Columbus, planning my trip to go hang with him on a yacht—sounded so sweet—but now everything was stupid and it was time to go back. I had to at least get wild on the way home. I figured I'd hit Hollywood and then see those dudes in Texas; then who knows what for the rest.

Minor got tossed out of Alfred's. Ricky stopped paying for drinks anyway, so I joined him; I mean, Ricky told me to get the fuck out, and I chilled with Minor to slam more brews. We posted up at the bar at an Applebee's and Minor was like, "Dude, you seen the 1969 Texas-versus-Arkansas game?" sounding pretty hammered.

"Yeah, dude," I was like.

"Sam," he was like, "I think that game is overrated."

"Naw dude," I said, trying to remember the game 'cause I was so drunk. "That pass by James Street was the tits." We ended up drunk as fuck with a $200 Applebee's bar tab.

The next morning while Ricky and Liana were sleeping, and as I looked pretty bummed as hell at the pile of laundry I had to help Ricky out with at the laundromat (which had always been sort of awesome 'cause we snuck tall boys into the laundromat and laughed our asses off), I decided to peace out. I looked out the window. "Fuck no," I was like, "I promised I wouldn't leave 'till I ate that burrito." I was thinking about the seven-pound suicide burrito challenge at a Mexican place in San Fran.

I chilled in SF for one more day. It was Sunday. It got hot; it was a bombass day; the sun turned red at three. I started eating that burrito at four. All that delicious carne asada and rice dripped out the sides of the burrito. About halfway through it wasn't delicious anymore, just hot and painful. My mouth was on fire. There was the end of the burrito, just a few more bites away, dripping wet and glorious with my money refunded and my picture framed on the wall where San Fran legends are born. But taking it too fast would mean vomit streaming out my mouth to shroud the table in half-digested beans, and a busboy would have to help wipe it up by hand and look slowly up to me with disappointment and disgust in his eyes. That was San Fran; and the hotties there for lunch watching me eat, waiting for me to win; and this burrito, and the salsa, and guac, and the seven brutal pounds.

I kept eating 'till I was sick; I thought I'd pass out, face down into the burrito. When the fuck will this burrito end? I thought, and ate desperately, as I had eaten at so many wing places in the world beyond. And before me was the final raw bulge of the burrito's tail; somewhere far beyond, badass, crazy Columbus had pictures of me plastered all over for burger and wing contests. There is something awesome about the burgers and wings of the Midwest; Cali is like too hung up on burritos, which are a drag to eat seven pounds of—at least that's what I thought of then.

CHAPTER TWELVE

BONER CITY

The next morning after I dropped a mad burrito dump, I packed my shit and peaced out while Ricky and Liana were still sleeping. I never threw that party on the old ghost ship—and it would have been an awesome fucking party—and Ricky and I were no longer tight.

In Oakland I slammed a Miller Light among some dudes at an Outback with a mediocre drink special, and I was getting my road on again. I hauled ass through Oakland to try to get to Fresno. A couple of rides hauled me south to Bakersfield. The first driver was mad crazy, this blonde dude in a pretty tricked-out ride. "Check out my toe," he was like and gunned it like hell down the road. "Check it out." He had it all bandaged up. "That shit got amputated this morning. Those dicks want me to chill in the hospital. I got the fuck out. Who gives a shit about a toe?" Fuck yeah, I was like, that shit is raw, and it was only gonna get rawer. The dude hauled ass into Tracy in a hot second. Tracy is a white-collar town; business dudes eat appeteasers at the local Fridays by the office parks. A ton of tech companies have offices there. The strips malls are long and beige. All the usual shit was there—Edible Arrangements, Office Max, Cosi, all the rest. The sun started to set, all purple over outlet stores and long parking lots; the sun the color of a Vikings jersey, slashed with scarlet, the color of the Ohio State Buckeyes.

I stuck my head out the window and hollered at a hottie in a Corolla. She was the hottest chick I've ever seen drive a Corolla. The crazy dude driving was a Systems Analyst with an IT company and he lived in Fresno; his dad had been a Systems Analyst too. His toe got all fucked in a company softball game, sliding into second, but that didn't make any sense to me. Dude dropped me off in Fresno. I pounded a quick MGD at a sports bar, and in walked this smoking Armenian chick, and like in a fucking dream, "Pour Some Sugar on Me" started playing on the TouchTunes, and I said to myself, fuck yeah, fuck yeah, this town rules.

I needed to bust south. Some dude in a Tundra picked me up. The dude was from Lubbock, Texas, and did some kind of multilevel marketing. "You want an amazing investment opportunity?" he was like. "Just take my card." He kept talking about all the money I could make selling for his company. "All you have to do is just sign up online and find five friends who will also sell, totally easy. After that, you just need to sell a very low minimum of inventory each week, and you'll have money rolling in. And the purchase price for the minimum inventory is extremely low. You think you'd be interested?"

I took his card and got off in Bakersfield. It got cold as balls. I put on the Adidas windbreaker I'd bought in Oakland and I was still cold as balls. I was standing in front of a shitty Red Roof Inn that looked like a real shithole. The cars blew by, headed to LA. I tried to get their attention. It was seriously cold as balls. I stood there until midnight, for two fucking hours, and got pissed as hell. It was like Stuart fuck-me-in-the-butt Iowa all over again. There was nothing to do except blow some cash on a bus for the rest of the way to LA. I hauled ass back to the bus station.

I had bought my ticket and was checking my phone when all of a sudden this Latina smokeshow rolled in. Her bus had just gotten in. Her rack was like unbelievable; her legs put me in Boner City; her hair was nice as fuck; and her eyes were big and blue and looked like they wanted to bone. I got super-amped, like I always do when I see a girl I wanna bone and need to figure out how. My bus to LA was about to take off. I grabbed my North Face bag and got on the bus, and then like magic I saw the Latina smokeshow sitting by herself. I grabbed the seat across from her and started working up my game right away. I was so in need of some action, so desperate, so wasted, so on-the-cusp-of-blueballs, that I got ready to spit game, the game necessary to lay a new hottie. I spent like five minutes adjusting my hat to the perfect angle.

Let's do this shit, let's do this shit or your nuts are gonna pop! Come on, motherfucker, let's do this! You some kind of pussy? Aren't you ready to get some action? And like a lifelong player I leaned over to her while she was trying to sleep and was like, "Hey girl, you wanna use my Adidas windbreaker as a pillow?"

She looked up with her face all hot and was like, "No, but thanks."

I sat back, sorta pissed; I checked my phone. I waited 'till she looked at me, to check out my abs that I let slip out from my shirt a little, and I went over to her again. "Can I chill with you?"

"Sure."

And I chilled. "Where you headed?"

"LA." I was into how she said "LA." Everything about her was boneable.

"Aw snap, I'm going there too!" I was like. "Thanks for letting me sit next to you, I was bored as fuck over there and you look like you like to have a good time." And we started talking about our past and whatever. Her deal was shitty: She had a fucking husband and a kid. The husband was a total douche, so she peaced out and was gonna go crash with her sister in LA. Her son was like back with her family or something; they picked grapes or something pathetic like that. She was pissed as fuck. Even though she had a fucking kid, I still felt like getting my grind on with her. We talked about a bunch of shit. She said she's never seen abs as chiseled as mine. Then she was talking about coming and hanging in Columbus with me. "Hell yeah!" I was like. The bus started balling downhill. In a way that was totally smooth, I started copping a feel, and we decided silently that she'd come and smash with me in a hotel in LA. I wanted to smash that shit so hard; I copped a feel all over her hot rack. Her little shoulders got me hot; I copped a feel and copped a feel. And she loved it.

"I love your triceps," she was like, feeling my upper arms. I promised her they get even bigger when I have more solid time for workouts. She was beyond hot. We'd said our shit; we just chilled in silence and thought about how we were gonna smash later. It was as awesome as that. You can go slay whatever kind of tang you want; this smokeshow was my jam, and that's legit. She'd totally noticed me checking her out before. "I thought you looked like a cut Big Ten bro."

"Hell yeah I'm a cut Big Ten bro!" I was like. We came in to Hollywood. In the gray, dirty dawn, like the dawn when Denzel Washington met Chris Pine in the train yard, in the movie *Unstoppable*, she felt my junk. I checked the scene outside: killer party houses and palm trees and In-N-Outs. It looked mega-tight; the land of hotties and parties, like the night-club of America. The bus let us off on Main Street, which was just as shitty as where you get off a bus in wherever-the-fuck—red brick, gross, assholes hanging around, buses driving by, the stank-ass smell of a big city.

But then I started to get all like a paranoid asshole, I don't know what my deal was. I started thinking that this chick, Talia, or Tali, was some kind of scheming bitch who made money by getting dudes on the bus to come with her to breakfast, then a hotel where a thug-ass pimp would like beat their asses or shoot them or something. I kept this bullshit to myself. As we were housing some breakfast I saw this thug-ass dude staring at me; I thought Tali might be giving him some kind of signal. I was crazy tired and was paranoid like I was high but I wasn't. All this paranoia made me act like a dick. "What's that dude's deal?" I was like.

"What dude are you talking about?" I dropped it. She dragged her ass; she ate slow as fuck; she chewed super slow, checked her phone, and kept talking, and meanwhile I was acting like a super pussy, worried about every move she made, thinking she was signaling to the thug-ass pimp. This was all so fucking dumb. I was ready to fight somebody as we walked around the streets. We nabbed a room at a DoubleTree and I locked the door as soon as we were in. I copped a feel. Forget about this crazy shit. We had to get our drink on and chill the fuck out. I checked like twelve blocks for liquor stores and finally I scored a pint of Malibu. I hauled ass to the hotel, getting stoked to beast. Tali was doing some chick shit in the bathroom. We took some shots. On the real, Malibu is for bitches but it felt good as hell to get a little crunk in my veins. I took my shirt off and we made out for a little. I started talking about my posse in the Midwest.

I was like, "You gotta meet this funny chick I know named Doric. That chick is like this tall-as-fuck redhead. She can show you all the tightest shit to do in Columbus."

"A tall-as-fuck redhead?" she said sorta like a bitch. "What's your deal with her?" She didn't get that I would never fuck a chick over five-eight. I tried to drop it. She wouldn't come out of the fucking bathroom.

"Let's fool around!" I kept being like.

"Some redhead? I thought you were like a cut Big Ten bro. I checked you out in your Hollister polo, and was like, he doesn't look like a dick. But you are! You're just a douchebag like every other guy."

"You're being insane."

"Don't act like you're not boning that redhead, 'cause I bet you totally are. You're a textbook dickhole douchebag like all the other dickhole douchebags."

"Come on, babe, I'm not a dickhole douchebag. I swear to fucking Christ I don't fuck chicks over five-eight. I just wanna smash with you."

"I thought you were a nice guy. Finally not a dickhole douchebag."

"Babe," I totally begged her. "I'm being real with you, I'm not a dickhole douchebag." Just before this I totally thought she was a hustler skank. This was ultra dumb. We were both taking turns being total assholes. I begged like hell, and then I realized that begging is stupid and I didn't need to deal with this and I straight-up told her that; and then I flew off the handle and chucked a glass of Malibu into a lamp and told her to get the fuck out. "Get the fuck out!" I'd lay mad nap bombs and forget it; I had my shit, my own awesome and clutch shit forever. It was quiet in the bathroom. I got some rest on.

Tali came out looking like she'd been crying or whatever. 'Cause she was some kind of irrational chick she figured that a dickhole douchebag wouldn't chuck Malibu into a lamp when he's trying to show he isn't a dickhole douchebag. She got totes naked in silence and got her hot naked body into bed. She was stacked. I saw her C-section scar; it was gross as fuck but I tried not to think about it or the fact that she had kids. Her legs were real hot. She was short as hell. I smashed it to her like crazy and hoped I wouldn't have to pay for that lamp.

CHAPTER THIRTEEN

ALMOST AS GOOD AS CHIPOTLE

For the next fifteen days we were total smash-buddies. The next morning we decided to road trip it together to Columbus; she'd be my in-town slam piece. I pictured crazy-ass times with Derek and Maryann and that whole crew—a raw time, a totally raw time. She was poor as fuck and my fave poker sites had been shut down, so we needed to pull down some cash for the trip. Tali wanted to get cranking with the cash I had left. I didn't like that freeloader bullshit. I took it easy and thought things over for a couple of days, as we checked out jobs on Craigslist, on my phone, until my cash got lower and lower. We had mad fun in our hotel smash palace. One night I couldn't sleep, copped a sleep-feel on my girl, and checked out the window. Some real shit goes down there. Outside the window I could see something right out of *The Wire*. A shitty old motel had some real shit going down. A cop car was there and a bunch of cops were questioning some shady dude. Some bitch was shouting from inside. I could hear all of it. I never saw so much shit go down. LA is the most fucked up and raw of American cities; Columbus gets XL-cold in the winter but people keep it together. LA is a fucking freakshow.

There were always real wild shit shows on South Main Street, where Tali and I would hang sometimes. Asshole cops were like all over the place. Super-raw dudes were wandering everywhere—all of it under the soft light of In-N-Out signs that signify the legit deliciousness that a burger can really be. The place reeked of weed, piss, burgers, and beer. Those awesome jams of Kanye floated from sick bars; it overpowered all the lame sounds of country in the American night. All these dudes looked like my bro Hammer. Thug-ass dudes cruised by; then long-haired lame-ass annoying hipsters straight off planes from Brooklyn; then old homeless dudes, looking for booze and some change; then an occasional hottie, and some hippy cocksuckers in Birkenstocks. I wanted to party with some of them, get real hammered, but Tali and I needed to scrape some dough.

We swung by a CVS at Sunset and Vine to see if we could get a few weeks of work. That area was a real clusterfuck. All these tourists were everywhere looking for movie stars but they never saw jack shit. A limo would drive by and they'd lose it trying to figure out who it was: some dude in sunglasses riding with a hottie. "Robert Downey Jr.! Robert Downey Jr.!" "No, Johnny Depp! Johnny Depp!" They were having the stupidest time. A bunch of gay dudes who were probably hairdressers or something walked by, probably checking me out. Some of the most amazing hotties I've ever seen walked around in short-shorts; they probably wanted to be actresses, now they were probably just blowing producers. We thought we could get some real stupid jobs at a movie theater. There was jack-shit anywhere. There were like a million cars on Hollywood Boulevard and these assholes were getting in wrecks constantly; everybody was headed to wherever-the-fuck—and then wherever-the-fuck after that. Black dudes hung out in front of restaurants, arguing like black dudes do in Columbus, Ohio, except they were like way louder and more pimped out. Tall, asshole preachers came by. Huge gross fatties ran across the boulevard to see *Jimmy Kimmel Live.* I saw Jonah Hill checking out cars at a dealership; he was inside the window, looking funny as hell. Tali and I slammed some drinks in a crazy bar downtown that had like an ancient Greek theme or some shit, with metal tits all over and huge stone statues with naked asses. People slammed fancy cocktails around waterfalls, probably looking sad 'cause they dropped too much cash on mixed drinks, which are a total rip. All the cops in LA were like pretty jacked and well-groomed; they'd probably come here to get famous and then just decided to be jagoffs instead.

Tali and I tried to nab jobs on South Main Street doing total bullshit like washing dishes, and we still got jack shit. We still had like no cash.

"I've just gotta get my clothes back from my sister and then we'll just hitch to Columbus," Tali was like. "Let's go." We hauled ass to her sister's place in a shitty neighborhood. I waited in a dark alley behind a burrito place because her sister would be pissed as fuck if she saw me. Dogs ran by. I checked my phone to see what was happening on Facebook. I could hear Tali and her sister arguing while I commented on my buddy's status. I was ready for whatever.

Tali came out and we took a cab to ESPN Zone, which is a mega sports bar in LA. What an awesome place it is, with leather chairs big enough to seriously kick back in, and the TVs blaring nothing but MLB, NBA, and NFL. We went up to the second floor and found Tali's friend Mariana, who had some of Tali's clothes in her hatchback. Mariana was a real hot half-black chick; her husband was super-black and a solid dude. He called out to the waitress and ordered some shots for all of us. I tried to pay for some of them, but he was like, "Hell no." They had two kids there. The kids ate chicken fingers; kids love ESPN Zone too. They high-fived me and thought I was pretty awesome. The wild awesomeness of ESPN Zone—the early rounds of NBA playoffs—howled and boomed from all corners. Dudes were shouting at the TV, slamming beers, just fuck it all and watch out. Tali got her clothes out of the hatchback and we peaced out. We walked by the Staples Center. A couple of scalper dudes whispered in my ears about Lakers tickets. Cheap-ass courtside seats. I was like, all right, I'll bite. His buddy came by and motioned me over to an alley, where I stood around like a chump as he was like, "Grab them, man, grab them."

"What the hell?" I was like.

He'd already gotten my cash. He was like just pointing at the ground. It was weird. There was something that looked like an envelope. Dude was being way too careful. "Got to look out for myself, cops are cracking down on scalpers." I picked up the envelope, which was sorta dirty, and went to grab Tali, and we headed over to the front gate to get into the game. We couldn't fucking get in. The tickets were bullshit. I wished I was less of a shit-for-brains about my cash.

Tali and I had to get real about our plan. We figured to just fuck it all and hitch to Columbus with whatever dough we had. She nabbed some cash from her sister that night. We had like enough to party but not to fly. So before we spent another night in the hotel I tossed my shit in my North Face bag and we got a ride to Arcadia, where there are some big-ass mountains or something. It was dark as hell. We were busting out into the American party. My hand on her ass, we chugged a few miles down the road. It was Saturday night. We chilled under a street-light, looking for a ride, when suddenly cars full of USC douche-bags drove by, flipping us off. "Fuck the Bucks! Fuck the Bucks!" they all shouted. Then they threw cans at us and were total dicks 'cause they saw my OSU T-shirt. A bunch of these asshole cars passed, full of dickhole faces and totally ugly chicks. I hated all those fuckers. Where the hell did they get off, making fun of us when everybody knows OSU has a way more solid football program, historically. We didn't give a shit. So natch we didn't get a fucking ride. We had to haul ass all the way back where we started, and the lamest shit was we wanted to grab a beer and went into the only open bar, which was a fucking Trojans bar, and all the assholes totally remembered us. Now they saw that Tali was a total smokeshow, a Latina hottie; and that this Buckeye had nabbed that ass.

With her hot ass shaking we busted out of that bullshit and headed up along the highway. I took the bags like a fucking gen-tleman. It was cold and my dick was freezing. I decided this was dumb and we should just go smash in the hotel tonight, and then figure shit out in the morning. We went into an Embassy Suites and grabbed a room—king bed, minibar, and all. We made out hard. We got real hammered and did it in the shower and smashed with the lights on and then with the lights off. I was proving to her my major-league sex boning skills, which she totally appreciated, and we finished the bone session early in the morning, breathless, then totally exhausted, like total porn stars.

The next morning it was time to get into gear. We were gonna pick grapes during the day, which would totally suck, but then just get totally wild at night, which would be sweet. Then we'd net some cash and be able to just take a fucking plane or something to Columbus. It was an awesome afternoon, cruising up to Bakersfield with Tali; we sat back, took shots from my Nalgene, copped some feels, and were just chill as fuck. We rolled up in Bakersfield at like 3 P.M. We were just gonna hit up some fruit picking places. Tali told me we'd probably just live in tents for the job. The idea of straight-up camping in Cali and getting hammered under the stars sounded like a fucking grand slam to me. But we still couldn't get jack shit and everybody sent us running around everywhere, like total bullshit. We found a delicious Chinese place and then headed out again with some General Tso's all up inside us. We rolled into a shitty Mexican part of town. Tali talked to people in Spanish about jobs. Now that it was dark, the area got bright as fuck: movie marquees, taquerias, bars, and a bunch of shitty cars parked wherever. A ton of poor-ass Mexican families were just chilling. My lady was talking it up with like everyone. This seemed like total hopeless bullshit to me. It was totally time to take a brew break, so we bought a case of Bud Light Lime at a CVS and went out by the tracks to get our al fresca drink on. We posted up on some crates and chilled out. There were just some gross trains around and a bunch of planes flying in from the airport, sorta like *Wayne's World*. It made for an awesome night, a raw night, a night for Bud Light Lime, a chill night, and a night to make out with your chick and shotgun and chillax. This we fucking did. She could totally hang and went beer-for-beer with me and even outdrank me and we rocked for a long-ass time. We just chilled there. Homeless dudes would walk by sometimes and take a piss, but usually nobody was around and I could even get to second-and-a-half base outside. Once we couldn't drink any more, we drunk-hiked to the road.

Tali figured some new shit out. We'd beast it to Sabinal, where she was from, and then we could crash at her brother's crib. I was like, "Whatever." When we were waiting for a ride Tali totally flashed her rack at passing cars to get their attention, and in like a hot second a truck stopped for us. The dude's rig was total bullshit and it like took forever. He drove slow as fuck. At the asscrack of dawn, the dude dropped us in Sabinal. I drank the last of the Bud Light Lime while Tali conked out, so I was like Terminator-hammered. We checked out the place—the scene seemed aight. We tried to text her brother and her brother's buddy. Nobody answered. As dawn busted open I just laid out all drunk in the town square and was like, "I love lamp! I love lamp! I love lamp!" This was from the movie *Anchorman*, with Steve Carell talking to Will Ferrell and all those dudes. Tali laughed. She thought I was pretty hilarious. I could lay there hammered and quoting *Anchorman* all day and she'd think it was awesome. But finally I figured shit would be all good once we met up with her brother, and I took her to a Holiday Inn and we dropped nap bombs comfortably.

The next morning I was too hungover to function so Tali went out to meet with her brother and I stayed in a crunk coma 'till noon. I woke up when this charter bus full of hotties with nice racks and Dolce & Gabbana sunglasses rolled by, looking real fine. "Holy shit!" I was like. "The West Coast is so legit!" They were probably going on like a college trip or something; maybe I could see them looking all fine on the way back.

Tali came back with her brother, her brother's buddy, and her fucking kid (ugh). Her brother was a pretty raw Mexican dude who could get pretty balls-out wild after some brews, he was pretty solid. His buddy was fat as hell and could get real loud and assholey. It was totally obvious that the dude wanted to fuck my lady. Tali's fucking kid was named Jimmy or something and was like seven and was total boner poison. So this was the crew I got up with, and shit started to get lit.

Her brother, Ritchie, had a pretty crappy Rav4. The crew piled in there and then we rolled out. "What's the deal?" I was like. Her brother's buddy Pedro talked the most. Dude stank like literal ass. Like for real literally. He made money by selling manure to farmers; so for real he drove around with a truck full of shit. Ritchie was sorta a baller and was always looking to party. Dude would always say shit like, "Aight man, aight—aight, aight!" And shit was aight. We rolled out to talk to farmers to see if they wanted to buy some shit.

Ritchie tossed me a half-full bottle of SoCo. "Hit this shit! We'll work tomorrow. Aight, man—hit that shit!" Tali was chilling in the back with that little boner poison kid; I looked at them and couldn't believe she had a fucking kid. It made me feel like my dick was crawling back up inside my body. I had to try to party even though there was a goddamn kid involved.

"What's up now, dude?"

"We'll find some farmer and grab his extra shit. We'll grab it tomorrow. Seriously, we'll make so much cash. Don't sweat it."

"We gotta make time for getting wild!" Pedro was like. I knew this was for real—everywhere I went, people needed to still get wild. We busted through Fresno and met up with some farmers in BFE. Pedro shot the shit with a bunch of old farmer dudes but shit-all came of it.

"We gotta drink!" Ritchie was like, and we busted ass to a Buffalo Wild Wings. Every Sunday, people love hitting up B-Dubs. They roll over with their whole family crew; they suck down wings and brews; shit's cool. Pretty soon the kids are tired as fuck and parents are totally hammered. They're all plowed. This is the scene at like every Buffalo Wild Wings I've been to. So we partied at B-Dubs. We all slammed some brews and watched baseball; that little boner poison did whatever with some other kids. Shit started to get dark. We'd done shit today. What shit were we supposed to be doing? *Mañana*, " Ritchie was like. "*Mañana*, aight, we'll pull some cash; slam one more brew man, aight? Aight!"

We piled our drunk selves into the Rav4 and headed to a sports bar. Pedro was the sort of loud jagoff who like knows everybody around. After we got hammered in the sports bar just the two of us rolled out to go pick up shit, but just ended up scoping for tail and trying to score some snatch for him and Ritchie. Later I had to just chill in the car while dude argued with an old Mexican at a 7-Eleven about the price of some Late Night Taco Doritos. We got the Late Night Taco Doritos; we ate those chips fast as hell and threw the bag on the sidewalk in front of the 7-Eleven. All kinds of hot ladies went past us on the street. I was like, "What's fucking happening?"

"Just chill, man," Pedro was like. "We're gonna pull mad cash tomorrow; we just chill tonight." Then we grabbed Tali and Ritchie and that little kid and cruised over to the Mexican part of Fresno. Some old Chinese dudes were checking out the scene; posses of Latina chicks walked around looking totes hot; Reggaeton blasted from the bars; lights were everywhere like Cinco de Mayo or some shit. We went into a burrito place and had big-ass burritos; it was almost as good as Chipotle. I whipped out the last of my party cash and paid for Tali and me. Now I was getting to be poor as fuck. Tali and I were like "Oh shit."

"Where we gonna crash tonight, babe?"

"Beats me."

Ritchie had gotten mad sloppy; he just kept being like, "Aight man, aight, aight man," like a drunk-ass zombie. The day had been hella-long. After all this we still had no idea what the deal was. The kid fell asleep and drooled on my Hollister tee. We rolled back in to Sabinal. Ritchie pulled into Texas Roadhouse real quick; he needed one more brew. There was a Super 8 behind the Texas Roadhouse. I asked the chick at the front desk how much it cost and it was hella-cheap. Tali was cool with it 'cause she wanted a hotel for the boner poison to crash in. We pounded a few brews in Texas Roadhouse, watched some drunk assholes sing with a Steve Miller Band cover band, and Tali and I went over to the motel to crash. Pedro kept hanging around 'cause he had no place to crash. Ritchie crashed at his dad's.

"You've seriously got not place to crash?" I was like to Pedro.

"Hell no. I used to crash with my girl Big Rita but that bitch tossed me out. I might just crash in my truck."

Reggaeton tinkled. I made out with Tali for a second. "*Mañana*," she was like. "You think things will be cool tomorrow?"

"Sure babe, *mañana*." I think that meant "tomorrow." I took Spanish in middle school but forgot most of that shit, but it probably means "tomorrow," or "around the corner."

The little boner poison jumped in bed with his clothes on and conked out; his shoes were full of sand, annoying fucking sand. Tali and I had to wake the fuck up and get the sand out of the sheets. I woke up the next day, body-sprayed, and checked shit out. There were some cotton and grape and whatever fields sorta nearby. I asked the chick at the front desk of the Super 8 if we could get another night. The cheapest room was vacant. I fished out my parents' credit card and moved our stuff into that room. The bed sucked and there was no minibar, but there was full cable with premium channels. We chilled there 'till Ritchie and Pedro rolled up in the Rav4. They brought some Natty and just wanted to get plowed in the motel room.

"Are we gonna make some cash?"

"Not this late. We're gonna pull mad cash tomorrow, for real; let's just chill and toss some brews today. You want some brews?" Today we have a few beers. What do you say, beer?"

You don't gotta twist my arm to get me to brew it. "Aight man—aight!" Ritchie was like. We were never gonna pull any cash with this shit. Pedro reeked.

That night Tali and I crashed in the Super 8 room watching *Entourage* reruns beneath the stucco ceiling. I was just about to get my sleep on when she was like, "You wanna smash?"

I was like, "What about the fucking kid?"

"He's asleep. He won't hear." But he wasn't asleep and my dick just doesn't roll that way.

The next day the dudes restocked on SoCo and came back in the motel room to get hammered squared. Pedro was too wasted to get out the door and slept on the floor of the room, wrapped in a couple towels and stinking like shit. Tali hated that dude; she said he hung around her brother so he could try to bone her.

Nothing was gonna happen for me and Tali without some party cash, so I went out the next morning to try to find like farm work or whatever. I checked out the farm that was sorta near the motel. The farmer was chilling with his fam in the kitchen. I told him I needed to pull some cash and the dude said that he'd throw down like twenty-five bucks for every hundred pounds of cotton. Since I'm a fit dude with mad cardio endurance I figured I'd nab like eight-hundred pounds every day and get a nice tan and workout on while I was doing it, so I was like "Hell yeah." He hooked me up with some big bags and told me I could start working at like dawn. I headed back to the motel feeling pretty psyched. On my way back this beer truck came by with its back door all open. It hit a pothole and dumped a couple cases of Bud on the road. I hauled those home. Tali was psyched too. "Jimmy and I can help you."

"Fuck no!" I was like. "I'm a fit dude!"

"Baby, picking cotton is crazy hard. I can teach you."

We drank some bonus Bud, and later on Ritchie rolled up with buns and brats and we had a sick cookout outside next to the hotel. There was this real hill-shit family crashing in the hotel room next to ours; the great-grandfather was old as fuck and couldn't work; his grandchildren and their children were busting ass every day picking shit for cash. I rolled out with that crew the next day. They were spitting some shit about how cotton weighed more in the morning 'cause it was heavier so you could nab more dough, but that sounded like bullshit. The great-grandfather had been a dust bowl player just like the old-as-fuck

Montana cowboy I rode with. That crew had been hanging in
Cali since that shit went down. They all worked like psychos.
They used to be super poor as fuck but now they were just sorta
poor as fuck. They thought that was pretty cool.

"You dudes ever headed back to Nebraska?"

"Hell no; fuck Nebraska. We're gonna settle down here."

We bent down and started picking cotton. It was awesome.
I could feel my upper body getting a real workout and the sun
was totally baking my skin to an awesome tan in the blue morning air. This was so much more awesome than a gym. But the
way I picked cotton was sorta lame. I took forever trying to pick
the white shit off the other shit; everybody else did it way faster.
And my fingers kept fucking bleeding; I needed gloves, or something. I saw this one old black couple working. They were crazy
fucking fast. My back started to hurt like hell. But it was real nice
feeling that burn in my arms and pecs. If I wanted to get some
pushups in I did, with my back all rippled and shimmering in the
sun. Migrant worker chicks totally checked me out. Tali and that
boner poison swung by in the afternoon and did me a solid. And
that fucking kid was faster than me!—and natch Tali was twice
as fast, being Mexican or whatever. They blew past me and left
me piles of cotton to put in the bag—all while I kept doing some
pushups. I threw them in feeling pretty stoked. I was getting
an awesome workout in and they were doing the work. They
did that all afternoon. When it started getting dark we peaced
out together. I dropped my bag full of shit on a scale; it was like
fifty fucking pounds, so I got like thirteen stupid bucks. I had
to borrow a bike from one of the workers and rode down the
highway to go grab some cheap food at a cheap grocery store.
LA-bound traffic blew by; Frisco-bound was all up in my ass.
I was pissed as fuck. I stopped to check my phone, had no service, and wondered why the fuck a dude like me had to ride a
bike and wasn't even able to afford some fucking beer. God was
being a dick to me. I should have known God would be a dick.
Chilling with Tali was cool though; she was always totally hot,

and I loved smashing with her, as long as the kid wasn't around. Tired as fuck, I reclined on the bed and watched some more *Entourage*. I checked my phone. Ritchie and Pedro weren't hanging out with us anymore and that was cool 'cause I was sorta sick of those dudes. Tali laid next to me, the boner poison was on the other side, and they played around, taking pictures of themselves on my iPhone. The Super 8 was pretty quiet. The episode of *Entourage* was pretty hilarious. Shit was cool with me. I copped a feel on Tali when the boner poison wasn't looking and we turned off the lights.

In the morning I was sore as fuck; I got up and went to the bathroom to groom it; then I put on my lacrosse shorts that had been all fucked up but Tali patched them up like a champ, put on my ragged Buckeyes hat, which used to be crisp as hell, and hauled ass over to the farm with my bag.

I was always just making like a really shitty amount of cash. It was just enough to get some shitty food on that stupid bike. Time flew by like hell. It was like my brain straight-up forgot all my crew in Midwest and my sick road trips. The kid was crazy annoying; he liked to bug me when all I wanted to do was chill the fuck out. Tali sat mending clothes. I was a total lame dude, not the partying king like I'd dreamed in Columbus. Word on the street was Tali's husband rolled back into town and was looking to drop me; I was ready for it. One night the family next door lost their shit and fucked some dude up outside the Super 8. From then on I made sure to work out my fight muscles in case those fuckers tried to start with us 'cause we're Mexican. They thought I was Mexican; but I'm just pretty well-tanned.

But now it was fall and I was getting bored. The family next door was sticking around. I was done, and besides I couldn't keep charging the room to my parents' credit card. We had to get the fuck out. "You should go crash at your dad's place," I was like. "Jesus Christ, you can't keep hanging with dudes in hotel rooms with a little kid; it's a huge drag." Tali cried because I was being a douche; I was just being fucking honest. Pedro rolled up in the Rav4 and so we headed over to her family's place to see what the deal was. I'd have to ninja-hide so they wouldn't see me. We started rolling out to Sabinal, but in like a second the Rav4 broke down, and it was raining like hell. We were all hella-pissed. Pedro cowboyed up and fixed that shit. He was a pretty solid dude after all. We had to blow up one more chug fest. We rolled into another Texas Roadhouse and slammed MGDs for a while. I was done with that cotton shit. I could feel the pull of the parties back home calling me. I shot my dad a text so he wouldn't cut off the credit card.

We busted over to Tali's family's crib. It was out in buttfuck wherever near vineyards or something. It was dark when we rolled in. I got out where they couldn't see me. Shit was bump-ing inside; a bunch of Tali's brothers were playing *Guitar Hero*. Her dad was chilling with some wine. The dude started shout-ing like hell over the sounds of *Guitar Hero*. They told her she was a total bitch 'cause she'd dropped that dickhole husband, ditched the kid, and rolled to LA. Her dad was pissed. But her mom calmed shit down, her dad seemed pretty pussywhipped, and they let Tali crash there. Her brothers started playing on Expert mode. I chilled outside and started to get kinda bored. On my iPhone I listened to that killer song "All Falls Down" by Kanye West; I jammed out to it in the bushes. It's not the words so much as the awesome beat and the way Kanye rhymes it, like a real player. The winds howled. My balls were freezing.

Tali and Pedro swung back and grabbed me and we went to go grab Ritchie. That dude was totally smashing with Pedro's old slam piece, Big Rita; we honked at him from the driveway. Big Rita bitched out and threw dude out. Shit was all sloppy. We just crashed in the Rav4 that night. Tali felt my junk, and was all like, "Don't leave." She thought she could like work picking grapes or something and be able to support me too; I'd hide in some farm-er's stupid barn near her family's crib. There'd be like fucking nothing to do but sit around and eat fucking grapes. Fuck that!

Tali's cousins picked us up the next day. I realized that like a ton of Mexicans knew that Tali and I were smashing and they were probably jealous as hell. The cousins were cool and pretty awesome. I chilled with them, shooting the shit, talking about who we were planning to draft in fantasy football. There were five cousins total, and they were all pretty solid. They seemed more like the side of Tali's family that wasn't out of control like her brother. But Ritchie was still a solid dude. He kept saying he was gonna come hang with me in Columbus. I pictured that dude on OSU campus, putting shit off and getting plowed. Dude was hammered in a field somewhere that day.

They dropped me down the road and then took Tali home. They texted me in a hot second and told me Tali's parents weren't around. I was able to chill up in that crib for the day. It was kind of a shithole; it blew my skull that the whole family all crashed there. It stank. There was no cable or WiFi. Tali was doing the dishes. I could see her sisters were totally checking me out. I couldn't blame them.

Once it seemed like her parents were gonna be back soon, Tali took me over to this barn pretty close by. We made like a makeshift rustic sex palace out of some blankets and hay and shit. There was this big-ass tarantula chilling right up over the bed. Tali said not to sweat that shit. I lay on the bed and remembered that tarantula in *Home Alone*. I went outside and checked my phone. In my phone were some funny pics on Facebook. Tali and the little boner poison were just chilling; we chugged some legit delicious Cali wine. Shit got dark. Tali had to have dinner at home but came back and gave me some mad good authentic tortillas. I used my phone as a flashlight. We beasted it in the barn. She got up hella-fast and went back to her house. It sounded like her dad was crazy pissed. I snuck over to the house to see what was going down. I hid near some trees and got my spy on. Her brothers were still tearing it up on *Guitar Hero*. The stars were out; smoke was coming from the chimney. It smelled like Chipotle again. I had just gotten laid. It was awesome. I hid there all stealth like some kind of action movie. I felt like Jason Statham; I was a total badass in the American night.

Tali was back and looked all pissed. I came out of stealth mode. "What's up, babe?"

"I hate my dad. He's making me go back to work. He's being a total dick. Sam, let me come to Columbus with you."

"How the fuck is that gonna happen?"

"Baby, please. I love you."

"Babe, I gotta peace out."

"You're such an asshole. Let's just smash one more time before you leave."

Back at the barn I boned her like mad under that tarantula. Could that tarantula tell how wicked mad I was boning her? We crashed out a while. She had to peace out around midnight; her dad sounded hammered, but then he must have passed out. I rested the hell out of my sexed-out self.

When I woke up the farmer who owned the barn came in and was like, "How's it going?" "Aight. Hope you don't mind me laying pipe here."

"Fella's gotta do what a fella's gotta do. You're with that hot little Mexican number?"

"She's crazy bangable."

"Sure sure. Her mom must have slept with somebody else to make such a hot little number." Then I had to hear him talk about his dumb farm for a while.

Tali hooked me up with some breakfast. I had all my shit in my North Face bag and was ready to roll as soon as I got a text from my dad saying the family card was still kosher to use. I knew he'd totally let me use it. I told Tali I was peacing out. She was being a total chick about it and was all sad and whatever. We made out real quick and she walked away. We stopped and looked at each other, and I thought maybe we'd smash one more time, but she kept walking and I almost had blueballs.

"Text me when you're in Columbus, babe," I was like. She was saying she was gonna come hang with me in C-Bus with her brother in a while. But we both knew that would totally suck for me and my rep. I stopped and scoped her one last time. She kept walking to the house, still looking totally smoking. I checked my phone. Hell yeah, time to get back to party fundamentals.

I headed back down the road, eating a Clif Bar I'd buried in my bag. I went over the tracks and finished the Clif Bar. I passed some buildings and whatever. It was time for some new shit. I checked my phone for a text from my dad. Nothing yet. I was pissed and waited. Then I finally got the text. He was sort of pissed; but I could use the card. "Shouldn't you be back in class?" he asked. It was all good. I was taking that shit pass/fail.

I strutted down the road and hoped a charter bus full of hotties would pick me up so I could make some time and get my game on. It was an impossible dream. I grabbed another ride. It was like the fastest fucking ride ever. It was a dude who drummed in a local Bon Jovi cover band. His new whip could push it past ninety like by accident. "I don't drink and drive," he was like and passed me a little bottle of Captain Morgan. I hit that and passed it back to him. "Fuck it," dude was like and poured one back. We balled into LA in like no time. Dude dropped me off right in front of the Hard Rock Café in Hollywood; ran in and chowed down a burger. Then I bought my bus ticket to Dayton. My dad wouldn't let me use the card enough to get to Columbus and buy beers. I figured I'd just get to Dayton with beers along the way and then figure shit out.

I had like four hours left to party in LA before I had to hop the bus. First I bought some Doritos to snack on on the bus. I didn't have much time. I got a six-pack and sat in the back of a Quiznos on Cahunega and got hammered and ate a Steakhouse Prime Rib Dip. As I chowed down the sandwich, I could see some mad-big searchlights from a movie premiere in the distance. The West Coast was getting wild all around me. And this was my shitty Hollywood party—my last night in town, and I was getting hammered on Modelo in the back of a Quiznos.

CHAPTER FOURTEEN

THE DICKHOLE OF BUCK CREEK

By the next morning I was hauling ass on the bus through Arizona with its big-as-fuck deserts. We kept rolling like through some mountains and whatever. I had a magazine I nabbed in a bathroom, *FHM*, with Megan Fox on the cover, but I'd already seen her more naked in *Maxim* so I just stared out the window. The road was like mad bumpy and it sorta made me carsick. At night I wasn't feeling so hot; at dawn I was feeling totally gross; in the bleak Sunday afternoon I thought, I was gonna chunk it way hard; at night I rocked my insides all over the bus shitter. The bus cruised on. I was headed to party in C-Bus in October. Everybody headed to party in C-Bus in October.

We rolled into St. Louis around noon. I hit some bars in St. Louis and checked out the chicks that came cruising in from the suburbs in the north—solid Midwest hotties of the American dream. Old bitches with their used-to-be-hot faces sat at the other end of the bar. Great pints of Miller Light went down my throat. The bus roared through the boring shit of Illinois that night; the moon illuminated the truck stops and Subways; I could totally have gone for a footlong meatball sub. I spat some game at some chick on the bus and we made out 'till Terre Haute. She was hot but annoying. When we got off to eat I could barely stand all her yapping. She bought me a footlong meatball; I pretended like I couldn't find my card. In exchange I copped some good feels. She came from Washington State, where she was playing in some stupid band. She lived somewhere in upstate New York and wanted me to hang there sometime. I said maybe we could smash in Columbus sometime. She got off in Indianapolis, and I slept my ass 'till Dayton. I was like more tired than is fucking possible. I still had like eighty miles to go 'till Columbus, and I was seriously sick of this shit. I walked for a while 'till I was out of Dayton; then I grabbed a few rides that got me to Springfield where it was raining like hell. I started walking again. I needed to get the fuck home.

That night I met the Dickhole of Buck Creek. He was this annoying old dude who kept talking about going to Canada. He kept hauling ass and telling me to keep up, and I followed him 'cause he said he knew a bridge ahead where we could cross. Dude was sixty and literally wouldn't shut up about whatever fucking bullshit he went on about for like ever. He had all these lame stories about the shit he'd done, but I could tell he was just a super annoying asshole homeless dude who just walked all over, hitting up shelters and sometime begging and whatever for cash. He was seriously a fucker. We walked a few miles along the boring Buck Creek. It's a real stupid place. It has like nothing cool once you get outside of the college. It's dark as fuck. Sometimes I'd get a text that would distract me from this assface. The dude needed to get a belt out of his bag so he made me stop and wait while he tried to get it. "I swear I had a real nice belt in here. Now where could I have left it?"

"Can we fucking move it?"

"I swear I had this belt!" He was like a champion motherfucker. He kept walking too close to traffic and almost bit it like a hundred times. I was so pissed. I was afraid he'd get splattered and then I'd have that fucker sprayed all over me. The bridge didn't exist. We finally split up near some tracks and, 'cause I was crazy sweaty from hauling ass everywhere, I changed shirts and put on some breathable performance Under Armour; a streetlight lit up my pecs pretty nicely. A car full of dudes passed by and probably wondered what kind of upper-body regimen I used. The crazy thing was, even though I'd been drinking like crazy, I still had sick abdominal definition; it was pretty awesome. It started to rain super hard. I got a ride back to Springfield and the dude driving said I was going the wrong fucking way. Then I saw that fucker standing by the road trying to get a ride—stupid asshole, stupid idiot, now a total jerkoff who could for real go get fucked. I told the dude driving the whole deal with this asshole and the guy stopped and tried to help the little fucker.

"Hey, buddy, you're going the wrong way."

"What?" the dickhole was like. "You can't fool me. I've been on these roads my whole life. I'm gonna get to Canada."

"This isn't how you get to Canada, this way goes to Dayton." The dickhole acted all pissed and stormed off like a bitch.

I always thought the best parties in America were in the West but as I got closer to the Midwest I remembered what a sick place it was. There are awesome times in the Midwest; it's the same awesome place Eminem got his start when he was just an underground rapper, the same place where Orlando Pace cut his teeth in the Big Ten, where the Cleveland Browns moved and then came back, before LeBron came to dunk. There weren't as many hot Latinas for a dude, just the German, Irish, and English hotties, not totally curvaceous but still with good bods.

I just crashed on a bench in Springfield that night; in the morning some dickbag cop made me move. I started my life as a solid dude and believed that things for me would always be epic. Then shit went south and I was hungry and hungover and pissed about how not-laid I was getting, and then I was all whining like a little bitch. I wandered around Springfield feeling totally drained. The sun was balls-bright and I couldn't find my Oakleys. I was so fucking hungry. All I had left to nosh on were the last of some pizza-flavored Combos I'd bought in Shelton, Nebraska, months ago; I sucked on them for some pizza flavor. I didn't know where the fuck I could find some decent grub. I crawled out of town with barely enough strength to check my phone for new texts. I knew I wouldn't find any good fucking food in Springfield. Fuck that place! I got a ride with this skinny dude who was on some bullshit diet where you're supposed to eat like nothing. I told him I was fucking starving and he was like, "You should just try this diet. Just lemon juice, cayenne, and honey." Dude was all boney, no tone, no definition, a total idiot. Why couldn't I have gotten a ride with some awesome fat dude who'd be like, "Let's stop at this Outback and have like twelve Bloomin' Onions." No, I ended up stuck with this dickwad on a cleanse. Eventually he started being less of an ass and grabbed some Cool Ranch Doritos from the back of the car. They were under a bunch of papers from his job. He sold some bullshit around Ohio. I inhaled that bag of D-tos. Suddenly I began to get real bad gas. I was just chilling in the car while he was doing bullshit sales calls in Mechanicsburg, and I farted so hard into his seats and laughed like crazy. Jesus Christ, that shit smelled bad. But the dude never noticed and drove me home to Columbus.

Suddenly I was all up in the middle of Ohio State campus. I'd gone like a million miles all over America and now I was back on OSU campus; right as a football game was letting out, being all like a hungover zombie in the middle of the absolute madness and fucking awesomeness of OSU with its thousands of students chugging to no end, the badass dream—grinding, smashing, partying, drinking, rocking, just so they could wake up in those shitty dorm rooms beyond Lane Avenue. The high towers of the main freshman dorms—the other end of campus, the place where true players are born. I stood in the quad, trying to get my shit together enough to pick up a hottie, and every time I started to spit game big crowds rushed by and swept the hottie away from my sight. I had nobody to give me a "welcome home" makeout. I had to get a bit of action. Can you picture a dude like me coming home and not getting any action? It was getting dark. Where were my usual slam pieces? I texted my usual slam pieces; they weren't around. They were partying, dancing on bars. Where the fuck was Derek? Where the fuck was everybody? Where the fuck were my slam pieces? I had to get to my apartment to lay some nap bombs and figure the plan for that night because I knew it could still be awesome. I had to hit on some fugly-ish chicks. I finally got to second with a gross chick who was hanging out by a tree. She might have had a moustache. I got the fuck out of there.

When I got home I ate fucking everything in the fridge. Ty looked up from the Xbox. "Motherfucking Sam," he was like. "You're back; you're fucking back. Where the hell have you been, bro?" I was wearing Under Armour and a hoodie; my North Face bag was still looking pretty good. Ty had decided to eat most of my protein powder while I was gone; it was a real stupid thing to do. Dude went out, and late at night I couldn't find any parties worth hitting up and just shotgunned alone on the couch. My half-finished P90X DVDs sat on the TV. It was October, and I'd have to get back to stupid school. Some rain started happening outside, at least I didn't get caught in that shit. Derek had been chilling here, crashed a couple nights in my room, waiting for me; spent afternoons watching baseball with Ty as they pounded down Natty Lights, which were now empty and stacked in a beeramid as tall and amazing as anything the Pharaohs built; and then he had peaced out, like a hot second before I rolled in, never fucking calling, then headed to San Fran. He had his own shit there; Carly had just gotten a place. I was too much of a dumbass to holler at them when I was in Mill City. Now it was too late and I had missed my chance to rock out with Derek.

Part Two
Aw Yeah

CHAPTER ONE

MUSCLE JUICE CHRISTMAS

I didn't chill with Derek for like a solid year after that. During that year, I hung around campus, finished P90X, and switched my major to Communications. At Christmas I went to hang with my brother in Virginia and chug a bunch of crazy strong eggnog. I had been Facebook messaging with Derek and dude told me he'd be chilling out East again; and I told him I'd be in Testament, Virginia, for Christmas with my family. So then one day I'm down there and all my lame Southern relatives were sitting around being stupid and boring about everything and talking about total bullshit, and a sick Jeep Wrangler Unlimited pulled into the driveway. I was all like, "Who the hell is that?" A beat-ass looking dude, all jacked and in a stained polo, stubbly, and hungover walked up to the front door and knocked. I opened it and it hit me that it was my dude Derek. That dude hauled ass from SF to Virginia in like less than a hot second after I'd sent him that last Facebook message. There were two people crashed out in the car. "Fuck me! Derek! Who the shit is in the car?"

"What up, what up, bro. Maryann and Todd Dinkel are chilling in there. Can we groom up and chow down up in here? We're balls tired."

"How the fuck did you get here so fast?"

"Bro, the Wrangler Unlimited can rip it up!"

"Where the fuck did you get it?"

"My grandparents gave it to me for my birthday."

Shit was crazy for the next hour. Shit was like beyond confusing for my boring Southern relatives who just stared at us like total jackwads. I could hear my brother and my aunt talking shit in the kitchen.

Now there were like a ton of people in this one house. And my brother was in the middle of moving so half the furniture was gone. They needed to take some of the remaining furniture to my aunt's place in Columbus, and they were just gonna use PODS or something. Since Derek is a champ, he volunteered to help out with his Wrangler Unlimited. Me and him would haul the furniture and shit to C-Bus in a couple trips and give my aunt a ride back. This was going to save some cash and be awesome. Everybody was on board. My sister-in-law threw down some grub, and the three busted-ass travelers got their eat on. Maryann hadn't slept since Denver. Still, she was looking hotter than I remembered.

Derek told me he'd been doing some mad smashing with Carly in SF for the past year; he got a personal trainer job at Crunch and pulled a lot of extra gym tail. He totally got Carly pregged up and had a fucking little girl, Amy. Naturally dude lost his mind with that going on in his life. His rich-ass grandparents gave him a bunch of cash and dude blew it all on this Wrangler Unlimited. He was totally stoked. He and Todd Dinkel had to get their party on. Derek tried to get Carly to chill and was like, "I'm going to Columbus to chill with Sam." But she was a big bitch about it.

"Why do you need to go now? Don't you care about me?"

"Chill out, chill out, babe—like—you know—Sam needs me to come party with him, and it's like beyond clutch that I— but I won't go into all this shit—'cause you know . . . Naw, babe, I'll tell you this shit." And he told her, and natch it made like no sense.

Todd Dinkel was also working at Crunch. He and Derek had just gotten fired for tying some asshole to a moving tread-mill as a prank. Todd had been smashing with this chick named Gabby who was pretty fucking loaded. Derek and Todd decided to be a couple of real hilarious assholes and bring Gabby with them so she'd pay for like everything. Todd tried to convince her, but the bitch wasn't gonna budge unless Todd like legit married her ass. For some reason that I still can't fucking believe, Todd for real married Gabby and Derek got ordained online and totally officiated that shit, and then they all beasted out of San Fran at like ninety-five MPH. They swung by LA and grabbed some sailor dude at a Subway so he'd throw down some gas money. Dude was headed for Indiana. They also grabbed some lady who had a fugly daughter. Derek chilled with the fugly chick up front and was actually kinda into her, he was like, "Hell yeah, man! Such a fugly face but a pretty solid body. Dropping off these assholes, they rolled to Tucson. The whole time Gabby kept bitching and saying she was tired and that they needed to stop like every five seconds and go sleep in a hotel as soon as it was later than seven. With this kind of bullshit, they'd never fucking make it to Virginia. They were losing huge amounts of party time. And to top it all off, the bitch wasn't even paying for that much. Derek and Todd totally abandoned her in a Comfort Inn and took off, like a couple of hilarious assholes.

Todd Dinkel was a solid dude and could totally act like a dick if Derek was acting like a dick too; Derek definitely flipped into douche mode around this time. They were hauling ass through New Mexico when Derek suddenly got a crazy mind boner for Maryann. That chick was crashing in Denver. He started taking the Wrangler Unlimited north, while the sailor in the back bitched, and rolled into Denver that night. He met up with Maryann at a hotel. They boned for like a half-day. They decided to get back together. Maryann was the only chick Derek smashed with that he was actually cool with hanging out with too. His dick almost blew up when he saw her again, so he begged like a fucking pussy to let him hit that shit. Maryann thought Derek was pretty hot so she got back with him even though he was sort of a crazy fucker. Derek tried to get the sailor to stop bitching, so he hooked him up with a hottie at a Days Inn. But the sailor turned that shit down and totally walked off to wherever and they never saw him again; dude must have taken a bus to Indiana.

Then it was just Derek, Maryann, and Todd Dinkel hauling ass through Kansas. It was snowy as all hell. When they were
going through Missouri, the windshield got so fucked that Derek
had to stick his head out the window; his Oakleys frosted over
and he looked like an arctic Terminator. He drove by his home-
town without giving a shit. The next day they hit some ice and
the Wrangler Unlimited spun like crazy into a ditch. A farmer
helped dig their asses out. This one dude they gave a ride to
Memphis totally fucked them over. Once they got to Memphis,
the asshole said he couldn't find the cash. They hauled ass
through Tennessee; the Wrangler Unlimited was sorta fucked up
from hitting the ditch. Derek had been going like ninety; now he
had to go like eighty or the engine would like explode or something. They crossed the Great Smoky Mountains and it was real
snowy. When they rolled up at my brother's crib they hadn't
eaten anything for like thirty hours—except for some Fritos and
Twizzlers.

They chowed down like mad as Derek, sandwich in hand,
rocked out my portable Bose iPhone speakers, listening to an
awesome Kanye remix I had downloaded, with Kanye's beats getting all fast and mixed with AC/DC that gave the track a totally
sick party vibe. My Southern relatives looked at one and another
and had no idea how awesome we were. "Why is Sam friends
with these characters?" they said to my brother. Dude had no
clue. Southerners outside of the major SEC schools don't get
mad partying, especially Derek's kind. He didn't give a shit. The
rawness of Derek had bloomed into a flower that was seriously
fucking crazy. When Derek, Maryann, Todd, and I took a quick
cruise away from my asshole relatives, I saw what a crazy fucker
he was becoming. Derek grabbed the wheel, checked his missed
calls, checked a text for a second, thinking, suddenly seemed
to get some shit in his brain and blasted the Wrangler like hell
down the road like in *Fast Five*.

"All right, bros," he was like, fixing his hat and reaching
down to feel if his phone was vibrating, as he always did when

he was at the wheel. "It's game time and we gotta figure out what the shit we're gonna get up to. Fucking crucial, crucial. Aight?" He almost hit a Saturn; there was a smoking cougar driving it. "Pop the hood!" yelled Derek. "Pop the hood, babe! Now think about this old hottie—just think about her." And dude slowed down the car so we could all check out the over-the-hill smoke-show driving along. "Hell yeah, check that out; I bet she has sexperience in that brain that I would give a nut-and-a-half to try out; to get all up on her and find out just what a mad sex vet-eran she is. Sam, I haven't told you this shit, but I once hooked up with a fifty-year-old in Arkansas for like a summer, when I was like seventeen. She was an awesome lay, but she was so married. I haven't been to Arkansas since that Christmas, when her husband chased me and my buddy with a fucking shotgun when he found out I was smashing his wife; I'm telling you this so you know I can fucking party in the South. Like for real—for real, bro, I get wild in the South, I get mad, mad wild—I was stoked when you sent me that Facebook message saying you were in the South. Fuck yeah, Fuck yeah," he was like, trail-ing off and checking his phone again, and suddenly blasting the Wrangler back to ninety and hitting the gas. He stared intensely ahead. Maryann wasn't being a bitch. This was the new and less-douchey Derek, less of a crazy douche. I was like, no way, he's more awesome. Funny shit spat out of his mouth when he told me about stuff that pissed him off; even funnier shit replaced this shit when he was stoked; everything he said was awesome. "Dude, you have no idea," he said, "Bro, we gotta find some time to—where the fuck is Carl? We all gotta chill with Carl, dudes, first thing tomorrow. Aight, Maryann, we gotta grab some grub to have food for the trip. How much cash can you throw down, Sam? We can throw all the furniture in the back and we'll haul ass to C-Bus. Maryann, babe, you can be up front with me, then Sam and Todd can chill in the back. Todd don't try any homo shit with Sam—I'm just fucking with you. And then we'll all go off to an awesome fucking time, 'cause it's game time and *we all gotta have an awesome fucking time!"* Dude checked his phone; he almost hit some trucks; he hauled ass into the middle of downtown Testament, pulling mad turns and hitting the gas like Dale Earnhardt Jr. Slam, he found a parking space in like a hot second, and he parked. He busted out of the car. Like hell he hauled ass into a GNC; we followed behind. He bought a bulk package of Muscle Juice. He had become totally obsessed with gaining mass; he seemed to be doing everything to increase it. He wanted to expand his neck, all the way out; jack out his shoulders; double his forearms; and all the time he was talking about how sweet he'd look with like fifty percent more mass.

It was mega-cold in Testament and they'd gotten what was like a ton of snow for the South. Dude stood in his Pony polo and Diesel jeans like some kind of modern badass cowboy. He came over to talk to Maryann; he backed away, pointing at her, "Hell yeah, lookin' good, babe! Lookin' good, looking hot as fuck!" He was totally insane, but like an awesome party kind of insane. Then he kept getting back down to business. We didn't come into downtown for any reason, but dude found reasons. He was like a fucking drill sergeant: Maryann went to grab some groceries; I had to nab brews; Todd got some jerky. Derek loved to chow down on jerky. He chewed a strip of Teriyaki flavor while checking his phone and talked. "Ah, the Cardinals just blew it in the third quarter again—fuck that!—fuck that fucking team!" He went to scope a hot black chick that just then passed outside the GNC. "Check that out," he was like, pointing at her ass and fixing his hat, "that little Halle Berry-esque hottie. Aw yeah!" The crew loaded back into the Wrangler Unlimited and busted back to my brother's crib.

It had been pretty boring hanging with my stupid relatives for the holidays and like talking and opening presents and whatever, but now shit was on again, and the bringer of shit was Derek Morrisey and shit was 'bout to get wild.

CHAPTER TWO

KEGSTAND

At night we loaded all the furniture into the car and said
we'd be back in like a day and half—we'd haul some
major ass both ways. Derek thought we could make it hella-
fast. It was a fucking blast; Derek's iPhone didn't have very good
service in the car so he kept waving it out the window like a
fucking pyscho to try to get his text. "I need my fucking texts!"
Everything was mega-cramped in the Wrangler. Bags of jerky
covered our laps. We didn't have the right cord to connect an
iPhone to the stereo. Derek had got this car brand new just like
a week ago but it didn't have Bluetooth. Derek had even sprung
for leather seats. Off we rolled, north to Charleston, on I-77, a
big interstate that was pretty chill. Derek shot the shit forever.
He said the craziest stuff, and leaned as far as me sometimes to
pound knucks, sometime dude had no hands on the wheel but
the Wrangler Unlimited kept going straight as hell 'cause it had
some serious good drift control.

It was totally crazy that Derek came, maybe even crazier
that I rolled out with him. I'd been chilling in Columbus going
to class and smashing with this Lisa chick, a racked-out girl who
I could sorta see legit dating. All these years I'd sorta been thinking about finding a chick I could like for real date. I couldn't
smash with a chick without thinking for a hot second, maybe
we could go to a restaurant sometime? I talked some about this
chick. Maryann was a total chick about it and needed to know
like everything. We hauled ass through Blacksburg, Beckley,
and Charleston, and up to Athens on the highway and talked.
"I·think I might wanna date a chick," I was like, "so I can like
get some action without having to hit the club every night. This

shit can't go on forever—all this frantic mad boning. I gotta get something locked down."

"Fuck dude," said Derek, "I think it's hilarious what a pussy you are about dating and all that other stuff in your soul." Some things were bullshit that night; but some things were pretty awesome. In Athens we went to a sick Ohio University party and got shit real. One of the dudes who lived there—it was late as hell—heard us talk about how much we could drink and offered to give us fifty bucks if we could hit a kegstand longer than his buddy. We took that fucking challenge. Todd Dinkel said he was unstoppable and stuck the tap in his mouth and I lifted his legs. Derek and Maryann took pictures with their phones. Then they were making out like mad in the kitchen; they fucked in the pantry. The dudes who lived in the house couldn't believe how long Todd chugged for. Dude sucked down beer for a solid two minutes. By sunrise the awesome specter of Columbus rose up from the frigid fucking snows. Derek pulled his shirt up over his head. He did a pretty hilarious vintage Cornholio impression. We busted through downtown and cut over to campus.

"Aw man, I wish I could get a hold of Hammer. That fucker, he never answers his phone." I tried texting him again. "Motherfucking Hammer. Dudes should have *seen* that champ in Texas."

At this point Derek had hauled ass like all over everywhere in less than a week and nothing had even started to get really lit up.

CHAPTER THREE

FROZEN TAQUITOS

We went to my apartment near campus and rocked some nap bombs. I woke up early, 'cause I had to get some pushups in. Derek and Maryann had boned in Ty's bed, and Todd crashed on my couch. Derek's jacked-up duffel was in the corner with Clif Bars hanging out. My iPhone lit up. I looked at the caller ID; it was Old Brad Lewis who was in New Orleans now. He was bitching about something. Gabby totally rolled up to his place and was trying to find Todd; none of this made any sense to Brad. Sounded like Gabby was being a super pathetic bitch. I was like, "Tell that chick to chill out 'cause me and Derek and Todd are gonna snag her when we come through." The bitch grabbed the phone from Brad. She was all wanting to know about Todd and shit.

"How the hell did you get from Tucson to New Orleans?" I was like. She'd used her parents' credit card and just took a plane. She was obsessed with Todd and needed to find that dude. I told Todd about it. Dude looked fucking worried, like his dick was gonna fall off or something.

"Aight," said Derek, waking up fast as hell, "what we gotta do is eat, stat. Maryann, find us something to eat. Sam, you and I gotta hit up Carl. Todd, mix up some protein shakes." I grabbed my phone to call Carl.

Derek looked at his phone and was like, "Oh shit, San Fran area code." He had a missed call from Carly. I was like, "Dude, you're pulling such an epic double smash!"

Derek cracked up. "Fuck yeah, dude!" He went in the other room and called her back. Then I hollered at Carl and told him to get the fuck over. Carl rolled up in no time. Derek and I got some snacks together for our haul back to Virginia. Carl kicked back in an easy chair, eating some of my frozen taquitos. For the first half-hour dude said shit; he was busy pounding taquitos. He had eased off his diet and exercise since the Denver Delts days; going on semester at sea had done it. On that boat, never wearing a shirt, he had gotten into some real shit with some dudes who partied legendarily. He had pictures on his phone of crazy nights on beaches. He said he almost died of alcohol poisoning like a chump a couple of times. Derek was playing *NBA Live 10* on my Xbox and was loving it—"Holy fuck LeBron looks real! Check this out! His dunk is like perfect—check out that pick and roll, fuck yeah." Todd Dinkel wanted to play *Rock Band*; he was all nagging like a bitch to play, nobody wanted to do that. Everybody thought that game was pretty lame. "Come on, who wants to take me on, come on, come on." Derek stayed focused on *NBA Live*; wearing no shirt; he was like, "Fuck yeah!"

Carl just sat there with his hungover-looking eyes. Suddenly he was all like, "I gotta ask something."

"What up?"

"Why the fuck are you all up in Columbus? What kind of fucked up shit are you into now? I mean, dude, what's the fucking deal? What's the fucking deal, bro, in thy shiny Wrangler Unlimited in the night?"

"What's the fucking deal?" echoed Derek still playing *NBA Live*. We sat and didn't know why Carl was being such a bitch; now it was awkward. We had to bust out. Derek announced it was time to haul ass to Virginia. Dude got his groom on, I microwaved all the frozen taquitos that were left in the box, Maryann packed the duffel, and it was game time. We dropped off Carl and told him we'd be back in time to party with him on New Year's Eve. Derek and me took turns driving and hauled ass to my brother's crib in like no time.

"This is like the first time in forever that just the two of us have chilled," Derek was like. And dude shot the shit all night. Like a motherfucking fireball we blasted all through Virginia and

rolled up to my brother's place by like nine. For the whole trip
Derek was crazy stoked about everything we passed, everything
we talked about, everything that people texted him. Dude was
fucking crazy. "And for real no one can tell us that Four Loko is
actually dangerous. We've partied with that. You remember, Sam,
when I first came to Columbus and Chaz Kerry and I drank like
five in a night? Wasn't that awesome? It's all cool, Four Loko isn't
bad for you, if you can handle yourself. All that bullshit about it
causing drunk driving is bullshit. It's *bullshit!*" He punched the
steering wheel; the Wrangler Unlimited kept on rolling. "And not
only that but we both know that some assholes just don't want to
let dudes get a good time on." At one point I bitched about some
of the bullshit that was going down—how my family wouldn't pay
for study abroad, how much I wanted Lisa to put out more, who
was cool but sometimes a prude. "That bullshit, you see, is what
happens when you can't get your party on. It's not worth getting
your vagina all sandy about. This fucking hangover!" he was like,
and pounded his head on the wheel. He pulled over and ran into a
gas station to score more jerky—that delicious, smoked jerky that
tastes so good in the car. "Since Denver, Sam, a lotta shit—man,
the shit—I've partied and partied. I used to be in trouble in high
school all the time, I was a little asshole—stealing brews as a psy-
chological expression of my need to rock. All my shit is straight
now. As far as I know I'll never be a little asshole like that again.
The rest who the fuck knows." We drove by some kid who threw
a rock at our car. "For real," Derek was like. "That little fucker
could make some dude crash and dude could die—he'll never get
a chance to party again. You see what I'm saying? We gotta fucking party. As we roll this way I am positive beyond doubt that we
gotta get wild—that even you, as you think about dating just one
chick at a time" (I knew this was prude shit)—"everything will
come together and you won't have to settle for just one vag and
we can keep rocking. Furthermore, we're awesome, we make it
happen; I can go anywhere in America and bone whatever chick
I want because it's the same in every corner, I know the bitches,

I know what they want. We drink and bone and go in the incredibly awesome rawness all over every side." What he said made no fucking sense, but I got his drift and his drift was awesome. Dude said "Awesome," like constantly. Derek had turned into some kind of philosophical player. The stuff he said now was pretty awesome but it totally led up to the weird-ass, jacked-up douche he turned into later.

We drove back to Ohio and even my aunt thought the crazy shit he was saying was pretty awesome. Since she was with us, Derek laid off the boning talk and spat some stories about being a personal trainer in San Fran. He told us like everything about being a trainer, and like every time we passed a fit dude he'd guess at what kind of fitness regimen they used, and one time he even pulled over and showed me crunches that can trick out your abs mad fast. Most of the time my aunt got her sleep on. When we were driving through Charleston, Derek sexted Carly. A hot second later, this cop got all on our ass with his sirens and the dude wanted to give us a ticket even though were weren't even going above fucking sixty. The dude just hated us 'cause we had Cali plates. "You guys think you can rush through here as fast as you want just because you come from California?" the cop was like.

We argued like hell with the dickhole and dude made us go to the fucking station where we tried to tell them is was all total bullshit. The fuckers were gonna lock Derek up if we didn't pay. My aunt offered to pay the ticket, but I didn't want to give these fuckers anything. One of the cops checked out our car while we were arguing and he saw my aunt just chilling in the back seat. She was pissed.

"Don't worry, I'm not some kind of criminal. If you want to come and search the car, go right ahead. I'm going home with my nephew, and this furniture isn't stolen; it's my niece's, she just had a baby and she's moving to her new house." She fucking owned the cop and he went back inside like a bitch. She just paid the fine 'cause otherwise we'd be stuck in this shithole; I'd gotten too hammered from a flask I was sucking on to drive. Derek swore he'd teach those fuckers a lesson, and he totally pulled it off, one year later he mailed a bag of his own shit to them. It was so fucking hilarious—a bunch of cops opening that bag of shit and they knew they got owned. My aunt told us about the cop that checked out the car. "He was hiding behind the tree, trying to see what I looked like. I told him—I told him to search the car if he wanted. I've nothing to be ashamed of." She was a totally solid lady; that was for real.

She started saying something about how men should all ask their chicks for forgiveness or something. Derek knew this was bullshit; he was for sure not pussywhipped. "I've pleaded with Maryann to understand that I gotta do what I gotta do and we should just smash casual-style—she gets it; her mind is stuck on some other shit—she can really be a bitch sometimes; she won't understand how much I gotta do my own thing, she can be a real drag."

"The truth of the matter is we don't need all of chicks' bullshit; we're good as fuck to them and they're just bitches back," I was like.

"But it isn't as simple as that," warned Derek. "Maybe someday a chick will actually be cool about stuff, but we won't even realize it when she does—you feel me?" Derek was drained as he hauled it through West Virginia; I drove some while he dropped some nap bombs. We rolled up to my crib in Columbus in the morning where Maryann and Todd were just chilling out eating some taquitos that fell out of the box in the freezer; they hadn't done shit since Derek and I peaced out. We went to my aunt's house in the suburbs and she made us some delicious fucking breakfast.

CHAPTER FOUR

SERIOUSLY,
WHERE THE FUCK IS MY PHONE?

I had to figure out somewhere else for Derek, Maryann, and Todd to stay since Ty was gonna be back in town soon. They could crash at Carl's place in South Campus. Derek and I dropped a whole bunch of nap bombs and then woke up to get wild on New Year's Eve. Todd Dinkel was drinking some SoBe in my massage chair. "Last New Year's I partied in Chicago. I got real wasted. I was chilling on the porch of a sports bar and this crazy good smell was all ripping up my nose from the bakery next door. They weren't open, but I knocked on the door and talked to the girl. She gave me some crazy good doughnuts. I hung out there and totally boned her over a mixer. I railed her all night. It was sorta like this one time I was chilling with my buddy Ed in Utah and this housekeeper came into my hotel room; she thought the room was empty. I was like, "What up babe!" We boned. I get random action like that all the time," said Todd Dinkel, looking smug as fuck.

"What the hell are you going to do about Gabby?"

"Whatevs. We'll figure it out when we get to New Orleans. Right bro?" Dude was trying to act all chill like a player but it was so obvious he was a total pusswad who loved that Gabby chick. "What's your deal, bro?" I was like.

"You know," Todd was like. "I just cruise along. I love to fucking party." He repeated it, the same kind of shit Derek always said. He had no clue about his life. He kept daydreaming about boning that baker in Chicago.

It started snowing like a bitch. My buddies were having a mad rager on campus; we were all going. Derek packed his jacked-up duffel, chucked it into the Wrangler Unlimited, and it was game time. Ty was hoping to smash with this chick he knew from home who was in town; he sat in our apartment and waited for her to call. We rolled through campus on the slippery streets. Derek was a mad solid driver; dude had done some crazy off-roading out West. We had the wires to connect an iPhone to the stereo now and we had sick beats to roll with. I had no clue where we'd end up that night; I didn't give a fuck.

As we were cruising through campus some shit started to haunt me. I had lost my iPhone again. I had it when Derek showed up, and now I couldn't remember the last time I had it and wherever I left it was like so close to my brain. I kept trying to remember where I left it. I asked people if they'd seen it. There was no way to even tell where it was when I called it with somebody else's phone because it was on vibrate. It haunted me and made me completely pissed. It was because of the pockets of my shorts. One time Carl and I played *Madden*, head-to-head, real intense, drinking, and I told him I couldn't find my keys; that I'd had them in my pocket; that now I couldn't find them. "When's the last time you used them?" Carl was like. We thought it over. I checked the lock to see if I left them there. That wasn't it. It was like something, someone, some fucking ghost or something just reached into my pocket and took my keys. It's like totally obvious looking back on this shit that it was just my pockets: the way they were shaped, things would fall out when I sat down. The one thing that we yearn for all the time is not losing your keys and phone like every five fucking seconds and having to spend so much time checking the couch and freaking out and this can only be fixed (though this sucks) by getting different shorts. But I love my shorts. I got so pissed about this while I was checking all over the Wrangler. I told Derek about this shit and he instantly sympathized 'cause he loses his phone with certain pairs of shorts all the time too; and because he also values shorts that look awesome and breathe more than shorts with a solid pocket structure, he, rightly, would just deal with that shit, and I was like, "I feel you."

We went looking for some of the raw players of my C-Bus posse. First we swung by my dude Tim Samford's crib. That guy can be sort of a downer; once in a while he suddenly flips into dick mode and ruins the fucking party. Tonight he was totally cool. "Sam, where did you find these totally awesome people? I've never partied with anyone like them"

"I partied with them out West."

Derek cranked up some beats, grinded with Maryann, and had an epic time. She grinded back. They must have grinded forever. My buddy Ivan McQueen rolled up with his crew. New Year's blew up, and kept blowing up for like the next three days and three nights. We took big crews party-hopping through the snowy campus streets in the Wrangler. I texted Lisa and had her come over to this one mad rager. That chick got all bitchy when she saw me get wild with Derek and Maryann—she didn't get how awesome I was with them.

"You turn into an asshole around them."

"Chill out, babe. We only live once. We're having an awesome time."

"No, you act like a dick and I don't like it."

To make shit worse, Maryann started getting all up on me; apparently she thought Derek was gonna leave her for Carly so she wanted to smash with me. "Come back to San Fran with us. We'll get it on. I'll smash with you like constantly." It was totally obvious that she was just trying to piss off Lisa and Derek, and I couldn't do that to my boy. This drama was bullshit. On the real, I totally wanted to rail her. After Lisa caught Maryann grinding all up on me, she went and chilled in the Wrangler Unlimited with Derek; but they didn't smash and just did some shots from the flask I left in there. Shit was fucked up, and shit was sloppy. I was gonna have to stop smashing with Lisa. Bitch was trying to fucking *change me*. She was with this boyfriend who was a dickhole and treated her like shit. I was willing to legit date her and like go to restaurants and shit if she left the dickhole; but she was too much of a bitch to dump him and the whole deal was fucked up, and anyway Lisa would never be more than a slam piece 'cause she doesn't get how wild I need to get and judges me like hell whenever I pass out naked in a Rubbermaid tub of jungle juice. I just gotta be me. I can't do anything except make an awesome time happen.

We hit parties that were legit off the chain; this one house party on High Street had like five hundred people. Dudes were freezing their dicks off on the roof. It was sloppy and wild—not a total orgy but close at times. There were some hot Asian chicks too. Derek grinded from chick to chick, grinding with almost every hottie. Sometimes we'd bust out to go grab more of my C-Bus crew in the Wrangler. My boy Denny rolled in. Denny is the fucking champ of my Columbus crew, like Derek is the fucking champ of the Western. In a hot second they got into some shit. Denny's chick all of a sudden nailed Denny on the jaw with a vicious punch. Dude was messed up. She had to drag his ass home. Some of my crew came in with ice luges. Outside, a straight-up blizzard was going down. I introduced Todd to Lisa's sister and the dude smashed with her immediately. That dude is like a snatch whisperer. He's six foot four, handsome, built, and smooth as fuck. He gets laid all over the place. That's just how dude rolls. Just before sunrise we totally pranked the Alpha Tau Omega house and then hauled ass to a crazy rager at Beta. Then we hauled it to Tim Samford's party. People were playing hold 'em and finishing the keg. I made out on a futon with some chick named Becky. Big crews kept rolling in from all over campus. Everybody, fucking everybody was piling in to the same crunk-ass time. The party kept bumpin'. Ivan McQueen is a real solid dude who says the funniest shit. He started being all "fuck yeah!" to everything, just like Derek was always being like, and dude still says that shit. While the Ying Yang Twins "Wait" blasted, I helped Derek do a kegstand. Derek was pretty fucking heavy to hold, too. He took his shirt off and just partied that way, even when we hit a fast blunt outside. Shit was off the chain. My dude Ronnie Gray texted and told me to come chill out at his crib near Dayton. His crib is nice, except he has to share it with his aunt 'till she dies. She's a huge bitch who kills parties like whoa. We didn't give a fuck and started up a mad rager there. That bitch just kept yelling at us from upstairs. "Go fuck yourself, you old bitch!" Ronnie was like. I wondered if having such a sick place would be worth dealing with that bitch and living in Dayton. He had a crazy pimped-out surround sound system—two systems, two rooms wired from floor to ceiling, and subwoofers like you wouldn't believe. He played the loudest scenes from *Armageddon* and pounded back brews. It was loud. Dude balls legit with music blasting and hotties all up on that. He rolls like a total pimp wherever he goes. He cranked shit so loud that the left-front speaker blew out as Bruce Willis detonated that fucking asteroid. He downed his Natty like a fucking savage. He crushed the can on his head, he tossed it, he grabbed another, he chugged it hard. We could barely understand anything he was saying with the speakers so loud. Derek just chilled with him, repeating over and over again, "Fuck yeah . . . fuck yeah . . . fuck yeah." He said stuff like, "That Ronnie dude is the rawest, most crazy of all. That's the shit I was trying to tell you—that's the shit I want to be. I want to party just like him. He's never a drag; he's rich as fuck; he puts on a fucking show; he makes it happen; he has nothing to do but watch *Armageddon* and chug. Bro, he's the tits! If you rock like him all the time, you'll finally get that shit."

"What shit?"

"*The* shit! *The* shit! I'll tell you—now's not the time, too much to do." Derek downed his Natty and went over to keep partying with Ronnie Gray.

Derek told me that he thought Ronnie Gray looked like Nic Cage. Derek and I went to see Cage in *Drive Angry 3D* in the middle of our long, crunked weekend. Nobody was in the theater, so we could totally drink our smuggled beers in peace. Cage came on screen, driving a classic car straight out of hell. He was an insane-looking badass with long hair, intense as fuck, crazy, with a total hardcore vibe that made you believe that he actually escaped from hell to beat ass. The chick in it, Amber Heard, was off-the-chain hot but never got naked. Then Cage began to blow motherfuckers up; bullets flew out of his guns; he totally fucked a chick in a middle of the shootout; and he began shooting dudes, still railing this chick. He swung her around; he threw her down on the bed; he blasted a dude in the face with a shotgun; his sunglasses were still on; he was amazing. It got awesome. The car chases got crazier, faster and faster; it seemed totally awesome, for real. Cage began to blow shit up; explosions rolled out behind him in great rich showers; you'd think being this awesome would be impossible. We got drunker and drunker in the front row. We shouted at Cage to "fucking drive!" Derek was amped up; he poured beer down his throat. "That's the dude! He's amazing! Jesus Christ! Jesus-Fucking-Nic-Cage-Christ! Fuck yeah! Fuck yeah! Fuck yeah!" And the ushers were conscious of what was going down, they heard every one of Derek's "fuck yeahs" and "get somes," but they were too big of pussies to try to take us on. "Fuck yeah!" Derek said. "Fuck yeah!" Cage smiled; he took aim. Cage rose from the ground, almost dead; this was the awesome part right at the end where he fucks everybody up. When the movie was done Derek pointed to the empty screen. "That was amazing," he said. On the wall outside the theater a poster for the movie hung; its golden glow made Cage look like some kind of amazing action god. Cage was God; he was awesome as fuck. It was a rainy night. It was real fucking wet. Derek was crazy hammered from all the beers we slammed. This night was gonna be a total shitshow. I didn't know what the hell was going on in my body, and suddenly I realized it was because I'd been downing Sparks for the past two hours; Derek had to drink that shit during movies. I thought about how things were getting totally off the chain—and how when shit gets off that chain it gets awesome forever.

CHAPTER FIVE

SNATCH-PHYXIATION

I peaced out and went home to drop some nap bombs. My parents called and told me that Derek and that crew were a bad influence. That was pure bullshit. I know me, and I gotta party. I needed to beast it out West and get back pretty fast so I wouldn't be on academic probation at school. Everything turned out totally awesome. I just wanted to go party and check out whatever crazy funny shit Derek got into, and since Derek was probably gonna dump Maryann for Carly, I wanted to bone his leftovers. It was time to get psyched. I nabbed some cash from the ATM and gave Derek twenty bucks 'cause I lost a bet for how many punches I could take to the stomach before puking. I don't know what Maryann was up to. Todd Dinkel, like always, came along for the party.

We had a ton of hilarious times at Carl's place before we peaced out. Dude chilled there shirtless and started giving us shit to be funny: "Now I'm not trying to be an asshole, but it seems like you all are acting like a real bunch of queers." Carl was sipping on some Jack. "I want to know what's up with all the gay shit you're doing. Are you all some kinda homos? Derek, did you leave Carly 'cause you're some kinda homo?" No answer— we cracked up. "Maryann, why are you hanging around with this big bunch of homos?" We cracked the shit up more. "Todd Dinkel, you've gotta be the biggest queer of all! Where's that chick you left? What the hell?" Todd Dinkel cracked the shit up. "Sam—how come you've fallen on such homo days and aren't even smashing with Lisa?" He poured some more Jack and sat facing us all. "I'm just fucking with you. I can't keep from cracking up for any longer. Aw fuck, that was pretty hilarious. I swear for a second you thought I was for real."

Around this time Carl was working on a party blog he hoped would catch on; the whole idea was to talk about all his crazy fucking stories. "It's sorta like Tucker Max," he told us; "but it's way funnier and realer." His crazy eyes glittered at us. Since things went down on semester at sea he had gotten into even more shit that he called the Don Pablos Disaster, when he kept hanging at Don Pablos for the crazy cheap margarita happy hours and at night would get so ripped that he didn't give a fuck; and he totally jumped off the indoor balcony onto a table of bitches. It was a real shitshow that had given him some legendary stories. He copped some feels on Maryann that he tried to play off as a joke. He was like to Derek, "Why don't you just hang with me at Don Pab's? Why you gotta hit the road so much?" Derek ran around, slugging Nattys and saying "Fuck yeah! Fuck yeah! Fuck yeah!" When it got dark, Todd Dinkel crashed on an air mattress. Derek and Maryann crashed on the futon, and Carl sat at his MacBook, posting on his party blog. I came over sometimes and checked it out.

Todd Dinkel was like, "Last night I walked all the way down to South Campus following this hottie and just as I got close to her I suddenly realized it was a dude—it was a fucking dude who looked like a hottie from behind." He said this kind of stuff to me without saying anything else. Like a day later when the topic had changed like a millions times, Todd was like, "Yeah, it was a fucking dude with a chick body."

All of a sudden Derek took me aside and was like, "Sam, I gotta be real with you—this is serious—I hope you're cool—we're cool, aren't we?"

"Hell yeah, bro." He was stoked. Finally he laid it down: He wanted me to bone Maryann. I knew he probably wanted to check out how Maryann boned other dudes. We were chilling in a Skyline Chili when he dropped that shit; we'd spent a ton of time cruising campus, looking for my dude Hammer. Skyline Chili is some of the awesomest grub in central Ohio; it gets better every time you eat it. The whole menu is delicious, even the salads, just a big-ass spread of chili and cheese and beans, from noodles to coney dogs. It's also full of gross fatties—big chicks pounding Sweet Tea that you wouldn't fuck with a stranger's wang on a stick. Derek walked in there with his stomach ready to chow on everything. There were coney dogs with mustard, coney dogs with onion, chili burritos, chili bowls, chili with noodles. It made sense for Derek to ask me to bone his lady at Skyline. All kinds of weird shit gets said over coney dogs—you can sense it in the air—you just get so fucking full and then say whatever is in your skull. For example, a coworker proposes not only to split a chili burrito but to fuck in her Sebring afterwards. I once fucked my coworker at a summer job after eating Skyline; it was aight and I still ate another coney after we were done. Derek thought that was pretty hilarious.

We downed our chili and rolled back to Carl's crib where Maryann was napping it up. Dinkel was probably trying to hit on more dude-chicks. Derek told her the deal. She was into it. I wasn't totes sure about it though. I had to get my head in the game. Derek was right there and shit was sorta homo. Maryann lay there, with Derek and me on either side of her, awkward as fuck, not knowing what to say. I was like, "Fuck dude, I can't do this."

"Come on, bro, you promised!" said Derek.

"Isn't this sorta homo?" I was like. "Come on, Maryann, isn't this sorta homo?"

"Let's do it," she was like.

I pretended like Derek wasn't there while she felt up my pecs. But like every ten seconds I'd notice that dude was there and I couldn't get anything up past a quarter-chub. It sucked.

"I can't do this. Why don't you get the fuck out and go in the kitchen for a hot second?"

Derek peaced out. She looked mad smoking, but I was like, "Wait 'till we can bone in San Fran; I can't get past a quarter-chub right now." I really couldn't get past a quarter-chub, she could tell. I was just trying to have a good bone but there was

all the weight of this sorta-homo shit weighing down on me. I
checked my phone. I went over to the kitchen and told Derek
I couldn't bone Maryann tonight; I crashed on the couch. I
heard Derek in the room, getting his beast on and going fucking
crazy. Only a dude who's a bonafide snatch addict can go to such
fucked-up extremes; asking another dude to beast his slam piece,
crazy with a completely shitbrained idea that watching your
friend bone your lady would somehow be awesome; not stopping to think that maybe you should take a fucking lap. This is
the result of years trying to drowning yourself in snatch; looking
at the boneability quotient of every chick passing by; working on
the steel hardness of your abs and thinking about the chick who
could grind against them. College is where dude promised himself the right to bone. Derek had never gotten that level of play
before ASU. Every new chick, every incoming freshman, every
TA was an addition to his history of bonings. He learned this
from his dad—old badass Derek Morrisey the Denver Nuggets
Marketing Director, chilling in skyboxes, working his game on
NBA cheerleaders, drinking, blacking out at after-game parties,
dropping hundos constantly across the West. Derek was destined
to die the sweet death of complete snatch-phyxiation. I wasn't
gonna get up in his grill.

Around 6 A.M., Carl rolled in and threw back some Jack.
Dude had sorta stopped drinking beer. "Fuck me!" Dude was
getting to be more of dick when he was liquor drunk—he was
totally a better beer drunk. Every day the world did its thing and
we were having our badass times at night. Maryann was pissed
at Derek for whatever; his iPhone was cracked. We needed to
bust out.

We rolled over to the bar where Derek and I first chilled
when he came to my door to learn how to play "Wonderwall"
and hollered at Old Brad Lewis. We heard Brad's bitching over
speakerphone. "Dude, what the fuck am I supposed to do with
this Gabby Dinkel chick? Bitch has been here for like ever, hiding in her room and saying shit to Jaimiee or me. Are you dudes

hanging with this Todd Dinkel dude? For fuck's sake bring the dude down and get rid of this bitch. She's totally cramping my style and she's not throwing in any cash for rent. This isn't a fucking La Quinta." Todd was saying everything would be cool but Brad could barely hear him since he was on speakerphone and me, Derek, Maryann, Carl, and the whole crew were getting real rowdy in the background. "Well," dude was like, "maybe you'll be less of a dick when you get down here." I told Ty I was heading out and made him promise not to eat my protein powder and then I took off for Cali again.

CHAPTER SIX

A HUGE CONTINENT-SIZED PISS

There was like an eighty percent chance of precipitation when we rolled out. We'd party regardless. "Fuck yeah!" Derek was like. "Let's light this shit!" Dude grabbed the wheel like he was trying to kill it and jacked the gas; he was ready to rumble, it was obvious. All of us got totally stoked, we'd never partied in the South when we weren't on spring break so this was gonna be sweet. It was game time! We hauled ass to the East so we could party down the coast on our way South. Big Easy, motherfuckers! We were ready to party. We were ditching the snowy bullshit of the Midwest to find the outdoor drinking and delicious grub of New Orleans at the pimped-out bottom of America; then we'd haul ass to Cali. Maryann and Derek and I chilled in front and had the realest talk about whether *Old School* or *The Hangover* was a better movie. Derek suddenly got real serious. "Now for fuck's sake, look here, motherfuckers, we must admit that everything in *Old School* was fucking hilarious and there's no way you can ever compete with that, and in fact we should realize that *The Hangover* wouldn't even *fucking exist* without the *funny shit* that went down in *Old School*. You feel me?" Dude was right. "Here we go, let's do this . . . what went down in Columbus? Let's get over it." Some fucking drama had gone down in Columbus. "Forget that shit, it's totally stupid. Now we're rolling down to New Orleans to chill with Old Brad Lewis and isn't that gonna be off the chain and listen to this dude drop the fucking beat"—he cranked the stereo and the Wrangler Unlimited rocked—"and listen to him get the party started and put down true beats and raw-ass times."

We all rocked to the beats and were on board with this shit. It was that awesome. The road flew by like we were in a rocket ship or something. Derek hunched his ripped neck, wearing a distressed polo that was rough and ragged like the American road, and drove that whip. He made my ass drive through Maryland; that was aight, except he and Maryann tried to steer while they made out. It was crazy; the stereo was bumping. Derek punched the dashboard 'till it got all fucked up; I did too. The Wrangler Unlimited was getting its shit tossed.

"Hell yeah, dudes!" yelled Derek. "Yo Maryann, listen, for real, babe, you know that I've got wicked stamina and I can beast it for days—now in San Fran we gotta keep crashing together. I know a sick-ass place for you—on a real awesome street—I'll be able to get over and hang with you like every couple of days for twelve hours, and *babe*, you know how hard we can smash in twelve hours, babe. Meanwhile I'll keep chilling at Carly's like no biggie, aight, she won't know. We can make this happen, we've made it happen before." Shit was cool with Maryann, she was totally looking to bitch-murder Carly. I thought I was going to start smashing Maryann in San Fran, but it was looking totally obvious that they'd keep smashing and I'd be totally slam-piece-less at the ass end of America. But I was like, "Fuck it," 'cause there's no reason to be a pussy like that when there's a million hotties lingering across the night like so many heavenly stars waiting to be boned.

We hit D.C. in the morning. There was some kind of women's rights thing going down. Great hoards of bitches clogged the streets as we tried to get through. There were old bitches, ugly bitches, even some actual hotties that maybe just looked hot compared to the ugly bitches; and then one bonafide smokeshow with a bullhorn. Derek slowed down to check her out. He just couldn't believe it. "What does such a hottie gotta hang with such bitches? There's probably hotties all over this town . . . Hanging with bitches . . . What the fuck . . . Pop the hood!"

Dinkel drove for a while Derek crashed in back. We told that dude to keep it cool. As soon as we all started dropping nap bombs, dude gunned it up to ninety, and not only that but the

dude went by a cop who was arguing with another driver—
Dinkel was flying in the wrong fucking lane. Natch the cop
busted ass after us like we were fucking OJ or whatevs. We were
fucked. We had to go with him to the station. Some dickhole
cop got all up in Derek's face; he was totally jealous of what an
awesome dude he was. The dickhole's buddy interrogated me
and Maryann. They were trying to bust Maryann for underage
drinking, 'cause she totally reeked of booze and looked young as
fuck. But she had a real solid fake ID. "I'm twenty-two," she was
like. They were still dicks. They thought we were up to something. They tried some amateur *Law and Order* shit and tried to
get us to fuck up. I was like, "We're all just chilling, and she's
totally not underage."

The cop tried to accuse me of stealing my wallet. Too bad
I've got like five gym IDs with my photo on them.

After all this bullshit, the dickhole was gonna make us pay
three hundo. We told them that was total bullshit; they didn't
give a shit. When Derek said that was bullshit, the dickhole cop
said he could bust Derek for some shit he did in Pennsylvania.

"That's so weak!"

"I don't care. Pay the fine."

We were fucked. Todd Dinkel was gonna try to go to jail
like some kind of white drunk Nelson Mandela. We thought that
shit over for like a second. The dickhole cop was still gonna try
to bust Derek for whatever Pennsylvania shit if Dinkel went to
jail. We just needed to get the fuck out. "Make sure to wear your
seatbelts," the dickhole cop said like a real dickhole. Derek was
crazy pissed. Everybody was all quiet. This was just so fucked
up. The cops knew we all had open container and urinating-in-
public violations out the ass. Cops are just like total fascists trying
to fuck with dudes who just want to have a good time. They're
a bunch of assholes; going around trying to break up every party,
and giving out noise violations even if noise violations don't
exist. Like N.W.A. said, "Fuck the police." Derek was so pissed
he wanted to mail a bag of his own shit to that dickhole cop.

"Pennsylvania!" he was like. "What the fuck did I do in Pennsylvania? Open container in State College, probably; ruin my good time and charge me with open container. Those guys are such dicks. They'll straight up take away your Wrangler Unlimited if you complain, too." We had to chill out and try to get over that shit. Around Richmond we started getting over that shit, and it got more all right.

It sucked we had to cough up all that cash. We needed to give some dudes rides so they'd give us some gas money. In buttfuck Virginia we passed some dude walking along the road. Derek stopped. I looked back and said he was just some homeless dude and probably had no gas money.

"Come on, it'll be hilarious!" Derek was like. The dude was a gross, ragged, crazy dude, walking along reading some shitty book he'd found in a ditch or something. He kept reading in the car; he smelled like shit and had way bad skin. His name was Hiram Simonson and he just like went all over the place and would beg for cash from other Jewish people.

He said that shit worked like mad and that he pulled mad cash. We asked him what that nasty book was. He had no clue. He didn't even look at the cover. He just read the words.

"See dude? See dude?" said Derek, posting pictures of the guy on Facebook. "I told you he'd be fucking hilarious. Totally fucking hilarious, bro!" We gave this Simonson dude a ride to Testament. My brother had moved to the other side of town so we didn't hang with him. We were on the same boring street with the Subway in the middle and the lame, loser Southerners doing whatever in front of the True Value.

Simonson was like, "So you guys need some gas money? Just wait here for a second and I'll find a Jewish family, get some money from them, and then you can take me to Alabama." Derek could not believe how fucking hilarious this dude was; he and I rushed off to buy footlong B.M.T.s for lunch. Maryann and Todd chilled in the Wrangler Unlimited. It had been like two hours and Hiram still hadn't come back. It started to get dark.

That dude wasn't coming back so we rolled out. "So you gotta believe, Sam, God is a funny dude, 'cause we came into this town again, and picked up that crazy weirdo who was such a fucking weirdo, and my friends are already posting mad responses like "WTF" and "Holy shit!" in response to the pictures I shared of him . . ." Derek kept laughing about it. He and I suddenly saw the whole country like a mad club for us to get into; and the bottle service was there; the bottle service was there. We kept hauling ass south. We gave another dude a ride. This dude told us about some amazing house party that was going down in North Carolina. "When we get there can you get us some trap? Hell yeah! Wooo! Let's do it!" We rolled up there like an hour later, right around party o'clock. We found the house and there was no fucking party. What the shit was that dude thinking? We asked him what his fucking deal was; he said shit. It was a big hoax; a long time ago, when he was doing whatever, he had seen a mad house party around here and he just made up that lie to get a ride. We decided not to beat his ass, but we def kicked him out 'cause we needed room for hitchhikers who would spot some gas money. This was the only right thing to do. We left his ass there.

I took the wheel and hauled ass through South Carolina and Macon, Georgia, while everybody else got some sleep on. I thought shit over while I blasted the Wrangler down the road. When am I gonna pull some trim? When am I gonna get back to partying? Everything would be clear soon. I was totally drained after we got through Macon so I woke up Derek to take over. While we stopped we took a piss outside and we got way stoked when we noticed that it was way warmer here. "It's fucking hot down here! Chicks won't be wearing as many clothes!" Derek's iPhone illuminated some grass and trees. I was amped; a car full of hotties blasted past us, going to Mobile. We had to hook up with them. I peeled off my shirt and flexed for them. A little later when we wanted some brews, Derek cruised into a gas station all quiet as hell, saw the dude inside was asleep, busted out, stole some beers, made sure the dude didn't wake up, and rolled off like a ninja with a 30-rack of Natty for our pilgrimage.

I dropped some nap bombs and woke up with Derek blasting beats as green shit flew by the window. "Where the hell are we?"

"Just rolled by the tip of Florida, bro—Flomaton, or something." Fuck yeah! Our crew was cruising down toward great soaring signs of barbecue restaurants and steakhouses. Like not even two days ago we'd been in shitty snowstorms in the Midwest. We regassed at a Shell, where Derek railed Maryann in the bathroom and Dinkel boosted a whole box of Slim Jims like it was nothing. We were hungry for some SJ's. As we rolled up in Mobile, we all went shirtless and started slamming some Nattys. Derek started telling some hilarious stories, and in the middle of it, dude came to a traffic jam at an intersection and instead of waiting he beasted the Wrangler straight through a gas station without dropping below seventy. People watching couldn't believe that shit. He went right on slinging funny-ass stories. "I'm for real, I started getting my bone on at age nine, with a chick named Maggie Mayberry in the back of a Showbiz Pizza on Grand Street—same street Carl chilled at in Denver. That's when my dad wasn't working for the Nuggets yet. I remember my aunt looking for me all like, 'What are you doing behind the *Jurassic Park: Lost World* game?' Yo Maryann, if I'd only known you then! Man! I bet you were still fucking stacked at nine." He laughed like hell; he stuck his hand in his pocket and checked his phone; he grabbed her head and made out with her while driving. She was into that shit.

Todd Dinkel kept staring out the window like a zombie, being like, "For real, I thought that dude was a chick." Dude was also probably pussing out about how he'd deal with Gabby in New Orleans.

Derek kept talking. "One time I went to this rave—I was like eleven years old, my dad was working late, I snuck out to party. I met these hot rave chicks, they gave me some E—I started to roll—I got super fucked up—I couldn't see straight for like weeks. I partied for hours, flying on E. All the way I kept making out with hot rave chicks—you know what a fucking mess those chicks are, I didn't know that shit at that age—clutching a span-dex-covered tit in one hand and the other on some other chick's ass. I'm not bullshitting you, this is for real. When the sun came up I was so thirsty I grabbed a two liter of Mountain Dew and slammed it in like a minute and chunked all over the ground.

"That's so fucked up," said Maryann, and kissed him. She checked her phone. He was into her.

As we started cruising by the sick beaches on the Gulf, an awesome thing started on the stereo; it was Kid Cudi, all mad beats, sick jams, with the rhymes just telling us to have a fucking awesome time! New Orleans was up ahead and we all got even more stoked. Derek took a pull off his can of Natty. "Now we're gonna get wild!" A few hours later we were all up in the Big Easy. "Yo, check this out!" Derek was like, all crazy pumped. "Let's do this!" He swung around a corner. "Fuck yeah!" He drove like a maniac and looked everywhere for hotties. "Check her out!" The hotties were so fine in New Orleans it seemed like it was a movie; and you could tell they wanted to party and really get wild, and drink, and smash, and do all kinds of shit 'till sunrise. We rocked out. "And check that ass out!" Derek was like, looking at another hottie. "Bro, I love, love, love trim! I think trim is the bomb! Let's pull some trim!" He spat out the window; he spun his hat to the side; he checked his phone. Great beads of sweat fell from his head onto his phone from being so fucking stoked.

We took the Algiers ferry to get across the river. "Now we gotta all get out and check out the city and chicks and see if there's a bar on the ship," Derek was like, grabbing his Oakleys and iPhone and leaping out the car like hell. We followed. We leaned over the edge of the ferry and checked out the big-ass river rolling down from the Midwest like a huge continent-sized piss—like if America had a wang in Minnesota and just let it fly. Bumpin' New Orleans got smaller on one side; old, boring Algiers got bigger on the other. Some hotties were hanging out in the hot afternoon, drinking Vitaminwater and looking so fine it made us all get half-chubs. Derek checked them out, sweating like a motherfucker in the sun. Dude started going around the whole ship with his lacrosse shorts sagging. He talked to some hotties. I thought dude would get with them right there. I heard him crack up all over the boat. Maryann found him. He told us all the shit, that those hotties had lame boyfriends, piled back in the Wrangler while everybody was all honking at us, and we rolled out, cruising through Algiers.

"Where are we gonna blow this up?" Derek was all like.

We decided first to slam some brews by the river and find where Brad was at. Some stupid kids were playing in the river; smokeshows were going by with short shorts and tube tops and killer legs. Derek checked out everything. He looked around; he nodded; he downed some Slim Jims. Big Todd chilled in the car, dropping a nap bomb. I sat on the fender. Maryann was taking a piss inside a Rite Aid. From the other shore where awesome dudes got wild every night, getting hammered and hooking up all over the fucking place, the river like some kind of party-killing moat keeping most of the fun out of Algiers. Boring, peninsular Algiers with all her shit that wasn't as fun as New Orleans was like pretty dumb in comparison. The sun slanted; bugs were all up in my face; I had to get Big Easy wild.

We cruised over to Old Brad Lewis's crib. There were like a ton of swamps everywhere. The house was in buttfuck nowhere, but it was a sort of awesome swamp-party pad; the grass was covered in red Solo cups, old beeramids leaned, old kegs sat on the porch. Nobody was around. We rolled up to the crib. I went up to the front door. Brad's wife Jaimiee answered the door while checking her phone. "What up, Jaimiee?" I was like, "It's me."

She knew that. "No shit. Brad isn't here now. Is there some kind of fire or something over there?" I couldn't see shit.

"You mean the fucking sun?"

"Of course I don't mean the sun, asshole—I heard sirens over there. Why you gotta be some kind of asshole?" I hated this; she could be sort of a bitch.

"I don't see anything," I was like.

Jaimiee went back to looking at her phone. "Same fucking Parker."

That was the bullshit she said to me; Jaimiee was my ex-girlfriend's roommate in Columbus. "Is that Gabby Dinkel chick here?" I was like. Jaimiee kept staring at her phone; I think she was pretty crunk since she was always drinking a shit ton of Smirnoff Ices. She used to be pretty hot, but she wasn't looking as hot now. Her pores acted up like crazy in New Orleans. Our crew rolled out of the Wrangler Unlimited and chilled in the house. Gabby was there and came over to her joke husband. That chick was gross. She was like a six-point-five at best and seemed like she didn't party. Todd adjusted his hat and was like, "What up." It was awkward as fuck.

"Where did you go? Why did you do that?" And she looked crazy pissed at Derek; she knew what went down. Derek didn't give two fucks; he was mega-hungry; he asked Jaimiee if she had some fucking protein up in there. Dude was drained.

Brad rolled up in the Rover and our crew was already all up in his crib; he was pretty stoked to see me. He bought this crib in New Orleans after graduation with some crazy dough he pulled down from some real smart sports bets. Dude pulled down occasional cash from freelance sports blogging, which was good dough but he was always spending mad cash on beer and weed—and his lady was also pricey as fuck, buying like a ton of Gucci shades all the time. They saved a ton of money by not having cable; they cancelled it and just paid for Internet. They had two TVs: a fifty-inch plasma with a PS3 connected; and a little forty-incher with a Roku box. He could still get live sports on them, which blew my fucking mind. Brad called his forty-incher "the Little Beast," 'cause it had a pretty vicious subwoofer. Brad came cruising home and rolled out of the car, and came over looking hungover, wearing sunglasses, an Izod polo, carrying a burrito, tall, lanky, and still smelling like booze from the night before, all like, "Shit Sam, you finally got here; let's go in the house and snag a brew."

I could fill a warehouse with the shit I know about Old
Brad Lewis; most importantly, dude taught people how to party,
and he was totes qualified to teach it because he lived his whole
life learning his "clutch-ass party essentials," which were totally
awesome. He transferred his ass to like eight different colleges
during undergrad, always trying to find which school had the
sickest vibe; he hooked up with the Provost at Michigan State to
keep from getting expelled; there are Facebook pictures of him
hanging with the 2007 LSU BCS-champs—huge dudes slugging
shots and laying babes; there are other Facebook pictures of him
in a Florida State hat, winning at flipcup in Seminole country; he
never hooked up with the Provost again. He was an intramural
basketball champion at Illinois State, an equipment manager at
UT-Austin, a beer pong master of Penn State. In Madison he sat
on porches, hollering at freshman hotties walking by. In Athens,
Ohio, he never went to class but managed to stay enrolled for
two semesters. At San Diego State he threaded his way through
the quads, looking for a party. In the Ohio State dorms he did
like five chicks at once. At Illinois State he planned the naked
mile, let word get out too much about it, and wound up running
ass-naked from the cops. He was like the grandmaster of partying. Now the final study was being all chill as fuck. He was now
in New Orleans, taking it easy and getting mad high.

There's this fucked up story about his time at Penn State
that illustrates some shit about him: He was having a pretty chill
house party and playing beer pong one afternoon before a game
when suddenly he took a shot and the ball missed the cup by like
a mile and everybody made fun of him, laughing. Old Brad got
pissed and was like, "This table is fucking bullshit!" and punched
a hole straight through the table. In his minifridge was a ton of
white wine. His friends were like, "Why do you have that in your
fridge?" and Brad was like, "I like that shit 'cause you can drink
a ton real fast." He was totally crazy. This one time I came to his
dorm room and the dude opened the door wearing full camo
hunting gear and smoking a cigar; he was frying up bacon and

was trying to make bacon spaghetti. He also experimented with brewing his own beer with bacon in it—that tasted like crap. He spent long hours watching *Band of Brothers*—"the most awesome shit ever," he called it. Since he moved to the South, he spent a ton of time trying to get good at barbecuing, and although he was always trying to grill, he never got much better. One time I was like, "Why the would you ever want to eat something with a dry rub?" and he was like, "When you dry rub it brings out the hickory flavors, you asshole." He had a bunch of parachutes that he used for building his sprint speed; his trainer was trying to help him get fast and found that Old Brad needed a sick combo of cardio and strength, each set getting more and more brutal with every day, ending with mad sprints with the chutes. The first set mostly just had some treadmill shit and some lifts; the last set was a fucking bloodbath. Halfway through he'd be totally busted, panting like hell, but he'd be like, "Some bastards finish their sets, some don't, let's blow this up."

Brad totally loved his days in college, before he graduated, when he could drink 'till dawn and chicks flocked to him from their dorm rooms and the campus was a total party zone where you could get wild like any way you wanted. He totally hated people who killed the party, like fatties and cops. He could teach like anybody how to party. He taught Jaimiee how to party, and me, and Derek, and even Carl Marcus. All of us would be total prudes without Brad. Dude was totally normal-looking and you wouldn't think he could get so wild, unless you saw him double-fisting with his crazy, jacked-up look with its awesome coolness—an undercover party agent ready to come out, guns blazing. He had majored in Communications at Ohio State; had majored in General Studies at SDSU, but he didn't care about any of it; and now he was chilling out and just wanted to get crunk-plowed and high on his couch every night. Dude chilled in his recliner. Jaimiee made us some margaritas. He always had the shades behind his recliner closed 'cause that window made a nasty-ass glare off the fifty-incher. On the TV was *Band of Brothers* and a hockey game in Picture-in-Picture. I kept being amazed by how fucking real World War II sounded on that shit. We all drank gallons of margaritas while we talked. Brad wanted to know what was up with our trip. Dude drained his margarita and pointed at Derek.

"Aight, Derek, I want you to chill the fuck out for a second and tell me what you're getting up to."

Derek could only check his phone and say, "Ah, you know, dude's gotta party . . ."

"Sam, what are you gonna get up to on the Coast?"

"I can only really hang there for a few days. I gotta get back to school."

"What's up with this Dinkel dude? What's his deal?" Todd was totally boning Gabby in the bedroom. We weren't sure if Brad would be pissed that some mad boning was happening in there. We didn't answer and Brad pulled out a vaporizer and said to go at it, dinner would ready soon.

"Smoking up before eating is pretty awesome. I once ate a rancid Arby's sandwich after blazing and it tasted like the most delicious thing in the world. I just got back from Houston last week, went to see the Black Eyed Peas with Jaimiee. We were crashing at my buddy's and one morning I woke up like crazy. That dude had the most incredible surround sound system I'd ever seen. Everybody else pays contractors like huge wads of cash to set up systems, but my dude just wired and tricked out the whole thing, saved a big pile of dough. I'd like to watch the Bastogne episode of *Band* on that shit, would be loud as fuck. A dude can't watch TV without a decent surround sound system." He opened his closet and showed us a ton of wires. Then he opened another closet and showed us a huge pile of speakers. In Columbus he once crippled his ear for a week after watching *Black Hawk Down*. "I've got the most amazing kicker now—a Klipsch P-312W subwoofer; look at this sick wood finish. I could blow the windows out of this place if I cranked it up and watched *2012*. Only thing wrong, the wood finish is like one shade off my shelving unit."

"I hope you never get that hooked up," Jaimiee was like. "How do *you* know how to wire that?" Brad was like, "Whatever;" he didn't give a shit about her bitching but he heard it. Their relationship was sorta weird: They hung out all the time; Brad liked to blaze up, he got high and watched *Band of Brothers*, she wanted to change the channel, she never could; by sunrise he crashed out and then Jaimiee would watch *The King of Queens* on DVD while dude snored. She loved that dude, but in like a sorta crazy way; there was never much fucking around, just like super intense and serious shit that there's no way I could deal with. Like real overbearing commitment-type stuff that might make a dude's dick drop off was just totally cool with them. I guess they were older; they'd been out of college and decided to get married and whatever.

Derek and I asked Old Brad if he could show us an awesome time in New Orleans. He was a total buzzkill. "New Orleans is lame as fuck. It's like a total letdown every time. The bars are totally boring."

I was like, "There gotta be some awesome bars around."

"Awesome bars don't exist in America. An awesome bar is something that doesn't exist anymore. Like back in the '80s a bar could be like a wild place where dudes would go after work, and there were chicks who wanted to hook up, the music was pumping, you could smoke if you wanted to, and beers were cheap as fuck. Now all you get is a bunch of lame uptight places, lame dudes, shitty drink specials, and owners who fucking hate having a good time; just a lot of fights at the wrong time and bitches that don't wanna hook up."

This was such bullshit. "All right," he was like, "I'll take you to New Orleans tonight and show you what I'm talking about." That motherfucker took us to the lamest places on purpose. Jaimiee chilled at home watching *The King of Queens* on DVD. I asked her if she really thought that show was funny; she said it was pretty good if you watched a lot of it. We all got in the Wrangler Unlimited and Brad thought Derek drove like an asshole. "Chill out, Derek, we'll get there, aight; whoa dude, there's the ferry, you don't have to drive into the fucking river." Brad thought Derek was becoming even more of a crazy douche. "That dude is totally gonna end up with alcohol poisoning or dying in a fucking car crash." He whispered to me. "If you go to Cali with that dude you'll never make it. Why don't you chill in New Orleans with me? We'll chill by the ocean and get hammered in my yard. I've got a Frisbee we could totally toss around. Some pretty nice hotties downtown, too, if you're looking for trim these days." He checked his phone. Derek wanted to check out more shit on the ferry. I went with him while Brad just chilled and checked his phone. It was foggy as hell and the water sorta reeked; we could see New Orleans glowing like a party beacon, beckoning with its bars and bands and hotties hanging from balconies in the crunked-out night. The iPhones of the ferry passengers shimmered in the darkness. My dude Big Jim Halverson had gotten arrested in New Orleans for indecent exposure; Mississippi Chad had gotten arrested up in here too; and as we crossed the river to the parties beyond I knew that awesome shit would happen and possibly one day it would be so awesome as to be The Shit. And what's pretty ironic is that the day after we took the ferry, Brad Pitt also took it, and we saw some pictures in the paper the next day.

Brad took us to every lame shithole in the French Quarter and we rolled back to his crib when it was barely midnight. Maryann got completely fucked up; she smoked pot, drank a ton of Red Bull and vodkas, dropped a Vicodin, and even asked Old Brad to score her some coke, and he didn't; he did give her another Red Bull and vodka. She was so totally fucked up that she was like a zombie and laid all comatose on the couch on the porch. The porch was sick. It was mad big and looked like you could have a crazy party on it. In the house Jaimiee sat watching *The King of Queens* on the forty-incher; Brad was in the living room watching *Band of Brothers* on the fifty-incher, clutching a beer in his hand and taking a drag off the vaporizer and sitting on

the nasty couch with a thousand booze stains; Todd Dinkel was
having a marathon bone session with Gabby in the guest bedroom; Derek was sending some texts; and I tried to make sure
Maryann wasn't fucking dead.

"Hey, you need some water? You gonna chunk it?"

"Shut uuuuuuuup. I'm fiiiiine."

Everybody kept texting everybody else to see where they
were in the house. I was sick of just hanging in the house and
went to find a fucking bar. I needed to chill somewhere and
maybe get a little action; instead of that I found all the bars
nearby closed at eleven. What kind of assholes close bars down at
eleven? "Fucking dickwads!" Old Brad would be like. But dude
just stays home all the time with *Band of Brothers* playing and
never takes advantage of the amazing party metropolis at his feet.
That didn't make sense to me. Who doesn't get wild when New
Orleans is like a hot second away? Maybe Brad was the fucking
dickwad.

DICK PUSHUPS

The next morning I was woken up by some loud-as-fuck commotion in the living room. Derek was helping Brad work on his surround sound system. Brad had taken out his surround sound wiring and was desperately trying to yank out all the knots in it. There were a ton of wires in like the worst knot ever.

"When I get these knots out I'm going to build a surround sound system that'll have like a *thousand decibels!*" Brad was like, all totally stoked. "Sam, do you realize that the systems you get a contractor to install are overpriced and generally introduce a fuckload of interference and distortion? Same with car stereos. These motherfuckers have invented wires and speakers that could make systems that are cheap as fuck and *amazing*. And watts. Americans are wasting their cash by the millions every year just getting systems with higher wattage that sound like shit. They could get lower-power systems with better dynamic headroom—and continuous power. You've gotta have decent continuous power—and signal-to-noise. They could get systems that would be amazing. They prefer paying contractors so everybody'll go wasting a ton of money and getting bullshit high-wattage systems and still ending up with distortion while they just need some decent wires and a solid subwoofer." He raised the ball of wires. "Don't you think this system will be awesome?"

Dude was always real amped up in the morning. The motherfucker got so high on his vaporizer that for most of the day all he could do was watch *Band of Brothers*, but he was totally amped in the mornings. Brad had some paintball guns so we shot those around in his yard. Brad said he'd seen this dude on *America's Got*

Talent who could shoot paintballs to like knock an apple off his assistant's head from like a hundred feed away. This got him going about dick pushups, which he thought would be the most amazing talent. "You could totally train that muscle. It's a muscle like anything else. You just need to be able to push yourself up by just like an inch, dudes. People would be so fucking amazed. Hahahahaha!" When he laughed he totally lost his shit and doubled over. He laughed about this shit forever. "Hey Jaimiee!" he yelled still cracking up. "I was just telling Derek and Sam about dick pushups!"

"Whatever," she was like and clearly didn't care. There were a bunch of clouds in the sky that looked sorta like dicks and were totally hilarious. Brad was mega-amped. "Did I ever tell you about my buddy Trevor? Trev was like the craziest fucker ever. He had like some totally terrifying motocross accident that like almost killed him but he recovered and just his brain was left just a little fucked up. He was still handsome as fuck and he'd get like mad play, but in the middle of getting some skull he'd just be like, "Shit, I gotta have some sliders!" Then for real dude would leave the chick, zip his dick back in, and roll out to White Castle where he'd buy like five Crave Cases. He'd start driving back and pound them in the car but then get too full and then he'd just toss the uneaten sliders out the window into other cars. They'd get all pissed and honk at him but he just kept slinging sliders. We'd like crack up about this joke we had where we'd imagine the dude like on a battlefield and like everyone has a gun but Trev is just throwing sliders at the enemy like they're fucking grenades! Dude, that shit is hilarious. Trev is the fucking man. It's nice as fuck out, right?"

And it for real was. Cool-ass breezes cruised in from the levee; it was def nice as fuck. We helped Brad measure the wall for the system inside. He showed us the entertainment center he built. He built it out of this like thick metal. "This could hold such a huge fucking TV!" he yelled, banging on the top of it like crazy.

At night, dude would sit in front of this entertainment center, drinking beer and catching Pringles in his mouth. He had like fifty tubes of Pringles. "I love Pringles. They're the best when you eat two flavors at once." He insisted on making us try Blastin' Buffalo Wing and Loaded Baked Potato together; he couldn't find any Blastin' Buffalo Wing. "Aight," he was like, "we can't try that now. Yo, my neighbors are the biggest douches." The neighbors had some asshole kids who tossed rocks in his above-ground pool. Brad totally threatened them with a rifle and they totally shit their pants and never tried it again.

Brad showed us this batting cage he'd started building in his yard. It was way too big for it to ever get finished or even to stand under its own weight. Dude bolted for the house all of a sudden to explode his prelunch nap bomb and vaporizer hit. He came out chill as fuck, and sat down in his recliner. The sunlight poked through the shade all weak as hell. "Hey, why don't you dudes try my hypobaric tent? Get yourself totally amped up. I always feel totally ready to fuck after being in there, hell yeah!" I couldn't believe dude had a hypobaric tent. The hypobaric tent is like a chamber for a dude to lay inside: just like airtight and regulated so the air is thinner inside. According to like modern sports medicine, this shit makes you have better endurance. People get tired because they don't have enough red blood cells. Old Brad thought by sitting in this shit he'd have more red blood cells and would be in peak shape. It was like some kind of cardio machine from space or something. Dude went in to drop a nap bomb and improve his oxygen absorption. "Yo, Sam, after lunch let's go hit up the off-track betting place in Graetna." That sounded clutch. He dropped another nap bomb after lunch in his chair, *Band of Brothers* on TV and Pringles in his lap. It was a raw sight, a king on his throne, a king who was fucking crazy but had it made. He woke up real fast and stared at me. He couldn't find his phone for a little bit. He was like, "Oh shit, it was in my pocket." Then he crashed back into nap mode in a second.

The two of us rolled over to Graetna in the afternoon. We took his Rover. Derek's Wrangler Unlimited was pretty new and nice; Brad's Rover was sorta janky. It could still off-road. The off-track betting place was down by the waterfront with a pretty sick bar. Louisiana dudes were hanging around checking shit on their phones. We slammed a brew, and Brad went over to this hottie hanging by a video slot machine. She looked all like she was into him and they were having a pretty solid convo and then her boyfriend walked up. Dude was totally denied. "Fuck that!" Brad was like. "That bitch should have told me she was with somebody. You know what I'm saying. Whatever." We checked out the horses. One horse was named Big Tryscha and that totally reminded me of this chick I used to hook up with. Old Brad was all like, "I'm gonna bet on Ebony Corsair."

I was like, "You know I used to hook up with a chick named Tryscha."

Dude thought about that real hard, like totally intense. He still bet on Ebony Corsair. Tryscha won like crazy and netted like fifty to one.

"Fuck me!" Brad was like. "Why the fuck did I do that, I've seen this before. When the fuck will I get this through my brain?"

"What are you talking about?"

"Big Tryscha is what I'm talking about. You had a vision, bro, a *vision*. Only dumbfucks pay no attention to visions. How do you know Tryscha, who you used to hook up with, just didn't momentarily communicate to you that Big Tryscha was gonna win the race? That name brought shit up in your brain; she used that to send a message. That's what I was thinking about when you said that shit. My cousin in Missouri once bet on a horse that had a name that reminded him of this chick he felt up in a bar, and it won and paid mad cash. The same thing just happened." He was pissed.

"Let's get the hell out of here. This is the last time I'll ever hit the OTB with you around; all this Tryscha shit sucks." He got all philosophical on the way back and was all like, "One day we're all gonna realize that we're actually in contact with old hookups, wherever they are; like we could know, if we could just like understand it, who we're gonna hook up with for the next fifty years and be able to avoid all kinds of grenades. When a dude hooks up with a random chick something happens in his brain that we don't know anything about but which will be totally clutch if scientists can figure it out. Those jerkoffs right now are only interested in like computers and whatever." Jaimiee thought this whole theory was pretty lame. She Swiffered the kitchen. Brad hit up his vaporizer.

Derek and Dinkel shot some hoops on Brad's halfcourt setup. I played too. We competed to see who was the most fit. Derek was off the fucking chain. He wanted to show us his vertical leap so we used a tiki torch as a bar and dude cleared it easy. Dude told us to hold it higher. We boosted it up so it was like five-feet high and dude could still clear it like nothing. He had a long jump that was like twenty-feet long, for real. Then we did a sprint. I can tear up the hundred like a bullet, but dude still humiliated me. The way Derek ran with his sweaty polo, his calves jacked, yelling "Fuck yeah! Fuck yeah, let's motor!" he looked like some sort of god, running faster than anybody. Brad busted out his paintball guns again and showed us where to shoot a dude to hurt him the worst. I showed them this sick wrestling move where you can flip a dude over from the ground and cause max pain. It was total Jet Li stuff. Brad showed me some other Jet Li moves. I imagined if some chicks could see this shit. We're such a jacked group of dudes they'd be totally amazed.

"Whoa, look at those guys! Can you believe how fit they are?" They'd say shit like that.

We partied in New Orleans. Derek had downed like four 5-Hour Energys and was going psycho. When we passed a Bally's he wanted to show me all his trainer shit. "You'll be a legit trainer before I'm through with you!" Derek, Todd, and me rolled into the Bally's; Maryann and Gabby just chilled in the car. We did sick reps for like an hour, saying what up to the training staff. They showed me how to make the equipment challenging as fuck, switching out a couple weights and blowing up the resistance. They showed us the break room, which totally had beers, good for getting crunked after training fatties all day. "Remember what I told you about all the chicks I smashed in the Columbus Bally's?" Derek was like. "This was the kind of place I'd make it happen."

We'd been gone for like a few hours so the ladies were total bitches when we got back. Todd and Gabby wanted to get their smash on in private so they grabbed a room in New Orleans. Brad was starting to get sorta pissed about all of us being up in his crib. Dude had just wanted to chill with me solo. There were empty energy gel wrappers and beer stains and bits of jerky all over Derek and Maryann's room; to make shit worse, that's where Brad had all his tools, so having them there was totally keeping him from working on his new surround sound system. Jaimiee was always bitchy from all the shit Derek was up to. We were waiting for my phone to charge; I'd let it run real low. Then we were ready to roll, the three of us—Derek, Maryann, me. Once my phone was charged I realized it sorta sucked to leave Brad's chill pad all of a sudden, but Derek was bored and ready to roll out.

As it started to get dark, our crew got into the Wrangler Unlimited and Jaimiee, Brad, Todd, and Gabby waved at us from the yard. It was peace out. Right before we left, Derek and Brad got in some drama over DVDs, Derek had wanted to borrow his copy of *Black Hawk Down*; Brad said no fucking way. This happened back in Texas too. Derek was always trying to borrow DVDs from people he barely knew. He laughed like hell; he scratched his crotch, felt up Maryann's leg, ate a piece of jerky, and was like, "Babe, you know that shit is straight between us in like the most clutch way or any way you can think of or imagine or dream . . ." and like whatever, and the car beasted out and we were off again for Cali.

CHAPTER EIGHT

WE'RE GOING STREAKING

You know how like sometimes when you leave somewhere you feel sorta sad?—it's sorta lame and whatever, but you know. We sorta felt that way about leaving Brad but we had to say "fuck that" and beast it toward our next badass adventure.

We rolled out through stupid Algiers, where like seriously nothing happens, and hauled ass toward Baton Rouge, crossing the Mississippi River at some shithole called Port Allen. Port Allen has like absolutely nothing in it except the stupid river and it was hard to believe that anybody would want to live in a place that stupid. Who cares about the Mississippi River? It's just a fucking ton of water.

As we were rolling, I looked out the window and saw some graffiti that said, "Fuck bitches. Make money" and I was like, "Aight, I will." We hauled ass through a bunch of broke-ass towns with stupid names across the Louisiana plains. We stopped at a Shell in Old Opelousas and I went to grab some snacks while Derek was gassing up. I could hear the attendant taking a dump in the bathroom, and it seemed like a real long-ass dump. Like a super thief, I took some two liters and Doritos and busted out the door. We were hungry as fuck. Derek stole some jerky and we were ready to roll—gas, oil, jerky, and Doritos—like Robin Hood. We rolled out.

There was like this big red glow up ahead of us; I hoped it was a Texas Roadhouse; no fucking luck. It was just like some stupid party where a bunch of idiots were parked around cooking on a big fire. Shit got mad spooky when we rolled into Deweyville. We were in some fucking swamps.

"Dude, do you think there might be some *Deliverance* shit up in here, with crazy Southern dudes trying to rape our asses?"

"No way dude!"

There were definitely some weirdos out here though. The road was like dirt with a ton of vines all over the place. We drove by this super weird dude who looked mad crazy and was all talking to himself and whatever. Who knows what his fucking deal was. As we rolled by, I looked back at him and dude totally like made eye contact with me in a creepy homo way. "Holy shit!" Derek was like. "We gotta get out of this *Deliverance* shit." The car got stuck in some mud. Derek switched off the dashboard lights as a joke. It was dark as hell and we could almost hear the slither of a million weird backwoods dudes. We could only see the lights of our iPhones. Maryann got totally creeped out. We fucked with her and told her there was a snake in the car. But on the real, we were sorta creeped out too. We had to get out of this creepy shit and get back to the warm embrace of familiar sights like Texas Roadhouse. The swamp stank. It was like somebody took a huge dump all over. Seriously gross. We got the Wrangler Unlimited unstuck, hauled ass down a road and got the fuck out. We saw great structures of off-ramp restaurants ahead of us. "Texas! Fucking Texas! Texas Roadhouse!" A huge Texas Roadhouse loomed like heaven in the delicious fucking air.

"Jesus Christ that sucked," Derek was like. "Let's nab some ribs."

After the ribs, we rocked it toward Houston. Derek spat some funny-ass stories about when he was chilling in Houston. "Your boy Hammer! That motherfucker! I'm like always trying to chill with him but he never returns my texts. Dude was off the chain in Texas. Sometimes we'd hit some bars and Hammer would straight-up vanish. We spent like forever checking all the bars to see where dude was." We rolled into Houston. "He was usually in this one totally gross club. Shit bro, he'd be grinding up on like any chick, regardless of what their face and body were like. This one night we tried to find him for hours and dude was like nowhere to be found. We had a VIP room reserved and like bottle service and everything. We lost our reservation 'cause we didn't have the minimum amount of people. I was pissed—I had to put a down payment on the reservation, this is the club right here"—we passed it and it looked pretty hot—"but the cool part was I met this super-hot deaf chick when we were looking for Hammer. She was on a business trip. She couldn't hear anything and talked pretty funny but her body was like off the charts. She read my lips all night, you know, you know? Brad was way hammered from trying to go shot-for-shot with some Mexican dude. Carl got high and sexted like crazy. Hammer finally texted me at like 6 A.M. He totally passed out in a Chipotle bathroom. Dude wanted to know if we could still get into the VIP room. I told him that shit was over. Even more crazy shit went down in Houston but I was usually blackout-drunk, so I've only got some blurry pictures on my phone to remember. But some of those pictures are amazing. There's a ton of naked tits in them."

This crazy dude on a motorcycle blew past us in the middle of the night, all in like awesome leather racing gear and riding a sick and loud sport bike, checking his phone in one hand and with this stacked hottie all wrapped around his waist, beasting it down the road like he was in *Torque* or some shit. Dude was gone in a second. "Oh shit! You see that hottie? Let's try to race that asshole!" Derek was like and gunned the Wrangler Unlimited. "Bro, it would be so fucking awesome if we could get sick motorcycles like that and pull that kind of trim. But those bikes are expensive as fuck and require like so much maintenance." He kept hauling ass.

Dude finally got tired after we were out of Houston so I got my drive on. It got rainy. We were deep into Texas and Texas is super big. It rained like a bitch. The road went through this little shithole town and somehow I got stuck in a dead end. I checked my phone and my GPS was fucked. From like nowhere, this big Chuck Norris-looking motherfucker with a badge and everything showed up next to the car. He was like a cop, or maybe a legit Texas Ranger. I was like, "How do I get to Austin?" Dude told me and I peaced out. Then all of a sudden I saw some car driving like the total wrong way down the road. I thought he wanted to play chicken; I'm not a pussy. Dude kept coming. I kept going. Shit was about to get real brutal so I pussed out and swerved off to the side of the road; I was embarrassed. The other car stopped and the douchebags rolled down the windows and looked at me. The driver looked like a real asshole.

He was like, "Chicken much?" I flipped them off. I was mad pissed that the assholes had fucking beaten me, 'cause normally I don't puss out like that. The asshole driver nodded at me like a dick and drove off. I punched the steering wheel.

"Derek," I was like, "wake up bro."

"The fuck do you want?"

"I lost at chicken and now we're stuck in the mud."

"How the fuck did that happen?" I laid it out for him. He was pissed. He opened the glove box and grabbed his dad's AAA membership card. He dialed the number and was on hold for like fifteen minutes; he finally got somebody. He told them we were stuck and they said they'd send a tow truck out. We waited there for like ever and it was mad boring. Finally the tow truck rolled up and pulled us out of the mud. Everything was fine now. It had taken like a couple hours and we were crazy bored.

I checked my phone, to see what was happening with my fantasy baseball team; and things were looking real bad. I had made what I thought were real solid draft picks. It turned out to be like the worst team ever; all my best dudes started getting injured and the rest were choking. It sucked. I wished I would have made better calls. Derek conked out so Maryann drove for a while. She kept looking back at me and like touching my thigh. She wanted to bone in San Fran. I wanted to tap that too much. Then I got my drive on—Derek was dropping hydrogen nap bombs—and I hauled ass forever through jack shit. Assholes on tractors did whatever. Poor-looking houses with trash in the yards were wherever. I just wished I made better draft picks.

At a 7-Eleven I stole some more jerky and beers while the cashier wasn't looking. Derek was psyched to have more jerky.

Stolen jerky was like way more tasty. "Fuck yeah, fuck yeah," Derek was like, shoving jerky in his face, "It would be fucking sweet to own a jerky factory, just make delicious jerky shit all day. If I had like a million bucks, I'd start a jerky factory; I'd be king, make like beer-flavored jerky; I'd get laid so much—fuck yeah! You feel me? Fuck yeah!" He took a picture of himself with his phone. "Yeah, what up! Fuck yeah!" Dude was like a fucking maniac. He got his drive on and hauled it like crazy to El Paso and just stopped one time to totally go streaking. He pulled over at this tourist trap place that had like Mexican or Indian ruins, got super naked and was like, "We're going streaking!" just like Will Ferrell. I was like "WTF?" He convinced Maryann to get all naked. I didn't want to be a prude and so I stripped my shit down too. We ran like fast as fuck through all these tourists and they couldn't believe what they were seeing: a total hottie with a nice rack running all naked with two dudes with pretty big dicks. It was fucking hilarious.

We just crashed in the car that night and I'm like ninety-percent sure that Derek and Maryann boned while I was asleep. By the time I woke up they'd finished boning and were driving through the Rio Grande Valley. I checked my phone and we kept hauling ass. What was sweet was that my fantasy baseball team had beaten Ty's that was favored to win. What was lame was that I was still in the fucking cellar. I was gonna have to have the most unbelievable season to make it to the playoffs. Fuck me.

"Howard Stern!" Derek was like. Dude had switched on his Sirius. Howard Stern was on; I hadn't heard him in ages. "This used to be the fucking shit!" Derek was like. "I used to listen to it like all the time in middle school and high school. Me and buddies would always try to call in. Dude did the craziest stuff with like strippers, midgets, whatever. Every clutch bro I've ever met, like anywhere; they listened to Stern, Howard fucking Stern. Dude was so hilarious. He was the best." We saw the program title crawl across the Sirius console. "Fuck man, fuck yeah!" Derek was like, so totally stoked. Totally ready to party, we rolled up into El Paso. We needed to party and get some drink on. It was late and all the bars were closed. We tried some liquor stores, but like nothing was fucking open. One dude was closing down but he refused to open up and let us buy a case. We banged on the door but he pretended like we weren't there. We walked around totally sober. It sucked. This one idiot we passed was totally scoping out Maryann. Derek and I got ready to beat his ass but decided he wasn't worth it. This sketchy young dude came up to us and asked if we wanted to come to a party at his place, and Derek thought this would be tight. "We've got like four kegs."

"Fuck yeah, bro!" Derek was like. They busted off. I thought this was dumb as hell; but Derek could probably hold his own in case things got sketchy. Maryann and I just chilled by the car. She got all up on me.

I was like, "Come on babe, I can't hit that right now."

She was like, "Come on. Derek's gonna dump me anyway."

I was like, "I can't smash my dude's lady!"

She was like, "Whatever. This is bullshit. Can I come hang in Columbus with you?"

"Yo, I'm not looking for relationship shit."

"We can just hook up. I'm not looking for relationship shit. I'll give you space. You can totally hook up with other girls."

"But you're gonna be staying all up at my place being all in my scene."

"You're being an asshole. Why do you and Derek have to be such assholes?" Derek showed back up, sorta buzzed and still a fucking lunatic.

"That was a totally sick party, aight! Real clutch. I used to go to a ton of parties like that, all with multiple kegs, an acceptable dude-to-chick ratio, just totally raw, fuck yeah, fuck yeah. . . ." Then dude revved the engine, checked his phone, and hauled ass like crazy out of town. "Yo, let's find some dudes to pick up! Hopefully they'll be awesome. Whoa! Fuck you buddy!" he yelled at this dude who totally cut him off and we all gave him the finger like mad. We could see some shit in Mexico across the fence and it looked like a pretty sick time but we had to bust some ass. Maryann stared at Derek and looked all like she wanted to bone him forever and like be in love and whatever, but she knew that a player like Derek could never be tied up to just one snatch because he was too awesome, too raw, too crazy; he'd party 'till dawn and get too hammered to resist the faint whiff of tang across a crowded bar, the scintillating sounds of hip hop pounding in his ears as his biceps flexed to show some random hottie how strong he was, and if she could just like get him to move to the suburbs and like lock up his dick in a box and like keep it forever then maybe she'd be happy but Derek could never watch his dick fade away into the cold air of commitment, becoming a speck among the dying stars. Dude needed to bone. Still, Derek would play that chick like he was mad into her or whatever and he'd like flex his shoulders as she touched them and bust out a big smile but it was fake and she knew it and he knew it and I knew it and maybe the universe knew it as he flexed and smiled and flexed and smiled on into the night.

As we were rolling out of El Paso we drove by this kid standing by the road. Derek wanted to give his ass a ride and pulled over. "Can you throw down some beer and gas money?" He had jack shit; he was in high school, skinny, sorta dorky, wearing like the tightest shorts ever. "This dude is hilarious!" Derek was like. "Hop in bro, looks like you like to get wild!" The kid didn't know what the hell was going on. He told us his parents were totally rich and owned like a software company in Cali and he'd hook us up with some dough there. Derek thought this was hilarious 'cause we'd gotten totally ripped by dudes like this before. "Fuck yeah! Fuck yeah!" he was like, "That sounds like so *legit*. Let's go find your totally fake rich parents, jackwad!" So we gave this dude a ride, and even though his shorts were mega-tight he was pretty solid. He just listened to our shit. He must have been totally pumped to get to ride with such awesome dudes. He was a big dweeb and was getting ready to apply to colleges. We asked him where he was looking.

"My reach school is Cornell, but I'm also looking at Carleton. I have some friends there who say it has a really amazing liberal arts program."

"Oh fuck me," Derek was like, "that sounds like the worst, the fucking worst, like there won't be any parties, any at all." Derek was right, that shit would suck. I was crazy happy that I went to OSU. Big state schools are the fucking business. For real.

We dropped some mad sleep in a Ramada in Arizona that night. I woke up first and took a quick jog and did some push-ups. It was nice in Arizona. The mountains were sick, there were like cacti and other desert shit, and it was a perfect temperature for cardio. After I did some cool down, it was time to roll out. I woke everybody up and I drove, totally tearing it up down the mountain super fast. I realized I was totally hungry. I'd done all that cardio and hadn't had any breakfast. We got off at the next exit and went to a Waffle House. It was mad good. I ordered like two waffles, hash browns, and a T-bone. I was totally full. I had some serious carbs and protein to keep me pumped. But then on the way out Derek checked out a waitress' ass and this big dude sitting at the counter got all up in our faces. He was like the waitress' husband and he was pissed. "It's cool, bro," I was like. Derek thought this shit was pretty hilarious. The big dude asked Derek "what the fuck were you looking at?"

"Bro," Derek said all cool, "bro it's all cool, we're just chilling." The big dude was still all pissed. Derek, all chill as fuck, raised his fist, like a calm-ass player, and invited the dude to hit the rock. The big dude paused for a second. He hit the rock.

"All right, all right," the big dude was like, settling down. "Just get the hell out."

"Aight," Derek was like and turned and walked out of the Waffle House. We were mad relieved. Some dudes get like crazy pissed when they see you check out their ladies in a Waffle House. "They're just assholes," Derek was like, "it's a fucking compliment that I want to scope your wife's ass. They just want to be

some kind of motherfucking hero, all defending their bitches'
honor and whatever. So stupid." We hauled ass over to Tucson.

Tucson is like pretty all right I guess. University of Arizona
makes it have some sweet party action but outside of that it's sorta
a snooze. My buddy Hank Higgins lived in a pretty sweet off-
campus house so we went to go say "what up" to him. When we
rolled up the dude was drinking beers in a kiddie pool. He was a
UA Wildcat, so Derek and him didn't get along so hot. Derek is
total ASU dude, so the two of them went at it about what school
is better and who has more solid athletics. Some of Higgins's
buddies were chilling with him out in the yard and they legit
almost tried to start shit with Derek. I tried to get everybody to
calm down before a straight-up rumble went down when Derek
said U of Arizona is full of ugly assholes. Finally shit got calmer
and we all chilled in the yard and grabbed some brews. Higgins's
roommate was grilling so we also had some sick brats.

After that we rolled up in a bar where we did some shots
and Derek almost got into more fights with some UA dudes.

We said peace out. Higgins was like "Shit, you dudes can
party," and looked sorta sad to see us go. We'd showed him our
raw party style and it was pretty obvious that he totally wished he
could hang with us. I knew he wanted to be at OSU and totally
regretted becoming a Wildcat. He just chilled in Arizona having an all right time but wondering what kind of totally amazing
times could happen if he would have stayed in Columbus and
gone to OSU; partying all night, hanging with us, just not giving
a fuck because Arizona is pretty fucking overrated when it comes
to partying and OSU will always be the fucking best. I was like,
"Hell yeah," and we hauled ass.

CHAPTER NINE

TIGHT SHORTS

We picked up another dude after we rolled out of Tucson. He was this dude from Bakersfield and told us his deal. "Man, I was supposed to start up this amazing company with my buddy from law school but the guy totally screwed me and made off with the cash—I put up a ton of money for it; I'm a day trader but I started thinking like, what if somehow you could make Facebook but for day trading? It was gonna be awesome but this jerk stabbed me in the back and now it's all over. If you guys can give me a ride to Bakersfield I can definitely get you some cash when we get there." This sounded sort of like bullshit again but we let him in. The car was fucking packed now. "So what'd you guys major in?" he was like, sounding like an idiot.

We started hauling ass around some serious mountains. We rolled though Mojave and shit started getting mad steep. The day trader kept trying to get us interested in his startup; the tight shorts kid seemed legit interested. The day trader said that the future of the web is social and that he had to synergize the worlds of social and finance but with an extreme pivot on the user, or whatever. He kept bringing up blog articles on his iPhone while he talked. Derek started cranking the whip up the Tehachapi Pass. We were like a fucking rocket. We were way high up. Then we headed down the other side. Like a badass, Derek threw the Wrangler Unlimited into neutral and straight up coasted down, like a fucking bobsled or something. I was like, "Holy shit." Dude kept coasting and would even pass other cars without any gas. It was like the Wrangler Unlimited was like an extension of him or something. This crazy U-turn came up and I thought we were all gonna bite it, but Derek threw the wheel to one side, we all leaned to the right like hard as fuck, and he straight up drifted around the corner. We bobsledded that shit all the way down to the San Joaquin Valley. It was like a million miles down, and we kept coasting like mad all the way, like if a bird had wheels and was shaped like a Wrangler.

This sick ride got us all pretty amped. Derek started spitting some stories about his times he'd hung out in Bakersfield when we started rolling through there.

He showed me his buddies' places where he crashed, apartments, houses, one sick condo that had a slide, Chipotles where he ate a ton of burritos, bars where he grinded with hotties, and this one place in the park where he got so hammered that he shat himself. Derek's Cali—raw, awesome, bumpin', a place where heavenly hotties flock to dudes all the time, and a dude with a solid build and a pretty cool sense of humor can live like a snatch king. "Oh shit! That place has such good ribs! I ate so many ribs there!" He showed me pictures on his phone of everything—topless chicks, crazy big burgers, hilarious drunk pranks. We passed by where Tali and me had chilled out at night getting hammered on a case of Bud Light Lime, getting to second-and-a-half base under the stars last year, and I tried to find some pictures on my phone of that night but I must have deleted them or something. "Oh shit! Dinkel and me partied over here and were competing like crazy to see who could smash with this hot RE/MAX agent. Jesus she was hot." Maryann was texting with one of her friends. The tight shorts kid said he could get some cash in Tulare. The day trader told us how to get to his brother's crib.

We rolled up to his brother's condo and the day trader texted him. There was no response. The day trader got out of the car and tried calling him. "This is so bullshit," Derek was like. "Everybody keeps screwing us. He's not gonna give us jack shit." The day trader got back in the car and told us to head over to this office park.

"Crap, I wish he'd pick up." He kept texting and calling. He might've though we were gonna kick his ass 'cause we were pretty big dudes. We got to the office park and he went inside for a while. He came out with his brother, who I guess was like a VP of some shit for an insurance company or something. He tried to get his brother to give him some cash. It was pretty obvious this dude was the fuck-up of the family. But his brother coughed it up and we got a nice wad of gas cash, which was solid. We peaced out.

Now we had to take Tight Shorts to Tulare. We hauled ass like mad. I checked my fantasy baseball team, they still sucked and I was ready to forfeit the rest of the season. I threw my phone down and just dropped some nap bombs as we cruised past Sabinal where I'd gotten all tan and smashed like mad with my Latina slam piece. Derek leaned way back in his seat and pushed it to like ninety-five. I was still deep in a nap bomb when we rolled into Tulare; people were saying shit as I woke up. "Yo, Sam! We took Tight Shorts to his house but his parents are like mad broke 'cause his dad's business' partner like made off with all the company's cash. This is like the same shit that day trader dude was saying. Like why the hell does this shit gotta keep happening to stop us from getting gas money from these fuckers?" Tight Shorts thought shit might get rough. We let him off and were like, "Peace out." He couldn't believe he'd gotten to ride with such a raw crew.

In a couple hot seconds we were rolling through Oakland and then San Fran busted out from like nowhere with all its hills and a bunch of water and whatever else all around it, full of bars and clubs and hotties and a pretty sick climate for outdoor sports. "Fuck yeah!" Derek was like. "We're here! Fuck yeah! The coast! No more fucking driving. We gotta stop driving and just get wild! Aight, babe, you go with Sam and find some place to crash and I'll hit you up tomorrow after I hang with Carly for a while and see if I can get my Crunch job back and you dudes just like find something awesome for tomorrow night on Yelp or whatever." We drove over the bridge and were all up in downtown. The buildings were all clean and tall and full of rich business dudes, sorta reminded me of *Wall Street: Money Never Sleeps*. We finally got out of the car and I felt like a gladiator entering the party arena; I was finally in town and ready to set up camp and get some shit started; the delicious burrito smells from everywhere got all up in my nose and made me mad hungry. We got our shit out of the car.

Then in like a hot second Derek was fucking peacing out. He was all blueballsing over Carly and needed to ditch us real quick. Maryann and me just stood there while the dude drove off. "See how he's a total asshole?" Maryann was like. "He'll fuck you over anytime he thinks he can go hook up with somebody hotter."

"For real," I was like, and felt sorta pissed. I left my phone and my wallet in the car. Derek totally took off with my phone and fucking wallet. "What the hell are we supposed to do now?" We carried all our shit around, like total poor people in the streets. Derek wouldn't fucking answer his phone; I used Maryann's phone and tried to call him, text him, e-mail him, send him Facebook messages, and I even like tried to friend Carly so maybe I could get her to get Derek to bring me my stuff—what the fuck was I supposed to do without my wallet or my phone?

CHAPTER TEN

THE BADASS BROSWARM OF HEAVEN

Maryann had hooked up with a dude who managed a Holiday Inn, so he was able to hook us up with a room. So at least we could crash somewhere. I was hungry as fuck, but Maryann was mad stingy with her cash so the two of us had to split one medium pizza when usually I eat one and a half mediums by myself. I texted Derek again from Maryann's phone and was like, "Where the fuck are you?" and "Give me back my phone and wallet." I decided Derek was a total douchehammer that year. I chilled in SF for a week and it was like the lamest thing that's ever happened. I had no cash and no phone and Maryann sucked and wouldn't ever buy me enough food to actually feed me. We went to Olive Garden and the bitch wouldn't even let me get anything more than never-ending salad and bread-sticks; I just wanted some fucking Stuffed Chicken Marsala.

We crashed in the hotel together for a couple days. Maryann didn't wanna smash anymore now that Derek peaced out; the whole time she was just trying to make that dude jealous. She bitched out like crazy at me. At night I'd try to spit some game at her to see if we could bone. I did my signature chick-catching move which is to like brush back her hair and then like sorta just move my finger like down her neck and then down her back and then just like real fast brush her ass like it's no big deal. "What the fuck was that?" she was like; she was being mad frigid.

"I just wanna get some action on because it's like boring as hell and you said all that shit before about how we could smash in San Fran but now we're here and all of a sudden you're being all bitchy and frigid when I'm trying to work some game and I just don't get what you're fucking deal is!" I was crazy pissed and hungry out of my fucking skull.

She went off and partied at a club that her friend owned. Bitch couldn't even get me in or spot my cover so I had to wait outside like an asshole, still fucking starving, and then like a million years later she came out all up on this old dude. Now it was totally obvious that she was a mad slut. She didn't even fucking acknowledge me even though I was standing like right there. She kept walking with the old dude and got in his stupid Acura with him. Now I was totally fucked.

I was mad pissed and super hungry. I walked by a Forever 21 and saw this chick walking out and she gave me like a crazy dirty look; she totally thought I was checking her out, which was true but I'm usually better at hiding it when my stomach isn't fucking digesting itself. I kept going. I got crazy with hunger and even though the chick was maybe a six-point-two, I seriously started thinking about her like she was nine-point-seven, and I wanted to bone her, and like date her, and like marry her and whatever and bone for the rest of our lives. I got crazy weird-amped about this. I imagined our lives together. She was a supermodel who passed through European cities looking all hot and making mad bank. I was a wide receiver for the Philadelphia Eagles, crazy fast and strong and famous and rich. Every night was an unbelievable party where Cristal flowed down long, shimmering fluorescent fountains and diamonds glimmered in the ears of my teammates and on the necks of all our hot wives. Velvet ropes swung open and I strutted in, a pinstriped god of the night, bringing an entourage trailing behind me like a comet's tail, clamoring for my attention and desperately seeking a single moment of my time in the VIP room so they could tell their friends that they hung out with me and that yes, he's just as awesome as you'd think. Whispers through the night carried my name from room to room, club to club, city to city, over nations, continents, and oceans. Who is this mighty player? Who is it that reigns supreme from his throne of cash, beers, and cars? "Baby, come on, just one more time," the hotties would say, pulling my pecs back into the beds of the world's choicest hotels, "Baby don't go." But I couldn't stay. I had to peace out. I had got my smash on. I had to fly away, off in my G6, fast as fuck, smoking cigars inside the fucking plane and feeling up the stewardess wearing pumps and a too-short skirt. Fuck yeah! More Cristal! Mile-high club! Through the clouds, crunked and awesome, I descended like a fucking eagle, gliding toward my amazing seventy-room mansion in Cali where every night my hottie wife reclined as a goddess upon my satin sheets in my big-ass bedroom with an eighty-inch LCD that shone so bright and crisp and clear it was like staring at the fucking sun except awesome. And I smashed with her forever and she didn't care that I'd boned a steward-ess eight hours ago and I would bone and bone and bone and before my eyes would pass all the hook-ups and smashfests of my life, like Tina and Tali and that Tryscha chick who tried to tell Old Brad to bet on that horse from across like the fucking universe or whatever. And in that moment, as I'm boning like hell, all becomes one and it all joins into a single rager across the planet with everyone awesome and everyone clutch all getting wild and crunked and sloppy together in a badass broswarm of heaven. I could hear Kanye blasting from inside my brain, drop-ping a beat that reverberated through my bloodstream and made me party from the inside out. I realized it wasn't really Kanye inside me, but the memory of Kanye, the untold countless times I'd rocked out with Kanye as a party playlist or sex-mix, all gath-ering together to create a perfect jam that now lived inside me and rocked out in my skull wherever I went. I had partied hard and drained keg after keg, like it was no big deal, and more kegs would be emptied and more after that, creating a ceaseless chain of steel kegs rolling down from porches and apartments and pickup trucks, plummeting down like rain on the dry ground of America that thirsts for just a drop of Natty, a drop of Coors, a drop of a fucking party. And as I continued to rock and to bring it and to get wild I would bring the party monsoon and soon great waves of light beer would rise up from all corners of the earth and charge toward those who can't party, who need to party, who should chill the fuck out and they would be enveloped in the chilly carbonated embrace of crunkness and they would float to the surface, smiles on their faces, and they would look to me in the sky and know that I had done them a solid, a solid that would be forever remembered for as long as the earth could turn and beer bongs could be lifted. And maybe Maryann was boning that old dude and whatever but I didn't give a shit because she was trash and a slut and who needs to get with a slut anyway. I just needed some grub, to slam some calories, to pack some protein up in my gut. There were places that served delicious wings dripping in delicious jerk sauces, places that would serve you an XL beer and ask you if you needed a refill after a few sips and you can look at them and just be like, "Fuck yeah." Somewhere Bloomin' Onions were being dipped into amazing mayonnaise-based sauces and dudes were looking over menus and deciding if one steak was gonna be enough or if they should order two. Somewhere Chipotle burritos were getting loaded down with barbacoa and guac and being wrapped and wrapped and eaten and eaten. Somewhere ribs were being smothered in delicious sauce in a Texas Roadhouse kitchen and then they'd be brought out to some hungry bros sitting in booths eating the complimentary peanuts and planning their awesome night and where they'd go and what they'd drink and who they'd bone.

CHAPTER ELEVEN

EDWARD FORTYHANDS

I was that starved and pissed when Derek finally showed the fuck up. I went with him to Carly's crib. "Where's Maryann at?"

"That slut peaced out." Carly seemed like way less of a slut-bitch in comparison to Maryann; she was more chill and way less moody. But I still kept thinking about wanting to bone Maryann. I crashed at Carly's for a little. She had a pretty hot view from her window so you could see like all of SF bumpin' below. Derek got this crazy job when we met back up. Dude was handing out free samples of Venom Energy drinks on the street. His boss dropped off like a ton of Venom that Derek had to hand out. I went with Derek around to like movie theaters and big office buildings where he posted up and handed out Venom. He was supposed to give out samples in busy areas to get people pumped about drinking Venom. "Dude," Derek was like, "this job is even tighter than that summer I worked for Steve. Steve sold timeshares in Colorado. Dude could sell to anybody. He threw sick parties in the model homes up in the mountains with like a ton of food and booze. This one time this loser family came up and they were totally not feeling it. Steve was still able to get some brews in their hands and get them having an awesome time. These losers totally partied and got hammered. They bought like two timeshares. Steve was the fucking man. I can't find that dude on Facebook. I got mad tail at those model homes. I totally copped a feel when I handed out some Venom today. You know? Fuck yeah!"

"Shit dude," I was like, "you could totally be the snatch king of San Fran." I couldn't believe that asshole could pull tang even while he was handing out Venom.

This one time he for real handed out Venom shirtless and this chick was all into it and he totally got laid in the copy room of her office. It was ridiculous. But dude got sick of that Venom shit pretty soon. His boss came by to see what his fucking deal was. Derek was chilling on the couch with a ton of empty Venoms all around. "Have you been drinking all of these?"

"Yeah," Derek was like, "but they taste like shit."

"You're gonna have to pay me back for those."

"Naw." His boss got crazy pissed and didn't know what else to do. He just grabbed the one unopened case and left. I was fucking over it all and Derek was too.

Even though things were getting lame, we still got pretty wild; we went to his buddy's place and played Edward Fortyhands. Edward Fortyhands is a drinking game where everybody duct-tapes a forty to each hand and you can't take them off until you finish your forty. All sorts of dudes play this game when they're looking for a pretty sloppy time, since you've either gotta drink hella fast or piss your pants. When you first get the forties duct taped onto your hands it seems pretty funny, but then you realize the shit you've gotten into. You take a few drinks and it seems like you'll be done soon, but you've got eighty ounces of Camo strapped to your palms and it's gonna get fucking rough; the night goes on and you drink more and more and you're just working on one and it's getting warmer and more full of backwash but you've gotta make it through. Shit gets gross near the bottom when you think maybe you should just start drinking from the other one 'cause it'll be less heinous, but that's a fucked up drunk choice 'cause then you've still got both hands incapacitated. Pretty soon you've gotta piss like a motherfucker but you can't get at your fly 'cause of the forties so you look around to everybody like, "C'mon bro, just get my fly, I can shake my dick out on my own" and since you're such a drunk cripple you don't get how homo that shit sounds and you wonder why the fuck you didn't piss before the game started. This goes on for a long time 'till you either man up and chow down on that Camo or you let out as little piss as possible into your cargo shorts and hope that it doesn't make puddles.

Derek stands out on the porch, all like, "Aw fuck! This is nasty!" and putting the Camo to his lips and chugging. "For real Sam, I fucking hate Camo. I fucking hate Camo." The other dudes around are making pretty good progress, getting through half their forty, then polishing it off and untaping one of their hands so now they can pee and use their phones but in a still pretty-awkward way, but still Derek is stuck back on his first forty because he hates Camo so bad and he swears and kicks shit over and wants to know why the fuck they didn't get Mickeys, or Olde English, or just fucking Coors, or anything other than Camo, and he keeps acting all like a little bitch and he won't just suck it up and enjoy the party 'cause everybody else is getting pretty hammered and having a good time and pumping their forties up in the air to some classic Poison but he just gets more and more pissed. Finally pretty much everybody is done with their forties except Derek, who still has both taped on him. Some dudes make fun of him and call him a pussy in a way that's like totally funny and not dick at all, but Derek gets mad pissed and punches this dude in the face with his forty-filled fist. Everybody looks at him all "what the fuck" but nobody gets how pissed he gets about Camo. He's had nightmares where he's trying to bone this chick, but he has Camo forties taped to his hands so it's like mad hard to bone right. He keeps trying to shake them off of him, but then the forties take on like a life of their own and start slamming Derek in the face. This was the kind of shit in Derek's brain when he laid that dude out. Usually if you punch a guy in the face with a forty there will be like a big rumble and that dude's buddies will try to take you out, but everybody looked at Derek, jacked, huge, and raging like a bull with two glass bottles attached to his hands and everybody decided not to get into any shit with that crazy fucker.

At that same party I chilled with this dude named Parker. Parker is this pretty funny dude who everybody said was related to Bill Murray. That sounded totally amazing so I asked him about it. The dude told me that Bill Murray was like some kind of uncle to him or something. Parker and me threw back some beers and he told me pretty hilarious stories about times he'd gotten hammered with Bill Murray, like these times they got wasted at a Cubs game and Bill Murray totally punched a dude and got away with it 'cause he's sweet. And like you'd guess, hanging with Bill Murray means you can pull amazing quantities and qualities of snatch so this dude has boned more than seems possible and kept slinging stories like mad about a chick he smashed here and another there and like all over the place. But then this chick he used to smash came up and was all pissed; she said that he was full of shit and that he didn't even know Bill Murray. Dude had like no response and it was mad clear that he had been telling me total bullshit for the past half hour. He was a total idiot. He totally blew. I was over this party and over all this Cali bullshit. Derek and I partied some more and then I needed to get the fuck out.

This trip to San Fran was total bullshit. Carly hated having me crash at her place; Derek was a dick and didn't give two shits where I crashed. I bought a twelve pack of Natty and dumped it in water bottles for the bus trip back; that shit was gonna taste mad skunky in just a couple days. We partied way too hard the last night I was in town and Derek found Maryann and we all hit some clubs but Maryann smacked this dude in the face who was hitting on her. His chick friends got crazy pissed and there was mad catfight action. But it was just bitchy, not sexy at all. Derek was acting like a grade A douche. This shit was done; I was over it.

I packed my shit and peaced out to Derek and Maryann. They tried to nab some of my water bottles full of Natty. I was like, "Fuck that." That shit was weak. We all thought each other were douchebags and didn't want to hang ever again.

Part Three

Bring It

I FELT PISSED AS FUCK

A semester later I thought I had totally exhausted OSU's party scene and my dad knew a dude who could get me into UC-Boulder without a bunch of hassle. I pictured myself getting wild Western style, just like I did back in Denver. But shit blew. None of my crew was still around Colorado—no Beth Riggins, Rob Riggins, Tom Grover, Becky Grover, Ryan Minor, Derek Morrisey, Carl Marcus, Todd Dinkel, Ray Jeffries, Timmy Snipes, none of my crew. I chilled around campus, checked out a bunch of frats that had been cool at OSU—they sucked at Boulder; this one party ran out of beer in like five minutes and nobody would fucking cowboy up some cash for more kegs. I paid for the whole fucking thing myself and nobody paid and still the party sucked. Jesus fucking Christ, why did I transfer?

Some weekends I'd go chill in Denver. I'd hoped that would be cooler than the bullshit in Boulder, but it was totally lame without my crew. I drove by Carl's old condo where we'd gotten hammered, and like as a reflex I checked in the window to see if the dude was Bowflexing up there. A dude either has a crew he can party with or he doesn't.

One night I went by Sports Authority Field and hoped it would be bumpin', but it wasn't football season so there was just some stupid concert happening; I wished for games and tailgates and hotties; it sucked that football season didn't last all year. I popped in Chipotle and got a carnitas burrito with hot sauce; I ate it and got fire shits. I wished that I had my crew with me, even just a couple solid dudes, anything except having to roll solo, a lone wolf. I'd always rolled deep with a crew; that's how I always got so wild and blew shit up. I saw some groups of dudes having a solid time inside a Buffalo Wild Wings; awesome times were there, with solid dudes and mad hotties; and crunked out vibes of a good fucking time. They high-fived and were totally pumped. A hot waitress brought their drinks, and one dude looked out the window and saw me and ran out of the B-Dubs and shouted at me—"What up, Garrett!"—but then realized I wasn't Garrett and went back inside to slam more wings. I wished I was Garrett. I was crewless, Sam Parker, lone wolf, walking past all this bullshit, this amazing-looking Buffalo Wild Wings, wishing like hell that I could high-five and slam beers with the awesome, party-focused, stoked bros of Denver. Seeing all these dudes get wild reminded me of Derek and Rob Riggins, who'd gotten wild up in here since birth. It killed me that I couldn't hang out with them now.

A little past the B-Dubs a rec league flag football game was going down at a park under the lights. Both benches yelled like crazy when their dudes would catch or not catch the ball. This huge crew of dudes were playing, all wearing Under Armour and slugging beer concealed inside of water bottles. I'd played rec league and intramural league sports forever but I'd never been able to get hammered during the game; the places I'd played had always been too uptight; you'd get kicked out if you smuggled beer onto the field. I was jealous as fuck. There were some hotties watching the game. The dudes would probably get laid after the game, and laid again, and again—flag football, beer, and tail. It was so stupid that I wasn't doing that shit! One of the QBs looked kinda like Derek. One of the hotties looked like Maryann. These dudes were having an awesome night in Denver; I felt pissed as fuck.

Past the park there was a sick apartment party going down, people were chilling on the balcony and throwing back Coronas and chilling out and occasionally hitting a beer bong. Some nice-ass cars rolled by and I could hear the bass beats of Kanye songs coming from them. Shit was awesome all around me and people were stoked and had crews that rolled five, ten, and twenty deep.

One of the hotties watching the game got all up on one of the players; the player groped her ass and grinned real big. I felt so pissed! I peaced out from that shit.

I went to smash with this chick that I sorta knew from Facebook. She told me some of her friends were road tripping to San Fran and was like, "You're bitching like crazy about wanting to hang with your crew; these guys can give you a ride over there." It was bullshit that she said I was bitching, but I was pumped to roll out to San Fran.

These two dudes were driving; they acted all like pimps but they were pretty lame chaches. We hauled ass like crazy to get to SF. We cruised some boring desert shit, then some more desert shit, a ton more desert shit, some mountain shit; then some more desert shit. As we passed some more desert shit I saw for the second time on my trip a cloud that looked like a dick and I was like, "That shit is so crazy hilarious." I took a picture of it with my phone and posted it to Facebook where I knew my buddies would see it and leave comments like "that's the most hilarious cloud" and "fucking awesome." LOL. We stopped for a Bloomin' Onion in Salt Lake City and then kept hauling ass. In a hot second, I was all up in SF again and it was late as fuck. I beasted it over to Derek's crib. Dude had gotten a pretty sick little house. I had to know what the hell was up with him and if we could get wild, 'cause I wasn't getting wild anymore; everything was lame and I was feeling pissed as fuck about it. I texted him from his driveway.

CHAPTER TWO

PISSMERGENCY

Derek texted me back, let me in, and was so totally pumped to see me. Dude was amped. "Sam!" he was like. "You're fucking legit. I never thought you'd roll up to *my* crib."

"Hell yeah," I was like. "I've been bored as fuck. What's up with you?"

"Pretty lame, pretty lame. So much shit has gone down I gotta catch you up on. Bro, let's lay this down and have a brew." I was cool with that and came inside. Me showing up was sorta like an awesome shark hitting a beach where it's all a bunch of losers swimming around, 'cause while Derek and I were slamming brews and hanging I could hear Carly getting all pissed and sad upstairs. Whenever I told Derek a story, dude was like, in a beyond-amped kind of way, "Fuck yeah!" Carly knew shit was gonna get wild. She'd gotten Derek pretty pussywhipped for the past few months; but now the awesome shark was all up in here and dude was gonna get wild. "What's her fucking problem?" I was like.

He was like, "She's been a real bitch lately, all nagging and fighting, turns into a huge bitch whenever I roll home past three, but if I chill here it's mad boring and she won't put out." Dude went upstairs to get her to chill out. Carly was all like, "You're an asshole; you're an asshole; you're an asshole!" While she was flipping out I checked out the crib. It was a pretty choice two-story place that wasn't hella big but was still pretty close to SF and had a sick view. Downstairs was an epic man cave that opened into a yard and everything. There was an all-right home theater setup. Derek's shoes were under the wall-mounted TV and there was still totally mud all over them from the time the Wrangler

Unlimited got stuck in the mud and we had to call AAA. He didn't have the Wrangler Unlimited anymore; he rolled it trying to take a turn at sixty. Carly got fucking pregnant again and had another kid; dude couldn't keep that shit wrapped up. It was mad annoying with her crying all the time. We peaced out for a second and bought some more brews. Carly finally shut up and fell asleep or something. I couldn't figure out what her fucking problem was; maybe she was on her period.

Right after I peaced out from SF last time, dude got a deafening mind-boner for Maryann and was sorta stalking her like a creep, and saw her boning like a million different dudes at her place. She'd always be bringing back some douchebag. Derek was pissed. He wanted to bone her and didn't want her to be such a slut. Then one night he drank like four gallons of Four Loko, the prime ingredient in shitshows—a guarantee for sloppiness—like a total idiot, and flew off the handle.

"At first it was sorta awesome," he was like, "I just like partied with my dudes and everything seemed to be like more off the chain than I'd ever imagined; I just kept throwing back Four Lokos like they were water. I started hearing this crazy noise in my skull and it was sorta like my eyes were going to explode but I still felt real chill. Then I went out onto the roof and then I fucking Got It, like everything that had ever come in my dome came back again and I was like some kind of crunked out Einstein 'cause I knew it all and understood everything and I just stood on the roof above the party and kept being all like, 'Fuck yeah! Fuck yeah! Fuck yeah!' Everybody below heard me and kept shouting 'Fuck yeah!' back at me, and this seemed like it went on for like five days but it was probably just five minutes. I was a fucking king; I knew how to party; I knew how to spit game; I knew how to chill; you know. I just like fucking got it for real. Then by my sixth can shit started getting brutal and my stomach turned and I could see like fireworks everywhere and everybody was trying to get me in a cab but I was like, 'Fuck no. Fuck no. Fuck no!' This dickhole called an ambulance like a total jerk. Carly was

having a girls night and didn't pick up her phone. I kept trying
to tell the dickhole not to call an ambulance but I couldn't say
anything and I just kept throwing up on pretty much everything.
I ran out fast as fuck, bought another ten Four Lokos and told
Maryann to come over and chill. She texted saying she would
come but then she didn't come and I got crazy pissed and at this
point I was like near-blackout but still amped from the caffeine
so I grabbed my lacrosse stick and sprinted to her place, threw
up like three times, busted down the door and made her take the
stick and I told her to hit me straight in the abs with it. She just
held it. I wanted to show her how fucking strong my abs were.
She wouldn't do it. I punched a hole through her toaster oven. I
was fucking *wasted*. It's legit. She'll back me up."

"What the fuck went down after that?"

"All that shit went down a while ago after you peaced out.
That bitch started dating some consultant who threatened to
beat my ass if I came around, but I'm pretty sure he's a pussy
and I can take him the fuck down, 'cause bro, I can drop almost
anybody. Even with my fucked up hand." Dude showed me his
hand. It was legit fucked up. "I broke my stupid thumb when I
punched Maryann's toaster oven at one-thirty in the morning—
I know the time cause the toaster oven's clock froze after I kicked
its ass—and I punched it way hard but the fucking glass shattered like mad and cut my shit up and my thumb lodged on the
mini broiler pan and some dickbag doctor set it totally wrong
and I had to go back in like all the time and I never washed
that shit 'cause I didn't feel like it, so part of it got infected and
those motherfuckers straight-up lopped off a little piece of my
thumb."

He showed me the pictures on his phone. It was nasty.

"Shit just got dumber after that. Carly couldn't get a job and
we had this other stupid kid so I had to work like double shifts
at Crunch where they made me do equipment maintenance and
wipedowns in addition to personal training, scrubbing the shit out
of nasty ellipticals and putting weights back on the rack, which

made me rebreak my stupid thumb on a barbell and now it's looking all fucked up again. You feel me? Fuck me, I'm a mess. I'm taking penicillin but it's totally giving me hives 'cause I'm allergic but
I'm not gonna wear some stupid medic alert bracelet. I can't even
get in a legit workout with my hand. I can't even get hammered
'cause there's like a five-hundred percent chance I'll rip off the
cast while I'm blacked out. I can't even spit game 'cause I'm losing muscle mass like crazy. I can't even play fantasy sports 'cause
I can't type or use a fucking mouse. I can barely text. I can't sleep
without Breathe Right strips 'cause some dude busted my nose up
at a karaoke bar a couple months ago. But for real—for real, I am
still ready to party and get wild and even though there's these two
lame kids all up in my grill I am still gonna get wild with you bro,
and for real, *for real* shit is gonna be awesome. Tomorrow I'll show
you the TV I'm gonna buy, it's sixty inches, has a 50000:1 contrast
ratio and a faint red back glow. I'm gonna mount it right above my
current TV and I can watch two things at once and like flip the
sound system between the two and it's gonna be all the way awesome. He gave me a high-five for going through P90X a fourth
time, this time in half the normal time. "That shit is awesome,
bro, we're all getting more raw with every day, and are getting
more ripped if we don't have shit wrong with our hands. You're a
solid dude, I think the way you make the home workout happen
is fucking legit and you've gotta have hotties flock to you if you
just wear a shirt that comes in tight around the pecs like I used to
have before this bitch and this fucking hand. Fuck! Fuck! Fuck!"
he was like.

The next morning Carly bitched out and kicked us out,
for real. Shit when down when Ray Jeffries rolled up and we
slammed some brews while Derek made sure the little kid didn't
die and did the dishes and whatever. Jeffries was gonna haul us
over to Mill City to meet up with Ricky Bronco. Carly got home
from work and looked all pissed about whatever. I acted all nice
to try to get her to shake the bitch off, and I was all like, "Hi" and
"What's up?" but she was still a bitch, a total bitch, and gave me

the shit-eye. Then things got awkward: She was all crying and shit on the bed and I needed to piss like a firehose and I had to go through the bedroom to get there. "Derek, Derek," I was like, "bro, can I piss in your sink?"

"What the fuck?" he was like, all wondering what the fuck I was talking about. Dude thought it would be pretty gay to have my dick out in his sink. I told him what was up with Carly and my pissmergency and dude was like, "Don't worry about her. She bitches out like that constantly." Fuck, I didn't want to get bitch-attacked by her. I bolted out to try to piss outside; I walked around the yard and up the street and there were always too many people around who'd be all looking at my package. I snagged a quick piss behind a FedEx office and headed back. Derek and Carly were bitching at each other like mad but at least my bladder was chill. A hot second later Carly chucked Derek's shit all over the place and told him to get the fuck out. What blew my skull was I saw a picture of Gabby Dinkel in their digital picture frame by the couch. I'd totally forgotten about that chick and she was probably chilling with Carly, always bitching 'cause the dudes they were with were too awesome.

Derek totally cracked the shit up and his kids made some annoying noises. Dude just strutted around grabbing his shit with his thumb all busted up, just chill as fuck like some kind of Buddha. He grabbed his jacked-up duffel full of energy gel and Clif Bar wrappers; he grabbed everything and threw it in there. Then he grabbed his CamelBak, the biggest CamelBak ever. It must've held like more than a gallon 'cause it was big as all fuck. It got mad heavy when you filled it to the top with Natty; shit got warm too. Derek ran upstairs to grab his phone charger. I pushed my shit into my North Face bag, and Carly just kept being like "Asshole! Asshole! Asshole!" while we got the hell out and lugged our stuff to a bus—it was gross as fuck but at least I had a crew.

It was like Derek's jacked-up thumb was totally what he was about. Dude didn't give a shit about anything like usual, but he still *gave a shit about getting legit wild*; like, I mean, dude couldn't give a fuck but still gave a fuck about partying and that was just his deal. He was all like, "Hold up."

"Aight, bro, you're probably sorta pissed or whatever 'cause we totally got booted a hot second after you rolled up and you might think I fucked you over or whatever—all pissed at me and you know, aight—but chill. C'mon, bro, chill."

I was chill. Dude looked like crap, his Hollister shirt was all stained, his Levi's were all torn up but not in a way that made them look distressed; he smelled like shit, he hadn't put on cologne or body spray in like forever, and he was holding his jacked-up thumb up at his chest 'cause his doctor told him to do it, but dude was still grinning like a motherfucker. He checked his phone.

"Why can't I load *espn.com*? Fuck AT&T. No fucking service!" He held his phone up to the sky and looked at it. He tried to hold it a different way. "My buddy got one with Verizon— have you ever had a Verizon plan? That is the shit. My buddy gets service like pretty much everywhere, even tunnels and elevators, for real." He finally got a couple bars, loaded *espn.com*, and pulled up the Giants game. He checked out the score all intense about it. "For real, Sam, I swear these fuckers are like trying to lose sometimes . . ." Dude got over that score pretty fast and started scoping for chicks. I was stoked I was out here. He needed a buddy to get wild with.

"What was Carly's deal? What the hell is gonna happen now?"

"Fuck if I know," he was like. "Fuck if I know. Fuck if I know." We tried to figure out how we were gonna get wild. Dude was a mess and I needed to make the call. Derek had gotten hella sloppy—I'd never seen a dude get so sloppy without getting hammered; totes crazy, jacked-up thumb, all covered in wicked B.O. that he could cover up in a hot second with just a fast hit of fragrance. "We should just like open a bar," he was like, "and then we'd never have to buy beer." Dude was fucked. I took out my parents' Discover Card and waved it at him.

"My parents have been stoked I've gotten fewer DUI's," I was like, "so they'll let me use this like whenever I want, so let's just go to Columbus—and then we'll go party in Cabo."

"Cabo?" dude was like. He got amped. "Cabo, fuck yeah—you for real, bro?"

I was legit. "We'll just use my parents' card, they won't fucking fight me. We can chill and scope mad Latina hotties on all the beaches; we'll hang out on the hotel balcony; we'll pound margaritas. Why not hop a plane to Cabo?"

"Fuck yeah," Derek was like, and then I saw him look sorta like a pussy for a second, the first time I'd ever seen him look sorta like a pussy, and I couldn't figure out what was up with him. There was total weak shit in his eyes, all weird and awkward, and we just stood there all awkward for a while. I sorta knew what was up.

"Are you afraid of flying?" I was like. I didn't wanna be a dick, but I had to ask. Dude didn't say anything but kept looking all weird as shit.

I couldn't remember if I'd ever heard about him flying and I could only remember him rolling up places in his Rover or his Wrangler Unlimited. I wasn't gonna let his bullshit fears get in the way of an awesome time—"Let's fly to fucking Cabo; I'll fucking pay for it." I was for real; I just wanted to get wild in Cabo. Dude kept pussing out. He was being all silent like a bitch. It hit me like a big-ass medicine ball that in some ways I was more raw than Derek, who I had always thought was like the rawest, and now that dude was dealing with that shit. We both thought about it. My brain was all thinking about how pretty awesome it was that I was so raw, in a bunch of ways, and I'd been this raw forever but always felt less raw in comparison; he was probably sorta pissed that he wasn't so raw. Then he got over it and started acting like less of weirdo. "Are you a pussy about flying?" I was like. That pissed him off. He hated that. Dude barely ever got pissed at me. For a second I thought we might rumble. Usually I'd think he'd kick my ass, but with his thumb

all jacked up I think I might have been able to drop him. Then
this megawatt hottie busted out of her apartment and cruised
past us in a mad-tight tube top and heels. We scoped that out and
couldn't believe the hotness that just got thrown down in front
of us, like bangable manna from heaven. She was stacked, for
real. Derek and I both sprung chubs. He took a picture of her ass
on his phone.

"Aight," Derek was like, putting away his phone, "let's do
this shit."

"Aight," I was like, "fucking Cabo!" Then we grabbed our
shit, I had to take most of it 'cause his thumb was all jacked,
and managed to hail a cab; we cruised downhill with our ripped,
tan arms hanging out the windows, two bombass heroes of the
Western night.

CHAPTER THREE

THE HOLY PIMP

We posted up at a sports bar and threw down the game plan— we were gonna party together and get wild forever. Derek kept checking his phone a bunch, sending text messages and looking at Facebook to see what his buddies were up to. "Looks like I've got some solid dudes chilling in Denver—we gotta go hang with those dudes; they're probably up to some real wild shit. You feel me?"

Fuck yeah; we were gonna get wilder now than we'd ever gotten before. First we were gonna party in SF for a couple days, then roll out in like a rental car or something. Derek said he was totally over Maryann but it was pretty obvious he still had a mind boner for her. Dude was gonna have an awesome time in Columbus.

Derek geared up in a fresh polo and a Yankees hat, I hit the ATM, and we texted Ray Jeffries to see if he'd haul us around SF and be a designated driver. Dude said he would. Ray was all up in San Fran, interning at a tech company and banging this blonde hottie name Denise. Derek thought her boobs were weird— dude thought this made her fugly 'cause they were like lopsided and too pointy or something—but her boobs were totally nice and she was hot. Ray Jeffries is sorta like a nerdy kinda dude without much of a build, but he's pretty solid and he'll totally do any favor for Derek 'cause he thinks Derek is real awesome. He just wanted to hang. He'd gotten in some kind of tangle with his chick Denise over driving us around and that bitch didn't want him to hang with us. He wasn't gonna get his dick cut off by her, so he came out with us anyway, but she kept sending him bitchy texts; he was totally pissed and just drove and like didn't talk; sometimes he'd blow through red lights while texting a response and we knew he was real pissed. Dude was all torn between his slam piece and his awesome former rec league football captain.

Derek was chill, and didn't give a fuck about his emo drama. We ignored Ray's bullshit and just chilled in the back of the car slamming some brews.

We rolled over to Mill City to try to hang with Ricky Bronco. The abandoned ship I wanted to throw a party on was gone, which was lame; and Ricky wouldn't text me back so we just went to his shitty old house but he had moved. This hot black chick opened the door; Derek and I spat game at her for a little. Ray Jeffries had barely any game and just chilled in the car, looking up shit on his phone. I texted Ricky one more time and figured "fuck it;" we'd gotten texts from that Gabby chick and it looked like we could probably crash at her place. Todd had totally dropped her ass, went to get wild in Denver, but that bitch was still trying to get him back by the balls. When we rolled up to her place, she was chilling on the couch watching *The Real Housewives of Beverly Hills* and eating some Yoplait. Some of Todd's posters were still around after he'd peaced out.

"He's gonna come back," she was like. "He's an asshole and can't do anything without my help." She got all pissed at Derek and Ray Jeffries. "He started hanging out with that Timmy Snipes guy. Todd and I were having like so much fun before that asshole started hanging out with him. They'd hang out in our kitchen and just play beer pong for like hours and talk about the stupidest stuff."

Derek cracked up. That was straight out of his playbook. Timmy Snipes totally started copying Derek's fashion and then rolled out to San Fran to hang with Todd Dinkel; I'm not kidding you here, Timmy got his dick caught in his work pants and dude had to get dick stitches, which sucks, but then got a heap of workers comp, which is amazing. With a ton of cash, they ditched Gabby and rolled out to Portland, Maine, which Snipes said was pretty awesome. By now those dudes were passing through Denver or they were already bumpin' it in Portland.

"Those guys will blow all their cash and then Todd will come crawling back," Gabby was like, staring at *Real Housewives*. "That asshole has always been an asshole. I wish he wasn't so hot."

Gabby actually looked sorta hot the way she was laying, with her hair covering the weird parts of her face and her clothes made her look pretty thin. Maybe she was aight. We let her hang with us when we went out to a club with this hottie Derek knew named Marcy.

So then Gabby, me, and Derek rolled over to Marcy's place. The chick had a pretty shitty place and the car was like a total piece of shit that maybe had four cylinders and crappy acceleration. We drove slow as fuck back to Gabby's place and we just chilled in her living room with Ray Jeffries and his chick, and everybody was all uptight, but Derek was being hilarious and drinking two beers at once.

"Why are you always such a jackass?" Gabby was like. "I got a text from Carly and she said you left. You have kids with her, you dick!"

"That's bullshit! She booted his ass!" I was like, ready to throw down. Everybody looked all pissed at me; Derek thought it was pretty awesome. "If you had to live with that kind of bitch, how do you think you'd feel?" I was like. Everybody kept looking all mad pissed, especially Ray's chick, who was ready to claw my face. They were all just being a big bunch of bitches and they thought Derek was some kind of asshole they could blame all their bullshit on. I checked my phone; I needed to bust out and hit some clubs—I'd just rolled in and needed to get wild.

"I'm glad Maryann dumped you," Gabby was like. "You've been a huge asshole forever. I can't even believe the sort of asshole things you've done."

And everybody thought Derek was some kind of asshole 'cause they just stared at him all mean and pissed, but dude just stood there and cracked up, for real. He finished his beer. His gross-ass thumb was even more gross-ass than before and the bandage was falling off. Then it hit me that Derek, 'cause he was such a raw dude and didn't give a fuck, was sorta the ultimate player, the ultimate bro, the sickest one anywhere.

"You're a total jackass to everybody and don't care about anyone. You just like always think with your dick and try to screw people over. And you're like such a douche about it. Like

you don't get that people don't have to go around like you trying
to act like some super awesome pimp."

Aw fuck. For real. Derek was the *Holy Pimp*.

"Carly is a total mess and she's texting me like crazy, but
there's no way you're getting back together; her last text said
that she was over you and that this time it's for good. Just stand
around looking like a jackass, just like a total dick."

This was total, total bullshit; I wanted to kick all their asses and I
totally could have taken everyone in that room. But it wasn't fucking
worth it. I wanted to be all like, "Just chill. Don't you get that Derek
is a funny motherfucker who loves to party and if some bitches get
upset it's just 'cause they're bitches. If needing to get wild constantly
is a crime then lock this dude up, lock all of us dudes up . . ."

All those fuckers were pussies. Gabby was the only one who
would actually grow the nuts to spit her bullshit to Derek's face. Back
in the day there were parties where Derek would have everybody
doing waterfalls to see who could chug the longest. Then shit would
get wild and sloppy and everybody got mad hammered. Still, Derek
would be a cool-ass player and like some kind of tang wizard he'd
have like six girls at once all up on his shit. And this was just during
high school. He taught his buddies how to party but then his buddies
got lame bitch girlfriends and now these lame bitch girlfriends were
all bitching out Derek for being the awesome fucking player that had
made shit happen for like a decade. She kept bitching about bullshit.

"So you guys are gonna go on a road trip to Columbus," she
was like, "then what the fuck are you going to do? You screwed
over Carly and now you're gonna go to some boring place like
Columbus? What a bunch of assholes. Columbus is the stupidest. I can't believe it."

If she was a dude I would have kicked her face in. You don't
talk shit about C-Bus. Everything got quiet; where a normal
person would feel all bad and apologize, Derek just checked his
phone, right in front of everybody, casual as fuck and all cool, his
ripped triceps flexing just slightly as he scrolled through his texts,
all like, "Fuck yeah, that's hilarious," like not even caring about all

those bitches that were there, and they couldn't believe that dude wouldn't get wrapped up in their bullshit drama. He was a *Bro*— the root, the soul of Broness. How hard could he party? He tried to show me how off-the-chain he could be, and all these bitches were jealous of me, getting to get so wild with him, hanging with him and doing crazy shit like they wished they could do. They were like, who's this dude from the Midwest who's out here putting the West Coast to shame? I was all about that.

"We're gonna party in Cabo," I was like, I knew they'd be extra jealous of that. Still, the bitches were real bitchy and totally getting off on that because they probably wished they could bone with Derek but dude would never do that, not just 'cause they were already smashing with some of his bros but because they were nasty bitches, and so that's why dude finished checking his texts, was like, "Peace out," and just straight up left, no joke. I saw him through the window checking *espn.com* on his phone. He left all the stupid bullshit back inside and just chilled out by the street with nothing in front of him but a night full of raw times and pure partying.

"Aight ladies, can we just chill out and go hit some clubs? This is stupid, and we need some chicks to hit the clubs with so we can get in. Derek is cool as fuck to hit clubs with, you know?"

"Derek sucks to party with," Gabby was like, and all those fuckers agreed with her.

"Take it the fuck back," I was like, "dude may be a little bit of a dick sometimes but he is the clutchest to party with because he has this sick vibe that we wish we all had and maybe one day something will happen and we'll get that vibe and then we'll all be so stoked that we hung with him so much."

They thought this was bullshit; those assholes just said that I didn't get Derek's deal, that he was the hugest douchebag in the world and if I kept hanging with him he'd douche all over me. It was obvious they were jealous. Ray Jeffries tried to side with the bitches and acted like he knew Derek's shit and that shit was a douchebag who could party. I texted Derek: "f tht noise letz prty"

CHAPTER FOUR

GUAC-FILLED DAWN

The bitches finally decided to hang and we got things started, riding in that shitty four-cylinder car. "Fuck yeah! Let's light this bitch!" Derek was like, and we piled into the ride and rolled out for some sick clubs.

We busted out of the car and got into a long, slow line, where we could smell the stank of chicken nuggets from the McDonald's across the street and hear the dudes up in the front of the line arguing with the bouncers trying to get in. Derek busted up through the line, pissing everybody off, all like, "Let's do this, let's do this!" A bunch of big pissed dudes stopped him and forced him back to the end of the line. It was a crazy long line that went like around the block and was just filled with a bunch of assholes all standing around checking their phones; it was so boring; there were like a ton of dudes but not that many chicks, and a lot of the chicks didn't look that hot. We stood around and checked our phones; we moved forward a little bit; we checked our phones some more; some people left the line so we moved up some more; we checked our phones. Low bass beats came through the walls and it sounded like things were wild inside and they must have at least a couple DJs who knew how to drop raw beats and sick scratches. Derek tried to accuse a dude of cutting in line, and I don't think this dude cut in at all. Derek was crazy intense and looked for real like he was gonna kill the dude if he stayed in line in front of us and Derek flexed his neck and brought his fist back ready to knock dude out and luckily this guy pussed out and left. Derek looked around and challenged anybody else to try and cut in front of him and was like, "What? *What?*"

Everybody was totally bored. Gabby and Marcy were complaining about how tired they were and said we should have gone to this other club that's easier to get into. Huge groups of people all rolled out of the club, heading out to other clubs or bars or whatever. "Let us the fuck in!" a dude in line yelled, but the bouncers didn't let anybody in when these dudes left and everybody in line got all pissed and was like, "What the fuck." "Fuck this!" Derek was like. He was standing on his toes, trying to see over everybody to see what the fuck was happening at the front of the line. Fuck, awesome shit was happening inside and shaking the walls with beats and making the wait worse because we were out here and everything amazing was inside. A big fat-ass bouncer was just standing at the front of the line, not doing fucking anything. "Yo! Let us in!" His buddy had a headset and was just looking at a clipboard, marking some shit with a pencil, then he went inside to do something—inside, where shit would be amazing, where all the awesome people were and with mad hotties probably all grinding up on everything. The bouncer walked down along the line and just looked at all of us; he looked like an asshole; who the fuck wears a Royals hat? He pointed at a couple chicks in the middle of the line and signaled for them to come out, and they did, and then he took them right into the club. Derek was like astro-pissed when he saw that shit go down, punching the wall, trying not to jump the bouncer, and the bouncer saw how pissed he was and just sorta cracked up at how pissed Derek was, and then these two hotties cracked up too; and then they went inside and we just stood there not moving and the beats from inside got louder and I thought Derek would flip out. He was raged up. The bouncer was just staring at him; he saw a dude who just wanted to get in and party and get wild but this jackass had the power and he was gonna flaunt it to try make his own microscopic dick feel a little bit bigger; I'm positive he had a microscopic dick 'cause why else would you be a bouncer unless you couldn't get into the club and instead you just wanted to stand outside and wave your pin-sized wang around at dudes who actually know what's up. "This is bullshit. Such fucking stupid bullshit!" Derek kicked the wall.

Then some more people left the club and the bouncer just stood there and didn't do shit except just stand in front of the door while everybody in line started feeling fucking broken. It got depressing. We sat down in line, giving up on this stupid shit; it was so dumb. We thought about going somewhere else. But we'd already waited this long, and if we left then we'd have totally wasted half our night and this club was supposed to be amazing. Some more people in front of us left and so we got to move up a little more but it sorta sucked 'cause then we had to stand back up just to move a few feet. I tried to text some people to see if anything else was going down but nobody responded. We had nothing to talk about and we just stood there. We moved up a little more. We waited. Some asshole tried to cut but everybody yelled at him. I texted some more people. Derek and Marcy and Gabby all tried to text their friends to see if they were inside and if maybe they could get us in. Nobody responded. Derek sighed. I played *Angry Birds*. I'd been having crazy trouble trying to beat this one level where all the pigs are wearing helmets or whatever. I tried to shoot one of the birds that curves around to the other side and then tap it at the right second so it would take out one of the pigs in a helmet and then hopefully he'd hit the box of dynamite and that would take out some other ones. I pulled back, I fired—the bird flew like crazy and I tried to tap it but then it curved back too soon. Then before I knew it, it didn't even hit anything and ended up like right back where it started. I was like, "Fuck." And the line wasn't moving and *Angry Birds* sucked and everything was stupid and why couldn't we just get into the fucking club and have a good time? The world was bullshit and stupid and the line moved slower and slower and I started to get pretty raged up. We saw a crew of dudes roll into a bar next door that was pretty chill. We had to get out of this fucking line so we left the chicks there to hold our place and went to grab a brew.

We rolled into the bar. We ordered some MGDs. The crew of dudes was getting pretty wild in the back. We went over to them and Derek was like, "What are you dudes up to? We've been stuck in the fucking line outside for like ever." They were all like, "We're just doing a hot second of prepartying 'till we roll out for a club a few blocks away. The shit there is way more awesome and there's like never a line. My buddy knows a dude who works there and you can totally get in and get drinks and whatever. What's your deal?" We told them we were partying in SF but were gonna bust out to Columbus and Cabo soon. "Aw fuck, I've never been to Cabo before but I hear it's like on par with Cancun. My girlfriend gets sorta uptight and she's never wanting to go down there."

"Bitches, man," Derek was like. "Where's she up at?"

"Watch it bro, she's my lady." the dude was like, all suspicious of Derek. "Don't try to be asking about my lady."

"Chill, chill," Derek was like. "I was just hoping she had some hot friends that were out tonight. I'm just looking for some action."

"Aight, I feel you. I've just been dealing with some real assholes lately who try to get up on my piece," the dude was like, finishing his brew. "My buddy's gonna go grab the car and then we'll give you a ride to this club if you want."

That sounded pretty awesome so we went back over to talk to the chicks. They'd gotten all bitched out about us leaving so they straight up left—what bitches. This stupid fucking fight broke out in the line: Some totally lame hipster dude thought this fat asshole was cutting in line and then the lame hipster shoved the fat asshole like a bitch and the fat asshole was all like, "Excuse me?" and the lame hipster was like, "Don't cut in the fucking line, dude." And then the fat asshole got all pissed that this lame hipster pushed him so then he grabbed the lame hipster's head and tried to like throw him down in a weird way that might have worked except the dude was way too fat so the lame hipster just like hit his big gut. The lame hipster tried to throw a punch but missed. The fat asshole pushed him up against the wall and totally started choking him and all these other dudes were standing around but they didn't stop that shit 'cause they didn't want to lose their place in line. The microdick bouncer finally broke it up and kicked both of them out of the line. "What the fuck?" the lame hipster was like. "Go fuck yourself," the fat asshole was like. I wished I would have taken a video of that shit on my phone. It was a hilariously stupid fight.

Those dudes from the bar rolled up; they were driving a badass classic Hummer. We loaded in. The dude driving gunned like fuck across the city and straight-up blew through red lights but all the other cars were terrified and didn't come close. Derek was stoked. "Dude can drive! Check out the mad drift he's pulling just totally chilling back in the seat and cranking the whip around corners like it's no big deal and is legit texting while he's doing it, fuck dude, fuck, I wish I could off-road with him—fuck dude—fuck. It's on, it's fucking on—let's do this! Fuck yeah!" The car drifted like a motherfucker around a corner and we were all up in front of the other club. We rolled out, the dudes just cruised into the club but the bouncer stopped me and Derek and was like, "Get in line" and the dudes didn't fucking do anything to help and just kept walking. We were like, "What the fuck?" and went to the back of the line, long as fuck like the other one, and we just stood there like total assholes, stuck in another stupid line with another dickless bouncer and we kept being like, "What the fuck? We were with those dudes!" And the bouncer didn't give a fuck and we just stood there totally pissed, 'cause nothing is worse than leaving one club with a line for another club with a line.

"This is the dumbest shit!" Derek was like, all pissed.

And it totally was. A bunch of high school kids with fake IDs were standing in front of us and were crazy annoying, all talking big but clearly they were just some sixteen-year-old ass-holes and just the fact that they were in line made me wonder if this club was like any good if sixteen-year-olds know about it and think they can get in. One of them kept bumping into me and it was crazy annoying and I finally gave him like a "don't fuck with this" look and he totally looked like he was gonna piss himself. Still, they kept being super annoying and I wondered if the whole club wasn't gonna be like this, a million teenage ass-holes acting all cool, drinks held high, spilling shit everywhere, and crowding the bar 'cause they don't know how to handle themselves. Any hotties would probably be underage and that shit is dangerous and gross most of the time. Derek stood next to me, checking for texts and hoping that someone would text him back with the lowdown on a more awesome place to be hanging, his fingers flying like crazy across the screen sending text after text and getting nothing in return. His phone blew up and he checked it but it was just fucking Gabby saying she was in the same line as us. Fuck, bullshit West Coast clubs, with their lines so long and the bouncers such dickholes, how the fuck could I possibly get wild? Some hotties came rolling out of the club looking all mad hot; they looked crazy good; I was like, "Shit I gotta get in there now. I gotta get in there now!" and I tried to go up to the bouncer and see what the deal was and that asshole just gave me some bullshit answer and told me to keep waiting. Derek sat in a pile in the line with his iPhone in one hand, staring at it, one side of his collar was unpopped and he looked like a totally broken dude with just one thing in his skull: He needed to get somewhere and get fucking wild and not be in this bullshit line. It was like a hurricane of bullshit and we were trapped in the winds. And those high school motherfuckers, with their fake IDs, got in the club and the bouncer didn't even give them any trouble and we still had to wait in the line, each minute becoming more bullshit than the last. It was so fucking stupid.

Like an hour later we gave the hell up and went over to some sports bar and just slammed some brews so we could at least get a little buzz on. It was a pretty lame place, but Derek pulled some awesome shit. The bar got mad crowded and Derek was trying to text Ray Jeffries about where we were at so we could snag a ride, but inside the bar Derek was getting like no GPS so he couldn't figure out what cross streets we were at so he had to like get outside the bar to get some GPS and figure out the deal but the bar was mad packed and there were a ton of assholes blocking his way. He got all like some kind of cross between a ninja and Jason Statham and like barreled out through the bar, jumping up on tables, pulling a sick slide across the bar, and straight-up diving between one dude's legs and did like a full-out flip over a dude puking outside to land like a badass on the sidewalk. His service still kind of sucked, so he held his phone up to the sky and spun around, try-ing to get a more exact position. There was a dude doing karaoke in the back and he was getting just through the second chorus of "Pour Some Sugar on Me," when he saw Derek pull those awe-some moves and was all like, "Whoa." Everybody in the bar was like fucking amazed by that shit, and then Derek plowed back into the bar, jumping over a dude, kicking off a wall, and totally swip-ing some choice asses on the way. In a hot second Ray Jeffries rolled up and Derek Jason-Statham-ninjaed it out of the bar. Shit was getting started again.

"Aight, Ray, I get that you've got a mad drama with your lady, but we gotta roll out to this sick bar across town 'cause my buddy is bartending there and he's only gonna be working for like ten more minutes so we need to get over there for some free drinks. You feel me? Fuck yeah! Tomorrow me and Sam are peacing out for C-Bus and this is like our last chance to get wild San Fran–style so you know what we gotta do."

Ray Jeffries got that shit; he blasted his whip through the streets and kept our party alive.

We crashed out around sunrise. We hung with this black dude named Wallace who got us pretty trashed on these shots he called "Prairie Fire," where you like put a bunch of Tabasco into tequila. "Burns like a motherfucker going in and coming out!" he was like.

We went over to that dude's place to drink some brews. He lived in a pretty crappy place with his girlfriend. They only had one TV and it was in the bedroom. We had to grab it and the cable box and move it out to the living room so we could watch it; Derek moved it and Wallace's girlfriend was pretty chill about it; she seemed like a pretty solid lady. She didn't get all bitchy to Wallace about being out late or being drunk as fuck; she was chill. We got everything set up in the living room and watched some FIFA and drank beers. It started to get light outside and we were gonna peace out. Wallace's gf totally took the TV back her-self and didn't bitch out at all. She was so chill.

As we crunk-walked home, Derek was like, "For real, dude, that's like the best kinda chick. No bitching, no complaining, like for real; that dude can roll up with a crew whenever and be totally crunked and drink some beers and do whatevs. He's the man, and nobody gets him by the balls." He sorta made two huge balls with his hands. We rolled out. We'd owned shit tonight. Some cops all looked at us suspicious but they had nothing. We grabbed some delicious burritos from this tiny place and ate them in the tasty guac-filled dawn.

This sorta older bro walked toward us with this younger, jacked dude. They were coming back from partying. The younger dude took out a flask and pushed it at the other dude but that dude like wouldn't take a hit and just checked some shit on his phone. "Shit, that dude is like Old Brad Lewis!" Derek was like. "All getting lame and not wanting to hit the flask when all his buddy wants to do is keep getting wild. Those dudes passed by us.

Delicious chunks of barbacoa floating in a burrito, we're all these crunked bros at the dawn of raw America.

We were ready to pass out; there was no way Gabby would let us crash at her place. Derek knew this trainer at Crunch named Evan Burns who had a place he lived at with his dad. Derek used to be tight with them when they were working together at Crunch, but shit went down, and so Derek wanted me to try to text him to see if we could crash there. It was so dumb. I had to send a bunch of texts to explain who I was and what was going down. I got confusing texts back from his dad; I guess dude had left his phone there. The dad remembered how hard they hated Derek, but he still let us come in. The place was mad shitty. At least the dad was chill enough to let us sleep in a bed instead of on the gross-ass floor. "I'm already awake," he was like and then did some shit in the kitchen. He spat some stories about when he was a personal trainer and how he even did some bodybuilding. I wished my dad would have been an awesome bodybuilder. I just chilled and thought his stories were pretty raw. Derek was totally zoned out and just checked his phone and was all like "for real" to everything the dude said. Then we blew up some sleep 'till Evan rolled in after his shift at Crunch. The dad kicked back some supplements to get ready to do some workouts. He downed twelve pills and two shakes and rolled out.

"These bodybuilder dudes are weird and have a shitty place but they're totally solid," I was like to Derek. "It was mad solid of them to let us crash here."

"For real, for real," Derek was like, totally zoned. Dude went to grab some jerky. I had to grab our bags from Gabby. The bitch was lying on the couch watching *The Real Housewives of New Jersey*.

"Peace out, Gabby, keep it real."

"Maybe when Todd comes back I'll try to party harder so he doesn't get all bored or whatever. Would he be into it?"

"I don't fucking know."

"Whatever."

"We're peacing out for Columbus in a hot second."

"Derek is such a dick."

She was un-bitchy enough to let me grab a shower and do some grooming at her place, then I grabbed the bags and got in a cab with a driver who I'm pretty sure ripped me off by like taking way too long of a route but I couldn't tell for sure 'cause iPhone GPS seems to fucking blow in San Fran sometimes. The city seemed totally awesome as I rolled through it for the last time, dudes eating, dudes drinking, a Giants game getting started, the mad crowds and tailgates of what is the most clutch thing about sports in America—and everywhere hotties streamed out of apartments, offices, and bars like the fog rolling over the bay. Only you can't bone fog. I was sorta bummed to have to peace out; I'd only partied for like sixty hours. Hanging with amped-up Derek meant that you party through the world like fucking crazy but like never stop to chill. In a couple hours we were beasting it back East.

CHAPTER FIVE

PARTY-SUFFOCATING
BOA CONSTRICTOR

We got a ride with this gay dude who was going to Kansas and drove like a real bitch; Derek was like, "This is such a lame Ford Focus;" it was mad slow and it was obvious the dude hadn't sprung for any of the optional features. "Gay as hell!" Derek was like, just to me. This lame tourist couple was in the car too and they wanted to like stop and see everything. They wanted to get out at Sacramento, which was like way too fucking close to where we started. Derek and I chilled in the back and tried not to talk to these idiots. "Shit dude, those Prairie Fires tore my shit up—I got mad hammered and then shit my face off; they were like the second-worst shits I've ever had." I asked him what the worst shits he ever had were. "Look, bro," dude was like, "it was like . . . shit. So I was mixing my liquor like a fucking idiot—this was back at ASU. I threw back a couple Jell-O shots 'cause I was hanging with some chicks, you know, and then I had like four beers and threw back a Jack and Coke 'cause my buddy made me one. Then my dude Connor comes up with a bottle of Jäger and was like, 'I bet Morrisey can't hold down nine shots of Jäger!' Everybody at the party stopped and was like, 'Oh shit.' They didn't think I could do it. Dude was pushing me, seeing if he could get me to puss out on a drinking challenge, to like shrivel my dick in front of everybody and run like a pussy, but I'm no pussy and so I took the challenge and drained those shots one after another until I couldn't see straight and my body was rebelling but I told my stomach that I'm the fucking boss and it's not gonna ralph, because that's just how I do, and you get that. So I drank it and didn't puke and made it home and ate a double

stack of pancakes on the way, but then I woke up covered in my
own Jäger-shit." I couldn't handle any more of that story; it was
totally gross.

I started spitting some shit I'd had up in my skull, like
pretty awesome stuff I'd thought about but never spat before.
I told Derek about this sports bar I wanted to open where you
could like get drunk and then play football against a robot; like
there'd be these robots that could sorta play football but it would
mostly just be a way to get drunk and beat the shit out of these
football robots. "Fuck yeah! Fuck yeah!" Derek was like. "I was
thinking of the same sorta thing but instead of robots you could
do like virtual reality drunk sports—listen to this. It's pretty fun
to play sports and stuff when you're hammered, but it gets real
hard and sorta dangerous, like this time my buddy Evan totally
snapped his femur trying to dunk after drinking half a case of
Coors. This is why—and fuck bro, I think this shit is so awesome. This is why it would be amazing if you had a bar with virtual reality sports where you could get hammered and then just
play simulated sports. That way if you totally tackle a dude head-
first with no helmet, it's just awesome and you don't end up in
the hospital and you can just keep playing and you never get
tired and feel like you're going to throw up because you're not
actually moving that much and you can still play with like a beer
in one hand. And for real, think about the mad cash you could
pull down because you like get people drunk and then they just
throw money at you to play the games, and it would be a way
better scene than Dave & Busters 'cause it would be more of a
bar so you wouldn't end up with stupid kids around; it would
just all be awesome dudes hanging around getting hammered
and playing virtual sports. You'd be rich in like five seconds and
I bet you could open like a million across the country and just be
drowning in dollars and then the hotties would naturally flock to
you. I just gotta get a business plan together and get some capital
on . . ." Shit sounded cool; we were on an awesome road trip;
we were amped.

"Oh, and there's some other shit," I was like, "'cause it's like one more awesome thing that could happen at this bar and it would be totally clutch. This one time my buddy smuggled a beer bong into a Buffalo Wild Wings and we ordered some pitchers and we actually started beer bonging in the *middle of a B-Dubs!* Natch, we got kicked out in a hot second, but just think if at our bar you let people use beer bongs; like they could rent them out and do legit beer-bonging in the fucking bar! It would be amazing and like no place else has that kind of shit and you'd— . . ."

"Fuck yeah! Fuck yeah! Fuck yeah!" Derek was like, totally amped. "I was thinking the same shit, except instead of beer bongs you'd have kegstands. Like beer bongs you could probably rent so then that would make more dough, but how totally fun would it be to get to do kegstands in a bar and like be able to have competitions and everything and make like a huge party out of it, and you could probably make removable mouthpieces on the keg so you could swap around without a bunch of like germs and whatever and maybe you could charge for those so you'd make some extra cash. . . ."

We were getting mad amped while we hammered out our business plan. Our ideas were so awesome that we totally forgot about the idiots up front and they were starting to get pissed at us. After a while, the driver was all like, "Will you guys just relax? You're kicking my seat." For real Derek was 'cause he was trying to show how to flip somebody up into a kegstand in a limited amount of space like in a bar and then I tried the same thing because finally getting this awesome shit out of our skulls was so amazing and off the chain that we couldn't stop getting stoked.

"Shit, bro! Shit! Shit!" Derek was like. "That is awesome, and it's awesome that we're roadtripping East—yo, we've never beasted it East together before; we're gonna light up Denver and figure out what the deal is with our crew, but we shouldn't give two fucks about that, 'cause we know how to *party* and have a solid *time* and we can make shit *wild*." Dude got all close to me and whispered like, "These fuckers up front, they suck. They're all uptight about shit and are just looking to get to the next place, and crash in some lame hotel, and then just try to get back to their stupid lame lives as fast as possible, never stopping to think of what an awesome time they could have. They act all like whiny bitches, stupid, weak, lame, and ball-less, and they're never gonna have a good time 'cause they'll be too busy worrying about bullshit and then making that bullshit into a party-suffocating boa constrictor that wraps tighter and tighter around them but they don't even notice it 'cause, and I'm being real here, they're such *bitches* and they're like trying not to get wild. They're always saying stuff like, 'Oh, no, I couldn't take another shot. I have work tomorrow. I'd love to stay and party, but it's getting very late and I have class in the morning. Me? Oh no, I don't particularly like beer . . .' Shit bro, you know what I'm spitting." Dude was all up in my face, trying to lay it down for me. He was crazy. He kept being all, "Fuck yeah! Fuck yeah! Fuck yeah!" in the back while the losers in the front were all pissed and annoyed and wished they wouldn't have picked up somebody so awesome. Shit was only getting started.

When we rolled in Sacramento we stayed at this Hilton Garden Inn and the gay dude got a room and invited me and Derek to chill with him, and Derek was totally fucking with this gay dude. It was hilarious but sorta homo. The gay dude was all saying like how he was glad he could chill with us 'cause we were cool or whatever, and then he started hinting like mad that he was a gay dude, which was already obvious from his car and whatever. Derek was all like, "Right on," and like messing with him and it seemed like this gay dude was totally into him. Then all super funny, Derek was like, "Let's hit some bars and look for chicks!" Just like that. The gay dude got all weird and awkward and just like checked his phone. We peaced out. Derek was like, "That was fucking hilarious! You see his face?" Now that the dude was all awkward he totally let us drive and we could haul some major ass.

We busted out of Sacramento and in a hot second were blasting through Nevada, totally rocking through the mountains so fast that the assholes in the back thought we were gonna bite it. We were in fucking charge now. Derek was stoked. Dude loved to drive. He tried to like reenact the opening scene in *Fast Five* where Paul Walker and that chick totally hijack Vin Diesel's prison bus. "The bus is like driving through the desert and the driver has no idea that some kind of shit it gonna go down, he's just like driving along. Then Paul Walker comes busting up and passes him but the driver thinks it's just some asshole driving fast. But then Paul Walker like throws on the brakes and spins that car around and then he just starts driving head-on toward the prison bus, like, like this . . ." and Derek totally swerved the Ford Focus directly in front of a truck coming the other way, and the truck started honking all like crazy and the idiots in the back started freaking the fuck out, and then Derek dodged it at the last second. "Like that, but dude straight-up took that prison bus down." I wasn't a pussy about it, Derek could drive. I swear to God, some of the idiots in back pissed themselves. They were afraid to say anything in case Derek went crazy. Dude kept hauling ass through the desert like that, reenacting awesome scenes from car movies, like how Nic Cage totally outguns the cops in that Shelby GT500 in *Gone in 60 Seconds* or like some of the awesome shit in *Transformers*, just like when it's just cars and not robots or whatever. We kept hauling ass through a bunch of shitty places in Nevada and by the time it started getting dark we were all up in Utah and could see Salt Lake City up ahead all glimmering with its stupid prude bullshit. I told Derek this funny-as-hell story about this time my buddy totally got his naked ass stuck in a dryer, and he didn't believe that shit but I showed him the video I took in my phone, with this dude pretty much naked and unable to get out of a dryer. Derek pounded his jacked-up bandaged hand on the steering wheel; the bandages were all starting to fall off like a mummy or something. "Fuck yeah, dude! That's hilarious! Fuck yeah! Fuck yeah!" Then dude pulled over like real fast and straight-up dropped a nap bomb. He was just totally chilling, all leaning against the door getting some mad rest.

The idiots in back were all pussed out. They were talking shit about my dude. "He's gonna kill us if he keeps driving like that. He's a total psychopath."

I wasn't gonna let that shit stand, so I laid it down. "Shut the fuck up. Dude is totally awesome and can drive better with just his dick than any of you could with both your hands, aight?"

"He's an asshole," the chick was like, being a total bitch. I was like, "Whatever," and just leaned back and dropped some nap bombs while Derek was getting his rest on. From the hill we were on you could like see Salt Lake City chilling out below and Derek noticed this lame, prude-as-fuck place he'd grown up in like forever ago.

"Dude, check it out, I was fucking born here, for real! Like all these losers just chill there and do their jobs and spend all their time not partying. You feel me? For real!" He was so stoked that I got stoked. How would we get wild? The idiot couple kept whining about driving. Whatever; we didn't give a shit. We chilled in the back and hit my flask. In a hot second those pussies got mad tired so Derek took back the wheel as we were rolling up in Colorado. We'd been going slow as fuck through some mountains in Utah and it was like days had passed. The idiots fell asleep. Derek flew fast as fuck toward Berthoud Pass, like way far away and mad tall, like where all the shit went down in *Clash of the Titans 3D*. He pulled some sick coasting shit—just like before, switching shit into neutral and just bobsledding it, leaving all these motherfuckers in the dust and just hugging the mountains like mad; then we could like see Denver chilling out below us—and shit was real.

The idiots were all pumped when we got out in Denver. We took our shit out and stacked it on the sidewalk; we still had to haul a bunch more ass. But whatever, we didn't give a fuck.

CHAPTER SIX

FACEBOOK APOLOGY MESSAGE

We had to figure out our deal up in Denver, and things were different this time 'cause we didn't have our deep crew. We could either chill and hang or get the fuck out.

Both of us were tired as fuck. We were taking a piss in the bathroom of an Outback and I was pissing in one urinal, then cut my stream and jumped over to another one, and was like, "Piss acrobatics!"

Derek was like, "Yeah, that shit's pretty funny, and I didn't know that you could just stop the flow like that with a little dick 'cause I always figured you needed a bigger dick because there's just like more room to stop the flow."

That shit pissed me off. "Little dick? My dick is like almost the same size as yours!"

"Yo chill, that's not what I meant, bro!"

"Fuck," I was like, "why you gotta talk shit about my dick size? My dick is totally above-average, and I can use it good as hell." We went back to our booth and the waitress threw down a Bloomin' Onion—usually Derek scarfed that shit down—and I was like, "Don't be some kind of homo asshole talking about my dick size." Then from nowhere Derek got like super pissed and just stormed out, like he was peacing out for good or something. Whatever, I was pissed; I wasn't gonna stand for that bullshit, so I let him know. But seeing that untouched Bloomin' Onion made me feel bad as hell. Maybe I was sort of a bitch—dude loves Bloomin' Onions—I've never seen him not eat a Bloomin' Onion. Aw fuck. But fucking whatever.

He just stood out there for like ever and then came back in. "Jesus Christ," I was like, "what the fuck were you doing out there, punching the fucking wall? Getting all pissed and making up more jokes about how I have a tiny dick?"

Dude looked all sad. "Naw dude, naw, dude, you don't get it. I don't know, it's like . . ."

"Just fucking spit it out dude." I stared at the Bloomin' Onion and wouldn't even look at him. I was pissed.

"I sent you an apology message on Facebook," he was like.

"Bullshit. You never apologize."

"What the fuck dude? Where do you get off thinking I never apologize?"

"You're too much of a douche to apologize." I felt like a total asshole saying all this shit. All the problems I had with my dude were on the table: I didn't even realize how mad pissed I was deep in my gut.

Derek was like, "Just check your phone."

I checked it and nothing was there. "It's bullshit."

"Just give it a second Sam, you know you have shitty data service." I totally did have shitty data service but I wanted to believe that he didn't send me an apology message but then I heard the notification ringtone from my phone and checked and he totally had sent me an apology message. I'd been mad wrong.

"Aw, shit, bro, my bad, I guess I was sorta a dick before. Sometimes I just get into dick mode. You know I get real sensitive about my dick size—it's like not that tiny but I worry about it. Don't tell anybody, but one time I tried these enhancement pills. Fuck, just forget it." The holy pimp noshed on his Bloomin' Onion. "I was joking about taking those pills! Seriously joking," I was like. "I was just joking about that shit so don't tell anybody. I can't have that shit getting around."

"Aight bro, Aight. Just take back saying that I'm a douche."

"I take it back, for real." The whole afternoon was this kind of bullshit bitch drama. Shit went down later when Derek and I crashed with the Sooner bros.

These were dudes from Oklahoma U that I chilled with when I was crewless in Denver before. The main dude had played linebacker for the Sooners and rolled out to Denver for Broncos training camp to try for the pros. He brought a bunch of his crew out to Denver so they could all party together once he was pulling mad NFL cash. After getting way too hammered one night the dude went to training camp and got a chance but was so fucking hungover that he blew it like mad. His dudes were real solid. One was trying to be an agent so he was interning for half the summer, but his chick Jenny was crashing at the place in Denver and she was like all wanting to be an actress or whatever; another dude was Jarvis and would say the funniest shit while we were all hanging around watching baseball, and then this other dude Louie was just the dumbest.

Dudes threw pretty sick parties. They just chilled and kept it real in their apartment and their landlord totally hated them because they were mad loud and threw their empties out the window. When it got dark you could see Denver from their window, all glowing like running lights on a tricked-out Range Rover, 'cause they had a pimped-out porch with a grill and a decent-sized hot tub where hotties basked in the early morning hours as parties wound down and kegs were emptied. Derek was pretty stoked at the scene and was pretty into Jenny, but I told that dude to fucking watch it and not step on a solid dude's slam piece, and Derek knew what was up. She was a totally solid chick and totally liked hanging with Derek 'cause she got wild and he got wild. She was all saying that Derek was sorta like her boyfriend. "Yeah, he has pretty cut arms too, just like you!"

So naturally we all ended up chilling at their place, slamming brews, cranking beats, and watching sports.

Shit started blowing up like a fucking blimp: The main dude—Frank-Rock, everybody called him—was gonna throw down on a new TV that he'd been talking about forever, and got a sick Best Buy gift card to increase his cash power. Derek took command getting the TV, 'cause he wished he had a huge sick TV to watch movies and sports on. Frank-Rock didn't know anything about contrast ratio or the difference between LED and

LCD or anything. But this dude refused to go baller once it was go time at Best Buy. Derek flipped out in the store and nearly ripped a fifty-inch plasma off the wall. "This shit is a fucking *steal* at fifteen hundred!" He was so pissed and thought Frank-Rock was being the biggest pusswad; he almost punched the dude in the face. "Fuck these stupid dickless pussies; some dudes are all talk; they'll just totally front like ballers, and then when it's trigger time, they grow big sandy vaginas and refuse to go baller— straight-up, that shit is the worst!"

Derek bounced back later that night after he got a text from his cousin Sean Brody saying he wanted to hang at some bar. Derek threw on a crisp party shirt and seemed pretty amped. "Aight Sam, here's the rundown on Sean—dude is my cousin." "Yo, speaking of, can your dad nab us Nuggets tix while we're in town?" "Aw dude, I tried to text him but I think he's traveling or something and the hotel he's staying at has real shitty service so I could try to e-mail him or something, but he's like never checking e-mail if it's not work, so you know. Aight, for real. Sean Brody and me were tight as fuck growing up and that dude is a hero. Dude would steal shot bottles of Bacardi from gas stations and one time he got in this fucking brutal fight with his brother and legit ripped off the end of his pinky. We got mad wild together. He was like the clutchest dude in my whole family. Now I'm gonna get to hang with him for the first time in like ever; dude is on break from grad school at Mizzou."

"Grad school? Sounds like a chach."

"No way dude, just wait'll you hang with him and hear the funny shit we did together—I've been getting wild for like ever, you know—and Sean has mad stories that I probably don't even remember 'cause I was young as fuck. I gotta hang with him, for real, I gotta!" This was like the third- or fourth-most amped I'd ever seen Derek. We chilled at this bar waiting for his cousin and hit on some chicks and did a couple Jäger bombs and whatever. Derek texted Maryann 'cause he saw on Facebook that she was gonna be in Denver around the same time. "Aw dude, back when

I was in middle school I would like post up on the corner right outside and try to get dudes to buy me beer; that dude down at the end of the bar, I swear to God bought me beer one time; I think he gave it to us for free like some kind of angel, and now like forever later we're totally chilling at the same bar and he has no idea what a fucking hero he is to me; isn't that shit crazy?"

Finally Sean rolled up, this lanky nerd-looking dude with glasses and pleated fucking khakis. Derek ordered three car bombs. "No thanks," Sean was like, "I quit drinking."

"WTF? WTF?" Derek texted me all stealth. "quit drnkng? fuck me wtf" Seemed like Sean thought Derek was kind of an asshole. We got in his shitty Elantra and Sean started being a huge dick to Derek.

"Okay, Derek, I don't want to go drinking with you or hang out or anything. I'm only here because you are really starting to embarrass me by posting all that crap on Facebook and sending me texts and everything. I'm not that kind of idiot anymore and I need you to stop it immediately." I looked over at Derek. Dude was crazy bummed.

"Aight, aight," he was like. His cousin kept hauling us around and even threw down for some burritos. Derek kept trying to get him to spit stories about partying back in the day and his cousin would start to talk and Derek would get pumped but the cousin didn't really give a shit. Like, how did this dude turn so lame? Derek's cousin dropped us by the dim lights of a lame sports bar. He made Derek promise not to text him or try to re-friend him on Facebook and busted out. It sucked that that dude had been such a dick to Derek and didn't get how awesome he was.

I was like, "No homo, but I think you're a solid dude. Sorry I was sorta a dick to you before about the dick stuff."

"Aight, bro, it's all good," Derek was like. We tried to hang at this lame sports bar. There were like no HDTVs, no darts, no draft specials, no wings, and the TVs weren't even playing sports. Ugly chicks hung together and danced all gross to the shitty music rising from the TouchTunes. Derek was wearing distressed Diesels and a Hardy tee and was definitely looking like the rawest dude in the place. One asshole who was still wearing his bicycle helmet was talking all loud about stupid shit on his cell phone. But there was this one crazy hot Mexican chick, short as fuck, almost to the point of being gross, but still with a mad rack and smoking face, and she was talking to the chicks saying like, "I'm gonna text Gonzalez and see if he can give us a ride." Derek was wanting to smash with her like crazy. He was totally bonering out over her. "Dude, she is hot, so hot . . ." He made me come with him and like stalk her after she left the bar. He kept pretending to be like texting or talking on his phone but was totally watching her. I tried to spit some game at a couple of her friends but they were bitches. Some dude, probably Gonzalez, rolled up in a shitty van and picked them up. Derek just stood there, all crazy. "Aw fuck, I thought my nut was gonna explode."

"Why the fuck did you puss out?"

"Aw dude, you know . . ." We went and nabbed a case of Natties and rolled up to Frank-Rock's crib to hang. We hitched some rides hauling the case. Jenny, Frank-Rock's buddy's slam piece, was mad hot and cool as hell. She had crazy nice legs that were like a supermodel or something walking all fine. Derek chilled in a recliner kicking back Natties and was like, "Fuck yeah, fuck yeah." Jenny knew dude was into her; she knew all dudes were into her. Earlier in the summer I had totally tried to hook up with her, but I couldn't do that to Frank-Rock's buddy.

CHAPTER SEVEN

BANGING THIS RICH CHICK

The rest of the night was pretty boring so we just crashed out. Shit got XL crazy the day after. Derek and I just chilled and cruised around Denver for a little and grabbed some food and some morning brews. We started heading back for Frank-Rock's place, but Derek totally bolted into a Dick's Sporting Goods and walked out with a bunch of energy gel like no big deal. Nobody even noticed. We were pretty tired, so we pounded the energy gel while we walked. "We'll get amped up pretty soon."

This rich chick I'd been hooking up with gave me a big-ass bottle of Johnny Walker Black. We threw that shit back at Frank-Rock's. There was this hottie that lived in the condo across from the porch and Derek had been trying to hit that for days. Shit got ugly. He kept flashing his iPhone at her window and showing his abs and I guess she wasn't feeling it. We were all chilling inside drinking some J-Dubs when like all of a sudden we saw this crew of dudes rolling up to the apartment. Derek ran in. "Aw shit dudes, I think her family is all pissed at me 'cause I was flashing abs too much."

"What the fuck? What do they want?"

"I think they wanna beat my ass. Whatever." Derek was hammered and didn't give a fuck. We went outside and posted up at the end of the building's courtyard. A bunch of dudes were coming up.

"That's the dude!" one of them said.

"Whoa, everybody chill," I was like. "What's the problem?"

The chick's dad was all holding a baseball bat and looking real pissed. "Your jackass friend has been bothering my daughter. I'm not gonna get the cops involved in this. If he bothers my daughter again I'm gonna take him out with this bat." The rest of the dudes were looking all ready to beat ass too. I was pretty drunk so I didn't really give a fuck, so I threw down.

I was like, "Look, motherfuckers, step the fuck off. That's my dude and if you wanna fuck with him, you're gonna fuck with me. Put away your fucking bat and get the fuck out."

"I swear to God I'll get him next time!" the dad was like. "He bothers her one more time and it's all over."

"Bullshit; you got nothing. Now get the fuck out." Derek was mad pissed. He was trying to text that chick. I was ripped enough that all these assholes knew I'd totally mess them up if they stepped. Derek and I went back inside.

"Fuck yeah dude!" he was like. "Let's get hammered!" We headed back to Frank-Rock and his dudes. Shit got weird and Derek got all pissed about something and threw down Frank-Rock's signed Elway football and shattered the glass case: The football was still all right. Derek didn't give a shit about Elway and thought he was overrated, but Frank-Rock fucking idolized Elway. Frank-Rock was mad pissed but I told him to throw a Natty can into Derek's nuts. Dude did it hard. Derek doubled over, in mad pain. Everybody cracked up. It was hilarious. Frank-Rock wanted to show us this hilarious scene from *Cedar Rapids* he kept talking about. "Fuck!" Derek was like. "If you would have bought that fucking TV it would have had Netflix Instant pre-installed and we could just watch that shit now!"

"That TV was bullshit!" Frank-Rock was like. Blah blah blah, and whatever stupid drama. Countless boring minutes ticked by as Frank-Rock searched for *Cedar Rapids* clips on YouTube from his shitty gray Dell laptop; there was no way he'd find them, 'cause of copyright and whatever. I was getting bored as fuck; I checked my phone a bunch and played a couple rounds of *Angry Birds*. Frank-Rock hollered at a cab to come grab us and take us to a bar and while we were waiting I got some texts from the rich chick I was banging. She had this older bitch cousin who thought I was a dick, and earlier that day I'd sent a Facebook

message to Old Brad Lewis, who was all up in Mexico City, telling him the funny shit going down with Derek and how blasted
we were getting. I was like, "I'm banging this rich chick who
totally gives me booze and some fat wads."

Like a total idiot, I was using Facebook while hammered
and totally posted it as a status update instead of a message. The
bitch cousin totally saw it and showed it to my rich chick as proof
of what a dick I was. So now my rich chick was texting me all
pissed and saying we weren't gonna smash anymore. The bitch
cousin started texting me at the same time all cocky and shit.
The cab pulled up and everybody was jumping in and Derek was
high-fiving with Frank-Rock and I texted back some mad nasty
shit about what bitches they were and what a shitty lay she was,
and like a total badass I told them both to go fuck themselves,
pocketed my iPhone and jumped into the cab to go get more
hammered.

Our crew rolled out of the cab at this country western
bar, a pretty hilarious place near the freeway, and started inhal-
ing shots. We were getting mad sloppy, and to make things even
sloppier there was this drunk dude at the bar who got all up in
Derek's face, and Derek flipped out from this dude's bullshit and
ran out and stole a shitton of energy gel from the store next door
then ran another block down and stole an even bigger box of that
shit. I looked out the window of the bar and saw sirens all flashing by the store and all these cops talking to the cashier about
the stolen goods. "Some jackass has been lifting energy gel all
over the place!" the cop was like. Derek just walked past the cops
checking his phone. The cops kept talking to the cashier. Derek
strutted into the bar and went shot-for-shot with this little dude
at his bachelor party. "Yo, come on, just five more Jägers!" Derek
hollered at him. "Dudes, I'm gonna steal a case of Natty and
we can get hammered for free and chill with Theo" (the little
dude) "and play mad beer pong." Dude peaced out. Then this
cop came in and was asking if anybody knew anything about the
stolen energy gel. Nobody knew shit. Out the window I saw

Derek sprint into a liquor store like a fucking ninja. In a hot
second he was back with a case of Keystone. "This is gonna be
better than the Natty," he was like. "The Natty cases were sorta
warm and I thought it might be skunky—I was like 'fuck that
shit' and grabbed the case of Keystone. I already pounded one.
Let's do it bros, let's pound this case." Dude was showing off all
his hard-ass criminal shit by jacking energy gel and Keystone. He
was sweaty and stoked and amped.

"Dude, the cops are getting all up on your ass."

"Fuck that, bro! Theo's gonna throw down with me, right,
bad-ass Theo?" Then Theo—who was a pretty little dude and probably had a low-ass alcohol tolerance—faceplanted onto the floor
and just made this like moaning noise, and then started to wretch
and beasted it to the bathroom to chunk it. Derek was pissed. Dude
grabbed his Keystone case and peaced out. Frank-Rock and I were
over that shit and called a cab. As the taxi drove us down the infi-
nitely awesome bars of Alameda Boulevard where I'd wished I'd
been partying for the past couple months, chugging and grinding
and pounding late-night burritos and booty calling slam pieces one
after another on my iPhone, Derek came from like nowhere on a
fucking stolen Vespa and started honking the horn and swerving
toward the cab. The taxi driver looked scared as fuck.

"It's cool, I know that dude," I was like. Derek got pissed
that the cabbie wouldn't high-five him out the window and
blasted off past us at a speed that was crazy fast for a Vespa, looking pretty hilarious on that stupid bike. Dude went down Frank-
Rock's street and pulled up in front; then like crazy he bolted off,
pulled a u-ey, and almost crashed into us while we were getting
out of the cab. We stood around waiting for him to come back and
he totally rolled up in the Vespa holding somebody's mailbox,
and like a crazy motherfucker, screeched to stop, drunk-rolled
into the house, and fell asleep like whoa. Dude just left a stolen
Vespa and a mailbox in plain sight in front of the apartment.

I needed to wake that dude up; the Vespa was a piece of shit
and I couldn't get it to start so I could hide it somewhere else.

Derek threw up real quick then went outside in just his boxer-briefs, and we both loaded on to the Vespa, which looked mad stupid, and hauled ass down the block until the Vespa totally bit it and wouldn't fucking drive anymore. "Shit's toasted," Derek was like and got off and just started walking back to Frank-Rock's place, like a half mile away, just in his underwear in the middle of the fucking night. We rolled up to the apartment and dude crashed out again. Shit was mad sloppy, Denver and everything, my rich slam piece, that Vespa, the Elway football, Frank-Rock, his place was mad fucked with all the partying, and I just wanted to drop some sleep. I kept getting Facebook notifications that kept me up forever trying to write back but getting like really sketch-ass service. The service in this part of the country, like it was in Wyoming, is shitty as hell and makes you crazy mad like a dude who just wants to hook up with a chick but always gets cockblocked by some assholes, 'cause like you're so close to being able to post a status update but you just can't. I just tried to send a couple, and luckily when I held the phone over the TV two great white bars appeared on the phone and my funny-ass status updates flew over the land from Denver across to all my crew in the Midwest.

CHAPTER EIGHT

A KEG OF SPARKS

We were hungover as fuck the next day. Derek got up and walked to the busted Vespa to see if he could still ride that shit. I was like, "Fuck that," but dude still went. He came back all scared and shit. "Fuck dude, somebody grabbed the Vespa and if it was the fucking cops they're gonna be all up on my ass 'cause they have my prints from when I got caught stealing a forty-pack of Magnums a while back. Shit dude, I was just trying to have a good time, aight? Fuck, we're gonna get mad busted if we don't get the hell out of here stat."

"Aight dude," I was like, and we packed our shit fast as hell. With my North Face bag still unzipped we said peace out to Frank-Rock and his dudes and went to the road where nobody would give a shit about the Vespas or condoms Derek stole. Jenny was all bummed to see us, or just me, peace out—I'm pretty sure she was still all wanting to smash with us, and I told her to hit me up if she was in Columbus.

"Derek has such a good bod," she was like. "Totally like my boyfriend. Except better arms. I hope he bulks up his arms like that."

I high-fived Louie, who was already hammered, and might have totally shat himself. We peaced out mad fast, early on Sunday, and we strutted away with all our shit. We hauled ass. We were mad scared that a cop car would drive up and bust us.

"For real, if the hot chick's dad with the baseball bat saw me jack that Vespa, we're fucked," Derek was like. "We gotta nab like a taxi or something and get the hell out of here." We were trying to call a cab, but our service fucking sucked. We felt like any second shit would hit the fan; the cops would check out the

Vespa and link it to Derek. We finally got some service and called a cab, but no cab came. We kept hauling ass. Cars started passing by, we were mad scared one would be a cop car. I saw this car that totally looked like a cop car and I was sure we were fucked and my parents would be crazy pissed and my dad would have to pull mad strings to keep it from sticking on my record. But the cop car totally turned out to be the taxi, and everything was all good.

We checked Craigslist on my phone and found a fucking bombass deal; this dude needed somebody to drive his beamer to Chicago. He was like moving there but had to fly out early or something. He just wanted some ID and for the car to get there all safe and shit. I gave him my ID. I told him shit would be totally cool. I was like to Derek, "Don't fuck this ride up, dude." Derek was mad stoked to drive that shit. We were gonna grab it in like an hour. We chilled on the grass near the Irish pub where I had chilled with some dudes a few summers ago after banging Tina Bellingfort, and I dropped an outdoor nap bomb with my headphones on playing Kanye. I totally ended up having crazy Kanye dreams. Derek scoped shit out. He spat game at this hottie who worked at Subway, said they could cruise together in the beamer, and woke my ass up to tell me about it. I was cool. It was all good.

We got the beamer and Derek grabbed it and immediately busted out "to get gas." We'd run into these two assholes from UConn and agreed to give them a ride for gas money. They wanted to know where the fuck Derek took off to with the car.

"Dude's just getting gas. It's all good." I went to the end of the block and saw Derek drive over to the Subway and wait there for the hottie, who had changed out of her Subway uniform; I could see her walk out and she looked fine as hell, and I wanted to party with them. She jumped in the beamer and they busted out. I went back and told the UConn assholes that shit was cool. I saw Derek haul ass through downtown with the hottie in the front seat, telling her funny stories and totally copping a feel after hanging out for only like five seconds. He took her to this alley and parked behind a Bally's where he used to work, and he totally boned her like in no time; she was all into him and he told her to come out to Columbus after she got her Subway paycheck and party at Ivan McQueen's crib. She was into that; her name was Becky or something. Derek finished boning, booted her out at the Subway, copped a feel, made out, and rolled up to where I was waiting with the UConn assholes.

"Where the hell have you been?" one of the assholes was like. "I thought maybe you ditched us."

"Chill the fuck out," I was like, "shit is cool"—I tried to convince them shit was cool because Derek was going fucking crazy. He chilled out for a little and even helped the assholes put their stupid suitcases in the car. The assholes had barely sat down, and I had barely opened my flask, before Derek gunned that shit, the engine roaring like a fucking eagle on crack. A couple miles later, I swear to God the speedometer busted 'cause Derek was rocking that shit so fast.

"Whatever, speedometers are for pussies anyway. I'm just gonna rock this whip as fast as I can." The ride was mad smooth so we didn't even think we were going that fast but we left all the motherfuckers on the road in the dust like crazy while we hauled ass up toward Greely. "I'm gonna take us to the Northeast 'cause, for real, we gotta hang with Aaron Wahl in Sterling, you gotta see this sweet-ass timeshare he has and this whip is mad fast so we like won't lose any time and can roll up to Chicago with plenty of time." Aight, it sounded like a plan. It started raining sorta hard but Derek kept hauling ass like crazy. It was a real sick BMW, like when they were mad clutch in the '90s, before they got sorta mass produced for pussies, all blue and with rims and a real sick sound system. The UConn assholes—Husky pussies—chilled in the back, and they would have totally shat themselves if they knew how fast as fuck we were going. They wanted to shoot the shit but Derek ignored them and downed a 5-Hour Energy and stayed amped. "That Becky chick is mad hot—we're gonna bone in Columbus—we're gonna bone like crazy once I dump Carly's ass for good—shit is awesome, Sam, we're fucking doing it. Fuck yeah!" I was stoked to be getting the fuck out of Denver, and we were getting the fuck out crazy fast. Shit got dark as we hauled ass down this little road that led to Aaron Wahl's timeshare in the middle of nowhere. It kept raining like a bitch and the road was crazy slick and Derek took it at like seventy, and I told him to chill the fuck out or we'd totally spin out, but dude was like, "Chill out, I got this."

"Fuck no," I was like. "You're gonna fuck this shit up and it's on my ID." He kept hauling ass like crazy on the mud and right after I told him that shit the road made a sharp left and Derek tried to drift that shit but he totally fucked up and the car fishtailed like crazy.

"Fuck me!" Derek was like, but didn't really give a shit about the car and tried to keep it going straight, and we spun like a motherfucker into a ditch. Shit got quiet. Cell phones didn't work out here. There wasn't anything anywhere. We'd passed like a gas station like ten minutes ago. I was crazy mad pissed at Derek and kept yelling like crazy. Dude kept fucking silent and went to the gas station in the rain to try to get some help.

"Are you guys brothers?" one of the UConn assholes asked. "He drives like a real dickhole, right? I bet he barely gets half the tail he talks about."

"He is sorta a dick," I was like, "but he's my bro, and he gets legit tail." Derek came back to the car with some farmer dude who agreed to help. He hooked up some chains from his tractor and pulled our shit out. The beamer was fucked-looking, all muddy and dented like hell. Greedy asshole wanted like fifty bucks for helping us. He had some hottie daughters that were checking us out from a distance. The hottest one was like standing half behind this tree but still the rain was getting on her so her top was kinda see-through and I swear to fucking Christ she was like for real the hottest chick that Derek and I had like ever scoped out.

She was sorta young looking, but I don't think she was like jailbait or anything, and she was mad thin but not like too tall, with her Forever 21 top clinging like crazy all up on her. With every chance I got, I flashed my abs. She stared at them with the crazy fascination of all the chicks across the American plains who've seen the ripples of my abs like waves, super muscular waves. She blushed with hotness.

I paid the farmer his fifty fucking bucks, flashed my abs at the prairie hottie one more time, and rolled out, keeping it more chill, 'till Derek got amped as we got close to Aaron Wahl's crib. "Shit dude, that chick was like scary-hot," I was like. "I'd like take a bullet in the nut to get to bone her for a while, and I'd go gay if she wasn't the best lay ever." The UConn assholes laughed at me. They were totally lame and total East Coast d-bags who talked a big game but didn't do shit to prove it and just sat on their tiny dicks drinking wine coolers. Derek and I didn't give a fuck about them. As we drove around this nice-ass lake Derek talked about chilling out here on spring break; he showed us this big-ass rock that he'd dive off and almost break his fucking neck, and these trees behind which he'd laid mad tail right near Aaron's place, which was pretty fucking nice; and where Gary Wahl, Aarons's brother, would run totally naked and drunk through the fields to fuck with all these geese hanging around, all like, "I'ma get you geese! I'ma get you!" "That dude cut his dick on a tree one time," Derek was like. "He didn't give a fuck. If somebody spilled a beer he'd get down on all fours and suck it off the ground. Had to suck down every drop to get as hammered as possible. A total shitshow. I gotta show you this picture of him asleep with his ass in the oven. I'd party here when I wanted a real awesome time. I was getting hammered here when I first posted those Facebook status updates that Chaz Kerry reshared to you." We turned left and started going up the long-ass driveway. A dude was totally passed out against a tree. "Oh shit! Tommy D! He's totally blacked out. We should fucking honk the horn and scare his ass! Fuck yeah!" We pulled up real slow to him and laid on the horn, and dude shot up like it was a nuclear fucking bomb, then saw it was Derek and got mad pissed, but then crashed back out and drifted off on the waves of crunkness. Then we saw the lights of Wahl's timeshare. Around the whole house was the awesome roar of a keg party in the middle of nowhere.

The sheer fucking scale of the keg parties in the plains is totally mind-blowing to a Midwest dude. There was like no end to the chicks, no end to the kegs, no bullshit at all except maybe a couple chaches chilling by a tree. The party that wrapped around the house and into the fields was a badass expanse of awesome that wouldn't stop rocking 'till sunrise. After we texted Aaron, who was making out with some chick by the lake, I strutted through the crowd, like maybe halfway in and then I couldn't move. The crowd was fucking crazy. Wahl told me they got a keg of Sparks, which I didn't think was fucking possible. He was a dude like our age, but dropped out of school, 'cause he got a mad inheritance when his dad kicked it. Him and Derek would post up at bars and scope chicks together. He seemed like an all-right dude and took us up to his room, which was sorta like a VIP room with shots and hot chicks, and was like, "Derek, what the fuck did you do to your thumb?"

"I punched this fucking toaster oven and shit got messy so the motherfuckers chopped a piece of it off."

"Why the shit did you fight a toaster oven?" He totally thought Derek was a dumbass. He checked his phone; he was getting mad text messages. "That's like such a classic you move."

Then his girlfriend brought over some pizza they'd ordered earlier. She thought it was sorta gross 'cause it had so much sausage on it: "I can't eat that meat lover's bullshit." But I fucking love meat lover's pizza. We ate like psychos; sausage flew everywhere as we ate like six pieces each. Wahl's chick was pretty hot but like all chicks that are with dudes who party all the time she sorta bitched about it. She kept telling us about all the people who had thrown up on their bed. Aaron Wahl just kept checking his phone. Derek kept housing pizza. He tried to get Aaron to believe that we had totally stolen the beamer and were like badasses on the run. Aaron didn't give a shit. Every time it sounded like cops were rolling up to the house he ran to the window to see if the party was getting broken up.

"You dudes gonna get wild in Columbus?" Even though he lived in the middle of nowhere, he thought Columbus was bullshit. That was bullshit. Aaron Wahl was a douche who thought Derek was a douche just like fucking Sean Brody—he like barely looked up from his phone to talk to us. Back in the day, he and Derek had gotten crazy fucking drunk all over the plains and chugged forties when the bars closed, but now he was a dick.

Derek checked his phone. "Aight, aight, we should peace out 'cause we gotta party in Chicago tomorrow and this is sorta gay." The UConn assholes thought Wahl was all cool and high-fived him and we peaced out. I turned and watched the keg party fade into the darkness. Fuck that shit.

CHAPTER NINE

A BEAMER FULL OF PLAYERS

In a hot second we were hauling ass down the interstate and Nebraska flew by fast as fuck in the night. We beasted it at like 110 down the highway, smooth as hell, no other cars, no cops, just a sick ride under the badass stars.

I was chill as hell; it was no biggie to rock it at 110 and chill and hit the flask and blow through all the bullshit towns— Ogallala, Gothenburg, some other shit, and some more other shit—so crazy fast it felt like we were hammered but we were just buzzed. The beamer was a sick whip; it held the road like I hold my liquor. It was like boning the road. "Shit dude, what a ride," Derek was like. "What if we had a sick whip like this, what could we get up to? Dude, you can drive down to Mexico and like get to the Poco easy as hell. We could just ride that shit like into South America and Brazil where chicks are hotter than anything and everybody is always partying! Fuck yeah! You and me, bro, we'd get hammered across the motherfucking planet in a whip like this 'cause, dude, our party can't be fucking contained. Can't stop this shit—you know? And dude, we gonna blow the fucking top off Chi-town in this piece! For real, Sam, this is gonna be my first time partying in Chicago, for real."

"We'll be total ballers in this rig!"

"Fuck yeah! And bitches! Bitches are gonna flock to this, on the real, I'm gonna gun this as fast as fuck so we can have more time cruising for bitches. Just chill and I'll take this shit like space-shuttle-fast."

"How fast are we going now?"

"Like 110 or something—it's still smooth as fuck. We'll obliterate Iowa tomorrow and then get our shit all up in Illinois in a hot second." The UConn assholes conked out and we shot the shit for a while.

I couldn't believe how Derek could be such a dickhole one second and then be like a totally solid dude—probably 'cause he had a sick whip to drive, parties to get to, and chicks to lay—just like that and no big deal. "I sorta flip into douche mode when I'm in Denver—that shit has gotten to be bad news. Denver Derek is a dickhole! Fuck me!" I spat stories about partying on this same road before. Derek had partied on it too. "Yo, back in high school, when I was like seventeen, I hauled ass out to Indianapolis to see the Broncos take on the Colts, which is always a pretty awesome fucking game. I rolled out in my dad's Range Rover and I knew I had to get a better fake ID 'cause the one I had was like from Hawaii and looked seriously stupid so I tried to call up this dude I knew in Nebraska to try to score a more legit ID. Dude hooked me up and as I went barhopping with this fake, this one cop saw me and thought I was way too young to be getting into bars and got all up in my face when I tried to buy some beer at a Conoco. He scanned my ID and it didn't fucking work and he totally took me back to the station where I had to wait with this real sketchy dude who was probably some kind of perv or something 'cause he looked like a total, total creep. The fucking cop interrogated me like I was some kind of criminal or something and kept threatening to call my dad or throw me in jail or whatever, but then I totally laid out some bullshit about how my dad knew the police chief and I could like get him totally fired and he shouldn't fuck with me 'cause I can totally end him and whatever, and dude pussed out and let me off. That motherfucker made me miss kickoff. I made the same trip a month later to see ASU take on Notre Dame—no bullshit cops this time and, bro, my dad like suspended the credit card on the way there so I couldn't buy any grub so I just like hit parties and raided fridges whenever I wasn't scoping tail. I will do fucking anything to check out a Sun Devils game."

I wanted to know what the shit he got up to in LA a couple years ago. "I started hooking up with this bitch at ASU, like the worst bitch I have ever hooked up with. I needed to drop that shit and drop it hot, for real; you know what I'm spitting. We were at a club, aight, and I just needed to get out of there, before I got drunk and started grinding and couldn't stop myself from boning. Another week of hanging with this bitch staring me in the face, I needed to get the fuck out of that club and get the fuck away from ASU for a while. I totally switched my shirt with my buddy so she wouldn't see me and took off, rolling up to LA in a couple of days where I was gonna crash with my buddy and wash the bitch off me, with some totally hot chicks who were chill as fuck and didn't pull all those bitch moves like needing to call me and whatever 'cause these chicks just wanted to party, and shit went down when my buddy Bentley and I were rolling down Hollywood Boulevard with some hotties and I told dude to take the wheel for a hot second while I got some make-out action from my hottie—'cause I was driving—but dude didn't hear me 'cause he was listening to his iPhone so we went off the road and totally smashed into this pole and I totally busted my nose up on the steering wheel. You know how my nose is all like Owen Wilson and whatever—sorta fucked up but still cool. Then I peaced out of LA and took my shit up to Denver where Maryann and me smashed for like the first time ever. Shit bro, she was all like finishing high school and just chilling in a Cosi and totally begging to be railed. After a couple Cosi lunches where I loosened her up we camped out in an Econolodge and we beasted for like ever in the third-floor corner room, the hottest most banged-in room in any Econolodge in America, I swear to Christ—dude bro, she was so fucking *bangable* then, you know, fuck yeah! Oh shit dude, there's a bunch of dudes in Nuggets gear, you know?" he was like, and checked those dudes. "Shit, my dad never texts me back about nailing Nuggets tix. What's his deal?" We kept hauling ass. Somewhere back where we'd been partying or where we were gonna be partying in the badass night his dad was probably chilling like a baller, for real— martini in his hand, bitches on his lap, cash all up in his wallet, and probably like a bunch of hotties all in his in-room hot tub stripping down for him.

I pounded knucks with Derek. "For real, bro, shit's gonna get wild now." Dude was gonna chill for real all up in Columbus. He was stoked. Shit was gonna be raw.

"Fuck, Sam, once we're all up in Columbus we're gonna eat Skyline Chili and get full as fuck. Fuck yeah, let's roll, let's roll!" The sick whip went fast; it blasted us through like a motherfucking rocket ship; it like tore the shit out of the road—the sickest whip. I opened my flask and drained it down; I was getting mad buzzed. Derek's jacked-up forearms strangled the steering wheel like he was trying to murder it.

"What's up with you?"

"Aw you know, you know, like the usual shit—thinkin' 'bout bitches."

I dropped some nap bombs and woke up in the middle of the boring scene of a bullshit morning in Iowa, and Derek was still hauling ass just as hard as last night; dude clung to curves at like eighty and pounded out the straightaways at like 110, but sometimes there'd be traffic and dude would have to crank it down to sixty. As soon as a window opened up, dude gunned that whip and passed like a million cars at once and totally blew past them. This idiot in a fucking Prius saw us blow past and like tried to race us. Just as Derek was gonna pass some dude, this idiot like blew by and cut him off and like flicked us off to try to piss us off. We weren't gonna get shit handed to us by a fucking Prius. "Check it," Derek was like, "I'll hustle this motherfucker for a little. Shit is gonna be awesome." Dude played dead so the Prius got out in front but then Derek gunned that shit and got right up to this idiot. Prius was pissed; he couldn't get it past a hundo. We saw the motherfucker through the window. He looked like a total lame-ass Chicago hipster riding with some chick who was mad ugly and like probably wrote poetry or some shit. Who the fuck knows how he could stand banging a bitch that busted, but dude kept hauling ass. He had a stupid fucking moustache, a total hipster from like the West Side of Chicago; he had those big stupid glasses. Dude must have thought that if he could race some raw dudes like us it would somehow make him more awesome, which was totally impossible, 'cause that dude was such an asshole. He was just an idiot. He totally almost crashed out a bunch of times trying so hard to beat us; he almost nailed a tree and kept doing dumbass passes on the shoulder, which are mad stupid and cheap. We fucked with this asshole for like eighty miles; I could not believe he cranked his Prius like that. Finally the hipster idiot gave up, like a bitch, probably 'cause his busted girlfriend was pissed, and we hauled ass past him and gave him the finger. We rode that whip; Derek had ripped his shirt off; I was pretty crunked from my flask, and the UConn assholes were crashed out. We noshed down some waffles at Denny's as my phone blew up with texts. Then we peaced out.

"Derek, you gotta chill out some 'cause it's light."

"Chill the fuck out dude, I got this shit." I knew this shit was dumb. Derek got all up on other cars like it was his job. For real he almost crashed into them trying to pass. He got all up in their grills, he almost scuffed bumpers as he swung it around corners, then he'd gun it like mad and pass the motherfuckers and almost totally bite it on cars in the other lane. Shit was getting crazy dumb. The roads were curvier and way more dicey, and when we were finally on a straightaway Derek jammed it at 110 and a whole bunch of shit I'd seen before flew by—a bunch of bullshit towns where I'd been stuck with that idiot Teddy forever. Everything I knew was flying by and I was mad scared that we were gonna bite it and get smashed into paste in bumfuck Iowa and never live to party, chug, or bone again. I felt sorta carsick.

"Fuck, dude, I'm gonna drop some nap bombs. This shit is dumb, for real."

"Pussy!" Derek was like and blew past this car mega-fast, fishtailed for a second, and kept hauling ass. I climbed in the back and dropped nap bombs. A UConn asshole climbed up front 'cause I told him to. Mad terrors that my awesome life was gonna be toasted filled my skull and I tried to just chill and pass out. When I was at parties I used to feel like an invincible god, with all the kegs and hotties laid out before me like a great rolling sea—now all I could think about was crashing into something and getting crippled so bad that my dick wouldn't even work again; all because Derek was such a fucking crazy douche driver. I tried to drop a nap bomb and just imagined getting totally busted and losing my dick. That would be so fucking lame. For real. I tried to chill. Derek kept hauling ass; dude wasn't gonna drop a nap bomb 'till we rolled up in Chi-town. We hit Des Moines like a couple hours later. There was a bunch of traffic so we had to go slower so I hopped back in front. Then we got in a totally stupid accident. This fat-ass was driving a Sienna with his whole family in front of us; he had like some cheap-ass bike rack on the back that he like probably bought at fucking Wal-Mart. The fatass slammed on the brakes and Derek was checking his phone so he didn't see that shit 'till too late, so we totally rammed the dude at like five MPH and kinda bent his bike rack. Shit-all else happened; just like a ding on the bumper or whatever. Derek and I got out of the car and got ready to fight the dude. It was pretty chill though and we just exchanged info and we didn't even have to beat ass, and the fat-ass somehow had like this smokeshow wife with like mad tits that Derek totally scoped. "Fuck yeah, fuck yeah." The fat dude took some pictures of the bumper with his phone and we peaced out.

A little later this cop came up from nowhere all blasting his siren at us and whatever. "What the fuck?"

This jerkhole came up to our window. "Did you just get into an accident across town?"

"Dude, we just dinged up some dude's shitty bike rack 'cause he slammed on the brakes."

"He said it was a hit-and-run and this car is stolen." We couldn't believe that fat fuck had totally acted like an asshole. It was sorta hilarious thinking about him whining to the cops through his fat face. We spent like forever trying to get a hold of the dude who owned the car. I kept trying to call him on my phone. Finally he picked up and I put him on with the cop. He was all like, "It's my car but I don't know what else these guys have done."

The cop was like, "They just got into an accident in Des Moines."

"I know—I mean that I don't know what kind of stuff these guys have been up to in the past."

Shit was fine and we hauled ass out of there. We rolled through Newton, Iowa, where I'd been pretty bored before. Then we blew through lame-ass Davenport and the stupid Mississippi; then Rock Island and all that other shit I'd seen before and had been pretty lame and I didn't really give a shit about seeing again. Shit started to look all Midwestern, with less desert shit and more Meijers and Waffle Houses. Illinois flew by fast as fuck like a laser or something as Derek kept hauling like crazy. Dude was getting sick of driving and was being even more of an insane motherfucker than before. We almost bit it trying to pull into Wendy's to grab some grub. There were like two cars trying to pull out of the parking lot and this other car driving down the frontage road in the other direction. There was no way to get into the parking lot without just waiting a hot second. But Derek kept hauling ass fast as hell toward the Wendy's and then cut the wheel fast as fuck, barely missed the car coming the other way and totally skidded up on the grass to the side of the driveway, almost nailed the sign advertising the Spicy Baconator, cut the wheel back, almost drifted into one of the cars pulling out, cut it again, busted over the curb and into the parking lot, slammed on the brakes, and screeched into a parking space, all in like two seconds and managed to just leave some tire tracks in the grass instead of like murdering us and everybody trying to get in and out of the Wendy's that day. I kept thinking about how we almost died trying to get a Frosty. We went through the drive-through and I dropped some more nap bombs.

The UConn assholes dropped some nap bombs too and Derek was like obsessed with rolling into Chicago before shit got dark. Outside a Speedway we picked up a couple of scruffy dudes who could front some gas money. Like a second before they'd just been chilling by a Speedway eating jerky and now they were all up in a pimped-out beamer going fast as fuck toward Chicago. One of the dudes just like stared at the road and looked scared as fuck, for real. "Shit," they were like, "it's like a motherfucking plane." We busted through small Illinois towns that had never seen such ballers before: A bunch of dudes in a sick ride, hauling ass, Derek not wearing a shirt and looking all jacked, me slamming a flask in the back seat—just like total pimps on their way to blow the shit out of Chicago, a beamer full of players set loose on America to get the party started. We grabbed some hot dogs at a travel plaza and people stared at us but they didn't give us any shit 'cause they knew we were for real. Derek didn't even put on his shirt in the travel plaza and just threw some cash at the chick behind the counter, grabbed the hot dogs, and we blew out of there. Shit started to get a little dark as we tore through Naperville, and we saw the sick lights of Chicago up ahead. We'd hauled ass from Denver to Chicago, which is pretty fucking far, in like seventeen hours, without the bullshit time with like cops or stuck in a ditch or at Aaron Wahl's stupid fucking party, hella-fucking fast, all with Derek driving the whole time. Which is pretty fucking awesome.

CHAPTER TEN

CAGE CHUGS

Bad-ass Chi-town sprawled before us like an ice-cold six-pack. We were all up on Clark Street hanging in hordes of hotties, some were standing by the curb, yelling at their douche-bag boyfriends, and others were adjusting their short shorts as they waited to get in to John Barleycorn. "Oh shit bro! Maybe Derek Morrisey's gonna get himself an apartment in this shit and move to like the epicenter of the party." The scruffy dudes got out and we rolled up to Wrigley Field. Pumping beats, the stank of beer, dudes pissing on the sidewalk all as the great red sign of Wrigley Field shined down on us with its thousands of tiny lights each announcing the upcoming free bobblehead day sponsored by Chase. "For real, Wrigley Field is tight, Sam! Fuck yeah!" We had to stash the beamer somewhere so we could start getting our party on foot. We stuck it in some expensive-ass lot and went to the stadium and had those UConn assholes take our pictures in front of it, and then those assholes went off to do whatever stupid shit. We saw this hot chick totally giving us the eyes, Derek spat game at her but it turned out she was just handing out postcards for some club and Derek got pissed. We were mad hungry and needed to bomb some calories. Tasty-ass Chicago with its deep-dish pizza around every corner calling our names. We nabbed a table at Sluggers and pounded pizza. Derek wanted to get with this hot cougar who'd been arguing with the bartender over why her flirtini wasn't covered by the drink special. She stormed out with her hot older rack all bouncing up all over everywhere. "Shit dude," Derek was like. "We gotta follow that chick, maybe hook up with her in the beamer; she's old but way hot." We just kept eating pizza and drinking beers then hauled ass down to Lincoln

Park to hit some more bars down there and scope more hotties. "Fuck dude," Derek was like while we were waiting in line outside a bar, "check this shit out, like sorta like a college town party scene but in a legit city. What a fucking awesome place—oh dude, and that hottie chilling at that hot dog place, looking all hot in that tube top and just eating a hot dog like she doesn't even know how boner-popping that is. Shit. Sam, we gotta make this happen."

"What do you wanna make happen, bro?"

"Fuck if I know, but we just gotta." This crew of pretty awesome-looking dudes rolled by slugging beer out of their Nalgenes. They rolled up into this Irish sports bar and so we followed. They posted up at the bar and just started ordering shots. We did shots with them. The dude who kept ordering shots was this jacked, funny dude who was like a student at DePaul, which I thought was sorta a school for pussies but I guess if you go there you have like mad access to pretty sick party scenes in Chicago—and this dude was just like, "Chug!" and all of us started chugging like crazy 'till he said to stop. Everybody called his buddy Prez, 'cause he was like a poli-sci major and did an internship in D.C., and so he had like mad smooth moves like some kind of politician and could totally get talking to some chick at the bar, totally smooth as hell, and make her think that he's like totally into her as he looks all concerned and nice and shit, even though he's just trying to hook up with her 'cause he's just as much of a player as any other dude in the bar. "Think about this shit dude, Prez could like be a senator or president or something someday, and think about what an awesome place America would be if that dude was in charge—if like the country wasn't run by tools who just care about like budgets and whatever, but by dudes who *just wanna party*. That would be amazing. Maybe beer prices would drop. Shit dude!" We all got hammered and started talking about what the funniest movies ever were.

It all started with *Old School* with Will Ferrell and Luke Wilson being crazy funny in what's still one of like the best movies ever; there was like *Animal House* before that, which I've heard is pretty awesome but I usually don't like shit that's old. Then there was

Anchorman, again with Will Ferrell, being so fucking funny and also with Steve Carell this time, who was like crazy random and hilarious—and *Anchorman* led to *Talladega Nights* and *Semi-Pro*, which weren't nearly as awesome as *Anchorman* but were still totally solid enough to buy on DVD and like get drunk and watch and whatever. *The 40-Year-Old Virgin* was totally amazing with Steve Carell going from like just some dude in *Anchorman* to being like the fucking man, with like Paul Rudd and Seth Rogen. Seth Rogen who was so fucking hilarious in shit like *Knocked Up* and *Superbad* with Jonah Hill who's also the fucking man and can't do anything that's not hilarious and was in *Forgetting Sarah Marshall* which was pretty good with Kristen Bell looking all hot and shit. And for real there's *The Hangover* and *The Hangover Part II*, which are both totally amazing and are like sorta on par with *Old School* because you watch them and think "This shit is so funny!" but then it just keeps going and keeps getting more funny until you think that you might like bust a nut or something from laughing so hard and then you just crack the hell up and keep repeating lines from it for like weeks afterwards. These were some of the most hilarious awesome movies ever.

Shit kept getting awesome, 'cause while we were all chugging and shooting shit about funny movies and whatever, this dude walked over to the TouchTunes, fed it one dollar, pressed a couple buttons, and then "Paradise City" started to blast; and when that shit blasts, everybody gets pretty stoked, 'cause it's a totally sick classic and there's no way you can just stand there and not pump your fist and scream along to it as you pound your beer—crunked as hell, with awesome guitars shredding in the night.

And then there were all the other dudes in this crew that we were getting hammered with. This one dude was like pretty wussy-looking and probably never worked out, but he would still spit game at these chicks and totally get them dancing with him. "Shit, that's a dude who can totally *grind* up on any chick!" This other dude was pretty fat and mad hammered, just staring into his beer, eating wings, starting to pass out, sometimes running to the bathroom to chunk it but still coming back to drink more and eat more wings. The TouchTunes just kept blasting awesome classic shit like "Welcome to the Jungle" and "Walk This Way." Everybody was rocking out. Clark Street hotties chilled at the bar, they got all pissed when dudes would spill drinks on them. Losers passed by the bar and wished they were having such an awesome time. Beats kept pumping. We kept pumping fists. In through the door walked this total fucker—a scrawny little asshole in like an off-brand Pony polo and a fucking Royals hat, dude wanted to hang out with this crew. They knew this asshole and didn't want to party with him. He walked up to the table and tried to grab a seat. We closed him off. We pretended like he wasn't there. The crew downed their beers, paid up, and got the fuck out. The little fucker wanted to party. He downed his beer, thought about trying to walk up to this chick who wasn't even very hot, and then just bolted out after the crew. Those dudes would never let him party with them, which was the right call 'cause he'd totally kill their reps. "All these dudes are awesome, sorta like Timmy Snipes and our dude Carl Marcus," Derek was like. We paid up and followed the awesome crew. They rolled into the Lincoln Park John Barleycorn and ordered some shots and partied there 'till shit closed down. Derek and I hung with them and got wild.

We peaced out for a second, grabbed the beamer, and cruised around to pick up some hotties. Everybody thought we were ballers in our big, pimped-out, legendary whip. Maybe 'cause he was getting too buzzed/hammered, Derek totally smacked the car into a freestanding ATM and then cracked the hell up. The car was getting totes busted; the suspension was fucked; there were mad dings all over it; it had weak acceleration. We started to look less like ballers since it looked all jacked up. We'd beaten that car to shit. It was a total shit-pile instead of a legendary whip. "Fuck yeah!" That crew was still getting hammered at the bar.

Derek got all quiet and just stared at the door and was like, "Sam, God himself just strutted up in here."

I checked it out. *Nic Fucking Cage*. Looking just as awesome as he does in his movies, fucking Nic Cage walked in the bar, probably 'cause he was shooting a movie somewhere close or something, his long hair blowing and his crazy-ass eyes like fucking lightning ready to set the bar on fire with badassery. All of us tried to get him to come over and have a drink with us. He fucking did. Like I'm not even shitting you, he came over and ordered a beer and legit chilled with us and we all slammed beers together in the tired glow of the bar's twelve TVs. Cage chugging and chugging as only Cage could, and all of us staring, slackjawed, 'cause God could fucking hang. His assistant came over like twenty minutes later and said they had to go. He peaced out through the door, old God Cage, and the crew was like, "Did that for real just happen?"

One of the dudes was like, "Maybe it was just a dude who looked like him."

It had to have been Cage. Shit was too awesome to be fake, too awesome to forget. We all tried to keep partying and chugging after Cage left, for real we did. We did shots and waterfalls and whatever. Sometimes a commercial that we all thought was hilarious would come on one of the TVs and we'd all toast it and chug and for a second shit was normal again. But it was weird, and awkward, and sorta lame, 'cause we'd been hanging with Nic Cage a second ago, and now what was up, how the fuck do you go on—and Derek told everybody to chug chug chug. At 4 A.M. they stopped serving brews and everybody cleared the fuck out into the Chi-town streets to go blow up some sleep until it was time to get brunch-hammered.

Derek and I were tired as fuck. We still had to drop off the beamer to the dude who owned it, his crib was some pimped-out condo on Lake Shore Drive that had like a garage and shit. We hauled ass over there and pulled the jacked-up beamer into a spot. The dude running the garage couldn't even recognize that shit. We gave him the paper. Dude was super confused. We need to beast out. Like fast. We nabbed a bus downtown and were in the fucking clear. For real, I never heard shit from the dude who owned it, 'cause he had our addresses but he never got pissed at us so I guess that was pretty sweet.

CHAPTER ELEVEN

GROSS-ASS SNO-CAPS

We had to keep rolling. We snagged a Megabus to Indianapolis. We'd bought way too many drinks and I was gonna have to dip into my parents' credit card. We hauled all our stuff to the Megabus stop. Derek's thumb bandage was getting super fucked up and all dirty and shit. We were for real the most hungover people in the Midwest that day. Derek slept like a motherfucker on the Megabus as it hauled ass down through Indiana. I spat some game at this mad hot farm chick whose rack was totally busting out of her shirt. But she kinda sucked. She just yapped about all the boring shit she does in the country and whatever. I could have dealt with it if I wasn't so hungover, but now it fucking pissed me off 'cause she was mad boring and I didn't know if I was even gonna get to first base with her. "You like to party?" I wanted to get her all hot and excited to like make out and bone. She just stared at me with this total boring prudeness that's probably the way all those farm assholes are 'cause they just sit around doing nothing except drinking lemonade and fucking goats. "You wanna hit my flask?" I wanted her to take it and slug back some and loosen the fuck up. She like didn't want to drink at all. She said some bullshit about how it upset her stomach, how it just didn't taste good, how she usually had the most fun when she wasn't drinking, and parties weren't really her scene, how she's really more into volunteer work—like bullshit where you stand around picking up trash or wiping homeless dudes' asses all day. "Don't you ever like wanna get wild?" I was like. She didn't give a shit. She just chilled at home and sat on her porch, probably pissing off every single dude in a fifty-mile radius. "You got a boyfriend?" She didn't have time for one because she spent all her time with her family or picking up trash. "Don't you party with your friends?" Her friends all started partying so she stopped hanging out with them. They had what sounded like sick field parties but she thought they were lame. Fuck me. "Don't you ever like go on spring break?" She built houses in fucking East Texas with some church group. "Aren't you bored? Don't you wanna get wild? Aren't you so fucking bored?" She wasn't. Bitch was frigid. She was gonna sleep. It was so bullshit. So many chicks were prudes. So many chicks sucked. It was total bullshit. She was mad hot and totally boneable, and completely sucked.

So me and Derek, with like a ton of time to kill before our next Megabus came, rolled out in lame-ass Indianapolis. We figured we'd go like see a movie or something. There's absolutely nothing to do in Indianapolis. Hammer got stuck here one time when his car broke down; he'd gotten totally hammered in an Arby's and got in a fight that ended with him almost drowning in Horsey Sauce. Dude was insane. He never returned texts and we'd like never see him around campus again. For a second Derek thought his dad might be here for a Pacers game, but that was next weekend. We threw down like fifteen bucks each, got 3D glasses, and sat down to watch *Transformers: Dark of the Moon* and we both totally passed out and slept there for fucking hours. It was a matinee show on a Wednesday so like nobody was there. Just a couple weirdos, some lame not-hot stay-at-home moms, and some dickhole teenagers who got the shit-hole deal of having to grow up in a place that sucks so hard that it makes Dayton look like a sick place to party. You could spend like a year trying to get wild in Indianapolis and you'd fail super hard. We saw some previews for *The Change-Up* and *Horrible Bosses*, which both looked pretty hilarious; then *Transformers* started with Shia LaBeouf and that super hot chick and all those robots. The movie played like three times while we were conked out. We watched that shit while we were awake and it just kept going while we were passed out; our skulls filled with insane-ass dreams about like Autobots and Decepticons and shit blowing up and that super hot chick, but like her head was on Shia LaBeouf's body. It made me keep having crazy-ass Decepticon nightmares for like weeks 'cause of the totally weird subconscious shit that streamed into my head as I wore those Real3D glasses. I heard Optimus Prime beat ass over and over again; I saw that hot chick's ass in the opening scene; I dreamed I was like flying through the air as shit was exploding and Optimus Prime caught me and then we like kept beating ass. Some bitch kept unwrapping candy and it was super annoying. I didn't want to be a dick and everybody else was too much of a pussy to say anything to her. When the ushers finally noticed we were passed out in there, I was like super unconscious with my Real3D glasses half-off my face while a couple of dudes cleaned the floor and left huge piles of shit near me—and they almost got that gross shit all over me. Derek thought it was pretty hilarious and he watched that shit 'cause he woke up before me. Gross-ass Sno-Caps and Sour Patch Kids, empty Buncha Crunch boxes and popcorn buckets, old-ass Mountain Dew, all this gross shit was like almost all up in my grill. If they would have spilled that shit on me I would have gotten so pissed I'd probably have beat the shit out of a dude and gotten in jail and then Derek would never see my ass again. Dude would have to party alone from coast to coast, looking behind every beer bong for a dude that could party as solidly as me, until he realized that I party like no other and so he'd come and visit me where I was locked up for beating ass so that I wouldn't have trash thrown all over me. What the fuck could I tell him from behind the bulletproof glass divider? "Forget my ass, bro, my shit is done. You gotta go get wild without me. I just couldn't have let some motherfucker push gross shit all over me." Freshman year the grossest shit ever happened. I was rushing, so all the Delta brothers were like making everybody chug like crazy to see who was good enough to pledge; I downed ten beers in an hour and ran to the bathroom and chunked it all over and then passed the fuck out, still holding on to the bowl. For the next like five hours, all these dudes came in and for real pissed all over me 'till I was totally drenched and I stank for fucking weeks. What kind of a dick-wad messes with your fucking hygiene? Fuck those people, fuck Delta, and fuck those assholes trying to push trash on me. They can suck all the dicks in the world.

A little less hungover, we rolled out of the theater and realized we'd missed the Megabus to Columbus. We chilled and grabbed some grub at a Waffle House and scoped some hot-but-probably-STD-coated chicks; then we nabbed a ride with this dude who was heading to Columbus and just wanted some gas money. He was like a pretty normal lame dude with like a family and bullshit. The pictures of his wife looked pretty hot, but she was probably a bitch too. Derek was totally tired and crazy so he was like a maniac. He hit my flask and punched the roof of the car. Like a hot second after we took off this lame dude realized that he'd just gotten into some serious shit by giving us a ride, but he tried to keep shit together and showed us like all the bullshit along the road in Indiana.

We hauled ass past Dayton and kept barreling to C-Bus. I started to think about how I'd been partying all across America again and again, like finding all the most awesome places, but like nothing was as sick as OSU, like there was no way I could ever for real be over that shit. The lame dude started to get tired and Derek drove fast as hell to Columbus, and we started to see people decked out in Buckeyes gear and now we were totally all up in the sickest state university in America. We rolled into campus. Shit was bumping, 'cause OSU doesn't know how to not be awesome. I texted Hammer but dude didn't text back.

Since I didn't have an apartment we just crashed at my parents' place in Worthington, but they were all busy like doing some kind of stupid yardwork or something, and were pulling weeds when Derek and me rolled up from San Fran. "Sam," my mom was like, "Derek can't stay here for more than a few days, understood?" They were such idiots. Derek and me strutted around through dark quiet boring downtown Worthington. He checked his phone.

"Shit dude, I was about to tell you some real funny shit, but then I got this text and now I don't know what I was gonna say, you know?" I knew what he meant. My parents were such assholes that they wouldn't let us use the car so we just walked around Worthington, but there was nothing to do, 'cause the only bar within walking distance closed at ten. We pounded knucks and swore we'd get wild more.

Like a week later we were hanging at this party on campus and I told this chick I knew named Isabel that she should totally meet Derek. I was hammered and told her he was a wide receiver at ASU and was probably gonna get drafted. "That is so cool!"

I texted Derek and told him to come to the living room where like everybody—A-Rock, my dude; Dub-Rock; Vic-Bomb, the funniest; Jinny Jones, this chick I used to smash with; Carl Marcus; G-Dex; and a ton of others—were chilling. "get 2 lving room stat" I texted. Derek came over all smooth. Like in an hour later, while everybody was all hammered, dude was nailing this chick in the guest bedroom and spitting all this game at her about how they should like keep smashing forever. She was this mad hot brunette chick. Like a total smokeshow and pretty racked out. A day later Derek dumped Carly's ass over the phone so he could hook up with Isabel without having to give a shit. And to top shit off, like a couple months later Carly had another fucking baby that was Derek's, 'cause for real that dude just can't wrap it up. He totally got Isabel pregged up too. So now this motherfucker had like a ton of kids all over the place and was totally out of his skull. We had to fucking cancel Cabo.

Part Four

Oh Snap

CHAPTER ONE

FINAL DROPS DRAINING FROM THE KEG

I had fucking owned it in a poker tournament and had a wad of cash. I was living with Ty again and threw him rent for the summer. As soon as it gets pretty warm in the Midwest I just can't resist the pull of sick parties that roar across the Mississippi and land in my sober ears in Columbus and I gotta roll out. So I rolled out. For the first time in a while I went solo and said peace out to Derek, who was chilling in C-Bus. He was working at the Bally Total Fitness near campus. Dude was one-hundo percent over school and was just hanging at the gym in his lacrosse shorts and muscle shirt, working, boning, and working out.

I'd hang with him around lunch time and shit was real slow. He just chilled in the break room, popping some supplements and watching TV. He was always watching some shit on TV. "Dude, there's some fucking *World's Strongest Man* on again, hauling rocks and shit, they're so fucking gross. Like why gain so much muscle mass if you're just gonna look like a fatty?" Seemed like he was sort of lame-ing out. He and Isabel had a place outside of campus. After he left Bally he'd just chill out in his boxers and smoke a ton of pot. This was the sort of lame shit he did all the time, this and watching porn. "I've been downloading a bunch of crazy shit on torrents lately. Check this out. Can you believe there's actually four chicks in there? I'm for real!" Dude wanted me to download this same porn, which was pretty shitty quality and the chick sorta looked gross. "Dude, I'll throw it on a thumb drive. It's awesome!" Isabel was just like checking some e-mail and sometimes would just walk through the room and wave. She seemed pretty chill. "Shit dude, isn't she awesome? Isabel is so clutch. She just chills and doesn't give a fuck what I do. I totally told her that sometimes I gotta take care of shit and she gets me. I'm gonna check Orbitz for some cheap-ass tix to the Catskills 'cause I hear it's mad chill there, then maybe we like get a pimp-ass house around C-Bus. You know? For real. Fuck yeah!" He pulled out his iPhone and changed the stereo to play some Kanye. He checked Facebook on his phone and cracked the shit up. "Oh my God. That's fucking hilarious! I can't believe dude posted how bad she is at sex!"

This was totally the same kind of lame shit dude had been suffocating in with Carly back in San Fran. He still had his jacked-up duffel under the bed, ready to go in case of bitch-mergencies. Isabel texted with Carly like all the time; they'd even like talk about Derek's package, at least Derek totally thought they did. Those chicks would like Facebook message each other about the crazy shit Derek was up to. Natch Derek was sending some cash back to Carly 'cause he ditched out on rent and like that kid and those other kids. To pull extra dough, he was getting into online poker, and was actually getting pretty solid. This one time he totally bluffed on a mad shitty hand and pulled in like a three-hundo-buck pot. We blew some of that shit on a road trip to a Browns game. The Browns can sorta be choke artists but we still got hammered.

This one time we were closing down the bar at Applebee's and Derek was like, "Fuck, like, it sucks that you're gonna peace out for a while; I haven't hung with you in forever." And he was like, "Columbus is a pretty awesome place, but for real San Fran is where it's at for me. Like, the whole time I've been here I've only been smashing one chick—like how the fuck is that pos-sible? Shit. But for real, roadtripping again sounds mad lame; we haven't like just chilled in forever." In C-Bus we were like con-stantly party-hopping all over the place with a deep crew that got mega-drunk. For some fucked-up reason, Derek totally wasn't into that shit anymore. He just wanted to chill at home in front of ESPN2 as he flicked through Facebook updates on his iPhone long into the night. "Isabel is like so fucking cool; she's totally chill with everything and she's always ready to smash. Like that's the thing 'cause eventually all the good bitches get snatched up. One day we're gonna be chilling in a bar, old as fuck, and at closing time no bitches are gonna want to even touch our shit."

"You think we're gonna lose our game?"

"It could totally happen. Like we could probably keep our game if we wanted to, and whatever. But dudes lose their game. You chase after trim for what seems like an eternity and then all of a sudden you're left trimless and old and you just can't bench anymore and your physique totally sucks." I saw where dude was coming from. He was thinking deep shit in his own weird-ass way. "So how are you gonna get wild, bro?—Cabo wild, Cali wild, Big Easy wild, club wild, crunked wild, just get wild. It's time to get fucking wild tick tock, you feel me? Wild o'clock." We finished our Steak Quesadilla Towers. "And for real, you've gotta always put your bros first. You're a total dickless pussy if you ever put a ho before a bro; that's fucking science. Real talk, Sam, whatever shit is going down, my duffel is always ready in case shit gets brutal. I'm always gonna be ready. Like you totally *know* I can sorta get lame and you *know* that's all whatever but if comes down to it and dude's gotta throw down then I just gotta knuck-up and throw down, aight? *You* feel me." We finished our Bud Lights. Bud Lights were being finished all along the Midwest and across the American night. People at parties in Columbus were downing Bud Light, dudes in Indiana were emptying cases, bars in Arizona were changing their kegs, drops of Bud Light were rolling down the continent's throat.

"Like," Derek was like, "I gotta do my shit how I do and just roll. My dad finally texted me back from Seattle—it was like the first time I've heard from the dude in forever."

"For real?"

"For real. He wants to know what's up with all these chicks I got pregs. I don't need that bullshit; if dude's never gonna hook me up with b-ball tix anymore then fuck him. I'd like to see him try to cut me off from the family credit card; my sister gave him so much shit and nothing ever happened. I never told you about my sis but she's pretty awesome although she can be sorta a bitch. We oughta hang some time."

"She hot?"

"Fuck you dude, fuck that. I'm not gonna tell you that shit, that shit is lame."

"But your dad is all up in Seattle?"

"Yeah, for like a Supersonics game or something."

"Fuck that team."

"Right on, right on. So like you feel me on why I gotta chill; you can totally tell I'm in more of a chill space."

"Yeah, whatever." Derek was just getting lame in Columbus. He didn't want to get wild. Applebee's stopped serving booze. We were gonna hang at my place before I peaced out.

We hung next weekend. I'd just gotten a second TV in the living room. We watched one baseball game on one TV, another on the other, and were getting updates on all the other games on our phones. "Aight, Sam, so like if Rodriguez goes four-for-four and Gallardo can get some more Ks and while that shit is going down Hamilton gets some RBIs, then my fantasy team is going to be kicking fucking ass and I'll be totally unstoppable. Fuck yeah!"

After the good games were finished we went and played some basketball with some buddies over by Westerville. We were driving so hard down the court that everybody else was all like, "Chill, you're gonna fucking kill somebody." We had way better verticals and totally owned everybody. We chugged a ton of Powerade. Derek elbowed a dude in the face once and it was hilarious. We went way too hard and then got too fatigued and started giving up real shitty turnovers; we were getting totally owned. It was like we were playing like Nic Cage in *Drive Angry*, all amped up and crazy and they were playing like Nic Cage in *Snake Eyes*, all cool as fuck. All the dudes we played with thought we were insane. We peaced out of that scene and found a shopping cart on the way back and we decided to do some stupid shit. I jumped in the cart and Derek started pushing it fast as hell down the road. Then he let me go and I just sped down in this shopping cart and started flying past cars and going faster and faster until I was about to hit the curb and fly in to a bush so I got into a crouch and got ready to fly as Derek was shouting "Fuck yeah! Fuck yeah! Fuck yeah!" and in one clutch moment I felt the cart lock with the curb and then I was in the air, flipping over with my aviators flying off and the collar of my polo flapping in the air like some sort of fucking awesome superhero who loves to party. I crashed into the bush, cut the shit out of my leg, crawled out, stood up, and pumped my fists in the air and Derek was like "I thought you were fucking dead!" and I was like, "Hell yeah!" and it was awesome. We went back to my place and Derek gave Ty a couple bucks from when he ate a bunch of his frozen Tyson chicken patties. Ty didn't even know that shit was missing. We Foremaned up some burgers. "Shit Derek," Ty was like, "I heard you've got like a shitload of kids now or something. What the fuck?"

"Aw, you know."

"Why the shit didn't you wrap it up? That's mad crazy." Derek chewed his burger and looked sorta bummed. Later that night we said peace out in the parking lot of a Fridays after a second dinner of Jack Daniels-glazed wings and Coors Lite.

"Are you still gonna be chilling in Columbus when I get back?" I was like. "For real, bro, I just hope that like someday we're both chilling in like the same apartment building, and we can just go out and get hammered together constantly and not worry about any other bullshit."

"For real, dude—that's exactly the sorta shit I want and just to get rid of all these pregnant bitches in my past and the pregnant bitches to come, the shit that Ty was bringing up before. Yo, I was mad bummed when Isabel got all pregged, but she was into it, so fucking whatever. Did you see on Facebook that Maryann is married to some dickhole in San Fran and is all preg?"

"Yeah. Fucking everybody is all settling down and shit." The final drops draining from the keg after all the liquor stores have closed; it was that kind of shit. The party's raging on the porch but the rain is coming down. Derek brought up a picture on his phone of Carly in San Fran with the baby out in a park and there was some blurry dude's leg in part of the picture. "Who's that dude?"

"Todd Dinkel, bro. Dude got back with Gabby, they're all settled and shit in Denver. He posted these pictures on Facebook."

Todd Dinkel, a solid dude who could bone any chick now totally tied down in Denver. Derek showed me more of the Facebook pictures. Like one day all our kids are gonna look at shit like these pictures and just think that their parents were pretty normal lame dudes who just went to work and drank O'Doul's and just pussed out in the great party of life, never knowing that long ago their parents had raged and been wild and boned more than you'd think a person could ever bone. That would suck. "Aight, peace out." Derek got in his car and turned it on under the long red glow of the Friday's sign. Other cars were pulling out around him. His headlights came on; his music started pumping, the bass thundering out through the windows. He flashed his brights. He stuck his head out the window and flipped me off, said something I couldn't hear. He cracked the shit up. He pulled out and got closer and closer to the frontage road. He flipped me off one more time. I flipped him off too. He slammed on the gas and sped toward the outerbelt and vanished into a stream of midsized sedans. I checked my phone. I had an awesome trip to get started.

CHAPTER TWO

A TIDAL WAVE OF NATTY

The next night, with Flo-rida's "Low" stuck in my head, I hopped on a bus; first I'd done some farewell partying in C-Bus; got hammered in the Arena District; got hammered at a minor-league baseball game; got hammered on campus and pissed on the side of the OSU stadium; made out with a chick in the back of a Potbelly Sandwich Shop, then got the fuck out. Hauling ass through the dark in Ohio, the bullshit fields of Indiana, and then into St. Louis, with like nothing to do except scope chicks around Wash U. The Mississippi kept flowing like a huge piss. The biggest piss. Listening to my iPhone as I rolled through Kansas, trying to get a signal so I could text in the shit-hole small towns of Kansas in the middle of wherever-the-fuck. Then things start to get hilly but the service is still pretty dumb.

This dude named Emory Gleason was sitting next to me. Dude had got on in Indiana and was like, "I totally hate this fucking Hoosiers T-shirt, you wanna know why?" He showed me this e-mail on his phone. He'd gotten expelled from Indiana University; he'd racked up about a million underage drinking violations in the dorms. He was young as fuck, probably a freshman. "When I get to Denver I'm gonna ditch this stupid shirt and get a new UC-Boulder one. Do you know how hard IU sucks? They'll bust your ass for anything. The campus cops are constantly trying to get you in trouble. I smuggled a keg into my dorm in a hockey bag and my RA totally narced on me and the campus cops came and tore up my entire room and found like five thirty-racks of Icehouse." He offered me some of the Easy Mac he was eating. Dude was such a freshman so he was like always eating Easy Mac. "Some people are real assholes at IU." He kept talking about how much he hated "assholes." "Anybody who leaves a guy hanging out to dry with the campus cops is a total asshole. I'll like punch a dude and tell him to stop being such an asshole. I hate assholes, you get me?"

"I'm not an asshole, dude."

"Anybody gets all assholey to me, my neck flexes, I get ready to beat ass. I ended up in IU because my dad went there and he's all about the fucking Hoosiers. I just wanted to go someplace on the West Coast where it's warm but he refused to have his son go anywhere except IU 'cause he's a total idiot. I wish I would have told him off and just like punched him in the face and done my own thing. So I just spent like a terrible semester at IU and I just gotta go to a more awesome school. Don't ever go to IU. It sucks. Everybody there sucks. When I got on the bus I came over and sat next to you on purpose, you know why?"

"Fuck if I know."

"You look like a dude who can party. If I had to sit next to one more asshole I was gonna rip their face off. Hate those assholes."

"Just chill, shit's gonna be fine."

"I'll chill. I just gotta get away from all the assholes."

He was gonna transfer to UC-Boulder and live with his cousin who went there. He bought the ticket on his dad's credit card without him knowing; who knows how the fuck he was gonna make tuition. He was a kid totally like Derek; he was just like way too amped for his own good; he got into shit everywhere; and even though he could party he could be a total douche.

"You wanna chill in Denver, Sam? Seems like you know how to hang and I don't want shit to go south."

When we rolled up in Denver I called my buddy and got Emory a legit fake ID. My buddy could tell that Emory was sorta a crazy douche. "Don't tell anybody where you got this. I'm being real here."

He was making a ton of fake IDs for freshmen in Denver and Boulder and didn't want his game busted up. Emory got a pretty good fake but wouldn't pay for one that scans. We rolled up to this bar Derek used to chill in—the ID totally worked there—and I texted Tom Grover. Shit was getting dark outside.

"ur here?" Tom texted back. "b thr in 1 sec."

A hot second later he rolled up with Steve Sharpford. They'd just taken a pretty sick trip to Amsterdam and were feeling sorta bored in Denver. They thought Emory was pretty hilarious and did some shots with him. Dude was throwing his dad's credit card all over the place like it was nothing. Like deja-fucking-vu I was back up in Denver with its awesome bars and delicious food. We blew up every bar around, a couple hotel bars, all the shit on the Sixteenth Street Mall, fucking everything.

Steve Sharpford had been wanting to party with me forever and now we were finally gonna get shit started. "Sam, for real, since I got back from Amsterdam I've been bored as fuck. I heard you wanna go to Mexico? Shit dude, can I come? I'll throw some cash your way for like gas or whatever."

Aight, shit sounded good, I'd party down in Mexico with Steve. He was a pretty cool guy from Denver who was into all that Denver shit like skiing and rock climbing and whatever. "Shit dude!" he'd always be cracking up like crazy, 'cause that was just his style. His dad was a total dick. He didn't want him to go to Amsterdam and didn't want him to go to Mexico either. Steve had like no cash to party with 'cause of his stupid dad. That night after we'd gotten plowed and had to keep Emory from beating the fuck out of a dude outside a Pizza Hut/Taco Bell, Steve just crashed with Emory. "I'm not going fucking home—my dad's just gonna be total dick about it. For real, Sam, I gotta go party somewhere else or like re-enroll or something."

So I crashed at Tom Grover's 'till Beth Riggins hooked me up with a room and we'd party there pretty much nonstop. Emory peaced out to meet up with his cousin and that's the last I heard of that dude and he never updates his Facebook so maybe he's doing awesome or maybe he's getting expelled all over the place again.

So I chilled with Tom Grover, Steve, and Beth and we'd just hang in Denver bars where the waitresses are pretty fit and there's pretty cheap beer and everywhere has like delicious bison burgers that aren't sorta rubbery like you'll get at a lot of other places but straight-up explode with fucking juicy-ass flavor and make you

want to shove more in your face even when you're full and hammered and think you can't take any more; and we still did some
awesome shit in the mountains like when Steve led us all on this
awesome rock climb where we got mad high up and my arms
burned like crazy. Most nights we usually finished up in Beth's back
yard where we shot a paintball gun at each other and shotgunned
tons of beers. It was a really awesome time and super fun shit just
went down 'cause we were all chill. Me and Steve tried to get Tom
to come party with us in Mexico, but Tom wouldn't cowboy up.

I was just about to peace out when my buddy D-Rock texted
me and was like, 'u hear whos comin 2 den?" Fuck if I knew. "Derek
bot a car and iz comin now." Suddenly I could see Derek, this fucked-
up shuddering crunked-out angel, beasting straight at me down the
highway, like a fucking bullet train, fast as hell, coming in like a post-
game Buckeyes football riot in Columbus, tearing shit up. I saw
his Hardy tee through the windshield with that winged skull with
gleaming eyes; I saw his mouth full of jerky; I saw his new Wrangler
Unlimited with thousands of empty Natty cans flying out of it; I saw
a tidal wave of light beer wash over the land behind him; it annihi-
lated everything with its cold crunked crush, destroying fields, cities,
bridges, and drenching the deserts in booze. It was a fucking tidal
wave of Natty. Derek had totally lost his shit again. He must have
thrown down all his cash on a new ride, 'cause dude doesn't drive
shitty rides. Shit was about to get crazy, for real. Behind him the sur-
vivors struggled to swim through seas of Natty. He hauled ass over
the whole fucking country, and in a hot second he'd roll up. We tried
to brace ourselves. Apparently dude was gonna drive us to Mexico.

"Am I gonna get to party with him?" Steve was like, all
pumped to meet Derek.

"We'll see what the deal is," I was like, sorta bummed. We
didn't know what was gonna go down. "Where's dude gonna crash?
Is he gonna be a douche? Should we find him some tail?" It was like
that big monster from *Cloverfield* was coming; shit had to be tied
down and everybody had to go into like Defcon One party mode to
make way for his mad wildness and totally fucked-up style.

CHAPTER THREE

LIKE A MILLION BEERS

S hit got real when Derek rolled up. I was chilling at Beth's place on a pretty nice-ass day. This is what's up with the house. It's like her family's house, but her mom was like doing some shit in Europe. Officially Beth's old-ass aunt Cathy was taking care of the place; she was like seventy-five but still pretty cool. She just like bounced from place to place out West seeing different parts of the family and like helping out wherever. She had some sons, but it sounds like they were all pretty big douches and they didn't even come by anymore. She was kinda hilarious to hang with. She'd get pissed when we'd shotgun inside and be like, "Why don't you all go shotgun in the yard?" There were like a billion people crashing in the upstairs. There was one dude named Tony who was trying crazy hard to get with Beth. Everybody said that he had graduated like top of his class in Dartmouth and has some sick-ass job waiting in Connecticut, but he just kept hanging around trying to lay Beth. He just sat in the living room staring at his iPad all the time and never even looked up when we'd say shit to him. You could tell he was listening like crazy, especially when Beth talked. This one time I totally nabbed his iPad from him and made him talk to us. He just looked all pissed and went upstairs, like an idiot.

Cathy sat and watched *Judge Mathis* while we chilled. Since she was in charge, she just had to make sure no shit got broken. Beth told some funny-ass story. Tom Grover, Steve Sharpford, and I all played hold 'em on the coffee table. Stupid Tony just kept fucking with his iPad. He stood up and was like, "I gotta go charge this," and went upstairs. Beth didn't want to hit that at all. She was mad into Tom Grover; but that dude was into a ton of other chicks. So we're all just chilling sorta like this, about to nab some dinner, when Derek rolled up in a new Wrangler Unlimited and busted out, for real wearing like a blazer and looking sharp as fuck.

"What up, what up!" he hollered from outside. He'd rolled up with Ray Jeffries, who'd been chilling in San Fran before but was back in Denver with his slam piece Denise. Dinkel, Gabby, and Timmy Snipes were up in Denver too. The crew was back together. I pounded knucks with Derek. "What's shaking bro?" Derek was like, "Looks like shit is pretty tight out here. What up, what up, what up," he was like to all of us. "Aw shit, Tom Grover, Steve Sharpford, what the fuck is up!" He met Cathy. "Hey. What up. How's it going? This is my buddy Ray Jeffries, a totally solid dude who came with me, yo! What up! Sup? Sup? You totally look like Milhouse," he was like to Tony, who just looked sorta pissed and confused. "Aight, aight. Sam, bro, what's the deal, when you wanna beast it to Mexico? Like tomorrow? Shit yeah, aight! So, Sam, I gotta peace out in like sixteen minutes to go say what up to Todd Dinkel, 'cause dude has my best razor, and then I need to send a bunch of texts and stop by the Denver Nuggets management office to see if my dad is around and can hook us up with some tickets and then for real I gotta go get a barbacoa burrito at the Chipotle near Sixteenth because I swear to God that is the best Chipotle ever and I've never had a better burrito anywhere than that Chipotle, you feel me? Aight! Aight. So like around six—like right at six, none of this late bullshit—you just post up here and I'll grab your ass and we'll go slam a couple with Ray Jeffries, do a power hour or two, just like some awesome pregaming before whatever shit you were gonna blow up with Tom and Steve and Beth before I rolled up. Oh, and for real you gotta check out how I rolled up in this tight orange Wrangler Unlimited out the driveway, and it really hauled ass 'cause I just stopped one time in Kansas to hang with one of my cousins, not that dickbag Sean Brody but my cooler cousin . . ." And while he was spitting all this shit like crazy, he was changing out of his blazer and into a Hardy tee in the den and getting some more product all up in his hair.

"What's the deal with Isabel?" I was like. "What went down in Columbus?"

"It's cool, Sam, I told her that like Bally is having a corporate event down here so I gotta go to it. I'm for real broken up with Carly, so like shit is totally cool; shit is totally straight; shit is totally awesome so we can just party, aight?"

I can't resist partying with Derek, so we got our shit together and decided to get wild one more time in Denver. It was legendary. Todd Dinkel's brothers were throwing a party over at their crib. The brothers are like IT guys or something. Their minds were blown by how awesome we got. There was a delicious five-foot party sub that we absolutely decimated. Todd Dinkel was doing pretty solid. "What's up with Gabby?"

"Shit's good," Todd was like, "Mad good. I got a job lined up for after I graduate."

"What kind of job?"

"Pharmaceutical sales rep. Gonna just swim in cash. Dude, Derek gets fucking crazier every year, right?"

"Hell yeah."

Gabby Dinkel was hanging out. While she was talking to some chick, Derek totally spilled his beer all over her. He was going totally crazy as we all stood around the keg in the kitchen. Todd Dinkel tried to fill up his beer. His brother was trying to get through. "Hell yeah! Hell yeah!" Derek was like, turning his cap to the side, slamming his beer, high-fiving everybody. "Fuck yeah, aight—this is mad awesome that the whole crew is back together and all this bullshit is fucking over and so shit is cool but it is still the same 'cause all of us are still looking to party and we gotta— we just gotta—aight hold my legs and I'm gonna hit this keg-stand." There was barely enough space for a kegstand. Denise and Ray Jeffries looked all pissed in the corner. Some of the people at this party were bitches. Then Derek kicked his legs up and froze in a kegstand with me and Steve holding his legs, and dude just chugged. He froze in this ultra-zen state to just suck down more and more beer. It was like he could just stay like that forever, even if we dropped him he'd just float there until he drank the whole keg and then he'd come crashing down like a monster truck, beer spraying everywhere. The kegstand ended and dude wiped the beer off his face and looked super amped and was like, "Fuck yeah! You dudes are totally solid for holding me up during that. Wasn't that awesome? It's totally like, Sam, I was hitting a beer bong like a couple weeks ago, you know, aight, fuck yeah!" He busted over to the living room and pounded knucks with one of Dinkel's brothers. "What up! I'm Derek. Shit yeah, I remember. What's happening? Aw man, check out that party sub. Is it cool if I hit that? For real? I'm balls-hungry." They told him to go for it. "Fucking clutch. Totally solid. A big-ass party sub for everybody and it's totally got some premium meats in it. Aw dude, this is so good, mmm, solid, fuck yeah, fuck yeah!" He just pounded that party sub, like at least one foot of it, telling everybody about how delicious it was. He grabbed a beer and chugged with a bunch of random dudes. He got amped about everything; it all seemed totally awesome. He ran around to everybody in the house and was like "Fuck yeah! That's awesome!" He got a text message that made him just like freeze and stare at his phone for a second. He replied and then waited for another message. He crushed his beer can 'cause he was so focused on it. "Fuck!" Everybody was looking at him like he was insane but he straight didn't give a fuck. He was totally a pimp, like the pimp I always knew he'd be; but even though pimps get mad tail and don't give a fuck, they can still be pretty sloppy douches, and when our whole crew rolled out to the bar at the Hyatt, Derek got mad sloppy.

You gotta know that the Hyatt, which is one of the choicest hotels in downtown Denver—they like give you bathrobes and hot breakfast and shit—was where Derek lived for a while. When his dad got the job with the Nuggets, they lived out of the Hyatt for a few months. This was his crib. He got super hammered at the bar like his badass dad must have gotten back in the day; he mixed light beer and dark beer and put fucking scotch on top of all of that. He was all like sweaty and sloppy and just staggered around the bar like hugging these random tourists and asking the concierge "where all the good tail" was. The rest of our crew was posted up at a couple of tables near the back. There were like a million of us, Beth, Daniel Douglas, Tom Grover, Steve, some dudes, Todd Dinkel, Timmy Snipes, and some more dudes. D-Doug was totally stoked: The hotel desk had a bowl of free candy and he kept coming back to the table with a ton of it. He said we should all send texts to Carl back in Columbus. We texted the most hilarious shit to him. His texts back made all of us crack the shit up. Derek and I did like a competition for kung-fu shit in the bathroom, like trying to break down a stall door with a single punch. The door was mad thick and I totally broke a finger but I was way too hammered to notice. Shit was sloppy. We'd downed like a million beers. Everybody was crunked. Drunk dudes on business trips all came and chilled with us. They probably got hammered in hotel bars like this all over the country. Everything blew up. We went to a fuckload of parties. The sickest was in like the top floor of this big condo building with a pool that we all sat around being loud as hell. It was mad nice and had a sick view of the mountains. It was like the most clutch of condos.

Later on just like me, Derek, Steve, Tom Grover, Todd Dinkel, and Timmy Snipes piled in one ride and refused to stop partying. We went to Hooters; we went to Taco Bell; we went back to Hooters. Steve Sharpford was beyond stoked to be hanging with us. He was all like, "This is off the *chain!* Fucking *tight!*" all loud as hell and raising the roof. Derek thought Steve was pretty tight. He was all "true dat" to the shit Steve was saying and pounded some more jerky. "Shit is gonna get mad wild, bro, partying Mexico-style with this Steve dude! Fuck yeah!" This was the last time we'd make shit happen in badass Denver, so we had to take no prisoners. We finished shit off in the basement of the house with a couple jugs of wine while Cathy watched some shit on TV upstairs. We picked up this black dude named Gonzalez who was like the only black dude in Hooters and was pretty awesome. He didn't give a fuck. Timmy Snipes spotted him at Hooters and was like, "Oh shit! That's Nick Cannon!"

Gonzalez looked over at us and was like, "What the fuck?"

"Are you Nick Cannon?"

Gonzalez was all like, "Nick Cannon is a total chump. Fuck that guy."

We all cracked the shit up and Derek was like, "Fuck dude, come hang with us!" and Gonzalez came to our table and plowed through some wings with us. We kept rocking in the basement 'cause we couldn't be stopped. The whole crew peaced out by 9 A.M. except for like Derek and Sharpford, who kept playing *Madden*. There were people upstairs waking up who heard dudes yelling, "Fuck yeah! Fuck yeah!" in the basement. Beth made us some sick-ass omelets. It was go time.

Derek needed to head to a car wash to get his ride looking good. He had a new Wrangler Unlimited Rubicon in Flame Red with a mad good sound system and OnStar. The only bummer was that he'd gotten TVs installed in the seats but they weren't working. "My grandparents are the fucking best," Derek was like. "They leased it for me but I think 'cause I fucked up the seats they'll probably just have to buy it." I MapQuested it on my phone—like a thousand miles to Mexico City, rolling through Texas, then like seven hundo down through Mexico 'till we roll up ready to get some cheap-ass tequila. Shit blew my mind. This was gonna be the rawest trip ever. We weren't just like partying in America, we were taking it *international-style*. We could see miles of Latina chicks lining the roads beyond the horizon, waiting for us to roll by in our sick whip so they could get all up on us. "Shit dude, we are finally gonna get *The Shit*!" Derek was like, all pumped. He pounded knucks with me. "For real, bro, for real. Fuck yeah!"

Sharpford and I rolled over to his place 'cause he had to grab his Wayfarers. His jackass dad was there who met us at the door and was all like, "Steven."

"Ugh. What?"

"You can't go."

"Jesus Christ. I'm *going*; why do you gotta try to stop me from doing everything awesome?" His dad looked like a total chach.

"What about school?" he was like. "When are you going to finish? I pulled hard to get you in at Stanford." This was such bullshit.

"Derek," his dad thought I was Derek, "my son is wasting his life. He only has one more semester to finish, and then I can easily get him into an MBA program. What he's doing is stupid. You can't go."

"Shut up," Steve was like, "My buddy is gonna get me in with this sports agent in a couple months. So just chill out." He grabbed his Wayfarers.

His dad got all pissed. "You are not using my card. You are *not* using my card."

It was pretty obvious that that was total bullshit, and we peaced out while his dad stood there looking all pissed in his stupid house in his stupid neighborhood wearing his stupid clothes. He was a total tool. He kept shouting. He was probably just jealous, 'cause he'd probably just taken four years to get through college and never had the awesome fucking time you can have when you're on the five-to-eight-year track.

"Dude, Sharp, your dad sucks."

"Fuck him!" Steve was like. "He's such a dick."

We drove over to his mom's place so he could grab some more clothes. She was a total MILF, but I didn't say that shit to my dude. She was in the kitchen and totally threw together a bag of grub for us. Steve was decked out in a Hardy tee and swim trunks that could pass for shorts, looking like a dude totally ready to head south of the border. He totally lived with his parents in Denver, which was sorta lame, but he was about to get shit started with motherfucking Derek. Derek rolled up a hot second later. Sharps's mom threw some grub in a bag for him too.

"Please be careful with my Steven," she was like, "I know there are a lot of bad people in Mexico."

"We're gonna be totally safe. For real," I was like. Steve kept talking to his mom so I shot the shit with crazy-ass Derek; he was talking all about how chicks in the East are different from chicks in the West.

"For real, they're totally different; in the East, chicks are all like high maintenance and uptight all the time; in the West they're like way more chill, but also tend to be less hot, unless you get out more on the coast, but then they get sorta uptight again; I think it's 'cause the air is like thinner out West or something so I think they have shorter periods." Seemed like Steve's mom was pretty chill 'cause she was like bummed to see him go, but she got that he needed to go do that shit. Dude was getting the fuck out to show his dad what was up. The three of us were gonna party and each of us were gonna show the world what the fuck was up. Steve said peace out to his mom and bounced. Peace out. Peace out.

We loaded up the ride at Beth's and peaced out to her. Tom was gonna nab a ride with us to his place. Beth was looking mad hot when we left; she was all thin but with a mad rack. She was pulling off a total smokeshow look. She looked kinda bummed to not get to hang with us anymore. She said she was gonna come and meet us with Tom—shit never happened. Peace out. Peace out.

We beasted out of there. We dropped Tom at his place sorta in the burbs and I looked back at him as we got further away. That dude just stood there for like two minutes making jerk-off gestures to get us to crack the hell up and we all cracked the hell up at that. His jerk-off gestures got farther and farther away, and he still kept doing them with one hand acting like it was jerking off back and forth and back and forth as we roared ahead and cracked the shit up until he was just a little speck and then there was nothing to see except big-ass road behind us that led back to the Midwest and my stomping grounds at Ohio State.

We finished cracking the hell up and hauled ass south toward Castle Rock, Colorado, as the sun got all red and shit and the mountains in the west looked like a Coors Light commercial during the Super Bowl. Way up in the mountains it looked like there were two people doing it, like straight up banging on the rocks, which would be awesome; but maybe it was just some mountain goats, which would make more sense but be less awesome. Mountain banging. That would be such awesome shit, to smash in the middle of rock climbing. And we peaced out of Denver, thinking about that shit, and how raw it would be.

CHAPTER FOUR

BLACK CAT BURRITO

We picked up some Chipotle. How the fuck can Chipotle, which makes burritos that taste so delicious and are so filling—the kind of burritos that are like three-hundo-percent tasty from start to finish—make a burrito as shitty as the one Steve Sharpford ate? He'd downed a carnitas burrito with extra guac and was just telling some funny-ass story when all of a sudden he started gagging and barfed like crazy out the window. The burrito had tasted totally fine. He hurled and hurled and then dry heaved for a little bit, and dude looked mad pale and sweaty. Derek and I were afraid we were gonna ralph too. We just had to wait and see if we were gonna get mad sick. It was so shitty that we were just like a couple miles outside of Denver, hauling ass to awesome times in Mexico, eating Chipotle, solid, reliable Chipotle like we'd eat a billion times before, and Steve got a totally rancid burrito that fucked up his stomach and made him ralph it up hard. "What the hell happened?"

"I have literally never heard of anybody getting sick from Chipotle."

"Fuck!" It was like a black cat crossing our path but in burrito form. We kept driving. Steve dry heaved a couple more times. We told him to cowboy up and deal. We hauled ass past some shit town and hit Colorado Springs when it started getting dark. A huge outlet mall shimmered overhead. Derek cranked it down the interstate. "I've chilled around here before," Derek was like. "I totally hit that outlet mall one time 'cause I was hoping the Nike outlet would have Nike+ but they didn't for whatever fucking reason."

We decided to see like who could go without pissing for the longest, and Steve totally already needed to piss when we started the game. "We gotta make time," Derek was like, "so if you can just

hold it in like a champ and just fucking deal with your bladder—
that'll be clutch and get us there faster. Hold it, bro, hold it," he told
Steve, who was totally already gonna piss, "like mind over matter."
Steve looked like he was gonna explode as we hauled ass into the
night. He tried to pretend like he was fine at first, but then shit got
harder and harder to hold in and he was all sweaty and jittery. He
tried to convince Derek to pull over. "Dude, come on, just like, can
you just pull over? Come on. I just really need to piss, like never
mind the game. Aight. Aight?" Steve was mad desperate. He seriously needed Derek to pull over. Derek was like the piss gatekeeper,
with piss veto power, and was laying down martial pissing law. "Just
hold it dude; just hold it." I got a text message, it was from Chaz
Kerry, who was chilling down in Miami Beach, where he was probably having a sick time too and maybe he was giving some dude shit
like Derek was giving Steve and Chaz had like no idea at the same
moment he was kicking back in Miami Beach that we were flying
like a fucking hawk straight down to Mexico while Steve pissed in
a bottle of Powerade. Sometimes text messages blow my mind. We
blasted into New Mexico where there was like nothing of anything
'till we swung in to a Subway attached to a Sunoco, fucking starving
for some footlong Sweet Onion Chicken Teriyaki subs, which we
got extras of to eat later when we got starving again. "Time to tear
up Texas," Derek was like, "Last time we tore it up East-West style.
Now we gotta hit it North-South. It's still long as fuck. We're gonna
be driving forever and just be in one state. That's fucked up."

We rolled out. Out of a big-ass dark field of nothing came
the first Texas Roadhouse we'd seen in Texas, which I cruised by
before. Its sign shimmered off parked cars stretched across its big-
ass parking lot. Looking at it sort of made me get hungry again. In
the bag next to me was another Sweet Onion Chicken Teriyaki
sub. I was gonna save it for later, but it was gonna be delicious; it
was like calling my name, 'till I couldn't stand it anymore and I
could smell it inside my brain—and I dug into that shit. Like six
inches later—it was still mad good even though it was colder—I
felt more full, and we cruised past Amarillo. There were brand

new Pizza Huts and bars, and gyms with big-ass windows and pretty nice-looking equipment. For like the whole time between Amarillo and Childress, me and Derek recited scenes from *The Hangover* and Steve thought it was hilarious and somehow he'd never even seen it. Once we got to Childress we took this little shitty road south and absolutely beasted it past a heaping shit-pile of nothing past some town with like nothing, nothing, and whole bunch of fucking nothing. Derek needed to drop some nap bombs, so we switched it up and Steve sat in front and I drove. The Wrangler revved and revved and gripped the road like a motherfucker. Shuddering reverberations of the Wrangler's subwoofer shook us to the core. Steve started needing to piss again but he still held it 'cause we weren't gonna stop for that shit.

Texas was super big; we were tired as fuck rolling through Abilene and were like "WTF." "Yo, can you believe motherfuckers live out here with like nothing to do anywhere? Jesus Christ, like for real I bet they all just hang around and fuck animals or something! Right? Fuck yeah!" Derek cracked the shit up and pretended like he was fucking a cow. Dude didn't give a fuck wherever he was. All these fat Texas dudes tried to ignore him as we rolled past and he was pretending to fuck a cow. We noshed down on some Long John Silver's near an off ramp. We all sort of felt like we were gonna chunk it after having about twenty butterfly shrimp each as we hauled ass toward Coleman and Brady—like deep as hell into Texas with pretty much nothing around except some trees, a creek, and an occasional Sonic. "Motherfucking Mexico is still far as fuck," Derek was like, coming out of his nap bomb for a second, "Just keep driving, aight, and pretty soon we'll be pulling mad Mexican trim by sunrise 'cause this Wrangler can fucking book it if you just hit the pedal—and if that check engine light comes on—just fuck it." And he napped back out.

I drove for a while past Fredericksburg, and like the little blue dot on my phone I was like all over the fucking map going back and forth and I was totally right near where Maryann and I had vibed all up on each other, and shit; what was her deal? "Chug!" Derek

hollered in his nap 'cause he must have been having a dream he was
at a San Fran party or at one of the Mexican ragers to come. Steve
really needed to piss again; Derek was seriously fucking with him
with this game and it was too hilarious to stop. He was about to
piss in that Powerade bottle again, which was extra gross because it
had been half full of Powerade, so it was like this sick fucking mix
of blue and yellow becoming a nasty-ass warm green that swirled
and stank. We all gagged from the waft of stank that came out of the
bottle and got all in our faces. We were all still pretty full of butterfly
shrimp and we could pretty easily ralph if we smelled that shit, for
real. The Wrangler Unlimited Rubicon hit ninety like no big deal.
We descended down the hills like mad. Gross-ass bugs were getting
the Wrangler all dirty. "Shit's getting real now, bros: the bitches and
the tequila. I've like never partied down here before," Derek was
like. "Fuck dude, my dad always talked about this shit when he'd be
here for Spurs games, that fucking dude."

Shit started to get hot as we rolled down this big-ass hill, and
San Antonio like shot all up in front of us. It was sorta like Mexico
but sorta still America. Shit was hotter; there were more taquerias,
and there were a ton of Mexican people. Derek drove and beasted
it into San Antonio. We blew past a shitload of suburbs and rolled
into the city. We stopped at a Chipotle to eat some real burritos.
Most Chipotles serve beer, but at this one people were like taking
advantage of it, buying like a shitton of beer and getting pretty wild
in the Chipotle. There were literally like a million people getting
hammered in this Chipotle. The sweet smell of Corona and barbacoa wafted in the air and wrapped us up in deliciousness. Some
hotties ate burrito bowls in the corner. "Fuck yeah!" Derek was
like. "*Ay caramba!*" We were ordering burritos, a ton of burritos.
Steve and me downed burritos, threw back some Negra Modelos
and already got a little buzzed up. We were almost done and then
Steve chunked it again and now dude had gotten sick off two different burritos. It was insane. Dude looked sick.

"Aight, bros, listen up—we gotta party for a little in San
Antonio but maybe we'll take Steve by the hospital 'cause he's

looking real nasty this time, and while dude is there, Sam, you
and me can go strut it and check out some of those bars over
there, it looks like a lot of hotties hang in there and you can
just imagine grinding up on them as the music blasts and the air
smells like tacos, so let's do this shit!"

We searched on our phones to find like a doctor or a hospital
or something. We rolled up to one in the middle of the city, sorta
near the River Walk, which is a pretty cool and chill place with like
water and trees and shit, and it would be cooler if there were more
like bars with patios on it, but I guess they wanted to keep it sorta
quiet, so whatever. Derek dropped us in front and I took Steve in to
see a doctor and Derek just chilled in the car and hit my flask a little.
The waiting room was mad gross and had all these Mexican people.
I thought about Tali, who was so hot. Steve sat there for like ever
waiting to see somebody and then finally he saw a doctor who said
that he had like an allergy to cilantro or something so the Chipotle
rice totally fucked him up. We couldn't believe he'd never eaten
Chipotle before. He took some Benadryl and chilled out.

While that shit was going down, Derek and I hit up San Antonio.
It was mad hot, but like a dry heat, totally not like it is in Ohio, which
gets so humid and gross. From like nowhere all these hotties just
appeared, texting on their phones in the dark. Derek just straight-up
scoped this out. "Dude, this shit is way tight!" he was like. "We gotta
check more shit out. Oh fuck! Oh fuck! A Buffalo Wild Wings!" We
needed to hit that up. A bunch of dudes were crowded around the
bar, watching ESPN. Derek and I got a pitcher and fed some dollars
into the TouchTunes and played Kanye and Kid Cudi and Shaggy and
pounded knucks. Derek started laughing at some shit.

"Yo, check it out, over by the bar, as we're bumpin' to Kanye
rap about being awesome and drinking down some MGD—check
out that dude, the scrawny dude hanging with the other dudes;
they're totally giving him shit; he's been getting shit for like ever.
Those other dudes are totally making fun of him and it's hilarious."

The scrawny dude was like trying to look awesome wearing this polo that was like way too big for him, and he was pretty

hammered, 'cause he probably couldn't hold his liquor that good. "Like for real, Sam, that dude's like Timmy Snipes, just in San Antonio. Oh shit! Look how they're stealing his hat! Ha! Fuck dude, that's hilarious. Like he totally wants his hat back, but they're not gonna give it back. Check it out!" We saw one of the bigger dudes hold it up so high that he couldn't grab it. He jumped and fell down. They all cracked the shit up. "Fuck dude," Derek was like, "that's funny shit." They lifted him up and wouldn't put him down, giving him mad shit. He was like "fucking stop!" He broke free and stormed out of the bar and stopped and looked back and flipped everybody off. "Shit dude, I wonder where the fuck that little dude is going and like why he hangs with those dudes and if he like scores any tail—aw dude, I'm getting hammered way faster than I expected!" We closed our tab and staggered out of the Buffalo Wild Wings, weaving through a ton of people who were now packing the place. Hotties lined the walls waiting for tables; they were on their phones; they were talking to each other; they were trying to get a drink at the bar. "I can't believe I've never chilled in San Antonio before! And Mexico's probably gonna be like fifty-times awesomer. Let's roll! Let's roll!" We hauled ass over to the hospital. Steve had gotten all the shit out of his system and was looking way less fucked up. We gave him shit for not being able to handle Chipotle and told him about the awesome time we had at B-Dubs.

It was game time to haul ass the rest of the way to Mexico. We piled in the Wrangler Unlimited and gunned it. I was tired as fuck and kinda drunk so I dropped nap bombs for a while 'till we rolled up to a Waffle House in Laredo at like 2 A.M. "Aight," Derek was like, "we've almost beasted out of Texas, beasted out of America; we're beasting into unknown territory." It was hot as fuck; we cranked the AC. There was no way we were gonna open the windows; we didn't want to get all gross and sweaty, so we just turned the Wrangler Unlimited's climate control down to sixty and leaned back in the chill breeze that blew in through the vents that kept us cold as we hauled ass to the Rio Grande.

Laredo was looking sketchy as fuck when we rolled in. Dudes with cabs and shady vans were chilling, like looking for some sketch-ass business. But it didn't seem like much business was happening 'cause it was late-slash-early as hell. It was like the basement of a frat party where all the sketchy dudes hang, where the sorta gross chicks get all up on dudes who are too drunk or too sketch to turn them down. I bet like almost everybody was like trying to smuggle drugs, *Scarface*-style. Dickhole cops and border patrol were like everywhere. The waitresses were not hot. You just knew that like right over the border was the awesome party of Mexico and you could taste the gallons of tequila being poured in bars across the night. Mexico was gonna be off the chain. We got mad hungry and when we piled in the Waffle House I really housed some grub. I took a T-bone to go for later. We were full as fuck and feeling a little tired. But we got mad amped when we hauled ass over the river and rolled up the border checkpoint. We were so fucking close to Mexico. Shit was like right there. We scoped shit out. It didn't look like Cabo, but it still looked pretty sweet. It was 3 A.M. and dudes were just chilling on the street getting hammered.

"Check those dudes out!" Derek was like, "Fuck," he was like, "Fucking pigs." The border cops came up to us and wanted us to pop the trunk. We popped it. We didn't want them to find the little sack of weed Derek brought. It was like not that much but it could still be some serious shit if it got found. "Fuck me, dude. Fuck me," Derek was like. We showed them our passports. They said to watch out for the tap water and then let us go. They like barely checked our bags. They were way less dicks than like American TSA assholes. These dudes were chill. Derek was mad relieved. He high-fived me.

"Dude, the cops here are amazing! Holy shit!" He slapped the steering wheel. "The fucking best." We hit an ATM to get some pesos. We weren't sure if we were getting screwed with fees, but we still got a shitload of pesos. We put those fat wads in our wallets and felt like ballers.

CHAPTER FIVE

FOUR HORSEMEN OF THE FUCKING PARTY APOCALYPSE

It was game time and we put our game faces on as we cruised into Mexico with like everybody looking at us wondering who those awesome dudes are. We saw awesome bars and cheap drinks and margaritas flowing like a river. "Fuck yeah," Derek was like.

"Aight," Derek was like. "It's go time. Let's do it. Watch out, Mexico. We're gonna have the rawest time. Fuck, how can you not have the rawest time in Mexico?"

"Fuck yeah!" Derek was like and we strutted up the street. We parked the car and we checked out all the bars and souvenir shops with super hilarious T-shirts. Old dudes sat in the stores and tried to charge us way too much for "I Ate the Worm" T-shirts. They thought we were just some tourists but we were for real looking to hang. We rolled up into this bar that was like blasting mariachi shit from the TouchTunes. Dudes in muscle tees and some lame-ass hipsters chilled at the bar, eating a bunch of burritos or something. We ordered a bucket of Coronas—the primo shit to be drinking in Mexico—for what was I think equal to like ten bucks. We just stared in awe at our amazing bucket of Coronas that were so cheap, and imagined how much fucking booze we could buy down here. Behind us were all the beers and kegs and handles Derek and I had ever bought: Nattys, MGDs, Popovs, everything. We were finally in the place with the cheapest beers ever and we'd never even imagined how cheap shit could be. "Just imagine how like all the Mexican people around think these are like normal prices," Derek was like. "And like imagine all the bars in front of us with even more beer that might get even cheaper when it's not as close to the border and imagine how we'll be having the same awesome times we'd always heard about from our buddies who would party here on spring break, who'd always sound like they were fucking lying about how good a time they had but now we can see it all in front of us in the buckets and buckets of Coronas that are gonna wash down our throats and make the awesome times blow up! How are we gonna get wild? What's our move? Let's fucking do it!" We slammed down the Coronas and piled back in the whip. I took a quick picture on my phone of the lights of Laredo just over the border, but I was like "Fuck that," deleted it, and got ready to party Mexico-style.

In a hot second we were hauling ass through the desert and it was like the fucking moon or something. Shit started to get light outside and we could see like some cactus and rocks and shit all around us. "It's like the fucking moon or something!" I was like. Derek and I were mad pumped. We'd been balls-tired in Laredo. Steve had come down to Mexico one time with some buddies, so he just dropped some nap bombs. Derek and I couldn't get any more amped.

"Aight, Sam, for real we're like party astronauts blasting off into the unknown. All the bullshit in the past—and the awesome times too—now it's fucking go time! So we gotta just chill and ride this whip with our party cups out so that the world, and I'm being real here, can let the keg flow into us! And you know, like American dudes have partied down here before, you know? Like for spring break. And bachelor parties."

"You know probably," I was like, "crews came down this way to party like back when our dads were kicking it, before you could get cheap-ass airfare to Cabo and so dudes would just drive, so like imagine this desert full of cars full of hammered dudes and hot chicks hauling it south to make awesome parties out in the Mexican sands . . ." "Aw for real!" Derek was like. "Fuck yeah!" he shouted, punching the steering wheel. "For real! Like we could totally just drive like a motherfucker straight down to South America. For real! Motherfucker! For real!" We kept hauling ass. Shit kept getting lighter outside and we could see like a ton of

desert with some little houses and shit. Derek cruised by looking for food. "Just shacks, dude, like nothing to do around this
part but get sand all over your dick. Boring." We rolled up into
another town that looked like it had actual shit. We wanted to get
there—'cause we were getting hungry again. "Shit dude," Derek
was like, "I just noticed that all the signs are like in kilometers
instead of miles. Fuck, are kilometers longer or shorter? I think
they're shorter 'cause I ran a five K and remember that it was like
three miles or something." It was like a thousand some kilometers
to Mexico City so I Googled the conversion and it turned out that
like a thousand kilometers was like seven-hundo miles. "Fuck! We
gotta get there!" Derek was like. I tried to lay some nap bombs but
Derek was being sorta annoying by punching the steering wheel
and being all like "Fuck yeah!" and "Let's do this!" and "Bring it!"
We rolled through someplace-*Hidalgo* at like 7 A.M. We cruised the
scene. Steve's phone woke him up. We rolled down the windows
and cranked some beats. The town was a shithole. All the buildings looked like they sucked. There were fucking donkeys walking around. The chicks might have been hot but they were all just
inside, checking us out through the windows. There was a big-ass
load of Mexican dudes walking around, probably going to work or
something. Super-old dudes watched us and were probably jealous. We just kept blasting our beats and cruising down the shitty
road. This crew of chicks crossed the street in front of us. One was
like, "What's up fellas?"

I punched Derek in the arm, all stoked. "What the fuck?
For real?" Derek was stoked too and was like, "Yeah dude, she
was totally into us, it was totally obvious; oh dude, for real, shit is
like too good to be true in this bomb-ass world. It's tang-heaven.
Shit couldn't be more awesome; shit couldn't be more clutch;
shit couldn't be more off the chain."

"Let's see if they wanna party," I was like.

"Yeah," Derek was like but kept cruising. He was pretty spaced
out, he was just too pumped about being in Mexico. "We're gonna
find like a million more hotties further down the road!" Still, dude

hung a U-turn and cruised past the crew of chicks. They said they
were going to work; they were totally into us. Derek gave them his
pimpest look. "Shit," he was like, whispering. "Bro! This is just too
clutch. Hotties, hotties. And like maybe I'm just tired as fuck, Sam,
but I'm just imaging how awesome it would be to live in one of
these shitty houses, 'cause even though you'd have some kind of
shit bed and probably like no AC, every morning you'd just wake
up with like nothing to do except work outside, then come back to
your house where your mad hot wife is like cooking up chorizo all
the time so you just throw back a Tecate, demolish a chorizo burrito, then like get your beast on for a hot second and then head over
to your buddy's house, and he's probably got a mad hot wife too
who cooks a ton of chorizo and everything is delicious and amazing. There's no bullshit here, for real. Everybody is chill, nobody
gives you shit about not going to class enough or like wasting your
parents' tuition money; it's just chill, people have a good fucking
time. Mexico is just all about chilling and living without a bunch
of bullshit. I think this is totally awesome." A born partier, Derek
existed to have a good time. He checked his phone, swerved back
onto the right side of the road, and kept cruising. We nabbed some
gas on the other side of town. A bunch of farmer dudes in hats
were just chilling outside the gas station slugging beers outside like
it was no big deal. Some dude walked by with a fucking donkey.
The sun gleamed through their beer bottles; drinking outside is
one of the most clutch things in life. We kept hauling ass toward
Monterrey. A Mexican Pizza Hut shot up right in front of us. At
first we thought it was like a mirage or something, but as we got
closer we could make out the sign, clear as fuck. We didn't know
that there were Pizza Huts in Mexico, but now here in front of us
with its big-ass sign and delicious smells was the same place that
had served us amazing pizza so many times during football games
in America. We had to eat that shit. The place was pretty empty. We
grabbed a booth. Trying to remember my middle school Spanish, I
checked out the menu. Pizza Hut in Mexico is like pretty similar to
Pizza Hut in America, mostly the same kind of tasty-ass pizzas with

stuffed crust, breadsticks, and all that shit; except they totally serve a Mexican pizza that has like salsa and shit on it in addition to cheese and sausage and whatever. We had to get it, so we ordered a Mexican pizza and our mouths watered as the waitress brought out all the awesome smells of a normal Pizza Hut pizza but intertwined with an off-the-chain aroma of pico de gallo that made you realize in a single moment how bullshit the idea of combination Pizza Hut/ Taco Bells are because why the fuck should you keep your tacos and pizzas separate when in one amazing genius move you can let the salsa rain down on the pizza and create a taste so fucking amazing that your face will melt. "Holy shit!" Derek was like. "That's so fucking good. Did you get a bite with sausage *and* salsa? It's so fucking tasty. Fuck yeah! I want to eat this like for the rest of my life— shit is *amazing!*" We thought about ordering some dessert pizzas too and checking out what kind of awesome sides they had, but Derek wanted to get cranking to Mexico City, and he knew there would be more delicious Mexican Pizza Huts ahead, and we'd have the sides there. Dude hauled ass like a motherfucker and didn't take a break. Steve and I were tired as fuck and needed to drop some nap bombs. I woke up for just a second past Monterrey and could see a Pizza Hut slowly fading into the distance, and my mouth watered.

We cruised our shit down into Montemorelos, which was hot as fuck. It was pretty boring in addition to being balls-hot. Now Derek wouldn't let me take a piss either. "For real, Sam, we *just* pissed." That was bullshit. I'd had like seven Dews at the Mexican Pizza Hut and now every five seconds my bladder totally throbbed. I tried to hold it in. Gritting my teeth hard as fuck, I stared out the window and tried to forget about that shit but everything outside was boring. It sucks when you have to piss so bad, and you just can't do anything about it. "Seriously bro, I'd love to stop for you," Derek was like, "but we gotta keep hauling ass and you just can't—for real you just can't—be stopping all the time to piss. You'll never get anywhere. A real dude never breaks the seal. While you're busy with your vag all in a knot about pissing, I've been just chilling and thinking what a killer time we're gonna have, and bro, if you could just like get all *Inception* in my head and see the mad shit I'm dreaming!" Dude was stoked. Even though this road was boring his brain was like blowing up with party shit—Mexico was his jam. He pedaled it down and we beasted it through all the boring bullshit at like ninety. "Bro, I'm getting legit tired now. Let's switch this shit up and you can take a piss like a pussy."

We pulled over and I started driving, feeling mad better now that I didn't have to piss so bad, for real. Shit got all green all of a sudden. Crews of dudes checked us out as we blew by. The cold-ass AC blasted. Then shit started getting uphill and the green shit turned into sand. Some place called Gregoria was coming up. My dudes were nap bombing it hard, and I was all over the wheel like fucking Willis in *Live Free or Die Hard*, and I was gonna beast it mega-fast. Not beasting it like America, in Ohio, or Indiana, or even Arizona; more like beasting it in a fucking movie, just a dude and his whip blasting into the shit that he was gonna blow up among the hordes of anxious hotties, waiting for him by the keg; the tube-topped shorties of legend, party cups raised in joy, hollering like mad in voices that echo across the campuses from ASU to OSU to FSU and then MSU, then to OU and UT and on and on to everywhere (except University of Michigan—GO BUCKS) until the reverberations break down the walls of frat houses everywhere so that crews of dudes spill out into the world ready to make shit happen. We were most definitely badasses and weren't like the chaches and hipsters that fucked up America's party vibe—we were real and clutch and could get wild and chill at the same time; we weren't douches, we weren't dicks; we were badass, beer-chugging bros and we started the party and kept it going. Anybody can party, but only we could *fucking* party. We partied like most people breathed. And all these Mexicans in the middle of nowhere had no fucking idea, thinking we were just some dickhole tourists cruising by; they didn't know how hard we could drop it, how real shit could get, they had no fucking clue. 'Cause when the party gets started and kegs are rolled out and thunder crashes down as dudes jump from the roof into the swimming pool, boring-ass chaches everywhere will stand in the sidewalk and look, pissed as hell and jealous as fuck of the awesome times they'd signed away years ago when they decided to be tools. This was the shit all up in my brain when I beasted it like hell to Gregoria.

When we were in San Antonio, I'd bet Derek that I could get him laid in less than twenty-four hours in Mexico. I was sorta joking but also sorta serious. We were pulling over to nab some gas when this kid came running up, all looking like shit, with a bucket and wanting to wash the windshield. "I am Vincente. I wash your car? Sixty pesos. Okay?"

"No way dude," I was like, "I want some *senoritas*," all kidding and shit.

"Yes! Yes!" he was like, "I know girls; I hook you up. Maybe later. Too hot now," he was like. "Only ugly girls when it's hot. Later tonight. Want a wash?"

I didn't give a shit about the wash but I was all about getting laid. I punched Derek. "Wake up, asshole, I said I was gonna get you laid—wake the fuck up, seriously; we're gonna get mad laid."

"Huh? For real?" he was like, waking up all fast. "For real? For real?"

"Hell yeah. This dude's gonna hook us up."

"Aight, let's do it! Let's do it!" Derek busted out of the car and pounded knucks with Vincente. Vincente's crew of buddies were all chilling by the gas station, checking their shitty phones, which probably could barely even text. "Shit," Derek was like, "isn't this raw as fuck? This shit *never* goes down in Denver. Vincente, where the ladies at? Where they at? *Donde?*" he was like. "Shit dude, does that mean 'where?'"

"Oh shit, ask him if he's got pot. Yo, kid, you got weed?"

He was totally holding. "Totally. I hook you up. Come on."

"Hell yeah! Fuck yeah! Let's do it!" Derek was like. He'd gone from sleeping to sixty in like no time and was all psyched as we headed down the street. "Come on! Game time!" I let some of Vincente's Mexican buddies take hits off my flask. They thought we were pretty awesome. They were all pointing at Derek and whispering about how raw he was. "Check that shit, Sam, those dudes totally think we're awesome. Hell yeah, we're like fucking kings down here!" We got Vincente in the car and we rolled out. Steve Sharpford had been asleep as hell but now he woke up and didn't know what the fuck was going down.

We hauled ass to the middle of fucking nowhere in the desert. The road was bumpy as shit but the Wrangler Unlimited Rubicon could handle it. We rolled up to Vincente's place. It was a total shitpile in the desert, with some dudes chilling out front. "Who are those dudes?" Derek was like.

"My brothers. Mother live here too. And Sister. Whole family. I married and live downtown."

"Aw fuck, your mom?" Derek was like. "She cool with weed?"

"She has hook up." And for real, Vincente got out of the car, said some shit to his mom, and then his mom straight up grabbed some pot that was drying in the sun. And Vincente's brothers just checked shit out and chilled. They were gonna come party with us. Vincente came back all smiling.

"Dude," Derek was like, "this Vincente dude is like the most solid little player I've ever met. Like for real, check his shit out. He's just chill and can totally hook a dude up." The windows were open and the AC was doing like jack shit now. It was mad hot.

"Crazy hot, right?" Vincente was like, climbing into the Wrangler Unlimted. "We smoke up and then shit is cool. Okay?"

"Hell yeah," Derek was like, trying to crank the AC up more. "I feel you, for real buddy."

One of Vincente's buddies came by with a bunch of weed just like on some newspaper. He gave that shit to Vincente and then just chilled leaning on the door, which was totally letting out the rest of the AC. Derek gave him a nod. It sucked that it was so fucking hot. Vincente rolled the fattest blunt that's like ever happened. It was like a straight-up cigar of weed—for real. Derek was blown away by how fucking huge it was. Hitting it was like being in a forest fire except there's no trees, just like a ton

of gonj on fire. And I don't usually get high ('cause it fucks with
your endurance) but it was Mexico so I sucked that shit down.
We got everybody in the car, cranked the AC, and baked that
shit. We were high as fuck. It got mad cold and it was like getting
toked in the fucking arctic. Another one of Vincente's brothers
came up and piled in the car and just like nodded and we nodded
back. The Wrangler was filling up with these Mexican dudes.
Shit was crazy. We were all so high as fuck that it didn't even
matter that we couldn't like fucking talk to each other; we were
just Americans and Mexicans getting high as fuck in the desert,
and it was amazing seeing how these dudes from the middle of
fucking nowhere could just like hang and party and blaze up like
pros. The Mexican dudes were all talking about us and checking
out how fit we were and probably feeling pretty jealous since it
looked like they probably didn't have much workout equipment
out here. And Derek and Steve and me talked about those dudes.

"Yo, for real, doesn't the dude in the back look so much
like George Lopez, but like a young-ass George Lopez the way
his hair is and he's like sorta making those same crazy faces? Shit,
like what if he's related to George Lopez or something—I'm for
real, don't laugh, like it could totally be possible. Shit, the dudes
are *real*. I've never hung with dudes like this. They're totally talking about our shit, like trying to figure out how a Wrangler full
of badass American dudes landed in the middle of their yard,
and the thing is we're not that different; like even though we've
got way better phones and are generally more built, we all still
love to hang and party and just blaze sometimes. Shit, what did
that dude say about me?" Derek tried to find out. "Yo, Vincente,
bro—is your brother saying some shit about me?"

Vincente took a big-ass long hit of the weed cigar and was
like, "Yeah."

"Yeah, but like, I mean, what is he saying about me?"

"Huh?" Vincente was like, sorta pissed, "You don't like
weed?"

"Naw dude, the weed is mad good. What's he *saying*?"

"We say stuff. You like Mexico?" It was hard as fuck to talk to these dudes sometimes. So everybody just chilled and got high and kicked back as we baked the Wrangler out like it was a fucking cake.

It was totally hottie o'clock. Vincente's brothers got out of the Wrangler, the awesome mom waved goodbye, and we hauled ass back into town.

Now that we were super high, the Wrangler Unlimited felt even smoother; like the smoothest fucking ride ever, like driving on a cloud or some shit, and Derek's neck flexed like a bodybuilder as he talked about the Wrangler Unlimited's Tunable Monotube Shock Absorbers and how they made the ride so fucking smooth. Vincente couldn't believe what a pimp ride he was getting. He told Derek to go left for the chicks, so Derek, popping a mad mind-boner, cut the wheel mega-hard and blasted us closer to the tang up ahead, all while Vincente kept trying to say shit that made no sense and Derek would totally make fun of him all like, "Hell yeah dude! For real! Exactly! I was thinking the same thing! Fuck yeah! Tell me more!" Vincente totally didn't get that Derek was punking him, so he just kept talking in Spanish. Derek was doing this shit so hard that I thought he could actually understand the dude for a hot second, like maybe he knew Spanish when he was high or something. And like for a hot second I thought dude totally looked like Nic Cage—a fucked up hallucination in my high-ass brain or something—and I like couldn't believe that shit and rubbed my eyes to see if it was fucking real. I was way too high to find where my aviators were so I just squinted through the sunlight to try to see better and with the sun blasting all up on his face he looked like Cage. I was too high to function; for a second the smooth ride made me think we'd like hit a ramp and were catching air. Just trying to check my fantasy baseball standings on my phone—which I needed to do to know if I had to make trades—was like super hard because all of a sudden my phone seemed way too bright and I felt like I couldn't keep my shit together and I might totally fuck up my team. I put down my phone. I felt delicious waves of air conditioning wrapping my body in cool-ass air, like all over me and into my brain; I was like an Eskimo. I looked out the window and it looked hot as fuck and we passed a cop and I totally thought I saw him switch on his sirens and come after us—total paranoid weed shit. The AC kept cooling my shit down hard. I spaced the fuck out and just started playing with the calculator app on my phone for some fucking reason and didn't snap the fuck out of it 'till the car stopped and everybody told me we were at Vincente's crib and the dude had already gone in and gotten his pit bull and was like showing it to us at the window.

"This my dog. He is name Perez, two years old."

"Shit dude," Derek was like, still looking a little Cage-esque in the fading sunlight, "that is like such a badass dog. Yo, Sam and Steve," he was like, "you gotta check out the dog and just think about what a badass he is and how he could totally fuck a dude up if you needed to, but you can train it to be nice as fuck to chicks so you can totally game it at dog parks with hotties." Dude was right as hell. And that dog was badass as hell. Vincente had to feed it raw fucking meat for dinner. All of us wanted to have a totally badass dog. We wanted a badass dog so bad that the dog like must have sensed that shit and like flipped out, first sorta barking and then straight up howling and like trying to break off its leash and fuck shit up and we couldn't do anything to stop it 'cause a dog like that is a fucking tank. The dog was crazy; Vincente tried to get him to chill; Derek cracked the hell up; I took out my phone and took some video of this shit. He barked louder and louder. "Shit dude," Derek was like, "your dog is a fucking beast!"

"He okay. Just a little crazy." Through the window behind Vincente we could see his sorta busted-looking wife, looking all pissed 'cause she probably hated that dog 'cause it was so badass. Vincente took that fucking beast back inside and told us to go to the right.

"Aight," Derek was like, and rolled through some shitty little alleys with people everywhere checking our shit out. We rolled up to this shady-ass strip club. It was a gross shit-colored

building. There were totally a couple cops posted up outside the
place, looking all ragged and bored, who just looked at us when
we went in and for real just chilled there for like three hours 'till
we came out and Vincente told us to give them both like a hundred pesos, 'cause Mexico is pretty fucked up like that.

It was like trim heaven inside. Chicks were grinding up on
poles on the stage; other chicks were grinding up on dudes by
the bar. In the middle was an ATM that had like no fee, which is
crazy, 'cause every strip club in America has ATMs with like ten-
dollar fees. That was an awesome idea. The dude who owned the
place was chilling behind the bar, and when we tried to use the
TouchTunes and it was broken, dude asked us what we wanted
to listen to, of course we were like "Kanye," and dude straight up
ran out and seriously came back with a fucking stack of Kanye
CDs and played them on the stereo. Like in a hot second this
whole fucking town could hear how wild shit was getting inside.
The thumping of the beats in the club—and this club had like a
crazy, crazy sick system with mad bass—was so raw that it blew
Derek and Steve and my mind as we realized that we'd always
thought we had sick systems in our apartments and cars, but we
had never gotten bass this crazy and bass this crazy was all we
wanted. It straight-up rattled our faces off. For real, the whole
town like showed up and tried to see inside, to see the bombass American bros grinding up on hot-ass stripper chicks. They
were all just standing by the door and the couple tiny-ass windows, all dirty and shit, looking jealous as fuck. "Power," "All
of the Lights," "Gold Digger," "Drive Slow"—and even more
raw Kanye tracks thumped and blasted in the dark, badass strip
club like the sound of the Four Horsemen of the Fucking Party
Apocalypse. The beats were so earth-shattering that I thought
for a second I was gonna throw up, but then I just got more
pumped. Kanye's rhymes were hot. *Late Registration* is my favorite album, the one that I've gotten wild to so many times; it's
seriously awesome. Kanye was all like "uh" and "yeah," "uh,"
and "yeah." Young Jeezy dropped it with slow-ass intensity.

The sick-ass bridge of "Power," from *My Beautiful Dark Twisted Fantasy*, made Derek freeze like a fucking zombie 'till he started doing his awesome robot dance, faster and faster, until the guitars and shit blew the fuck up and as the beats kept rolling. Derek raised his beer and started pumping his fist, amped as fuck like he was actually seeing Kanye live. I raised my fist too; I heard new sick beats as "All of the Lights" started and it felt like Kanye was playing inside my skull.

Once "Monster" started dropping we got our grind on for real. We were stoned and hammered and we scoped the hell out of the strippers. They were actually not that gross of strippers. The hottest one was like sorta Mexican-looking but kinda looked Indian too, and wasn't gross at all. She was like model-hot. Who the fuck knows how any chick who's model-hot ends up stripping in the middle of Whereverthefuck, Mexico. She was also sorta a bitch. She yelled and got crazy hammered. She straight-up threw back a million shots and like didn't give a fuck. She did this bullshit move where she knocked over our beers so we'd have to buy more beer. Looking all fine in her stripper gear, she grinded all up with Derek like it was her job and it sorta was. Derek was still high as fuck and like couldn't believe with all the Kanye and strippers that this wasn't a fucking dream. They bolted to the VIP room. I got this fat busted chick all up on me, and she got all pissed when I asked her what she weighed. She left to grind up on another dude and then this okay-looking chick latched on me and like wouldn't stop giving me lap dances. I wanted to get the fuck away from her and grind with this crazy hot Latina chick who was just like chilling at the bar on a break or something. I couldn't get away from this lap-dance leech. Steve was grinding up on some chick in a sequined outfit that was totally coming off fast as hell. Shit was wild. Dudes came into the club and just watched us get wild.

Pretty soon the boyfriend of the Latina chick—a real jackass-looking dude—rolled up and got in some fight with her. Once I saw she had a gross-ass boyfriend, I was totally over her.

I went with the lap-dance leech to a back room, where, even though I usually have a "no strippers" policy, with Kanye dropping it hot through the walls, we beasted it like mad for like thirty to forty minutes. It was a little VIP room with some couches and dim-ass light, with a bucket of some beers in a corner. All around me I could Kanye thumping and thumping, and it was like I had my Kanye sex-mix. Steve and Derek were hooking up with other chicks in the other VIP rooms. My chick wanted like three-hundo pesos, which is I think like twenty-ish bucks, and then wanted a big-ass tip and said some shit in Spanish that I didn't get. I was drunk and didn't give a shit; I had like a million pesos. I threw some bills at her. We kept grinding outside. The crowd outside was big as fuck. The cops still didn't give a shit. I went with Derek's model-hot chick into a second bar that was still part of the strip club. There were like a couple dudes at the bar just talking and not doing any grinding. Kanye was still blasting like fuck in here too. The whole fucking world was bumpin'. Model-hot got all up on me and had me buy her drinks. The bartender cut her off. She kept like screaming at him to let her have one, and when dude finally served her she like spilled it everywhere not on purpose, and she looked hammered as fuck. "Whoa, chill," I was like. She kept falling off the stool like an idiot so I had to hold her up. She was for real the drunkest chick I've ever seen. I got her another drink, 'cause she was annoying as fuck about it. She pounded that shit. There was no way I could hook up with her. The lap-dance leech wasn't as hot but wasn't as much of a mess. Since this chick was all fucking sloppy and like spilling shit all over me, I wanted to get the fuck away, for real. I still totally wanted to hit on the Latina chick.

That Vincente dude, he just chilled by the bar and gave us some high-fives 'cause he was stoked to have such clutch American buddies. We did some shots with him. Dude was totally wanting to grind up on this chick but he was a mad prude 'cause he had that sorta-busted wife. Derek did like a million shots with him. I hadn't even noticed how totally hammered

Derek had gotten. He was so crunked that he couldn't even use his phone when he got texts. "Shit, aw fuck," he was like, trying to push the keys. The wildness wouldn't stop. It was like a badass spring break dream in the middle of Mexico from a movie—hotties and drinking and boning. I smashed with my stripper chick real fast; Derek and Steve totally smashed each other's chicks; and everybody outside was all wondering where the fuck the party went. Somebody kicked the AC up a notch inside.

In a hot second it was gonna start getting dark in wherever-the-fuck we were. The Kanye never stopped; the owner must have put that shit on repeat. I kept scoping the hottie Latina chick like mad, and how, like a total smokeshow she walked around looking all hot and even the bartender wanted to get with that action. Out of all the strippers in the world she was probably the hottest, unless you're in Miami maybe. Latina chicks have rad bodies. I like never, for real, never went up and spat game at her. I felt like her assface boyfriend was gonna come back any second, and getting in a fight while I was that drunk and stoned sounded like a shitty fucking time. I was popping a total mind-boner for her while we were there; it was like I needed to hit that but I couldn't hit that and that shit made me pissed as fuck as I just stood there like a total pusswad not making a move, even though I had a good fucking reason. Like Derek and Steve totally didn't spit game at her either; she was too short for Steve and Derek didn't want to fuck with that boyfriend either. I saw Derek totally scoping her and like getting ready to swoop in like a hawk and make shit happen, and then the boyfriend came back just as he was gonna go over and so he stopped and looked all pissed. Why do chicks gotta date such dicks?

Vincente started freaking out and made us come over to the bar.

"What the fuck?" He spoke all in Spanish and we didn't understand shit. Then dude got the check from the bartender, who looked kinda pissed, and showed it to us. It was like five thousand pesos, which is like four hundred bucks, which is kind a shit-ton of money to drop on a strip club that's not like nice and in America. We didn't really give a fuck and wanted to keep partying, even though we'd dropped like a fuckton of cash we wanted to hang with these strippers who were like so hot in the middle of nowhere 'cause we'd found this amazing hottie oasis in the middle of the desert. But shit was starting to get dark so we had to peace out; Derek knew we had to peace out but wanted to keep partying, and then I finally gave orders to roll out. "There's gonna be a ton of awesome shit on this trip, bro, this is just like the start."

"Fuck yeah!" Derek was like, getting amped, and went to say peace out to Model-hot. That chick had blacked out and was a total fucking mess by the bar. There were still crowds of people outside trying to figure out what the shit was going down; they were probably so fucking jealous, and then I looked at my phone and didn't recognize the carrier and I remembered that we were totally in fucking Mexico and not just in some kind of awesome smash-filled drunk-ass house party in heaven.

We hauled our drunk asses through the door; we didn't know where the fuck Steve was; we texted him and dude texted back that he was still inside and didn't want to leave. New chicks were rolling in for the night and he wanted to light shit up again. When that dude gets hammered he loves to party and when that dude gets hammered he's like glued to hotties. And the hotties won't fucking let him go. Dude said we had to stick around and grind up on the new chicks 'cause he said the ones working nights were probably first string. Derek and I grabbed that dude and pushed him the fuck out of there. He was all waving to everybody and trying to give his number to the chicks; he was high-fiving like everybody outside and all the dudes were high-fiving him back and thinking he was all awesome and shit. All the people outside thought we were like famous or something; people took pictures and shit. Derek threw some cash at the cops and tried to get them to pound knucks, which was pretty hilarious. Then dude busted into the Wrangler Unlimited, and for real all these strippers we'd been hanging with came out and said peace out and were all like getting one quick last grind, even Model-hot who got out of her crunk coma for a second, and that chick totally threw up—some shit she probably always did, being such a mess. My lovely Latina lady was inside, probably with her idiot boyfriend. Shit was done. We rolled out and left a trail of crunk-ass chaos and bloated bar tabs behind us, and shit wasn't even that dark outside. "Fuck yeah!" Derek was like, posting some shit to Facebook.

Vincente thought we were awesome and felt awesome 'cause he was hanging with us. "You want food?" he was like. Fuck yeah; we were hungry as balls.

And dude pointed us to the weirdest and most amazing thing ever: This restaurant that served buffalo wings just like in America, full of dudes hanging around eating wings and slamming beer and watching sports and whatever. The only real difference was they were like mostly watching soccer, which is sorta stupid but all right if you've got enough beer. Me and Steve grabbed some wings and some beers and refueled like hell. Derek just got a burger or something and was talking to Vincente about whatever and Derek ate like half of Vincente's fries. But Vincente was pretty cool with that shit. After we pounded some wings it was time to say peace out to Vincente and Derek was sorta bummed 'cause he thought Vincente was a solid dude and a pretty awesome wingman to party in Mexico with.

Vincente was mad bummed we were leaving. "Come hang in Gregoria again?"

"Hell yeah, dude!" Derek was like. Dude even offered to give Vincente a ride to come party in the states if he wanted to. Vincente wasn't sure about that shit.

"My wife and dog—and money—I think about." He was sorta a prude but he was still pretty awesome and he waved at us as we rolled out. Behind him was the crazy Mexican buffalo wings place.

CHAPTER SIX

AMERICAN BALLERS FROM THE BADASS HEART OF CIVILIZATION

All of sudden the road beasted downhill and there were trees all over the place and as we were hauling ass a ton of bugs kept slamming into our windshield. "Fuck yeah!" Derek was like, and turned on the stereo but the stereo wasn't working. "What the fuck? What the fuck? Shit, what the fuck?" Dude messed with the knobs and punched it and tried to fuck with the fuses. "Shit, we're gonna have to make the whole ride without any more beats, that's gonna be such fucking bullshit, like we're never gonna get to rock out to anything and that's gonna be the fucking *worst*! Shit, no fucking stereo. What the fuck, bros, what the fuck?"

"I've got my laptop in the back. I could try to just play music from that."

"That thing has no fucking bass and you can barely hear it! Fuck that. This sucks. Whatever." So we just kept hauling ass through the dark without even any radio and shit was awkward 'cause Derek was all mad about the music and he was totally sure it was because one of us had fucked with the stereo. "I told you fuckers! I told you not to fuck with it! Seriously!" I knew that was bullshit and tried to ignore him and check my phone; I hadn't gotten any texts or anything but I didn't want to deal with that. From like nowhere the stereo suddenly started fucking blasting and the beats got heavy and now we were rolling again as we hauled ass through some tall-ass trees.

"Holy shit!" Steve was like. "Holy *fuck*!" Dude was still high as balls. We had no idea dude was still so high and all the stereo bullshit didn't matter to his stoned-ass self. We all cracked up.

"Fuck it! Let's just haul ass like a motherfucker through the jungle, we'll just crash in the car, let's do this shit!" Derek was like.

"Steve is so fucking high! Steve, how much did you smoke? Dude has gotten mad wild with the pot and the strippers and beer and the wings and those loud-as-fuck Kanye tracks that blasted so mad that it shook my shit—fuck yeah! Steve is so fucking high!"

We went shirts-off windows-down and cruised like hell through the trees and shit. Nothing was around, just trees and shit forever, tons of bugs, crawling on all kinds of shit, and it stank mad hard but eventually we got used to it. "It would be awesome to have like a sick jungle party," Derek was like. "For real, why don't we just like get crunked in the jungle with some hotties?" Then we were rolling into Limón, this shithole in the jungle with just like some houses or whatever, all dark as hell, with a bunch of dudes chilling around some shitty houses—looked pretty lame.

We stopped for a second in the jungle shithole. It was as hot as a pair of balls inside a cup under full lacrosse pads doing sprints at summer two-a-days in Tampa. There were a bunch of people chilling out talking and some chicks that came by to see what we were up to but they were way too young and pretty fugly anyway. They would be jailbait if they were hot. We asked at the broke-ass general store if there was like a Best Western around but nobody knew what the fuck we were talking about 'cause nobody spoke English in this dark-as-fuck jungle shithole. We were crazy tired and needed to crash out somewhere so we just drove to some deserted road outside of town and tried to sleep it up there. It was crazy fucking hot and Derek wouldn't let us idle the car for the whole night. He just straight-up crashed in a blanket on the ground like it was no big deal. Steve crashed out in the front with the doors open but it was still hot as fuck. I was in the back, beyond fucking hot and like drowning in my own sweat. All like, "Fuck that," I got out of the car and just stood there in dark shitty heat. It was quiet as fuck; all the assholes in this town were used to sleeping like this. How the fuck was I ever gonna crash? Mosquitoes were like all up in my shit. My brain got an awesome idea: I could just sleep on top of the Wrangler Unlimited 'cause it's metal and all cool. It was still hot as fuck, but the roof felt cool for a second and the bugs seemed a little less annoying, and I realized that the jungle fucking sucks. Trying to sleep in that stupid fucking heat felt like being stuffed in a fucking locker and then having dudes piss all over you as hazing for the varsity team. For real like it wasn't just like the weather was sorta dumb, like annoying or stupid or whatever, but it seriously fucking sucked. My cargo shorts were like soaked through. Bullshit clouds of bugs bashed into my face while I tried to crash, and they were crazy annoying. There was no data service, so I couldn't check my phone. I could down a couple Ambien and just lay there and still I'd never be able to fucking fall asleep. Dead bugs were all up in my nose; live ones kept stealing my blood; I felt like bugs were all over me and I wanted to chunk it from the rank, nasty smell of the jungle, which was probably making all my clothes in my North Face bag stink like hell. Why the fuck didn't I pack any OFF!? I changed into an Under Armour shirt to try to wick some of the gross-ass sweat off me. Derek was snoring and had totally been able to crash. Steve was crashed out too. Why the fuck couldn't we have just idled with the AC?

There was some stupid cop who was wandering around with a flashlight checking shit out in the hot-as-balls night. He started coming toward us with his stupid flashlight and I got ready for some bullshit. He flashed his light at us. I looked at him like ". . . the fuck?" In a voice that told me he was total pussy, he was like, *"Dormiendo?"* pointing at Derek sleeping in the road. I think that's the word that means "around the corner" or something.

"That doesn't make any fucking sense."

We just like stared at each other for a second and then he just like turned away and went back to the town. All cops are idiots, but at least the ones in Mexico are pretty fucking chill. No bullshit, no dickwad stuff, no asshole moves: He knew he was just some idiot with a badge in a jungle shithole, for real.

I laid back down and tried to use the roof rack crossbar as a pillow. I didn't even think about how nasty the top of the car was, I was already gross as fuck. I hocked a loogie to get some

gross shit out of my throat. It wasn't just phlegm; it was like a
nasty-ass paste of bugs and snot. There was no way I was gonna
sleep. Some animals started making some noises 'cause it must
have been getting early or something. Still hot as balls, no wind,
no sleep, which sucked. Everything was still dark as fuck. From
out of nowhere I heard some rumbling in the dark, and then I
heard a car getting closer. It got louder and louder. What motherfucker drives through the jungle now? Then I saw shit that was
like a total hallucination: A Monster Energy Drink van, black
with the green Monster logo, rolled down the road like straight
toward where Derek was sleeping. Inside there was probably a
ton of free promotional Monster Energy Drinks. They probably
weren't gonna hand them out now, they must have been way
lost, but I still waved at them and tried to get them to toss me
one. They got crazy close to Derek. The driver saw him at the last
second and swerved, honked real fast, and kept rolling, engine
humming, into the jungle on the other side, and all I could think
about was how awesome it would have been to get some free
Monster Energy Drink. The sound of the van drifted away. What
the fuck was a Monster van doing in the middle of the fucking
jungle? Do they do promotions out here? I told Derek when he
woke up. He said I was full of shit. Then he remembered dreaming about almost being hit by a van, so I told him that shit was
real. Steve Sharpford got up. In a hot second we were sweating
balls again. Shit was still mad dark. "Can we please fucking start
the car and get some AC?" I was like, "My balls are melting!"

"Aight!" We hauled ass out of there and rolled down the highway with the AC blasting. Shit got light outside and we could see
a ton of swamp shit all around us with crazy-ass vines all over the
place. We kept hauling ass next to some railroad tracks. There was a
big cell phone tower that made it seem like maybe we were in fucking civilization for a second. We nabbed some gas and kept getting
butt-rushed by bugs that were flying like little fuckers all over the
place and frying their faces off on the light bulbs and dive-bombing
at us; some of them were for real like a foot long and looked like

they could eat a cat or something, but still the worst were the mad clouds of mosquitoes that were still trying to get all up in our blood. I went fucking crazy to swat them all down and then they were all crawling all over my feet which was extra-gross; I ended up hiding in the car like a total puss-wad, feeling like there were centipedes all over my junk. "Let's get the fuck out!" I was like. Derek and Steve didn't give a shit about the bugs; they grabbed some Powerade from the gas station and downed it like no big deal. All their clothes were totally fucked with dead bugs and nasty blood, just like mine were. I dared Steve to lick his shirt.

"Oh shit dude, that is a rank-ass taste," Steve was like. "Fuck, I gotta get this shit out of my mouth."

"You're a total asshole," Derek was like. "That shit is totally gross, but I'm pretty sure some Axe will cover that shit up if you just spray it on thick enough." So we baked out the car with Axe, kicking the ass of that nasty bug shit.

There was a huge mountain up ahead, steep as fuck. Once we got over that shit we'd be like a hot second away from Mexico City. We hauled ass up the mountain and were like five thousand feet up there and it was mad scenic and you could see this huge river. It must have been like the Mississippi of Mexico or something. All the Mexican people by the road looked all weird. They were like Indians, but in Mexico, and it was like some weird little like universe cut off from civilization. All these guys were all short and sorta fat and hella-tan with totally shitty teeth; they were always lugging a ton of shit around. They were like for real farming on this big-ass mountain. I guess they were just like doing farm shit. Derek slowed down and took some pictures with his phone. "Holy shit! It's like the fucking stone age!" At the top of this one super-big mountain, there were totally bananas growing. Derek jumped out and had me take a picture of him pretending one was his dick. There was a crazy-ass shack on the ledge we were on that totally looked like it was gonna fall. Derek's picture looked pretty hilarious and he was amped to post it to Facebook once we had service 'cause it would get likes from our buddies that were miles below us in America.

There was this little girl all staring at us in front of the crazy-ass shack, sucking her thumb and trying to figure out what our deal was. "Yo, she's probably totally freaked seeing like a car and shit up here!" Derek was like. "Yo, hey kid, what's up? What the hell do you do here?" This kid just kept staring and wouldn't say shit. We'd talk and take pictures with our phone and she just kept standing there. "Shit dude, like what is up with her? Like *for real*, she's just lived here in buttfuck nowhere on a mountain—and there's probably like nothing at all to do around here. Her dad probably like farms somewhere on this mountain and is boring as hell and they all probably just sit around all bored as hell. She's like never gonna go somewhere that's actually fun, like somewhere where they don't just sit around and like fuck goats or whatever. Just imagine how crazy boring this place must be! And there's probably even more boring shit farther away 'cause at least this place has a road going through so sometimes solid people like us cruise through. Dude, she's all sweaty and shit," Derek was like, pointing at her. "It's like totally gross, like they're always sweating 'cause it's constantly balls-hot here and like they probably don't take showers or whatever, they probably smell like ass for their whole lives." She was mad sweaty, and she was just a kid. "Jesus, that's gotta be so gross! Like when you have a bunch of people together they must be so fucking gross!" Derek kept hauling ass, like taking pictures of shit with his phone and saying some pretty hilarious shit about how weird all these people were. He was sorta being a dick but it was funny.

We got higher up and shit got a little less balls-hot and we saw all these like Indian chicks walking along the road. They all waved at us and wanted to talk to us; we checked that shit out. They were trying to sell us some stupid-ass little crystals they found. They were so sweaty and sorta fat so we didn't scope them at all; and some of them were like way too young and some others were like nasty-old. "These chicks are busted!" Derek was like. It was like they'd all been fucked up pretty hard by an ugly stick. We couldn't imagine how anybody would ever wanna hit that shit. But they totally thought we were pretty fine. We flashed some abs real quick 'cause we couldn't resist. They'd probably never seen abs so well-defined in their mountain shithole. "I bet these chicks have no idea what a fit body looks like—I bet they're used to all their dudes looking flabby as hell."

The girls probably wanted to get all up on our shit. This one little girl was all grabbing at Derek. She was saying some shit in some weird-ass language. "Aight, aight, aight," Derek was like. He popped the trunk and looked inside his jacked-up duffle— the same busted-ass American duffel—and grabbed a couple Clif Bars. He handed them to this kid. She thought they were crazy delicious. All these other busted chicks all crowded around and wanted to try some. Then dude grabbed a crystal from her hand 'cause "chicks back home will probably think I'm like super sensitive and worldly when I show it to them and tell them the story." He grabbed the biggest one. And threw another Clif Bar her way. They got so stoked; it was like we gave them iPads. The girl noshed down on the Clif Bar. All of them thanked Derek and tried to touch his abs. He stood in the middle of them with his ripped neck shining in the sunlight, taking pictures of them with his phone, and it was like he was some kind of badass god descended from the mountain to deliver Clif Bars to his flock. We got back in the whip. They were mad bummed when we left. They just stood there and kept waving at us for like ever as we hauled ass away. Derek laid on the gas and they ran after us like weirdos. "Aw dude, this is hilarious!" Derek was like, trying to take pictures out the back while driving. "How fucking pumped can they possibly get over some stupid Clif Bars? What's their fucking deal? Yo, do you think if I slowed down they'd just tail us forever?"

"Prob," I was like, 'cause they were crazy.

We busted it to the fucking top of the Sierra Madres. There were bananas and shit all over the place. It was super foggy. We blew by all these weird little shit towns, full of poor-as-hell Indians checking our shit out and wishing they'd been born in the U-S-of-A. Their lives were shitty, boring, dumb. They stared at Derek, this crazy motherfucker in a Wrangler Unlimited Rubicon, not knowing what the hell was going on. They were all begging like pathetic losers. They came out of their shithole houses to try to get some cash and food from a trio of American ballers from the badass heart of civilization, and they didn't even realize that we were never gonna share our fucking cash with them. They didn't know how fucking expensive drinks were back in the U.S. and how they could decimate your bank account if you were an idiot who just threw your money around instead of saving it for a rainy day party and so we needed that cash, probably worse than they did. The sick-ass Wrangler Unlimited just rolled, rolling past all of those losers and left them in the dust.

This big-ass flat patch was ending. The sun was bright as fuck; the sky had like no clouds; and it looked totally hot as fuck out there, like a desert on crack. Steve drove while Derek dropped some nap bombs. My phone made a noise, 'cause there was data service all of a sudden, and I checked, all pumped. On Facebook, my buddy Connor had posted this hilarious video of him peeing on the shoes of this drunk dude on his porch, and it was the funniest shit ever. "Bro, bro," I was like to Derek, "get the fuck up and check out this video, wake your ass up and check this funny shit that Connor sent, just check it out!"

He woke up all fast, looked at the video for a hot second just as Connor was starting to pee, and went back to nap territory. But he totally described the video to me when he woke up later, all like, "Fuck yeah, dude, that was mad hilarious. Oh, dude, when he was pissing . . . oh man . . . oh fuck." He cracked the shit up, he rubbed his eyes, he almost cried from laughing so hard.

We were almost at the fucking finish line. There were big-ass fields all over the place; a crazy wind blew all up at us and made the Wrangler swerve for a second as it started to get dark. We all started to get some data service. "Mexico City, bros!" It was game time. Like 2K miles of hauling ass from Denver to the cheap-as-fuck drinks of Mexico, and we'd almost fucking made it.

"Dude, you wanna groom up somewhere?"

"Naw dude, we'll just Axe it up, for real." And we showered in Axe on our way into Mexico City.

After we hauled ass up a mountain real quick we had a beyond-sick view of Mexico City, all chilling out in this big-ass crater like the kind of shit Bruce Willis tried to stop in *Armageddon*. We gunned it down there, past another Mexican Pizza Hut, right through some shithole called Reforma. I caught up on all the shit on Facebook I'd missed since we lost data service. There were some hilarious pictures that people tagged. Naw, I couldn't blow my battery on that shit right now. Miles of text messages showed up; it was gonna take forever to get through all that shit and reply to people. I wondered if I was getting charged for roaming. From like nowhere the city busted up and we were like in the middle of a ton of bars and restaurants and shops and whatever. This biker we almost hit yelled at us. Nasty-ass construction dudes walked by, all greasy and shit. Crazy fucking Mexican cab drivers almost hit the Wrangler Unlimited and sped off like psychos. It was loud as hell. No one had a decent muffler. The cars were shitpiles and everybody drove all crazy. "Whoa dude!" Derek was like. "Fucking watch it!" Derek gunned the whip and totally messed with these other drivers. He was driving like just as much of a psycho as they were. He almost drifted it into this crazy traffic circle where there were like a million cars all blasting in from like a million directions, busting ass in and out and almost like murdering us, and he was mad amped. "This is some real *Death Race* shit! It's fucking off the chain!" This ambulance hauled ass like crazy through everything. American ambulances drive sorta like pussies, taking it all slow at intersections and waiting for people to get out of the way; these fucking psycho Mexican ambulances just tore ass, and people just had to stay the fuck away because the ambulances just don't give a fuck and gun it like hell down the road. It tore past us and we saw it keep ripping it up ahead, like never slowing down. Mexicans are psycho drivers. The buses like didn't even stop for people, for real. These Mexican bros would chase shit down and try to like jump on fast as hell. The bus drivers didn't even wear shoes and just looked like real hardasses and talked on their phones and gunned it like total psychos. I took a picture of one of them on my phone. His face was totally busted and he was like looking at my phone right when I took it and it was hilarious.

There were a shitload of tourists downtown, all walking around with fanny packs or backpacks on backwards and taking pictures and checking their maps, some of them buying some stupid tourist shit on the street to take home to their lame friends. You could like go down a shitty alley and there'd just be like a crazy tiny bar in some hole in the wall. There was like a shitty gutter in the bar and that shitty gutter was just like full of shit. You'd have to grab a drink and then get back over that shit. I had this delicious drink that was like coffee and rum and so it was sorta like Four Loko with the caffeine and the booze. Mariachi was like all over the place. Nasty-ass hooker chicks were chilling along the shady streets with busted faces and guts that stuck out from their tube tops in the night. We got a little hammered and staggered through this weird shit. We chowed down on these delicious steaks that were super cheap but I swear to God it was like the same quality as Ruth's Chris with the tenderness and the flavor and the perfect fucking cooking—but the sides weren't as good. But they had cheap drinks and would give you an XL beer or a crazy strong Jack and Coke for almost nothing. The city was bumpin'; the city knew how to party. Drunk American dudes lost their shit all over the place. Whole crews of dudes leaned against dim alley walls, supporting themselves as they chunked it into the ancient streets. Their Hardy caps fell off; they dropped their phones; Mexico was totally sloppy. Pretty much everywhere there were people cooking up crazy tasty carne asada and making burritos and tacos with mad good salsa and sour cream. This was the clutch and final awesome unconquered party scene that could get you hammered and feed you burritos and where we knew we would get wild at the end of the road. Derek strutted around with his phone to his face, texting rapidly, the screen glowing, and took us into a ton of bars 'till around sunrise and into a field with a ton of tequila and a dude that didn't have toes, 'cause we had to get wild.

Suddenly I got like mad sick and blacked out. Fucking water. I tried to cowboy up and get my shit together. I knew I was in Mexico, crazy far from Ohio State and all my buddies, and I knew that I'd partied hard before and been more hungover than you'd ever think is possible but this was way worse and I felt like shit and I was losing valuable party time. Derek was going out and getting hammered all over Mexico City while I was dying on some chick's couch. Then like barely a couple days later he was peacing out. "What the fuck, bro?" I was like.

"Aw dude, aw dude, you're a mess. Steve'll make sure you keep your shit together. Aight, for real, this is what's up: Isabel totally knows I'm not at a conference for work and I gotta get the fuck back to Columbus if I don't want her to like bitch out and withhold sex forever."

"That's so lame!" I was like.

"You're so lame, bro. I'm over this shit anyway. I'd love to hang, but you know. Maybe we'll party here again." I felt like a fucking cobra was in my stomach. When I opened my eyes that fucking dick was there with his jacked-up duffle giving me a "peace out" nod. I didn't get how he could be such a massive cocksucker, and dude totally knew what a cocksucker move he was pulling, and like couldn't even look me in the face, and just tried to pound knucks with me. "Aight, aight, aight, I gotta roll out. Sick-ass Sam, peace out." And dude peaced out. The next day I could think straight and realized that dude for real peaced out on me. He was already hauling ass alone past all those Mexican Pizza Huts, totally lone-wolfing it.

Once I got my shit together I knew he was a total fucking douchebag cocksucker, but then I had to admit what a crazy motherfucker he was, how totally raw and crazy he was to leave my ass in Mexico, so he could go party in the states and make sure he kept getting laid and whatever. "Whatever, fucking douche, it's aight."

Part Five
Peace Out

CHAPTER ONE

IN THE LAND WHERE THEY
LET THE BROS PARTY

Derek beasted it outta Mexico City and partied with Vincente again in that crazy fucking strip club and gunned the Wrangler Unlimited up to Lake Charles, Louisiana, until he got pulled over and busted for DUI, which was totally inevitable. He texted his dad who pulled some strings and got him out and paid for a plane to Columbus, so Derek fucking grew a pair and went by air. As soon as dude landed in Columbus with his license gone, he got his smash on with Isabel and they got a new apartment near campus; like a hot second after they signed the lease, saying some bullshit about how Bally was having another offsite for its best personal trainers, which was such total bullshit because personal trainers never have to do that shit; dude emptied out his SkyMiles and beasted off again across the jacked-up continent to San Fran to get his smash on with Carly again. So now dude was pulling his second double smash, this time cross-country.

A little later I hauled ass back to C-Bus from Mexico City and one night at an Outback just over the border in McAllen, Texas, I was finishing up a Bloomin' Onion under the soft glow of the American League Divisional Series on a forty-inch plasma with the final flakes of delicious breading sticking to my fingers when I heard a seating pager buzz behind me, and no shit, this huge fucking dude in a Hurley tee with a Miller Lite in one hand and the pager in the other walked over to the hostess and as he passed he gave me a nod and was like, *"Keep it real, bro,"* and went and got his table with a couple buddies. Had I not been keeping it real enough in all my raw times across America? I finished my beer and hauled ass to Columbus, and a few days later I was standing on the porch of a house on campus and kept banging on the door 'cause I thought my buddy Brayden was having a party there. But like this hottie opened the door and was like, "Who are you?"

"Sam Parker," I was like, and sorta flashed some abs in the cold Columbus night.

"Wanna hang out?" she was like. "I'm just watching some Netflix." Natch, I came in and she was just chilling on the couch, the chick who was just mad chill but also super-hot that I'd always wanted to get with. We became total smash buddies. We decided that I'd try to actually graduate by winter break and we'd go move our shit to San Fran; I'd probably get a job in like sales for a startup or be an agent or something. I texted Derek and told him the plan. Dude texted back this big-ass text that took up like seven separate texts, with all this weird shit about what he'd done back in the day in Denver, and dude was gonna come out here and go with us to San Fran. I had a couple months to cruise through my pass/fail classes and started actually going to class to get that shit done. But like from nowhere, Derek just rolled up, like a month-and-a-half early, and if I didn't get my school shit done, my parents would legit cut me off.

I was coming back from the bar late as hell and rolled back to my chick and wanted to show her some hilarious pictures I took of that night on my phone. She was just sitting on the couch looking all secretive and shit. I showed her a couple hilarious pics from my phone and then I noticed a bag of jerky on top of the TV. It was totally Derek's favorite flavor: Jack Links KC Masterpiece Barbecue. Dude flying tackled me from out of nowhere. He was fucking crazy. He jumped off me and cracked the shit up and pounded knucks and was like, "Aw, aw, dude you gotta hear this shit." We waited, wanting to hear that shit. But dude couldn't remember the shit he was gonna spit at us. "For real—aight. Yo, Sam—Lisa, what up; I'm all up in this; I gotta peace out; aight, one sec, fuck yeah." Then he like just spaced out and checked his phone for a little. "I gotta be real as hell; you feel me; you read me; oh, check this pic out." And we waited.

He couldn't find the picture in his phone. "Aw fuck," he was like, sorta pissed. "So for real; I guess I deleted it—or whatever."

"Why the fuck are you here so early, bro?"

"You know," he was like, a total fucking space cadet, "early bro, yeah. What's . . . what's up; like, what's up is . . . I got this cheap-ass flight—Delta—turns out flying isn't so bad—but a ton of connections—in LA and Dallas—got a ton of jerky in SFO and just noshed that down during the trip." Dude grabbed his bag of jerky. He threw back a couple pieces and offered us some. "It's fucking delicious," he was like. "For real, Sam, I gotta tell you so much funny shit 'cause so much funny shit has happened and for real I drank like five Red Bulls in the Dallas airport and then I had a *ton* of drinks on the plane and *I gotta* tell you about shit that went down in Mexico when you were sick as fuck—but like you know. Aight, you feel me?"

"We feel you." And dude recapped his whole trip here and all the shit he did in LAX, like how he hit on this chick in an airport bar, had a Wolfgang Puck pizza for breakfast, got his flight delayed and then had another pizza and hit on this chick again—how hot she was, how tall she was, how they snuck in to the American Airlines Admirals Club and he totally banged her there; dude went on for like a couple hours about all this shit, and once he finally got to the part where he flew out of LAX he was like, "Oh, but dude, you know when shit *really* went down— for real—was in Dallas, on layover there for a while—slamming Red Bulls—eating some more Wolfgang Puck pizzas, delicious fucking pizzas—got so fucking crazed on Red Bull, hit on some more chicks—for real. So many fucking hours in airports for like an eleven-hour trip all to fucking *party* with you, bro."

"What's up with Carly?"

"She's cool, bro—I ain't whipped. Carly and I are super chill, for real."

"What's Isabel's deal?"

"Aw like—like—like—I'm gonna get her to come and crash back in San Fran—you know? Fuck dude, maybe that's dumb." Then dude backpedaled and talked all like a super puss, all like,

"And like, for real, you know, I wanted to hang with you and your lady and—you know—it's clutch hanging with you." He crashed in Columbus for a couple days then found another long-ass cheap flight on Kayak to go back across the continent with like three layovers, ten fucking hours in coach on flights too short to have in-flight movies. Natch I had to get school done so my parents wouldn't de-ball me so we couldn't move our shit West with him. He took Isabel out to eat at a Red Lobster and they fought like crazy over some popcorn shrimp and that chick totally stormed out. I got a text from Carly, 'cause Derek had lost his phone somewhere. "whr iz d at? im crzy sad n miss him. we r all waitin 4 him." So like that chick was still into Derek even though he'd pulled total, crazy-ass dick moves, and even though her text was sorta lame, I guess it was pretty solid of her to not be a bitch.

The last time I saw him it was under pretty weird circumstances. Ricky Bronco had gotten his trust fund unlocked and rolled up in Columbus like a baller. I wanted to party with Ricky and Derek together. We chilled, but Derek was being a total weird asshole and Ricky was like, "fuck that." Ricky had tickets to a Train concert at the Value City Arena and made me and Lisa go with him and his slam piece. Ricky had gotten lame and become the sort of homo who goes to Train concerts, but dude still wanted to be a baller, so he wanted to do shit with *style*, or fucking whatever. Dude lined up a limo to take us over there. It was balls-cold outside. The limo was pulled up in front of my crib. Derek stood at the limo with his jacked-up duffle, about to head to the airport to catch his first flight.

"Peace out, bro," I was like. "I wish I didn't have to go to this fucking Train concert."

"Could you like give me a ride to the airport?" he was like. "We could do some shots in the limo, bro, and taking a cab all the way out there is mad expensive . . ." I asked Ricky about that shit. He was all like, "No way," he thought I was a pretty solid dude but he thought the dudes in my crew were super douchey. I didn't wanna pull the same dick moves on Ricky I pulled at Alfred's in San Fran with Ryan Minor.

"Fuck no, dude!" Stupid fucking Ricky; he was wearing this dumbass T-shirt: it was like a Train concert shirt from a couple years ago, with all the cities they went to, and it was even fucking autographed, since Ricky was such a total homo about Train.

Derek wasn't gonna get a ride with us so I just stood out the sunroof of the limo and flipped him off as a joke. The limo driver was a dick about me standing out the sunroof. Derek, looking like a crazy motherfucker in this huge-ass puffy North Face parka he brought 'cause of how balls-cold the Midwest gets, took out his phone, and the last I saw of him he was staring at his phone, probably reading a text, and then texting back. Hot-ass Lisa, my cool-as-hell slam piece, who I'd told crazy stories to about how awesome Derek was, got pretty bummed.

"We're just gonna leave him here? That seems shitty."

Old Derek has peaced out, I thought, and was like, "Dude can handle himself." And we busted out to the boring Train concert that I didn't give a shit about and the whole time I just kept texting Derek to see how his long-ass trip through like a million airports to get back home was going, but dude never texted back.

So in America when the beer bong comes out and I chill on my buddy's big-ass porch watching dudes take long, long drags over the Columbus night and think about how all that badass land hauls ass in one crazy rager to the West Coast, and all those parties bumpin', all the chicks looking fine as hell all over the place, and all across the Big Ten I know by now the bros must be partying in the conference where bros party the hardest, and tonight is gonna get mad sloppy, and don't you wanna hit this beer bong, bro? the plastic tubing must be drooping and spraying the Natty Light on the prairie, which is just before shit gets crazy and envelops the earth, fills the rivers with light beer, shakes the mountains and echos across the ocean, and fucking nobody, for real nobody has any idea how big shit's gonna blow up except that it's gonna be legendary, I wanna party with Derek Morrisey, I even think of his dad who never hooked us up with Denver Nuggets tickets, I wanna party with Derek Morrisey.

ABOUT THE AUTHOR

Mike Lacher writes and builds funny things on the Internet at *mikelacher.com*. His work has been featured in *McSweeney's, The New York Times Magazine, New York Magazine*, WIRED.com, *The Huffington Post*, and the *Toronto Sun*. He has a totally weak alcohol tolerance and can't hold a kegstand for more than like two seconds.

DAILY BENDER

Want Some More?

Hit up our humor blog, The Daily Bender, to get your fill of all things funny—be it subversive, odd, offbeat, or just plain mean. The Bender editors are there to get you through the day and on your way to happy hour. Whether we're linking to the latest video that made us laugh or calling out (or bullshit on) whatever's happening, we've got what you need for a good laugh.

If you like our book, you'll love our blog. (And if you hated it, "man up" and tell us why.) Visit The Daily Bender for a shot of humor that'll serve you until the bartender can.

Sign up for our newsletter at
www.adamsmedia.com/blog/humor
and download our Top Ten Maxims No Man Should Live Without.